Kate Thompson was born in Belfast. She came to Dublin to study French and English and had a successful career as an actress and voiceover artist before ditching the day job to write full time. Her five previous novels, *It Means Mischief*, *More Mischief*, *Going Down*, *The Blue Hour* and *Striking Poses* have been widely translated. Kate divides her time between Dublin and the West of Ireland, is happily married and has one daughter.

A Perfect Life

KATE THOMPSON

BANTAM BOOKS

LONDON • NEW YORK • TORONTO • SYDNEY • AUCKLAND

A PERFECT LIFE
A BANTAM BOOK: 0 553 81577 6

Originally published in Great Britain by Bantam Press,
a division of Transworld Publishers

PRINTING HISTORY
Bantam Press edition published 2003
Bantam edition published 2004

1 3 5 7 9 10 8 6 4 2

Set in 11/13½pt Baskerville by
Falcon Oast Graphic Art Ltd.

Bantam Books are published by Transworld Publishers,
61–63 Uxbridge Road, London W5 5SA,
a division of The Random House Group Ltd,
in Australia by Random House Australia (Pty) Ltd,
20 Alfred Street, Milsons Point, Sydney, NSW 2061, Australia,
in New Zealand by Random House New Zealand Ltd,
18 Poland Road, Glenfield, Auckland 10, New Zealand
and in South Africa by Random House (Pty) Ltd,
Endulini, 5a Jubilee Road, Parktown 2193, South Africa.

Printed and bound in Great Britain by
Cox & Wyman Ltd, Reading, Berkshire.

Papers used by Transworld Publishers are natural, recyclable
products made from wood grown in sustainable forests. The
manufacturing processes conform to the environmental
regulations of the country of origin.

For Marian

Acknowledgements

I confess that taking people out to lunch is my favourite way of doing research. For this book I lunched with three people whose advice and expertise were worth their weight in gold. They were: Paul Berry, whose glorious flower shop on Patrick Street, Adonis, was the inspiration for Dannie's Florabundance; Maureen Hughes, casting director – thanks for the insider knowledge and that last glass of champagne (!); and Deborah Pearce, who juggles motherhood and a highly successful career with enviable éclat.

Thanks also to Cathy Kelly for being Cathy Kelly, to Hugh Morton for not being Roydon Sneyde, to Ciarán Hinds for the book and the videotape, to Helen Hutton for letting me sit in on the dance workshop, to La Joaquina for the fantastic display, and to Eileen and Peter Colquhoun for guiding me through some scary psychological landscapes. Thank you to the staff at Morehampton Clinic – again!

Thank you, Ali Gunn and Jonathan Lloyd at Curtis Brown, for – er – gunning for me.

Thanks to Declan Heeney, and, of course, to Gill and Simon Hess for looking out for me.

Thanks, of course, to the team at Transworld, especially Beth Humphries for being meticulous, Sadie Mayne for understanding me when I seem to be hailing from the planet Zog, and Francesca Liversidge for her remarkably insightful editing and her invaluable friendship.

Thank you to the booksellers for their continuing support, to those people who have written to say lovely things about the books, to the sisterhood of the RNA, and to my family and friends for their encouragement.

Thank you to the twin apples of my eye – beloved Malcolm and Clara – for putting up with unwashed dishes and laundry and the inevitable boo-hooing when the going gets tough.

Finally, thank you to the High Queen of popular fiction for the masterclass over the phone that despondent Saturday afternoon. This book is dedicated to Marian Keyes.

Chapter One

Calypso O'Kelly was serenely stuck in gridlock, filing her nails and talking cheerily to her secretary, Iseult, on the speaker phone. It was impossible not to be cheery around Iseult. The pretty thing had a sweet voice, a mass of curly black hair, brilliant blue eyes, and a dazzling smile. Couriers, clients and cleaners alike all loved her so much that sometimes Calypso might have felt jealous. But then, there was no need for Calypso to feel jealous about anybody, really, because she had a perfect life.

'How much longer are you likely to be?' asked Iseult.

'Around twenty minutes, by the look of things.'

'Oh! You lucky thing! Enjoy it!'

'You know I will. Bye!'

Calypso loved the morning gridlock. It meant that she could spend her time going through casting briefs and consulting her diary while listening to Radio 4. At that hour of the morning she would have preferred to listen to something rather more mindless, but Radio 4 had gravitas, and it was useful to be in the know about gravitas-type stuff so that she could make worthwhile contributions to dinner party conversations.

Today's diary reminded her to send thank-you notes to Liam Neeson and Neil Jordan, to set up a casting session for next week, and to respond to an e-mail from shit-hot Hollywood film director Jethro Palmer. It told her that she had a lunchtime meeting with film producer Noel Pearson, and that she was attending the theatre this evening for the opening of a new Tom Murphy play. It reminded her to take out a subscription to a glossy new Irish arts magazine that she knew her husband Dominic would love, and it screamed at her to *MAKE A HAIR APPOINTMENT!!!* She also noted the list of phone calls that had to be made before midday. She was glad to see that she had a window before lunch that she could use to get a nail repaired.

The pages of her diary were more crowded than Jennifer's in *Harpers*. In the driver's seat of her nifty little Mercedes convertible, Calypso stretched like the cat who'd got the cream. Oh! How she loved her job! She loved the wining and dining and sociability of it, she loved the thrilling rush she got every time she discovered new talent, she loved the buzz she got out of telling an actor he'd got the part, and – because she was secretly a fan of *Hello!* magazine (she read it when Dominic wasn't around) – she loved the fact that she often met real live celebrities.

The traffic slid forward six feet. Calypso put on the handbrake for the hundredth time that morning, opened her case and extracted a casting brief for a new movie. She ran her eyes down the list of characters required. As usual, the male characters outnumbered the female characters by a ratio of around five to one. All the female characters bar one were under thirty: 'hotel receptionist – early twenties'; 'first clubbing girl – late teens'; 'second clubbing girl – late teens'; 'Stanley's girlfriend – mid-twenties'; 'Stanley's mother – early sixties'.

OK, thought Calypso. Let's check out what age Stanley is. Chances are he's at least ten years older than his nameless girlfriend. She was right. Stanley, the movie's lead role, was stipulated as being in his 'early forties'. In real life, how many twenty-something girls were involved with men in their early forties? She didn't know a single one – apart from her, of course. Dominic was considerably older than she was. But in the male-dominated fantasy world of film, the older the guy, the younger in direct proportion to his age was the doxy that swung off his arm. Had been that way since Bogart and Bacall – and even now in the new millennium, it looked like it always *would* be that way. Woody Allen was a classic example. He'd been getting away with it for decades.

Calypso had escaped from the acting game at a fairly early stage of her career. She had seen what the future held for her, and noted how someone had once described actors as 'walking milk cartons with expiry dates everywhere'. Thank heaven she'd been such a smart cookie! Friends of hers in the business who were barely out of their twenties were having a tough time of it. She'd had to make serious efforts not to look appalled when a director had recently described a twenty-eight-year-old friend of hers as 'past it'.

But that was mild compared to some of the remarks she'd been privy to after an actor or actress had delivered the words 'thanks very much indeed, it was lovely to have met you' with a shaky smile, and backed out of a casting session. She knew how it felt to be a fly on the wall in a jock's changing room: had done since an occasion long ago when one evening she had as near as dammit *been* that hypothetical fly.

Gazing out of the car window at the terminally stationary traffic, she recalled now the conversation she'd overheard in the men's loo of the Dublin Theatre Festival Club just over a decade ago . . .

She was under the table in the Festival Club – not because she'd drunk herself there, but through choice. A producer from a UK television station was visiting Ireland, checking out the talent. He'd met Calypso at a casting session, and now, completely rat-arsed, he was staggering around the Festival Club with his tongue hanging out, hunting for her. Calypso had dived under the table to avoid him.

'It's OK – you can come out now,' came a friend's voice from above.

She emerged, laughing. 'Well, thank God for that! I'm bursting for a pee.' Still laughing, Calypso headed for the Ladies like a heat-seeking missile. The queue that was snaking out of the door set her zipping in the opposite direction. Without so much as a second thought, she hit the men's loo across the corridor. One surprised gent was tucking himself away as Calypso darted past into a cubicle, sending him a bright smile as she swung the door shut. She heard the outer door to the loo open and shut (he hadn't washed his hands! she observed), and then open and shut again as someone else came in. Two someone elses: two lubriciously laughing someone elses.

'*Very* cute piece of ass,' said a familiar voice.

'You speaking from experience?'

'Oh, yeah, oh, *yeah*!' More lubricious laughter. The sound of flies being unzipped and porcelain sprayed. 'She got a bit above herself once – thought she could make it without putting out – but as soon as she heard I was casting students as extras in the Christmas show, she got spooked and changed her mind lickety-split.'

'Ha. Did she get the part?'

'No. Snooty bitch got her come-uppance. I cast the succulent Ms Calypso O'Kelly instead.'

Calypso froze.

'Hey! She looks like a real goer!'

'Haven't hit base there yet. But I'm working on bringing her to her senses. Or should I say – to her knees. Ha ha ha.'

'Ha ha ha.'

'Hey – did you get a load of that blonde in the silver shimmery thing?'

'The one with the great tits?'

'Yeah. Her name's Zsa Zsa – can you believe it? I brought her back to my joint last night and . . .'

It got worse. Calypso had never heard men talk that way about women before. The description of what had been done to poor Zsa Zsa was so graphic that she felt like being sick. Finally the outer door to the Gents opened and shut. They hadn't washed their hands either.

Calypso sat there, staring unseeingly at the graffiti on the cubicle wall, thinking harder than she'd ever thought in her life. How she would have loved to have swung open the door and confronted them! How she would have loved to have stood there with an insouciant hand on her hip, letting a contemptuous look linger on their undone flies, before turning on her high, high heel and declaring: 'You honestly think I would put *that* in my mouth?'

But she knew she'd done the right thing by resisting the temptation to confront them. She had acquired new knowledge, suddenly. Knowledge was power, and power was control. And what had happened so shockingly just now had determined Calypso's future with the blinding flash of a *coup de foudre*. She had made one of those monumental decisions that occasionally descend from out of the blue with gob-smacking, life-changing force. Knowledge. Power. Control. Control was *self*-empowerment, and Calypso was going to wrest back the control over her own life that until now she had relinquished so unthinkingly to others. To those others who 'knew what was best for her'. To the teachers and the 'mentors' and the producers and the directors – all of them, *all* of them men. From now on, *Calypso* was going to make the decisions about whose offers of assistance she'd accept and whose she'd reject.

The sudden, surging sense of liberation she felt at the knowledge that *she* could call the shots – why shouldn't Calypso O'Kelly kick ass with the best of them? – almost made her reel. She would have her work cut out – of course she would, she knew that – but Calypso had always been a hard worker. She'd worked hard at trying to please her parents, she'd worked hard at school, she'd worked hard at her theatrical training. She had determination on her side, and ambition, and the dazzling optimism of which only those who have not yet hit twenty are capable.

As she let herself out of the cubicle and went to the basin to wash her hands, the name of her new business flashed into her head and she almost laughed out loud at how good it sounded. *Calypso O'Kelly Casting.* Oh, *yeah*!

The door to her office boasted a plaque with *Calypso O'Kelly Casting* engraved on it in classy, understated letters. Calypso swung through it into the reception area and gave Iseult a bright 'Good morning!'

Iseult's 'Good morning!' back was even brighter.

'Anything new?' asked Calypso, hanging her coat on the stand and kicking off her shoes, as she always did when alone with her staff in the office. She always put them on again if she was expecting visitors, though. She hated her feet so much that she even found revealing them to her beautician when she went for pedicures humiliating.

'Jethro Palmer phoned. I've booked a table in Le Blazon for tomorrow evening. Neil Jordan wants you to phone him. Nothing urgent. Oh – *Individual* magazine rang. They want to do a profile on you and Dominic for their "Power Couples" slot in the May issue.'

'Cool!'

'The editor asked if you could ring her back to confirm today. I have an outline here of the kind of stuff they want.' Iseult tore a page from a Post-It pad and handed it to Calypso.

'Crikey,' said Calypso, scanning the Post-It page. 'They want to know which of us first brought up the subject of marriage and how romantic was it? I'll need to be a bit economical with the truth there. Dominic actually proposed to me when I got locked in a hotel loo once upon a time. He ended up sliding the ring under the door.'

'Couldn't he have waited till you got out?'

'No. He was dashing off to catch a plane. I had to wait for ages before they located the head porter. Luckily there was a copy of *Newsweek* in there. I kept myself amused by drawing Mickey Mouse ears on every picture of a politician I could find.'

'Who wore them the best?'

'Guess.'

'Dubya?'

'Got it in one. New mugshots?' Calypso indicated a pile of manila envelopes that had been stacked on her desk.

'I guess. Hand-delivered this morning by Postman Pat. He really is called Pat, you know. I got chatting to him one day. He's awfully sweet.'

'Iseult, you think everyone's awfully sweet. You'd probably think Osama bin Laden was sweet if you met him.'

'He *looks* sweet. He's got eyes like Po.'

'Po?'

'In the *Teletubbies*.'

Calypso smiled and raised her eyes to heaven, then reached for a paperknife and slit open one of the envelopes. 'Oh, no. Silly fellow. No SAE enclosed.' She considered the ten-by-eight shot the envelope had contained. 'Still, he's not bad-looking.'

'A contender for the bodice-ripping epic?'

'Sadly, no.' She handed the photograph to Iseult, who raised a questioning eyebrow. Calypso responded with a resigned nod, and the actor's mugshot was consigned to the waste-paper basket.

She hated having to do this, but in purely practical terms it was the only alternative she had: she received so many unsolicited packages these days – some came from places as far flung as Australia – that returning photographs simply wasn't an option. The cost of the postage would run to hundreds of euros – it was amazing how many actors didn't bother to enclose SAEs.

Quickly she scrutinized the other mugshots that had arrived in that morning's mail in the vain hope of spotting a face that might be right for the new star she was seeking. Not one passed muster, not one had the all-important 'Wow' factor.

The 'Wow' factor was as much of a mystery to Calypso now as it had been when she had first started out in the casting business. No matter how stunningly gorgeous or how talented a performer, if you didn't have that thing the camera loved, you simply wouldn't hack it. Directors nowadays were all on the lookout for the next hot actor or actress who oozed 'Wow'. It was a rare and elusive commodity, and as valuable as a treasure trove.

She shook her head and handed the photographs over to Iseult. 'I'd love some coffee when you've a minute, Iz,' she said. 'And would you mind nipping into the Pen Shop for some of that handmade paper later? I'm out of it, and I've thank-you notes to get off ASAP.'

Picking up her briefcase, she padded through to the office, sat down at her reassuringly oversized desk and switched on her computer. She swung round in her leather-upholstered chair while she waited for it to boot up, still feeling a bit cat-who-got-the-cream-ish, and wondering who she'd get to do her make-up for the photo session with the *Individual* photographer. The girl in Nu Blu Eriu, probably. That meant she could have one of their rose-petal massages beforehand.

Viv, Calypso's casting assistant, put her head round the door just as Calypso's screen-saver – a photo of her cream Burmese cat, Marilyn Monroe – materialized. Viv was as deadpan as Iseult was bubbly. She was shrewd, efficient, and – most importantly of all – she had an excellent eye for talent.

'Calypso, hi! Sally Ruane was on to me earlier. She wants you to get back to her ASAP.'

'Did she say what it was about?'

'Don Juan's Double.'

Don Juan's Double – the bodice-ripper Iseult had referred to earlier – was causing Calypso many headaches. Although she'd got hold of the right actress for the female lead – a rising French star – she had not yet been able to find the all-important male. Another casting session for unknowns was to be held the following week, and the chief reason she was meeting Jethro Palmer, the director, for dinner tomorrow was so that she could run some more established names by him. Unfortunately, there were availability problems with all of the more desirable candidates. 'Desirable' being the operative word. The 'Wow' factor was required bigtime on this project.

As soon as Viv's head disappeared back

around the door, Calypso picked up the phone and speed-dialled Sally's number. The agent was a good friend and had as canny an instinct for casting as Calypso. She was generally a very laid-back individual, so the fact that she'd used the ASAP word meant that something was up.

Sally's secretary put her straight through.

'There's a guy you gotta see, Calypso.'

'Yeah?'

'Yeah. He is a serious contender for the lead in *Don Juan's Double*.'

Calypso immediately uncapped her fountain pen. 'Shoot.'

'His name is Leo Devlin.'

Calypso smiled to herself as she tried out the name on the Post-It pad. 'Good name,' she said.

'That's just for starters. This boy is going all the way, Calypso. This boy is a hot property.'

The familiar thrilling feeling of excitement started its tingle in the pit of Calypso's stomach. It was a sensation as potent as poteen. 'Fill me in,' she said, trying not to sound too uncoolly intrigued. 'What age range?'

'Mid-twenties.'

'Colouring?'

'Dark.'

'OK.' Calypso covered the mouthpiece with her hand and mouthed thanks to Iseult, who had come in with her coffee. Then she helped herself to the tiny amaretto on the saucer and touched the tip of her tongue to it, relishing the way the biscuit dissolved on her taste buds. 'How did you find him?'

'I'd been tipped off about him. I saw him last night in *Liaisons Dangereuses*.'

Calypso had heard no word of any production of *Liaisons* currently running. 'Who's doing *Liaisons*?'

'Thespius.'

Thespius was an amateur outfit, set up to nurture fresh young talent. The fact that it was located out of town meant that Calypso and others scouted for talent there only if rumour of some remarkable newcomer was doing the rounds.

'Last night was a showcase, a one-off. He played a blinding Valmont. I got to him first, thank God. There were no other agents in at the show. I signed him immediately.'

'You *what*?' It was virtually unheard of for an agent to sign talent that way.

'You heard right, Calypso. You've got to see him.'

'I'm convinced.' Calypso opened the desk diary. 'Let's see. We're running a session next week. Iseult could put—'

'Next week's too late. He's out of the country from the day after tomorrow.'

'Oh *shit*. What for?'

'He's doing the backpacking thing. You're

going to have to see him today – or even tomorrow. I know it's Saturday tomorrow, but this guy is worth compromising your weekend for. Trust me.'

'I do trust you, Sally – but hell's teeth! *Back*packing! Couldn't he postpone—'

'I asked him. He wouldn't consider it. He's not working at the moment, and he's determined to do Vietnam before real life constraints come calling. I told him that if he wanted a career as an actor he was missing out on a golden opportunity.'

'And what did he say to that?'

'He said the idea of becoming a professional actor had never occurred to him and – wait for this – held no especial appeal. He's been working as a carpenter's apprentice until now. Can you believe that I actually had to *persuade* him that signing with me was a good idea? It's the first time I've ever had to practically *beg* someone to let me represent them.'

Calypso was becoming curiouser and curiouser. 'OK,' she said. 'I'll see him this afternoon.'

'I'll call him and get back to you ASAP.'

Less than two minutes later, Sally was back on the phone.

'He says he's busy this afternoon.'

Hell's *teeth*! thought Calypso again. Most young actors would beat a beeline straight to her door if they thought there was even an outside chance of meeting Calypso O'Kelly!

'And that the only time he has free is from around seven o'clock tomorrow evening,' continued Sally. 'Can you see him then?'

'I'm having dinner with Jethro Palmer in Le Blazon tomorrow evening.'

'Business or pleasure?'

'A bit of both. We've a lot of catching up to do. I haven't seen him for nearly three years.'

'How would you feel about Leo joining you?'

Calypso considered. 'I don't see why not. Actually – it's a bloody good idea, Sally. It means we'd be killing two birds with one stone. I'll ask Iseult to tweak the booking.'

'Perfect! What time should I tell him to be there?'

'Eight o'clock. By the way, Le Blazon's got even more chi-chi since they headhunted that new chef. I hope this geezer won't find the ambience too intimidating.'

The agent laughed down the phone. 'I'm not sure that Leo Devlin would find *anything* intimidating, Calypso.'

'You're intriguing me. I'd love to get a preview. Can you courier over a mugshot?'

'He doesn't have any.'

'He doesn't *have* any? *Every* aspiring actor has a set of ten-by-eights.'

'I told you. He doesn't consider himself an

24

aspiring actor. I can e-mail you a shot I took last night. It doesn't do him justice, but it'll give you an idea.'

'Cool. Will you do it ASAP?'

'ASAP.'

Calypso put the phone down. While she waited for Sally's e-mail to download, she knocked back her coffee, nibbled her little biscuit, then put in a quick phone call to the agent of the French actress she had cast in *Don Juan's Double*. She hated having to do this because her schoolgirl French was embarrassingly inadequate, and because French women always made her feel so *small*. She adored Paris, and had once thought about investing in a *pied-à-terre* there, but the thought of having to compete on a regular basis with chic Parisiennes had put her off.

Ping! Sally's attachment had finally downloaded. She'd titled it 'Check it out!' Calypso clicked on the paper clip icon, and the photograph took shape on her screen.

Wow! Oh, *wow* . . . Calypso steepled her fingers and held them against her mouth. Then she leaned back in her chair and studied the face looking back at her from her laptop.

Leo Devlin was the most blatantly sexy boy she had ever laid eyes on. He was dark-haired, with sculpted cheekbones and the sulky mouth of Michelangelo's David. And his eyes! His eyes were as impenetrably black as Heathcliff's. They regarded her from the screen with an intensity that was almost disturbing, as if he were looking into her soul.

'Calypso?' Iseult's voice came over the speakerphone, distracting her from the treasure trove she'd just downloaded. 'Rosa's here to see you.'

'Rosa! Send her right in!' Calypso stood up from her desk. 'Hey, babe!' she said as her friend Rosa Elliot came through the door. 'How's it going?'

'Hey, you!' Rosa slung her bag on the chaise longue and came forward to give Calypso a hug. Then she held her at arm's length and gave her the once-over. 'Well, Calypso O'Kelly, you are a total disgrace. You've been shopping again. Those are brand new threads, aren't they? I saw them in the window of Brown Thomas last week.' She shook her head and made a 'tch-ing' sound. 'How typical of you, girl. Butter-coloured suede! It's going to cost a fortune in dry-cleaning bills.'

'Mm.' Calypso gave her a guilty look. She always felt guilty wearing expensive new things around Rosa because Rosa was a cash-conscious single mother. She was also Calypso's best friend. They had met at Trinity when they were first-year theatre studies students, and had shared a flat that was a total kip: but in those days they hadn't cared two hoots about the kippishness because they were hardly ever there. There'd been too much fun to be had elsewhere.

Now she tried to divert attention from her suede trousers by saying: 'Come and see what I've found!' She moved back to her desk and angled the screen on her laptop so that Rosa could see her new discovery.

'Wow!' said Rosa, and Calypso clapped her hands.

'That's exactly what *I* said! He's beautiful, isn't he?'

'Mm.' Rosa put her head on one side and gave the image on the screen the once-over. '*Very* mean and moody. Very, *very* sexy. Irish?'

'Yep.'

'Who's his agent?'

'Sally Ruane.'

'Sally gets lucky again. I must be the only dud on her books.' Rosa checked her watch. 'Have you time for a quick coffee? I'm between gigs and I want someone to keep me amused.'

'What am I? The court jester?'

'Yeah. And I'm the Queen of Sheba. Please come, Calypso. I've been doing voiceovers all morning and that means I've had to smile sweetly at some truly obnoxious advertising people. My jaw muscles are aching. Butler's?'

'Sure. I've just had one, but I'll keep you company.' Calypso swung her bag over her shoulder and led Rosa through reception. 'We're going to grab a coffee, Izzy,' she said as she slipped into her shoes. 'I'll be back in ten or so.

Hey – why don't you nip into my office and get a load of the pic Sally e-mailed? And ask Viv to have a look, too. I think we may be on to something.'

'Will do, boss.'

In Butler's, the café across the road from Calypso's office, Rosa ordered latte and a selection of their chocolates on the side, and Calypso had water.

'Want one?' Rosa held out the dish of chocolates.

'I'd love one, but I've had my sweetie ration already today. I had an amaretto with my coffee earlier.'

'And that's *it*? One teeny-weeny amaretto is all you allow yourself for the entire day?'

'Yeah. I really pigged out on holiday. Dominic will divorce me if I get any fatter.'

'My dear Calypso, you have no need to worry. I think you look fantastic. How was Tuscany?'

'The usual. Pretty fab. Too much lazing around and way too much food. I've been trying to fit in a gym session every day since I got back. How do you do it, Rosa-belle? Look at you – sitting there pigging out on chocolates. How dare you not be a big fat lump.'

'Ashtanga yoga.'

'Really? Are you taking Ashtanga classes?'

Rosa laughed. 'Joke. Where would I find time to fit in Ashtanga yoga classes, you dimwit? It's all the running round after Lottie that keeps me fit.' She bit into another chocolate, and said: 'So. Tell me more about your new discovery.'

'The actor on my laptop?'

'You wish.'

Calypso returned her wicked smile. 'I'm having dinner with him tomorrow evening.'

'Oh? Business or pleasure?'

'Business, of course. I'm keeping my fingers crossed that he'll be right for the epic.'

'*Don Juan's Double*?'

'Mm.'

'What's his name?'

'Leo Devlin.'

'Hey! He's even got a cool moniker.'

'Damn right. This boy's got everything going for him – touch wood.' Calypso put out a hand and touched the underside of the table. 'Unlike just about everybody else I've seen for that part. D'you know something? I got a stack of ten-by-eights in the post this morning and every single one of them had to go in the bin.'

Rosa shook her head. 'It must be such a weird feeling to have the kind of power you have, Calypso. I so envy you! I'd love to be able to tell some of the gobshites I have to work with to go stuff their job.'

'Actually, sometimes I'm not sure that I *enjoy* being powerful,' said Calypso, looking thoughtful. 'It's a double-edged-sword thing. I can never be sure whether people come on to me on social occasions because they genuinely want to, or because they're sucking up to me.' Calypso had given up going to opening nights for that very reason. She couldn't handle actors fawning and flirting and competing with each other for her attention.

'What about someone like that Leo Devlin dude, though? Wouldn't it be hard to resist *him* if he came on to you?'

'Absolutely not. I pride myself on my professional propensity for detachment and imperviousness,' announced Calypso in a mock-snooty voice.

'Ooh. What big words you use. Where'd you learn those?'

'Dominic, probably. Or Radio 4.'

'Yikes.' Rosa made an embarrassed face at the *Teletubbies* theme tune that jingled loudly from her mobile. 'Bloody Lottie keeps changing my settings for a joke,' she said. 'She put that awful theme tune from *Home and Away* on last week and it went off in front of the world's coolest copywriter. Excuse me.' Rosa pressed 'talk', and then said, 'Hi, Dannie! What's up?'

There was a series of 'mms' and 'OKs' and 'no problems' before Rosa said 'See you later', and stuck the phone back in her bag. 'That was Dannie,' she said.

'How is she?'

'Busy. She's started doing commissions – business has really taken off for her.'

'I'm not surprised. She's got to be the most inspired florist in town.'

'And the most inspired homemaker. She was driving past that retro shop on Baggot Street earlier today and she saw a fantastic embroidered bedspread on display in the window. She wanted to know if I might get a chance to pick it up for her before someone else nabs it. She's big into retro stuff – you should see what she's done to her apartment, it's really beautiful.'

'All retro?'

'Yeah. It's really – um – what's the right word? "Feminine's" too fluffy. Kind of "womanly", I suppose. Like a courtesan's boudoir. We should get together again soon, the three of us. We haven't done it for ages.' Rosa drained her latte, then looked at her watch and made a face. 'I'd better get on.' She scanned the bill and slapped Calypso's hand when she tried to contribute two euros for her water. 'Get me next time,' she said.

'Thanks. What's your gig?' asked Calypso, getting to her feet.

'A new telly ad for Grant & Wainwright.'

'A nice earner?'

'Yep. D'you know, one of the mothers at the school gate asked me what the rate for a telly commercial was the other day and her jaw nearly

31

hit the deck when I told her. I had to remind her that the fee might have to keep some actors going for a month.'

They had left the café and were standing on the footpath, waiting for the pedestrian light to turn green. 'Do the Grant & Wainwright voice for me,' urged Calypso. 'It always makes me laugh when I hear it come on in the ad break.'

Rosa shook back her hair, and said, in her best soft-sell purr: '"Sleek. Silken. Smooth. Sexy. *Iridescence*. From Grant & Wainwright."'

'Excellent! How many takes to get it right?'

'With a bit of luck, not many – as long as I don't have to lip-sync. And it had better bloody not be many. I've a rash of gigs lined up today, and if there are any hiccups I'll be late for the school run.' The green man lit up, and they crossed. 'Bye, Calypso m'dear. Will we do that girly night soon?'

'Sure. My gaff?'

'No. Mine. That means I won't have to bother with a babysitter.' She gave Calypso a waspish smile. 'Good luck with your new actor tomorrow. Looks like you're on to something there.'

'Keep your fingers crossed. Send Lottie a hundred kisses from me.'

'I'm not sure she deserves them. She was like a bag of cats leaving the house this morning. Love you.' Rosa leaned forward, gave her friend a kiss on the cheek, and then she was gone.

Calypso ran up the stairs of her office building. She always chose to do this rather than take the lift because she knew it burned up loads of calories. Rosa might think she was looking fantastic, but she, Calypso, knew what she looked like with no clothes on. Back in reception she raised an enquiring eyebrow at Iseult. 'Well? What do you think?' she asked.

'Oh, Calypso – he's gorgeous!'

'Knew you'd fancy him!' She gave her secretary a cat-like smile, then slid off her shoes and went back into her office. Sitting down in her chair, she swung round again, assessing. Was it time for a make-over? No. She'd had the joint redecorated just over a year ago. However, she'd have to get the cleaners to do something about that mark on her beautiful powder-blue chaise longue. And the fish tank needed cleaning, and those flowers were looking a bit past their best-before date. She'd ask Iseult to run out to the local florists. No. She'd call Dannie. It was about time she put some business her way, now that she was doing commissions. Reaching for the phone, Calypso simultaneously clicked on her mouse and regarded the face still smouldering at her from her computer screen. She put her head on one side and narrowed her eyes back at Leo Devlin, then laughed out loud and blew an extravagant kiss at the digital image of the man she had yet to meet.

'*And then a really weird thing happened. Just as she'd finished the little drawing of the house in the very bottom right-hand corner of the page, the map on the wall turned to dust and the door of the room swung open.*' Rosa raised her eyebrows, gave her daughter a sphinx-like smile, then leaned forward to kiss her on the forehead.

'Mum! No, Mum! You can't stop there! Go on, go on – *please* go on!'

'No, Lottie. It's way past your bedtime. You got an extra ten minutes of the story tonight. Anyway, I can't go on because even *I* don't know what happens next. I haven't the first clue what's behind that door.'

'You must have an *idea*.'

'Nope. Not an iota. That's the beauty of making it up as you go along. It means the story's as exciting for me as it is for you.' That was a fib. Rosa actually kept a notebook in her bag so that she could jot down ideas for Lottie's story any time they came to her.

She got to her feet and pulled the duvet up under her daughter's chin. Her little flushed face and shining eyes made Rosa's heart swell with love suddenly, and she bent to kiss her again, smoothing out the thick, blond hair. The pillowcase was torn on one corner and there was a bit of pillow poking out, she noticed absently. A self-tear, too, which meant it couldn't be mended. A new pillowcase and matching duvet cover were in order. Lottie had had these for years – in fact, Rosa recalled now, her own mother had bought them for her not long before she'd died, around the time Lottie had graduated from her cot to a bed. Funny how you remembered stuff like that. Stuff like where duvet covers came from. It had been the Brown Thomas winter sale, and Rosa's mother had bought towels for her, too. Rosa couldn't afford duvet covers and towels from Brown Thomas now, even at the sale price. She'd have to go to the Bull Ring on Meath Street for something cheap and cheerful.

'Good night, baby. Sweet dreams, sleep tight—'

'And don't let the bugs bite. Good night, Mum. Love you.'

Rosa blew another kiss from the door, and turned out the overhead light. The night light stood sentinel in the form of an illuminated rabbit that had been another gift – this time from Lottie's munificent fairy godmother, Calypso.

The noise the child's bedroom door made as she shut it behind her was another punctuation mark in the routine of her daily life. Rosa wandered into the sitting room, realizing that she was feeling very, very tired. In the corner of her eye she noticed the screensaver on her computer blank out. It was as if it had chosen this strategic moment to remind her of its existence, and of all the real life things connected with it. She really should sit down in front of it and sort out her accounts – at least two bills were overdue – but she'd spent the latter half of the afternoon stuck in traffic, ferrying Lottie from school to her Irish dancing class, and then to the dentist; right now sums were the last thing she felt like doing. Anyway, she wouldn't be in a position to pay any bills at all until the cheque came through from the Definite Article Advertising. The woman in the accounts department had told her when she'd phoned today that it was in the post. But that's what she'd said last week, too.

Rosa steeled herself, then moved to the dining table and touched the mouse to reactivate the computer. It was an ancient one that Calypso had given her when she was upgrading, and it took for ever to access files. As she waited for the sluggish machine to emerge from hibernation she thought of the new suede trousers she'd seen Calypso wearing, and how much they must have set her back, and she felt even more disheartened. She loved Calypso, she really did, but when she'd married Dominic something in the dynamic of their relationship had changed.

She remembered the first time she'd seen the town house in Ranelagh where Dominic had installed her best friend, nearly a decade ago. He'd bought the joint sight unseen: extended, refurbished and ready-furnished from the top-of-the-range computer in the office down to the leather armchairs in the sitting room and the sleek cutlery in the kitchen – even the aroma-therapy candles by the Jacuzzi had been positioned with the precision of a set-dresser, Calypso had told her. Rosa had looked round at that beautiful kitchen (where she knew very little cooking would ever get done), at Calypso's azure-blue units, glass-brick walls and stainless steel island topped in granite, and she had burst into tears. 'It's so *beautiful*!' she'd wailed. And as Calypso had given her the conducted tour of the house, Rosa hadn't been able to stop crying, and repeating: 'It's just so, *so* beautiful!'

Rosa knew that the beauty of the house wasn't the only reason she'd wept. She had wept too because she'd known how divergent their lifestyles would inevitably become. Their student days when they'd larked around and taken the piss out of grown-ups like Dominic were well and truly gone for ever. Of course, another reason why they were gone for ever had been evolving inside Rosa's eight-month-pregnant belly even as she followed Calypso from room to room so that her friend could show her how her latest toy – the zapper-on sound system – worked. And as Calypso had danced ahead of her, zapping and laughing, Rosa had found it hard to believe that not so long ago her friend had been a struggling student actress like her . . .

* * *

'Carbohydrates!' pronounced Calypso. 'That's exactly what I need.' They were setting up for the lunch shift in the restaurant that provided them with part-time work and minuscule wages. Calypso was making sure all the cutlery was smear-free; Rosa was filling bowls with mayonnaise from a catering-size plastic container. The smell of food drifted up from the kitchen. 'I want pasta for breakfast. With bacon. And piles of Parmesan. If I can sneak the precious Parmesan out of the kitchen, that is. I don't care about the calories, I just want the cure.'

Rosa looked up and gave her a wan smile. 'Hangover *that* persistent?' she asked.

'Yeah. That herbal remedy you recommended is crap. Also, it tastes disgusting. No – pasta's definitely my cure of choice for today.'

'Where did you end up last night?'

'In Lillies. It was vile – I've never seen it so crowded. You were right not to come, and your virtuous behaviour has been richly rewarded.'

'Yeah?'

'Yeah. You are not suffering from a hangover. Although,' Calypso put her head on one side and gave Rosa a look of narrow-eyed assessment, 'I'm not convinced, somehow, beloved, that you didn't sneak out somewhere and sink a few. You're looking easily as peaky as I feel.'

'Am I? That's because – that's because . . . Oh God! Because the smell of cooking's making me feel sick.' She clapped her hands over her mouth. 'Oh, Calypso, I think I'm going to – no – I *know* I'm going to –' Rosa had turned nearly as green as the napkin Calypso was polishing her knives and forks with.

Seeing that the situation demanded immediate action, Calypso slung a clatter of cutlery back in the drawer, grabbed Rosa by the hand and dragged her towards the Ladies. They reached the loo just in time. Rosa doubled up and heaved into the bowl while Calypso held her hair back from her face, making reassuring sounds and averting her eyes. When it got to the dry-heave stage, Calypso unrolled a few metres of loo roll, soaked it under the tap, squeezed it out, then knelt down on the floor where Rosa half crouched, half slumped, and proceeded to gently swab her face. Rosa no longer looked quite as bilious, but there was sweat on her face and her eyes were wet with tears.

'Hey,' said Calypso. 'You don't end up like this after a quiet night at home with your mum, Rosie-baby. You must have contracted some kind of—'

'Pregnant,' said Rosa, in a raspy, dead-sounding kind of voice. 'I think I'm pregnant.'

Calypso sat back on her heels and covered her mouth with her hands. 'Oh, Jesus,' she said. Then, cautiously, after a pause: 'Is it Profound Dave's?'

'I don't think so.'

Calypso bit her lip. 'You mean it could be the Brad Pitt lookalike? The bloke you met at Theresa's wedding?' Rosa had told her very little about the dude at the wedding, and Calypso suspected it was because, while the liaison had sounded gloriously romantic, her friend was ashamed of having acquiesced in such time-honoured walkover fashion to a one-night stand.

Rosa nodded. 'Yes. I think it's more likely to be his. There was a split condom.' She gave a laugh that was half-wry, half-manic. 'Although it's immaterial, isn't it, whose it is? I'm not likely to see either of them again in my life.'

There was a pause while each of them chewed their lips and avoided eye contact.

'I even took the morning-after pill, Calypso. That's what convinced me there was no chance of my being pregnant. Plus the fact that I had a kind of a period—'

'A *kind* of a period?'

'Yeah – you know, spotting – around the right time. It was light, but it was enough to reassure me. You know my periods have always been wonky, anyway . . .' Rosa's voice trailed off, and she chewed her lip even harder. 'I know what you're going to say. You're going to say that I've been in denial. You're going to say that I've been putting off making the big Real Life decision that's facing me.'

Calypso drew in a deep breath, then let it out slowly. 'Well. It would seem that way, wouldn't it?' She knew Rosa's feelings about abortion. Rosa had never known her birth mother. She had been adopted, and any time the subject of abortion came up for discussion she had always pointed out that, while abortion might be a legit solution for her girlfriends, it was a seriously dodgy moral option for her. Calypso cleared her throat quite unnecessarily. 'Have you done a test?' she asked.

'Not yet.'

'I'll hold your hand.'

'Thanks, Calypso. You always were a chum.' Rosa leaned forward to aim a kiss at her friend's cheek, then changed her mind. 'I'll postpone kissing you until I've spritzed with Gold Spot. I'm sure you could do without further close contact with someone who's just barfed down a loo.' Smiling, she got to her feet and brushed away any dust that might have accumulated on her bum.

As Calypso stood up their eyes met, and the unspoken question had to be asked. 'What are you going to do, Rosa?' she said.

Rosa gave a bright smile. 'I'm going back to work, of course.'

Calypso laid a hand on her friend's arm. 'You know that's not what I meant,' she said. 'I meant, what are you going to do about the baby?'

Rosa looked scared for about a sixteenth of a second before assuming the stubborn expression that Calypso knew so well. 'I'm going to keep it,' she said.

In her sitting room Rosa stared at the figures on the computer screen. They seemed to her like grotesque Munchkins going 'Nyah na na nyah na! You'll ne-ver pay us!' The sheaf of bills on the table yoo-hooed at her too, and she tried to ignore it. She knew that she'd have to ring that bloody woman in accounts again next week when the cheque still hadn't arrived in the post.

Her adoptive mother Ursula had always told her not to take stuff like that personally, not to let the bastards get to her, and Ursula had been very wise. When Rosa had made the decision to do the theatre studies course in Trinity, Ursula had pointed out the pitfalls of a profession where income was notoriously erratic. In fact, neither Rosa nor Calypso had gone back to Trinity after that first year. Calypso had made herself apprentice to a casting director and married Dominic shortly thereafter, and Rosa had become pregnant and latched onto the voiceover bandwagon that had supported her and Lottie ever since. Ursula had encouraged Rosa to keep her options open by taking night classes in other skills so that she'd have 'Something To Fall Back On' if the work ever dried up. Rosa smiled as she remembered the way those words had sounded in her ears like a mantra: *Something To Fall Back On* . . . And then she remembered how Ursula had looked when Rosa held her hand as she lay dying, and the smile vanished. She had lost both her mother and – several years earlier still – her adoptive father to cancer. Ursula's had been intestinal. Fast, fierce and excruciatingly painful.

She didn't want to think about it. Feeling a surge of mutiny, she shut down her computer and turned the television on instead. She zapped away fly-on-the-wall documentaries and depressing news footage and soap stars screaming at each other until she came to tropical fish on the Discovery channel. Mesmerizing eye-candy. Or a glass of wine and a book. That's what she wanted this evening. Turning off the television, she headed for the kitchen to pour herself some wine.

In the kitchen the dishes looked at her as tauntingly as the sheaf of bills had in the sitting room. Was there *no* escaping real life? Oh, hell – at least the dishes didn't require any brain power. She'd get them out of the way before settling down with wine and chick fic. Filling the basin, she automatically reached for the switch on the radio. Her own voice came back at her, advertising some unnecessary bathroom product. It was a voiceover she'd done over a year ago. Good! That meant she'd be due a residual fee for second-year usage.

The jolly, upbeat bathroom cleanser ad (*Rely on Cleanrite to keep your workload light!* – what a bitch it had been to record, what with all those r's and l's tripping her up!) came to a pingy end, and Nat King Cole slid out through the speakers into Rosa's kitchen. She immediately lunged for the 'off' button. She hadn't been able to listen to that song since it had played at a friend's wedding nearly ten years ago . . .

Rosa was feeling pretty damn good. She was at the wedding party of one of her posher fellow students. It had been going for some hours now, in the garden of a fabulous country house hotel. She was sipping white wine, and she had just stubbed out a spliff of excellent, excellent Thai grass which made her feel floaty and sexy and kind of *at one* with the universe and everyone around her. She was sitting on the edge of a fountain weaving a daisy chain and swinging her legs, watching beautiful people in beautiful clothes waft around the grounds, and there was blossom on the trees. The smell of it drifted to her on the balmy night air, and fairy lights glimmered in the branches, and there were stars up there in the deep blue velvet of the sky. And Nat King Cole was playing over the speakers. And all she was lacking, Rosa thought, as she trailed her hand along her forearm, loving the sensation of the fine hairs rising at her touch, all she was lacking was a beautiful man to dance with.

She'd just split up with her boyfriend, whom she had taken to calling Profound Dave as a joke because she'd begun to suspect that, under the cool veneer of profundity that he chose to adopt, poor Dave was actually pretty vacant. Now the vacancy was waiting to be filled. Rosa set her daisy-chain crown on her head, knocked back the wine in her glass, then wandered on bare feet towards the marquee for a refill.

Oh, God! There he was! There *he* was, standing by the entrance. The guy who looked like Brad Pitt, the guy with the fantastic physique and the merest soupçon of a slouch, the guy with the faint trace of golden stubble and the tousled golden hair. She'd spotted him earlier, and had cast covert glance after covert glance in his direction, hoping he might notice her. Not a chance! He had too many distractions in the form of the women who were hanging onto him – laughing exaggerated laughs at his remarks, tossing back flirtatious hair and toying insinuatingly with the thin straps of their party frocks, looking meaningfully at him from under mascaraed lashes.

'Who is he?' she'd asked Calypso.

But Calypso had just shrugged and said:

'Some pal of Sean's from London. Why don't you go for it, babe?'

Rosa had just laughed. 'Get real, Calypso. A bloke like that wouldn't look twice at someone like me.'

So Calypso had kissed her on the cheek and said, 'You look amazing, sweetie-pie. You look like a fifteen-year-old waif in your Ghost frock and daisy-chain coronet.'

'No! I don't want to look fifteen, Calypso! I want to look like a worldly and sophisticated goddess-type. I want to look like you. How do you manage it?'

'Hard work,' said Calypso matter-of-factly. 'Anyway, you have the rest of your life to look worldly and sophisticated, Rosa. My advice to you is to take advantage of the fact that you look like jailbait while you have the chance.'

Now she turned away from the Brad Pitt lookalike in case he should see her staring, and when she turned back, he was walking across the lawn to her, smiling.

'I was watching you earlier. Sitting on the fountain like something out of a fairy tale,' he said.

'Yeah?' said Rosa, dropping her eyes and realizing that she sounded like a cerebrally challenged adolescent. She coloured and tried to cover her confusion by sipping at her wine – then saw, of course, that her glass was empty and she must look like even more of an eejit.

'Allow me to get you a refill,' he said. And yes, his voice was educated and chocolatey, and yes, his denim-blue eyes had a shockingly knowing glint in them, and yes, when he took the glass from her she felt a *frisson* as his fingers brushed hers, and yes, she *knew* she was going to end up in bed with him tonight, and yes – it was the finest, sexiest feeling in the world.

They slow-danced to Nat King Cole, they shared the wine in her glass, they allowed their bodies to fuse ever more closely as the dance became slower and slower, and when he brushed her earlobe with his lips she knew what he was going to ask her, and of course she said 'yes'.

They glided across the lawn, they floated up the staircase of the olde worlde hotel and they dissolved into bed. It was the most exquisite thing she had ever experienced. And when, after a lifetime of indescribable pleasure had passed, he'd extracted a condom from his jacket pocket and asked if he could enter her, of course she'd said 'yes' again. And when she'd woken from a slumberous half-dream around dawn and found him standing looking down at her with his jacket slung over his shoulder and she'd asked him was he leaving, of course, of *course* he'd said 'yes'. He had a flight to catch, back to London, where he lived. And she knew with absolute, blinding certainty that there was no point, no point whatsoever, in asking him for his address, just as he didn't ask her for hers.

She watched him from the upstairs window as he strolled down the driveway towards the car park and out of her life, his jacket still slung over his shoulder, and she realized that they hadn't even asked each other's names. And when he'd disappeared from sight she saw the lovely garden of the country house hotel in all its post-party squalor – the litter, the glasses, the passed-out party-goers, the bedimmed fairy lights. The reality. Turning back to face the room feeling deflated, Rosa debated whether she should have a shower or whether she should go back to bed for some kip. And as she bent to retrieve the condom from the floor beside the bed she saw, with a flash of fear, that it had split.

'Mummy mummy *mummy*!'

Lottie was calling her in a voice that made her sprint from the kitchen. Within seconds she was by the child's bed, stroking her forehead, smoothing her hair, saying in her lowest, tenderest, most reassuring croon: 'There, there, baby. There, there, my little love. Sh, sh, sh. The nightmare's all gone. It's Mummy here, who loves you. The nightmare's all gone . . .'

And later that evening, after she'd got the dishes out of the way and curled up with an undemanding book and a glass of wine, she remembered how Ursula had used to sing to her at night if she was fretful or sick; she recalled the stories she had told her before she went to sleep – stories which were not unlike the stories Rosa now told Lottie – and suddenly she missed her mother so much she wanted to cry.

What would Ursula think of her now, she wondered? She'd had such high hopes for the daughter she'd adopted. How would she feel if she could see her now, slugging back indifferent wine in a city-centre flat, with no social life to speak of, and no significant other? She looked at the framed photograph of her mother that she kept on the mantelpiece. Her dark eyes gazed back at Rosa's hazel ones, her generous mouth was curved in a loving smile. Being adopted, Rosa had inherited none of those physical traits – she would have loved the bee-stung lips, but had to content herself with a hateful Cupid's bow. What she *had* inherited was enough money from the sale of Ursula's house and effects to buy her flat. Her own home was her inheritance – that, and lots and lots of love.

Her home. Somehow, this flat had never really felt like home. She thought of Calypso's des res, and she thought of Dannie's fabulous bird-of-paradise nest, and she looked around at the sitting room she'd furnished with the usual suspects – bits and pieces of stuff picked up in Habitat sales as and when she'd had the money

– and she thought that, actually, this was more a space for living than a home. She remembered the house she'd grown up in, with its garden and garage and Aga, and the attic where she'd had a playroom. That, she thought, was what a home should be.

The bell gave its familiar tinkle, as if announcing her arrival, and the heady scent of lilies greeted Dannie Moore as she pushed open the door of the shop she'd christened 'Florabundance'. The flowers banked up in buckets all round her seemed to preen as she made her way through the shop to the back room to dump her bag and fill the kettle. This was the time of the day she loved the most, the early morning when she had the place all to herself and could fiddle about to her heart's content, getting ready to face the world. She loved to imagine her flowers sleeping at night, bunched up together with their silly faces hidden under furled petals, then starting to wake as the sun came up: chrysanthemums shaking their tousled manes, impish orchids sticking out their tongues at each other, dotey begonias in pots fluffing out their frilly frocks, macho red-hot pokers checking out their tackle. Sometimes she reminded herself of Alice when she steps through the looking-glass and discovers that flowers can talk – 'when there's anybody worth talking to'. She had always loved the bossy Tiger-lily's remarks about daisies: 'The daisies are worst of all. When one speaks, they all begin together, and it's enough to make one wither the way they go on!' It was lovely to be able to indulge in whimsy from time to time – especially since she hadn't always had the opportunity. In her past life, whimsy had been severely frowned upon. In her past life, in the television station where she'd worked, too much whimsy and people looked at you sideways, as if you were doolally.

She re-emerged into the shop and threw an eye around, trying to decide what to do first. Should she light a fire in the tiny, cast-iron grate? It was shaping up to be a sunny day, but in Ireland you never could tell. Ach, might as well, she thought, as she threw a shovelful of dry pine cones, turf and sticks into the fire basket. It wasn't to heat the place so much as to provide one of those cosy touches her customers loved. The shop – which had once been a family grocer's and had remained unchanged for years – was small, but, as far as she was concerned, perfectly formed: a pocket Venus! It still had loads of original features: an ancient scrubbed wooden counter, bare oak floorboards, crumbling plasterwork, a stained-glass fanlight above the door, and, of course, the cast-iron fireplace with its gorgeous ornamentation of embossed butterflies, berries, birds and blossoms.

The fireplace had been encrusted with several decades of paint when she'd first seen it, but the detail had been decipherable under the dingy, once-white layers.

This was the feature that had made her mind up for her five years ago when she was on the hunt for premises. It had seemed like a sign to have discovered a fireplace covered in flora and fauna; sometimes she felt it was the shop that had found her rather than the other way round. The first thing she'd done after she'd signed the lease was to strip away the paint. It had taken a week of knuckle-skinning, nail-breaking work, but it had been worth it when the fireplace was finally revealed in all its original Victorian glory, gleaming with fireblack.

Dannie could have done with more space now that business was booming – or, as her customers liked to put it with a cheery 'ha, ha', *blooming* – but she wasn't prepared to sacrifice the unique ambience of her shop for the sake of a few extra square metres in premises with less character. Anyway, the fact that the place was always so crammed with flowers only added to its appeal. While many of the florists in town were still stuck in the postmodernist groove so well travelled in the nineties – that stark Zen look favoured by their feng shui-conscious customers – Dannie's preference was for abundance: she loved the look of hundreds of blossoms jostling for space on her shelves and drenching the air with perfume.

A thin stream of smoke started to spiral its way up the chimney, and, as the pine cones took, she sat back on her hunkers watching fire burgeon in the grate like surreal, speeded-up footage of flame flowers in autumn. Contentment swelled, and, as ever, Dannie welcomed the warm feeling which, even after all this time, was still quite new to her. *Her* shop. Her dream. Five years ago, that's all it had been. The dream of a culchie from Connemara who'd fetched up in London . . .

The horn of the black taxi was pumped again, several times in rapid succession, and finally – after much effing and blinding from the driver's seat about the standard of driving in London – the cab swung round a corner and pulled up outside the building in Chiswick where Dannie had her flat. She paid off the still-muttering, road-enraged cabbie, gathered her bags together and ran up the steps to the front door, tucking a carrier bag under her chin as she rummaged in her bag for keys.

Once inside her apartment she dumped the carrier bag in her bedroom, her briefcase in the spare room that doubled as her study, and her Tesco bags in the kitchen, along with the flowers she'd bought. Star Gazer lilies – *not* the freshest, she'd noticed, and way overpriced – but she hadn't had much choice in the end-of-day florists, and she hadn't had time to be picky. She did what she could with the flowers, put music on, and legged it to the bathroom to run a bath. On the way past the open door of her study, she saw that her fax machine was spewing paper. She'd been warned that she'd more than likely get a 'send later' fax from a PR company in LA. Feck, feck, *feck*! Work was the last thing on her mind right now. She'd ignore it. There were more important things to consider this evening. Dannie was at the most fertile phase of her cycle, and damn *right* was she going to take advantage of the fact!

While her bath was running, she threw together the antipasti she'd bought earlier. Finger food had been the obvious choice. After all, she intended spending most of the evening in bed with her gorgeous fella, making a baby. It had taken a lot of cajoling, but she had finally, finally persuaded Guy that a baby was a good idea. How lucky that the most fertile day of her cycle had coincided with the day before he was off on an assignment again! Once upon a time she had thought it was romantic to have a boyfriend who was a war correspondent – handsome, dashing, brave, etc., etc., etc. Her heart leapt up every time he appeared on the news looking world-weary and narrow-eyed and – oh,

God! There was only one word for it! – *manly*. And when he signed off with 'Guy Fairbrother, northern Afghanistan' (or wherever it was he'd been posted), she wanted to swoon. Now she switched the news off when he came on. It was just another worry in her already stressful life.

Dannie was a highly regarded researcher on a high-profile weekly television chat show. She had an excellent salary, a stylish home, and she was enjoying a relationship that had all the potential in the world for becoming permanent. Until, that is, the happy couple stumbled across that booby trap in life known as 'irreconcilable differences', when she decided that she passionately wanted a baby and Guy equally passionately refused to oblige her by giving her one. But slowly, subtly, she'd worn down his resistance, like a guerrilla warrior who won't give up. And now D-Day had arrived.

She bathed, rubbed in the body lotion Guy liked best, and checked the clock. It was nearly time. She applied a little, very discreet make-up (he hated the stuff), and checked the clock again. It was time. She slid into the kimono she'd treated herself to that day in a retro shop that she passed on her way to work. It had been sick-makingly expensive, but the garment had sung the most seductive siren song to her that she had ever heard. She'd spotted it in the window last week, and every time she had walked past on her way to work, she'd heard its sweet voice calling to her. 'Dannie! Dannie Moore! Over here! Look at me! Try me on! You don't have to *buy* me – just try me on!' So she'd gone and tried the feckin' thing on, and that, of course, had been her undoing.

Dannie didn't often indulge her graw for pretty things. Growing up in Connemara on a working farm surrounded by seven older brothers meant that girly stuff had been a no-go area. She'd always been a tomboy. Even when her father had had her carted off to an all-girls boarding school, girl stuff hadn't impinged much on her – especially since the pupils had to wear their fierce-looking uniforms seven days a week.

Weekend visits home weren't encouraged: Dannie's da had made it quite clear that if he was forking out a small fortune for her school fees, he was going to milk them for all they were worth. Her board and lodgings were paid for, and she'd damn well make the most of them. Her favourite brother Joe sometimes came and sprang her, and would take her off to Clifden or Galway for a bit of fun and a sneaky visit to a pub, but she hadn't ever enjoyed much of a family life.

It was from Joe that she had found out all about their mother, a stunning Italian teenage hitch-hiker that her father had picked up one sunny day in the tiny village of Kilrowan, and whom he'd married three months later. It had been an extraordinary alliance by all accounts: the taciturn Irish farmer and the dark-haired beauty who bore him seven boys and then died giving birth to her, Dannie. She'd been named for her mother, Daniella, and had inherited her continental looks. But Dannie had never bothered about the way she looked. She was perfectly happy, when not in uniform, to deck herself out in nothing fancier than Docs and dungarees. She was one of the lads, and on her holidays she worked as hard around the farm as any of them. Since one of her duties was to clean the pipes of the milking machines at the end of the day, a running serenade in the household was, inevitably, 'Danny Boy'. Her brothers thought that the line about the pipes calling to Dannie was a hilarious joke, and they sang it at her *ad nauseam*.

She'd have been quite content to stay on in Connemara after she'd finished school, but her father had insisted that she 'better herself ', and Dannie had always done as her dada told her. She knew it was because she felt guilty about having been the cause of her mother's death. Frank, her father, had never got over losing his glorious, exotic wife. Dannie also knew that, as the years had gone by, the similarity to her mother had become more and more pronounced, and she suspected that her father couldn't handle it. So off to Dublin she went to get her degree at UCD, and then to London to land her groovy job as a television researcher. She'd only been back home twice since.

Now, as Dannie recalled growing up in the wild West of Ireland, she wondered if London was really a suitable environment to rear the child she was about to conceive.

She checked the clock for the third time in ten minutes. Guy was late. She replayed her favourite track on the CD. She poured herself a glass of wine. She lit candles. She fiddled with flowers. This was OK. He'd been held up before. But *tonight* of all nights! *Jaysus!* She tried to resist the impulse to check the clock again, but couldn't. He was running late by over half an hour. He always phoned when he was this delayed. Maybe she should phone him? She moved towards the study and dithered. No. Not yet. She didn't want to look too needy, too desperate. Needy women were every alpha male's pet hate. She would read her fax, so she would. She'd divert herself with a little business, and by that time *surely* he'd have arrived.

She picked up the thin sheet of paper that lay curled on her desk top, and smoothed it out. *Dear Dannie*, she read, and immediately her focus zoomed in on the signature. *Guy*. She swallowed, pushed her hair back from her face and moved like an automaton to the kitchen to retrieve her glass of wine, reading as she went.

Dear Dannie,

I know you never thought I'd take the coward's way out, and believe me, neither did I. But I also know that if I tried to do this face to face with you, I'd wimp out. Your quite irresistible charm is such that I'd end up in bed with you, and you'd have your baby, which I understand is your all-consuming need right now. But I can't do it. I can't bring a child into this world. It would be morally an entirely wrong thing for me to do. We've talked about it a lot lately, and you know my feelings on the subject. I've seen too much horror, Dannie, and too much anguish. And consider this. I'm not going to be there enough for you, to provide the kind of support you're going to need. The worst-case scenario that's been haunting me is of me getting blown to bits in some war-torn region of the world and you rearing our baby on your own. I'm sorry, so sorry. You'll have your baby some day – how could a gorgeous, minxy woman like you not get what she wants?

Please know that this is no easy thing for me to do. You've always told me I'm brave. I'm not brave – this fax bears testimony to that. As far as I'm concerned, this is the most craven thing I've ever done in my life. Sorry. Love, Guy.

The music she'd put on the CD player came to an abrupt end and the ticking of her biological

clock reverberated around the walls of her taste-
fully furnished Chiswick apartment. Dannie
scrunched the fax paper in her hand and
dropped it in the bin. And then she started
crying.

She spent the weekend in a living nightmare. On
Monday she went into work feeling knackered
and empty. It was a strange feeling. After all that
emotional wrestling she'd expected to experience some kind of catharsis, whether it be
murderous rage, or weepy regret. She'd
certainly never expected to feel *empty*. Standing
by the water-cooler, trying to make sense of this
new emotion, she observed the comings and
goings of the staff and made a huge discovery.
No-one was smiling. *No-one*. Every single person
streeling round the corridors of that huge, ugly,
soulless building looked almost shifty, as if they
expected someone to sneak up behind them and
slide a knife between their shoulder blades. By
the water-cooler, she tried a few smiley opening
gambits. 'Lovely day, isn't it?' 'Did you watch the
match on Saturday?' '*Corrie*'s gone downhill a
bit, hasn't it?' Without exception, her chatty
remarks were met with surprise, followed by
suspicion, followed by an indecipherable grunt
that could have been 'yeah'. Dannie was no
Pollyanna, but to her mind this weird socio-
phobic behaviour indicated that something had

gone very wrong in her workplace. Something was rotten.

She dumped her polystyrene cup in the overflowing bin and headed towards her office, passing row upon row of shoulder-high partitions. Stopping off at her PA's plot to pick up some printouts, she noticed a stuffed teddy bear leaning against the computer wearing a T-shirt which bore the legend: FUCK OFF. I'M HAVING A BAD DAY. What was going on? How had she never noticed the misanthropy before, the misery that pervaded this building like fog? She stood back and surveyed the acreage of cordoned-off office space, and suddenly a long-dormant memory from her childhood flashed across the screen of her mind's eye and almost made her reel.

She was aged ten, on a day trip to Inisheer, the tiniest of the Aran Islands off the Galway coast. She was standing on a hill looking down over a landscape that was covered in a maze of drystone walls, each one built to mark the boundaries of the farmer whose field it was. The occupants of this vast office space were as jealously territorial as any Irish peasant, she realized – only they had no vast expanse of blue over their heads, no salt wind in their faces, no sound of the sea in their ears. And all at once Dannie felt so wretchedly homesick that she wanted to hunker down right there on the floor of the corridor and cry.

Later in the day she did cry, in the privacy of her office. She'd been on the phone to yet another of the celebrities who were to appear on next weekend's talk show treadmill. She'd had a list of routine questions in front of her, and as she asked one of the most standard questions of all: 'Tell us! What amusing anecdotes do you have for us?' and felt the celebrity on the other end of the phone stiffen as they realized – as they always did – that they couldn't remember a single amusing anecdote to save their lives, she was suddenly aware that she felt about as interested and as animated as the apathetic junior in her hair stylist's who parroted questions of the 'where are you going on your holidays?' variety.

The very next day she walked into the CEO's office and informed him that she wanted to accept the voluntary redundancy package that had recently been offered to contracted employees of the television station. He expressed concern; understandably so. After all, Dannie was one of their most valued researchers. Guests warmed to her vibrant Irish charm – she had a rare talent for drawing people out of themselves and making them feel relaxed. Had she been headhunted elsewhere? No. The CEO looked puzzled. Was she experiencing – er – problems in her personal life? No, she lied. It was none of his fecking business. Well, then. Did she feel the need for something more *challenging* than the work she was presently engaged in? No. Something *less* challenging, then? Was her work-load perhaps too stressful? No. Then why, exactly, did she want to leave? Because she was deeply unhappy. 'Well,' said the CEO, with an unctuous smile. 'Let's think of a way to make you happy.' What could they do to persuade her to stay? A salary hike? No. The CEO shook his head in disbelief. What other perks, incentives, in*duce*ments could they offer? Nothing? He gave her a cynical look. 'Come *on*, Dannie! There must be *some* way of making you happy?'

'There's not,' said Dannie. 'Just look around at the people who work here. They're all steeped in misery. No-one could be happy working here.'

For a moment or two the CEO looked at her as if she was speaking *as Gaeilge*. Then he leaned across his desk and gave her the kind of fierce glare that might once have made her quail. But now it didn't bother her at all. She just noted with detachment that he looked like a trapped rat. A rat who, from behind the bars of its cage, is jealously watching an erstwhile cell-mate making a bid for freedom. 'Well, if that's your attitude, Ms Moore,' he said in a voice icy with disdain, 'I think we'll be very glad to get rid of you.'

So Dannie had worked out the remaining weeks of her prison sentence, and in those few hours of the day that were left to her after she'd met all her deadlines, topped up her energy levels (i.e. had a processed lunch in the canteen) and commuted (an hour and a half minimum), she worked on her escape plan. Which involved intensive weekend courses with an acknowledged doyenne of floristry in the UK. And after she'd flown to Dublin to view at first hand the old grocery shop she'd seen on the Net, she knew that freedom was finally within her reach.

Now, in the grocery shop she'd transformed into a temple to the Goddess Flora, she lobbed another log onto the fire and stood up. Outside on the street, traffic was starting to build, and the first of the early morning pedestrians were straggling to work, most of them looking as miserable as she once had in her commuting days in London. That was another of the advantages of setting up where she had – she didn't have to commute any more. She'd found a flat just across the road: she could see it from where she stood now. It was a standard, decade-old two-bed city-centre apartment, but she'd camouflaged the modern interior by draping fabric strategically anywhere she could. Having spent most of her childhood in study rooms and dormitories, and most of her adulthood in what she now considered to be Loser Land, she'd discovered her sybaritic side. She'd raided retro shops and charity shops for old curtains, rugs and pillows in brilliant, Byzantine, jewel-like colours and had transformed her current bedroom into a Sultana's boudoir with stars on the ceiling. Lottie, the little girl from the flat one storey down, had gasped and gawped and gazed in awe when she'd first seen it, and had wondered out loud if Dannie wasn't really a princess.

And there was Lottie now, pulling up the blind on her bedroom window with one hand and rubbing her eyes with the other, clearly still half asleep. Lottie squinted when she saw Dannie waving at her, then laughed and waved back before moving away from the window to ready herself for the school day. Dannie wondered how Lottie's mother Rosa was: the two women hadn't seen each other for a while. Maybe she'd phone later and see if she was free to go for a coffee.

The shop bell announced the arrival of the first of her assistants, the fax machine began to whirr, and the working day was off to its official start. When the phone rang, Dannie let the answering machine pick up. 'Dannie? Dylan Moody here. Could you send a dozen Baccaras to the usual address, please? With a note saying – um: "Thanks for a truly amazing evening". And another bouquet to my home address. Orchids or something. And – um – just say: "Happy birthday, darling" on the card. Much obliged. Stick it on my Amex. Thanks.' She and her assistant Laura exchanged a knowing look and a smile, but refrained from comment. Because Dannie hadn't got to become one of the busiest florists in Dublin through being indiscreet.

As she took a tube of barrier cream out of the drawer under the counter and started to slather it over her hands, she found herself wondering about the woman who would receive a dozen Baccara roses a little later on that morning, and she felt a small stab of envy. After all, Dannie Moore hadn't had flowers from a man in a very long time.

Chapter Two

As a special treat, Calypso answered the door to her husband on the morning of his return from London wearing absolutely nothing at all apart from a little YSL Touche Eclat to conceal the early morning blotchiness of her skin, a discreet application of mascara (her eyes looked so tiny without it!) and a light spray of Chanel 19. She took his breath away, as she'd known she would.

'Welcome home, darling!' she sang.

Dominic groaned as he followed her upstairs, pulling his clothes off. 'Jesus, Calypso – I don't have time for this! I'm just off the red-eye and I've a meeting in half an hour!'

But of course he had time for it, Calypso knew, because Dominic never took very long.

Afterwards she slid on a kimono and wandered down to the kitchen to make her breakfast coffee while Dominic showered. She would take it easy today. She had nothing to do until her facial at four o'clock, and then dinner with Jethro and the New Boy this evening. She should try and manage a workout, but she'd been to the gym every day this week, and her trainer had told her that that was overdoing it. She was allowed to be lazy today.

Saturday morning sun was streaming in through the sliding glass doors, and her cream-coloured Burmese cat was stretched out along the step, basking. 'Darling, darling Marilyn Monroe,' she cooed, draping the cat over her shoulder and talking cat language to her as she heaped Illy into the coffee machine. She could hear Dominic upstairs, issuing directives on his phone. In a minute or two he'd come down to kiss her goodbye before heading off to his meeting. He'd be wearing a shirt by Paul Smith and a suit by Hugo Boss, his hair would be still wet from the shower, he would smell of Aqua di Parma, and he would look amazing. Especially after the sex – sex always gave his patrician face the kind of glow that even his Clinique scruffing lotion couldn't.

Calypso turned the dial to 'Espresso', then peered at herself in the mosaic-framed mirror that hung above the coffee machine to see if the sex had given her skin a glow. Sadly not. The only glow about her complexion was the artificial one that came courtesy of Yves Saint-Laurent. She didn't care. Having been married so young,

Calypso hadn't had many men in her life – but she'd had enough to know that sex was over-rated. However, because she knew that – like all men – Dominic loved a good ride (and because she was no eejit), she was always more than happy to oblige him.

Dominic swung into the kitchen looking exactly as she'd predicted he would look. 'Yeah, yeah, yeah,' he was saying into his mobile. 'Yeah. Next Thursday, then? Excellent. Bye.' He slid his phone into his pocket, grabbed his laptop case and planted a kiss on his wife's shoulder. 'That was glorious, darling. What a way to welcome home a busy husband! You are such a clever girl. Any coffee going?'

'Of course.' Calypso filled a travel mug with coffee and broke off a banana from the bunch in the fruit bowl. 'Here. Take this with you. It's great for topping up your energy levels. Full of potassium.'

She followed him out to where his car was parked at the rear of the house, and watched while he zapped locks, automatic gate, and car roof. Then she handed over coffee and fruit and received another kiss through the open driver's window. She smiled at what he said into her ear as he peeled his banana, she smiled as she waved goodbye, and she smiled as the gates slid shut. Then she turned to smilingly survey her Zen garden.

Calypso wandered along the tiled pathway on bare feet, stretching, enjoying the sensation of the heavy silk of her kimono against her skin, and reminding herself to feed the koi she'd recently had installed in the pool – the existence of which she had so far managed to keep secret from Marilyn Monroe. She wanted to sigh with pleasure when she surveyed her beautiful garden, her beautiful home! It had been designed specifically to serve as a turn-key base in central Dublin for someone too busy to cope with the hassle of renovations. And that busy someone was Dominic to a T!

The co-owner of a chain of cutting-edge art galleries in London and New York, he and his two partners had decided to expand, and Ireland, with its booming economy, had seemed the obvious next choice. Because he had Irish roots and no family in London, Dominic had been put in charge of the Dublin gallery a decade ago. He had bought this house, set up his gallery, ensured that invitations to his openings were many times more valuable than gold dust, and that his name dominated the arts pages in the broadsheets and the society pages in the glossies. At one of his exclusive openings he had seen a vision in gold, a stunningly beautiful girl with the name of a goddess, and he had promptly wooed and wed her and installed her in her temple at this exclusive address in Dublin 6.

Lucky, lucky Calypso O'Kelly! Hadn't she the life of Riley?

A construction worker with builder's bum was ogling her from the roof of a building down the laneway. Calypso shot him a cross look before drifting into her kitchen and shutting the door. She hated whatever it was about herself that made men want to stare. She remembered what her mother, Jessica, had said to her when she'd told her that she and Dominic were getting married. 'It won't last,' she'd said. 'I hate to be so brutally frank, Calypso, but a man like Dominic is going to see through you in no time at all. A pretty little wannabe, married to an alpha male like him! If I wasn't able to keep your father, darling, I can't see how you're going to manage to keep Dominic.'

Calypso had flinched, but said nothing, and, as punishment for her mother's remarks, Calypso rarely saw her now. She loved it when stuff was written about her in the social pages of the Sunday papers, and childishly hoped that Jessica would see it. Because every time a photograph of Calypso and Dominic appeared in the paper, she knew it was a slap in the face for her mother. The perfection of her life was Calypso's revenge.

Her mother's dagger words came back. Ow! Sometimes her heart skipped a beat when she wondered if Jessica might be right. After all,

Calypso's and her mother's beauty combined hadn't been enough to keep her father from absconding . . .

Her mother had worked hard at keeping her father. Calypso remembered how he would come to take her out for weekend jaunts after he and Jessica had separated. Jessica would visit the hairdresser before he arrived, and spray herself with perfume, and then she'd dress Calypso in her prettiest clothes, brush her long hair until it looked like burnished corn-coloured silk, and tell her to 'try hard to be good for Daddy, and do everything he tells you, because maybe then he'll want to come and live with us again'. And Calypso would come back with her McDonald's plastic toy as a souvenir of the afternoon spent with Daddy, and watch anxiously as her parents had a drink together like civilized people, and then her heart would start to flutter like a small bird trapped behind her ribs as her mother issued the usual invitation to her father to stay to dinner, and he would look at his watch and say, 'Thanks for the offer, but I've really got to dash.' And then he'd kiss Calypso on the forehead this time and be gone out of the door, and her mother would go into her bedroom and exchange the pretty dress she'd been wearing for a tracksuit, and wipe the make-up off her face. Later, over a supper taken in front of the television, she'd drink the bottle of wine she had bought to share with her errant spouse, having consigned his portion of painstakingly prepared beef Wellington to the bin. The sound of the knife scraping against the plate told Calypso more eloquently than many words that she'd let her mother down again.

Thus had she learned from an early age not to believe in her beauty. People had always told her she was beautiful, but to her, beauty was a worthless commodity. Its nickel-plated currency might have been useful to her if she'd continued her acting career, but she'd soon sussed how specious its face value really was. Sometimes she even wondered if her beloved Dominic had married her for the way she looked. She knew he took enormous pleasure in wearing her on his arm like an accessory when they went to nobby dos. He also adored the fact that she bore the name of a goddess, and referred to the place between her legs as his 'shrine'.

So Calypso's bathroom cupboards were full of expensive lotions and potions, age-defying creams and wrinkle busters, skin-peeling face masks and cellulite-reducing body lotions, and pills that promised glowing skin, gleaming teeth and glossy hair. Being worshipped as a goddess was all very well and good, but maintaining the divine infrastructure was bloody hard work. Calypso O'Kelly bore her beauty like a burden.

* * *

It was nearly time to go. Calypso was feeling unsettled now. Dominic was late, and she was never happy going out unless he had first checked out what she was wearing. He had an incredible eye. She'd had an hour's pampering by her favourite beautician earlier in the afternoon, but even that hadn't been enough to convince her of her 'fabulousness'. She put the finishing touches to her make-up, then wandered into her dressing room to change for dinner. This evening she selected a tight, stretch linen skirt; very high, slender, ankle-strapped heels that were hideously uncomfortable but had quite a flattering effect on her feet, and a discreetly sexy silk blouse. A push-up bra went underneath the blouse, and her favourite pashmina went over it. Thankfully, Dominic was passing the front door as she high-heeled her way out.

'Hey! You look sensational,' he said, pulling over and rolling down the window of his sleek convertible.

'Do I?' asked Calypso uncertainly, turning round so that he could get a rear view. 'Are you sure my—'

'No, darling. Your bum does not look big. It actually looks amazing. Jennifer Lopez, eat your heart out.'

'Oh! What a lovely thing to say! You're a saint

and an angel!' She swooped down on him to give him a kiss.

'Who's having the pleasure of dining with you this evening?' he asked.

'Jethro Palmer, at Le Blazon. And some hot new talent Sally's been raving about. I hope I'm not going to be disappointed.' She scanned the terrace, located her taxi, and waved at the driver before bending down to her husband and giving him another, more lingering kiss. 'It may be a late one,' she warned him. 'Jethro's really fired up about this *Don Juan* project. Don't wait up, darling.'

'I won't. I'm knackered.'

As Calypso slid into the back seat of the taxi, the driver held the door open for her. She noticed his eyes take in the way her tight skirt rode up over her thighs, exposing the lace top of her stay-ups. She flushed as she gave him the address. He'd made her feel uncomfortable again. Jennifer Lopez wore 'sexy' well: Calypso was never a hundred per cent sure how to carry it off.

Jethro was at the table when she walked into the restaurant. He stood up when he saw her, gave her a great bear-hug, and said: 'Hell, ma'am. You're more beautiful than ever.'

'And you're a great big flatterer.' The waiter slid Calypso's chair out from the table for her, and she sat down, smiled at her date and indicated the champagne flute in front of her. 'You've even remembered what my favourite tipple is! Aren't you clever?'

'I've always known how important it is to pay attention to detail. It's one of the reasons I'm successful. You know as well as I do that actresses love it when you remember that kind of bullshit, Calypso.' He gave her a smile worthy of Jack Nicholson at his most charming, then raised his glass in a toast. 'Here's to our next project. I'm looking forward to working with you again, Ms O'Kelly.'

'Me too. It's always a pleasure working with you, Mr Palmer.' Calypso raised her glass back at him. They small-talked for a while, and bantered a bit, and then: 'Tell me more about the actor who's joining us,' he said.

'Leo Devlin? I can't tell you very much because I haven't met him yet myself. All I know about him is that he's a carpenter whose only acting experience to date has been in amateur productions. He does, however, come highly recommended. Did you get the photograph I e-mailed you?'

'I sure did. He's a good looking son-of-a-bitch.'

'Sally Ruane – his agent – said it didn't do him justice.'

There was a pause. Jethro's gaze had slid away from hers and was now directed at something or someone on the other side of the room. 'It didn't,' he said.

'Sorry? What didn't what?'

'Do him justice. He's just come in.'

As Calypso turned, her professional sang-froid very nearly failed her. Jesus H. *Christ*! she thought, biting down on her lip. She found herself averting her eyes and smoothing down her skirt as she prepared to greet the youth who was moving towards their table. The boy was almost too gorgeous to look at. Every single diner in the restaurant clocked him, then looked away.

Leo Devlin had black hair, anthracite eyes, a predatory profile – and a body to die for encased in black jeans and black leather jacket. He carried himself with such breathtaking insouciance that a couple of women old and savvy enough to know better stopped with their forks lifted to their mouths and gazed open-mouthed at him as he moved across the room, then turned to each other and burst into a fluster of girlish giggles.

Halfway across the floor he paused and surveyed the room, searching for Calypso, thrumming lazy fingers against his thigh. The *maître d'* approached, discreetly handed him a tie, then nodded towards the table where Calypso and Jethro were waiting. Leo's eyes met hers. For an instant Calypso felt like a small animal caught in a huntsman's sights, but then

Leo Devlin smiled and inclined his head, and the curious sense of threat that had pushed up her pulse rate subsided a little.

He continued towards them with an un-hurried stride, extending a hand. Calypso felt something inside her melt as he ran his eyes briefly over her, assessing her the way men always did when they met her. She saw the tip of his tongue part the curve of his lips as he took in her tight skirt, but the unsettling effect he was having on her was nothing like the unpleasant sensation she'd experienced earlier in the evening when the taxi driver had ogled her legs. Oh, God! Calypso flinched visibly as she made contact with his hand, and hoped he hadn't noticed. Sweat broke out under her arms; she felt suddenly, thrillingly goosebumpy. Hell's teeth! This boy had 'Wow' in spadefuls.

'Leo Devlin?' she said. 'I'm Calypso O'Kelly.'

'I know. I'm pleased to meet you at last, Ms O'Kelly,' he replied. His voice was low, sexy, a little rough around the edges. Easy enough for a voice coach to polish up, thought Calypso, switching back into casting director mode with difficulty.

Beside her, Jethro had risen to his feet. Calypso quickly withdrew her hand from Leo's and turned to the director. He was wearing an expression that conveyed wry amusement. 'Well, well,' he said. 'If you photograph as

78

charismatically as you look, pal, we might just have found ourselves our principal,' he said. 'I'm impressed already.'

The fact that he was dining with a couple of influential big shots didn't seem to faze Leo Devlin at all. His demeanour during dinner was relaxed, good-humoured, urbane. He asked all the right questions, laughed easily at anecdotes, and told some good ones himself. He had a keen line in self-deprecating wit, telling Jethro – when he asked about his family background – that it would make a more maudlin tale and a better movie than Frank McCourt's.

'You don't strike me as someone with a deprived background,' remarked Jethro. 'You're clearly a highly educated son-of-a-bitch.'

Leo laughed. 'The university of life is a pretty damn dandy institution,' he said. 'It even taught me how to spot a fine wine. This Bordeaux is exceptional.'

'Nothing can beat a good Château Lafite. I reckon we could use another bottle.' Jethro looked round for the sommelier.

'So. Your childhood was poor but happy?' Calypso said, to fill the momentary lapse in conversation.

The look he gave her made her feel as if she'd just uttered the most mawkish sentiment on the face of the planet. She could feel herself blushing.

'Let's just say I was poor,' he said, looking her directly in the eyes. She looked away, and took another sip of wine.

She knew she was drinking too much. She'd been drinking quickly, nervously, in the hope that the alcohol might help to restore her equilibrium, which, of course, it didn't. She was deeply unsettled by the fact that she found this man so sexually attractive. It had never happened to her before. She had met hundreds of gorgeous, ultra-sexy actors in the course of her work, but this was something new, something totally unprecedented.

He knew it. He played her the way an angler plays a fish. He was agonizingly sparing with eye contact throughout the meal, focusing most of his attention on Jethro. The fact that he withheld his gaze from her was, she knew, intentional. Occasionally he would bestow a glance on her as one might bestow a gift on some charitable case, but his looks in her direction were rare and valuable enough to make her consider them something devoutly to be wished. She was particularly put out when he didn't notice the very famous rock star on the other side of the room blowing a kiss at her. Calypso was used to being lionized. She'd never been treated this way in her life, with the kind of – what was the right word? – the kind of offhandedness Leo was demonstrating.

When Jethro excused himself to pay a visit to the john, Leo looked directly at her over the rim of his wineglass for the first time, and smiled. He loosened the tie that the *maître d'* had given him, but he said nothing. He just narrowed his eyes at her in an amused way, and raised an eyebrow.

Calypso flailed around, hoping that some topic of conversation would come to her. The two women who'd practically orgasmed when he had strolled into the restaurant earlier were well-oiled now. They were trying to attract attention by getting ready to go in an ostentatious fashion, continuing to ogle Leo shamelessly, but Calypso could hardly make a conversation piece of *that*. She finally ventured something inane about the artwork on the walls of the restaurant. Leo nodded, then made reference to some French painterly technique.

Calypso hadn't a clue what the French term meant, but she lit on the fact that his pronunciation was so – well – *French*. A subject of conversation at last! 'I noticed earlier, when you ordered from the menu, that your French accent is impeccable,' she said.

'Thank you. That's because I spent a year working in Paris.'

'Paris!' said Calypso. 'The most divine city on earth! I toyed with the idea of buying a rather *bijou* apartment there, but then I realized that I couldn't bear not to stay in my favourite hotel!'

As soon as the words were out of her mouth, she wanted to hit herself on the head. How fatuous and fluffy she must have sounded! '*Divine* city! *Bijou* apartment! *Favourite* hotel!'

But Leo gave no indication that he found her remarks risible. Instead he bestowed a look of intensely flattering interest on her. 'Where in Paris do you stay?' he asked.

'The Pavillon de la Reine, in the Marais.'

Leo smiled. ' "The Queen's Pavilion". I should have guessed. It's a beautiful hotel.'

'You've stayed there?'

'No. I used to work in the Marais.'

'What did you work as?'

'I was a kitchen porter in a hotel not far from the Pavillon.'

'Oh!' Calypso felt her face flare up. Change the subject – oh, change the subject, quick! 'But I understand you're working as a carpenter now?'

'Yes. Coincidentally, I recently finished work on a house two doors down from where you live, on Palmerston Terrace.'

There was a moment of astonished silence as Calypso took this information in. 'How – how do you know where I live?'

'I used to see you every morning, zapping the locks on your gate. I love the little Merc you drive. Very nifty.'

'Oh. Thanks.' Calypso remembered now that

she'd had to complain to the owner of the house that she couldn't drive in or out of her back gate without being the subject of wolf whistles and lewdly graphic gestures from the building workers. The thought that Leo might have been one of the perpetrators made her feel a flutter of perverse arousal.

Silence descended again. 'That house must have needed a lot of work,' she babbled. 'I heard it was in pretty bad nick.' Wow! In*spired*!

'Yeah. It needed complete refurbishment, but it's very special now. The kitchen's going to be featured in next month's *Irish Interiors*.'

'Really? What's it like?'

The smile he gave her made her feel like a small child. 'The lady of the house wanted a country feel to it, so we went for lots of tongue and groove.'

Oh, God! Calypso dropped her eyes to his work-roughened hands, and watched as he poured more wine. He raised his glass, then looked at her directly. 'May I propose a toast?' he said.

'Certainly,' she replied, glad of another opportunity to make small talk. She raised her glass back. 'What'll we toast to?'

'To our liaison, of course, Ms O'Kelly,' he said. 'May it prove a fruitful one.'

'To our liaison,' she parroted, maintaining eye contact with an effort.

She was spared having to say anything more by the arrival of a waiter, who materialized as if out of nowhere and inclined his head towards Leo. 'Excuse me, sir?' he murmured silkily. 'The lady who has just left the restaurant – the blond lady who was dining there –' he indicated the table that the giggling women had recently vacated '– asked me to give you this. She says you may remember her.' He passed a folded sheet of paper to Leo with such masterly discretion that Calypso knew he'd been tipped lavishly for the service rendered. Then he backed away as smoothly as he'd approached.

Leo raised an eyebrow. 'I've never seen the woman before in my life,' he said, before unfolding the paper. Calypso watched his face as he studied the contents. A smile began to twist his mouth. His black eyes got blacker. Finally, he gave a robust laugh. 'Well, well,' he said. 'It's a very generous offer, but I don't think I'll take her up on it.'

'What does she say?' asked Calypso.

'I'm not sure you want to know.' Leo crumpled the note and tossed it aside just as a kiss descended on Calypso's shoulder.

'Calypso! Beautiful woman!' It was the rock star.

'Darling! How are things?'

'Things are fine. How are things with you?'

'Fine, likewise.' She turned to Leo with a big

smile, like someone presenting an award. 'Allow me to introduce you. Leo, this is—'

'No introductions necessary,' said Leo, extending a hand. 'I don't imagine there's anyone on the face of the planet who doesn't know who you are, man.' He and the rock star shook hands and exchanged pleasantries, then the rock star's entourage rolled up and there ensued one of those social kerfuffles that Dublin specializes in. When the heavenly bodies finally made their exit, Calypso sat back down and found that Leo was no longer at the table. Oh! What on earth made him decide to take a trip to the loo when he had an opportunity of shooting the breeze with the *crème de la crème* of Dublin society? How bloody blasé could you get?

She tapped the tabletop with her beautifully lacquered nails. She *hated* sitting in restaurants on her own! Where was Jethro? Why was he taking so long? As the *maître d'* held the restaurant door open for a diner to pass through, she caught a glimpse of the director in the foyer, talking on his cellphone. Shit! How long was she going to have to sit here like a wuss? She wished the waiter would bring a menu. She didn't need to see it – she had no intention of having dessert – but she'd rather appear to be consulting a menu than staring into space like Norma No-Friends.

As she sat there trying hard to look

unconcerned, her gaze fell upon the scrunched-up piece of paper lying on the linen tablecloth. She cast a surreptitious look to left and right, and then, without hesitating, took the note, dropped it into her handbag, and indicated to the waiter to come and clear away their plates. He did so with silky efficiency, then returned to brush crumbs off the tablecloth into a miniature silver dustpan.

'You might bring another bottle of Bordeaux,' Calypso told him. She shouldn't have any more wine, she knew, but the small act of felony she'd just perpetrated was making her feel reckless now.

'Of course, madam,' said the waiter, bowing and retreating just as Leo returned to the table.

He sat down opposite her, registered the pristine tablecloth, then raised an eyebrow. 'I'm impressed by his efficiency. But he might have asked my permission before he cleared away my personal correspondence.' He raised a hand to call the man back, and Calypso went into shock.

'I think – um – I think—' She hadn't a clue what to think. She could hardly say: Oh, I nicked your note, Leo. So instead of saying anything, she automatically raised her glass to her mouth and took an unwisely hefty swig. It went straight down the wrong way and made her choke so violently that she felt wine spurt out of her nose and tears spring to her eyes. Grabbing a napkin, she held it to her face, then dropped it immediately, the better to fight for air.

'Are you all right?' queried Leo, all concern, as he indicated to the waiter to refill her water glass. 'Here. Let me help.' He was at her side in an instant, his hand on her back, rubbing the silk of her blouse. Calypso continued to cough and cough and splutter and wheeze, but even in her distressed state she was intensely aware of the physical contact.

Now Jethro was back, and saying in a worried voice, 'Hey. Does she need the Heimlich manoeuvre?'

'No. She's choking on liquid, not food. She'll get over it. It's a frightening experience, but not life threatening.'

He was right. After several more mortifying moments of gasping and sobbing for air, with Leo alternately rubbing and pounding her back, the paroxysms subsided and Calypso's breath started to come more normally. At last she was able to speak, although her voice sounded like Marge Simpson's, and she was stupid with mortification.

'I'm sorry,' she said, wiping away tears with her napkin. 'How embarrassing!'

'Don't worry about it,' said Leo, with a re-assuring smile.

'Maybe we should call a cab to take you home?' suggested Jethro. 'You've had a bad fright,

Calypso, and we've done all the talking we need to.' Another little flurry of activity erupted among the staff as he instructed the waiter to call a cab immediately. 'What address should we say?' he asked.

She heard her voice reply without being aware that she was speaking. 'I'm in Ranelagh. Near Palmerston Park.'

And then Leo said: 'That's not far from me. I'll go with her.'

No! 'That's not necessary,' she said.

'Of course it is,' said Leo. 'You're still in shock.'

And then Jethro was expressing regret that the evening was being terminated so abruptly, but it was great meeting you, Leo, she heard him schmooze, and our people will talk, and enjoy Vietnam.

And then Leo had taken her by the elbow and was escorting her out of the restaurant and down the steps to where the taxi was waiting.

'This is very good of you—' she started to say, but Leo raised a finger in admonishment.

'Don't bother to make small talk, Calypso. Not after what you've just been through. You should be saving your breath.' He held the door of the cab open for her, and she slid in.

In the back, they sat side by side without touching and without speaking. The fingers of Leo's left hand caressed the velour of the seat between them, as one might caress a lapdog. It was having a catastrophic effect on Calypso. She felt dizzy from wine and shock and something else she was too terrified to contemplate. The cab pulled up outside a block of flats.

'This is where I get out.' Leo turned and looked at her for the first time since they'd got into the cab. She knew that he knew what she was thinking. There was a long silence, and then: 'Perhaps you'd like to come in for coffee?' he said. 'Or tea. They say that tea's good for shock.'

She couldn't trust herself to articulate a reply. Instead she just nodded.

'Cat still got your tongue, Ms O'Kelly?' He leaned over and trailed a rough thumb down the side of her cheek. Calypso felt her face flare, and she stiffened in indignation. How dare this – this – *boy* take liberties with her!

He opened the cab door and swung his legs out. Then he stood there, thumbs looped into his belt, looking down at her where she still sat, irresolute and resentful.

'Changed your mind?'

'Um. No. Actually.'

He helped her out, then paid off the driver, ignoring her protestations that she should pick up the fare. As he guided her through a gated archway and along a gangway flanked with identical doors, he laid a light hand on the small of her back. Stopping at the last door, he unlocked it, then stood back to allow her to precede him. Once inside, he threw a switch.

Even in the full glare of the overhead light, Calypso barely registered her surroundings. A flat, perfunctorily kitted out with flat-pack furniture, including the mandatory sofa bed. A kitchen through an archway, a couple of doors off, a standard framed Man Ray reproduction on the wall, a coal-effect gas fire. A backpack was stowed in a corner, the *Rough Guide to Vietnam* sticking out of one of its myriad pockets. She stood vacillating in the middle of the room, unsure what to do next.

Leo switched on a table lamp, and killed the overhead illumination. 'Let me take your shawl,' he said, taking hold of a corner of her pashmina and pulling. He circled her, trailing the length of rose pink cashmere away as he did so. The garment slid off her shoulders in a way that made her feel almost indecently exposed. When he'd completed the circle, he casually dropped her beautiful pashmina over the arm of the sofa, then moved towards the kitchen and proceeded to pour water into a kettle.

The jerk of disappointment she felt almost floored her. 'Um. What are you doing?' she asked.

Leo looked at her over his shoulder and raised an eyebrow. 'Making tea, of course,' he said. 'I suspect you'd prefer leaf, but I'm afraid I've only bags. Is that OK?' He indicated the sofa with a nod of his head. 'Take a seat, Ms O'Kelly. Make yourself comfortable.'

Like an automaton, Calypso moved to the sofa and sat down stiffly, watching Leo while he slung a tea bag into a mug, helped himself to a beer from the fridge, and snapped the tab. She was feeling intensely uncomfortable now, and beginning to suffer heartfelt regret at the idiotic impulse that had made her accede to his invitation. He was leaning against a kitchen unit, watching her. His imperturbability made her feel even more awkward. For the umpteenth time that evening she cast around for something to say. 'Is this your flat?' she attempted.

He gave her an amused look. 'No. I couldn't afford a gaff like this. It's a friend's. I'm caretaking it for him.'

'Oh. It must be very convenient for you, living so close to home. I mean – town.' What *was* she rambling about?

'Yes. You must find that too.' Leo poured hot water into the mug, gave the contents a perfunctory stir, then dumped the tea bag in the sink. He dipped the wet teaspoon into a bag of sugar.

'Oh – no sugar for me, please.'

'Now, now, Calypso. You're recovering from shock, remember? Tea with lots of sugar's the only man for shock. Very hot –' a pause; 'very sweet –' a smile; 'tea.' He moved towards her, handed her the mug, then sat down on the sofa beside her.

Her heart was beating too hard. She took a sip of disgusting tea, then another one.

'You keep koi,' he said.

'I beg your pardon?'

'Koi. Those ornamental carp from Japan.'

'Oh. How – how do you know that?'

'That corner of your garden is just visible from the attic bedroom of the house I was telling you about – the one with all the tongue and groove. I used to watch you feed your exotic fish.' He gave a little laugh. 'I felt jealous. I only ever had one goldfish and that died.'

'You watched me feed my fish?' Calypso often fed her fish wearing very little clothing. She had no idea that she might be watched.

'And a very fetching sight it was, too.' He gave her that smile again. 'Don't worry – the rest of the garden is perfectly secluded. But you were the subject of some fairly appreciative remarks from the lads I was working with, especially during that last hot spell. They kept making excuses to visit the attic when koi-feeding time came round.'

Another swig of tea.

'Hey!' He put a restraining hand on hers. 'Don't knock that back too fast, Calypso. Remember what happened in the restaurant.'

She didn't like being reminded of that. How hideous she must have looked, all red-faced and gasping for air, with red wine dribbling from her nose! She tried to make light of it, now. 'I must have looked a sight! All flushed and panting.'

He echoed her light laugh. 'Don't worry. In my experience it can be quite a good look.'

Oh, *God*! Calypso took a final swig of tea, then set her mug down on the floor.

'Finished?'

'Yes.'

Leo rose to his feet and looked down at her. Calypso knew her face was scarlet again, and that he must be able to hear her stupid, ragged breathing. Oh, God. What was going to happen now? Was he going to kiss her? What would she do if he did? How would she respond? She sensed that once he started kissing her, she wouldn't be able to stop kissing him back. She was feeling excruciatingly, squirmingly aroused – she had never felt such an ache of lust for anyone, ever, in her life before. His gaze trailed down her body, from her parted lips to her breasts, all pushed up and with the nipples shockingly erect, and thence to her thighs, where she knew a tantalizing hint of lace-topped stocking showed below the hem of her skirt.

'In that case,' he said, retrieving her pashmina and draping it around her shoulders, 'allow me to escort you home, Ms O'Kelly.'

Oh! Before she could collect herself or even register what was happening, Leo had strolled to the door and was holding it open for her.

Feeling as if she was in a bad dream, awash with humiliation, Calypso rose to her feet, ungainly in her heels and hampered by the tightness of her skirt. She moved stiff-legged to the door, tugging her pashmina round her, busying her agitated fingers with the knot, terrified that he might see the expression of gobsmacked disappointment on her face.

'There's no need, you know,' she managed to say as she slid past him, 'to walk me home.' Covered in confusion and shame, she just wanted to run away, back to her beautiful house and into the safe arms of her wonderful husband.

But Leo insisted. 'When I'm with a lady,' he said, 'I behave like a gentleman.' And as they left the flat and headed back down the gangway, Calypso realized that she was actually absurdly glad for the opportunity of spending extra minutes with him.

A youth was approaching from the opposite direction, clearly pissed.

'Good night, I take it, Eamonn?' remarked Leo, as they passed him by.

'Cracker. For you, too, obviously.' He eyed Calypso lecherously, looking her up and down. 'Scored again? Sexy piece of ass. You're a jammy bastard, Leo Devlin. Give her one from me, won't you?' Calypso had never before felt so keenly mortified. *Scored again*, the geezer had said. She was simply the latest in a long line of pushovers. She felt like a slut, a harlot, a strumpet, a *slapper*.

'Hey,' said Leo sharply. 'Mind your mouth, man. You're talking to a Palmerston Princess.'

The walk took ten minutes. Calypso stewed. Each minute that passed was more agonizing than the last. She was abject, desperate. She asked how long he was going to be away. He shrugged. 'Depends on how long funds last,' he said. Oh . . . 'Two weeks? More?' 'Haven't a clue.' She asked how she could keep in touch, but he told her he would be incommunicado. He'd let Sally know when he was back. 'We're definitely interested, you know – in you for the movie.' 'I know. That's cool.' 'We'll need to test you, of course, when you get back, but that's really just a formality. The part's 99 per cent yours.' 'No big deal.' 'You've got a potentially very exciting career ahead of you, Leo. And the sort of money you've probably only ever dreamed of.'

The sceptical look he gave her almost made her flinch. 'I've never dreamed about money in my life, Ms O'Kelly,' he said.

They had reached the laneway that ran parallel to the rear of her terrace. Calypso hesitated, then turned into it. Leo paused. 'You're going in the back way?'

Again Calypso hesitated. She looked down at her hands, twisting her plain 22 carat wedding ring, then she looked up at him. 'Yes,' she said.

He narrowed his eyes at her. 'You want me to see you to the gate.' It wasn't a question.

'Yes.'

'You want a good-night kiss.'

'Yes,' she said again; then added 'please', despising herself. She couldn't meet his eyes. She walked quickly towards the gate, then turned to face him.

Leo moved towards her and leaned his hands on the slatted wood, one on either side of her face. He remained that way for several moments, looking hard into her eyes. Then he inclined his head, brushed her left cheek with his lips, and breathed into her ear. Calypso remained mute, lips parted, eyes shut, yearning for him to kiss her properly. She waited and waited, and then, frightened to let him see how unguarded she appeared, she allowed herself at last to look at him. When she did, she knew that she was lost. What was worse, she could tell by his expression that he knew it too. He was regarding her with amused recognition, as if seeing something in her soul that he alone in the world could identify. He smiled at her, and then he touched the side of her face and slid his thumb into her mouth. It was the erotic equivalent of an intra-venous drug. Calypso shut her eyes and sucked as hungrily as a baby. 'How fucking, fucking perfect you are,' she heard him murmur before he finally extracted his thumb. Her limbs were rag-doll limp. She almost fell when he took a step backwards and raised his hand in a gesture of farewell.

No! Calypso felt drenched with something akin to desperation, but she sensed – no, *knew* – that it was of paramount importance not to betray it. Somehow she managed to keep her voice steady. 'You're going?'

'I am. I've an early start in the morning.'

'Of course. Well – enjoy your holiday.' She busied herself with a little purse-rummaging business, extracting her key and shutting the clasp with a sharp click. When she looked back at him she had managed to rearrange her features into a businesslike expression, as if she hadn't just spent the past few hours in a state of fairly advanced sexual arousal. 'You'll call me when you get back from Vietnam, of course?'

'I will.' He took another step backwards.

'That's a promise, I hope?' She hoped that investing the words with school-marmish rectitude might make them seem less abject.

'I never make promises.' He continued to move backwards, not taking his eyes off her, still smiling. Then: 'Sayonara, princess,' he said. And

97

Leo Devlin turned on his heel and walked away with long, rapid strides, without once looking back at her.

He rounded a corner and was gone. Calypso finally turned away too, feeling very wobbly. She let herself in through the gate and teetered into the house. In the hallway she took off her shoes, then crept up the stairs to the bedroom. Dominic was asleep, the book he'd been reading still open in his slack hand. She slid her kimono away from where it lay on the ottoman at the foot of the bed, then backed out of the room on silent feet and shut the bedroom door behind her.

In the downstairs shower room she changed into the silken robe before going into the drawing room and pouring herself a large, anaesthetizing cognac. She curled up on the big cream suede sofa with Marilyn Monroe, trying to take comfort from the cat's loud purring, from her unconditional, unjudgemental adoration. What had she just done? She had just performed an act of quite flagrant lunacy, that's what she'd done. She'd made the biggest mistake in the book. She'd fucked the talent. Or near as dammit. What on *earth* had made her do it?

The answer was staring her in the face. Him. Leo Devlin. *He* had made her do it, and she knew she had to see him again. He had tapped into something in her psyche she had never known existed, and now she knew about it, she wanted more. She was in his thrall now, and if she didn't see Leo again, didn't fuck him, she'd be like an addict denied a drug.

Oh! What was she thinking of? What had become of her? Calypso had never *fucked* anyone in her life. And she'd certainly never had a liaison in a *laneway* before. How beyond sordid! And then she recalled the effect Leo had had on the giggling women in the restaurant, and knew that they would have done exactly what she'd just done if the opportunity had arisen.

She remembered the note. Feeling even more full of self-loathing, she unclasped her evening bag and took it out.

Dear Tall, Dark & Devilishly Handsome, she read.

It may interest you to know that I'm sporting a Brazilian. Fancy checking it out? I'm staying in the hotel across the road – Room 505. If you're free later, why not drop up for a glass of champagne, a line of coke and a little soixante-neuf? I need someone to fuck me senseless tonight, and I suspect you're the very man for the job . . . XXX

Oh! Calypso scrunched the paper into a tiny ball. Then she quickly drained the rest of the brandy, toppled Marilyn into her basket in the kitchen, tossed the note in the bin and headed for bed, trying unsuccessfully to obliterate the words she'd just read.

As she leaned towards Dominic to slide the

book from his hand and switch off his bedside light, he stirred, then murmured something and turned towards her, reaching for her. His mouth found her breast at once, and before she could think of some way of dissuading him, he'd initiated sex.

Calypso took a deep breath, then cooed and rubbed herself against him like a cat, preparing herself for yet another performance. She always faked her orgasms, and had, in fact, got so good at it that if porn films figured in the Oscars she'd have been a contender for best actress. She'd read about the joys of sex in countless magazines but had never understood why such a tedious act got such good press, and she'd certainly never felt curious enough to ask questions. She hadn't a clue how her girlfriends felt about it. She couldn't understand women who talked openly about such things – she and Rosa never had. As far as Calypso was concerned what she got up to in the bedroom was nobody's business but hers. Those awful American television dramas where women all sat around drinking tequila and discussing penis sizes struck her as quite bizarre. And when someone had asked her if she'd seen the *Vagina Monologues*, she'd very nearly laughed in their face. To sit in a theatre and listen to a celebrity drone on in an 'ironic' self-referential fashion about vaginas was her idea of entertainment hell. She'd rather go to a Tupperware party. It wasn't that she was prudish – far from it. She'd just never understood what all the fuss was about.

Until now.

No! Don't go there!

But she couldn't stop herself. As she wound her legs round Dominic's back, she found herself replaying mental footage of Leo Devlin, up against the gateway, his black eyes boring into hers as he'd slid his thumb between her lips – and suddenly poor, perfect Calypso O'Kelly found herself crying out with exquisite pleasure as the rush of the first real orgasm of her life overwhelmed her.

For the next few weeks she had difficulty functioning. She couldn't concentrate. She was uncharacteristically testy both at home and in the office. She resisted Dominic's sexual overtures for the first time ever, pleading tiredness as an excuse. She made frequent excuses to make phone calls to Sally Ruane just so that she could say as a casual afterthought before she terminated the conversation: 'Any word from Leo?' The response was always in the negative.

One morning her phone rang as she came through the lift doors on the fifth floor of her office building. She glanced at the display before she picked up, and her heart lurched. An unfamiliar number was registered. Could it be Leo?

'Hello?' Her voice was breathy with anticipation as she moved down the corridor.

'Hello. Is that Ms O'Kelly?'

A woman's voice. Shit. 'Yes. This is Calypso O'Kelly.' Juggling her business case with her satchel, she tucked the phone between her jaw and collarbone and opened the door to her office. She never got to find out who was on the other end of the phone, because it fell to the floor as she entered reception. There, sitting on the reception desk, smiling down at a pink-cheeked, flustered-looking Iseult, was Leo Devlin.

The pair looked up at the sound of the phone hitting the floor. 'Hello, Calypso,' said Leo. 'How's it going?'

She knew she had suddenly gone at least as pink as Iseult.

'Oh. Hello, Leo,' she said in a very strange voice. 'How was Vietnam?'

'Pretty damn spiffing.'

'Good.' She busied herself with 'arriving into work'-type things, listening while Leo joshed with Iseult. He was reading horoscopes from *heat* magazine, embroidering them with such outlandish predictions that Iseult was in fits of laughter. Calypso hung up her coat, picked up the desk diary and – resenting Iseult's merry chortles – scanned today's page with unseeing eyes. She kicked off her left shoe – No! Keep your heels on, you klutz! Keep your heels on and your head high – and, finally, when she felt a little more in control, she turned to him and said: 'When did you get back?'

'A couple of days ago.'

'*What?* Why didn't you phone?'

'I had things to do. I was jet-lagged. I forgot. Various reasons.'

Calypso wanted to say: You promised, and then remembered that he hadn't, so instead she said: 'We're well into pre-production. You could have done me the courtesy of getting in touch ASAP.'

'I'm terribly sorry, Calypso. I had no idea you wanted me *that* desperately.'

She tucked a strand of hair behind her ear, then picked up her mobile phone and switched it off. 'Well. Would you like to come through to my office?'

'Sure.'

As she led the way across reception, heart thumping, she heard Iseult say: 'Can I bring you anything? Coffee? Tea?'

'Nothing for me, thanks, Iseult. What about you, Leo?'

'No stimulants necessary, thanks,' he said. And the smile he sent Iseult as he slid off the desk made her go pinker still.

Calypso held the door open for him to precede her into her office. 'You'll field calls for me, Iseult, won't you?'

'Certainly.' The secretary returned Leo's smile, dimpling. 'But you do remember you've a meeting with Jethro? He wants to bring it forward to eleven o'clock, if that's OK.'

Leo glanced at his watch. 'That's only half an hour away. I'd better let you get on with things, Ms O'Kelly.' He aimed a light kiss at her cheek, then moved towards the door.

'Wait! I can let you have twenty minutes, Leo,' said Calypso, trying to keep the desperation out of her voice.

He shrugged. 'Another time. It was nothing important.'

'Oh. Well. I'll see you out.'

'No need. Bye-bye, Calypso. Farewell, fair Iseult. Incidentally – I meant to say it to you – I love your T-shirt.'

'Oh! Thank you!' Iseult pinkened again as the door shut behind him. Then she turned to Calypso and sighed. 'I think I'm in love,' she said.

Chapter Three

'Rosa? It's Georgia here from Nesbit & Noonan recording studios.' The receptionist needn't have bothered announcing her identity. The initials N&N that had flashed across the display on her mobile had told Rosa who was calling before she picked up. Every single recording studio in town was listed in her phone's memory. 'Can you get in here ASAP?' Georgia went on. 'There's been a script change on that commercial you recorded last week for Reflex, and they need the job done in a hurry.'

'Absolutely.' This was Rosa's automatic response when she got a call to do a voiceover. You simply didn't *ever* turn down work. Her second automatic response was: What to do with Lottie? She glanced at her watch. 'Georgia, I can get there in half an hour if it's cool to bring Lottie. I'm just on my way to pick her up from school.'

'It's cool. See you later.'

'Later.' Rosa thanked her lucky stars it was Georgia in Nesbit & Noonan, and not Suki in Online who'd called. Georgia was fun and relaxed about Rosa bringing Lottie into studio with her if she wasn't able to access the brilliant network of mothers at the school gate. The Motherhood was a real lifeline – there was usually someone willing to help out by taking Lottie home to play with their offspring; but Rosa hated having to ask too often. Most of the studio receptionists were OK with Lottie – apart from snooty Suki.

Lottie was waiting for her by the school gate. She ran to the battered deux.chevaux when Rosa pulled up and flung herself into the back seat. Before the car had even pulled away from the kerb, the child had come out with a Niagara of words. 'Mummy Mummy, Jake Mulholland has a new gerbil and he brought it in today in its cage and it's *soooo* cute and it had this wheel to go round on and Jake let us all have goes holding it and I think it liked me the best because it tried to snuggle into my armpit and we were all laughing and I was like "Hey! Get off" but it wouldn't and Jake had to bribe it with food before he could get it to go back into its cage and he says that they're quite cheap really and they cost hardly anything to feed and can I have one, Mum? Can I?'

Rosa checked her rear-view mirror. Lottie's face was reflected in it, looking back at her expectantly. 'Lottie, no. If I get you a gerbil, who will end up having to feed it and clean its cage? Me, that's who.' Rosa indicated right, then slid into traffic.

'No, Mum! *I* will! I promise! I'd love to look after a little cuddly gerbil.'

She had never known a child so mad about animals. As far as Lottie was concerned, every defecating cur on the street was a Crufts candidate, every mangy stray cat was picture postcard perfect. Now Rosa refused to look when she heard the words 'Oh! Look! It's *soooo* cute!' from the back seat of the car, because she knew that if she *did* look she'd see a dreadful aberration of nature – some unthinkable cross between Great Dane and chihuahua and Rottweiler, or a mobile hairball.

'Lottie. You'll get bored with it and you won't play with it and it'll go mad like that polar bear stuck in the zoo who just paced up and down all day. It'll go round and round on its wheel and the wheel will squeak and drive *me* mad, and you *won't* clean the cage and the pong will mean that *I'll* end up doing it for you. The answer is no.'

'But Mum—'

'The answer is *emphatically* no.'

There was no response to this. Lottie knew when her mother used the emphatic word that

107

there was very little point in wasting her breath. A mildly explosive sound of indignation came from the back seat. 'Was that a snort or a fart?' queried Rosa.

'It was a snart,' said Lottie. Rosa smiled at her daughter in the rear-view mirror, but Lottie was looking out of the window. 'What's that bimbo doing?' she asked in a curious voice.

Rosa glanced to her right, where a model dressed in cowboy boots, a stetson, a tiny skirt and a gingham shirt tied at the front to reveal maximum exposure of cleavage and belly was linking arms with a giant hamburger. Well – a human wearing a giant hamburger costume. A ponytailed photographer was shooting away, obviously thinking he looked like something out of *La Dolce Vita*.

'They're advertising a special offer on hamburgers. See?'

The giant hamburger was pointing to a placard that said: *New Chargrilled Buffalo Bill Steak Burger Challenge! Get Your Mouth Round Two And We'll Give You One Free!*

'Ee-yoo. Gross. More like "Get your mouth round one and we'll give you a free sick bag."' Lottie was studying the model. 'D'you think *she* thinks she looks good?'

'Probably. She probably thinks she looks like Madonna in her "Music" video. Do *you* think she looks good?'

'No. I think she looks like a slapper. If I had to choose, I'd be the person under the hamburger.'

'Wouldn't you feel a bit stupid?'

'Nah. Nobody would know it was me. For all you know, Mum, the person under the hamburger is making rude faces at the photographer and muttering imprecations like: "Hah! Suckers! Just give me the money and let me zoom off to my next gig where I'll earn more dosh being a banana or a sausage."'

'Imprecations? That's a good word. Where did you learn that?'

'School today. Ms Whelan said she'd been muttering them all day. Where are we going? This isn't the way home.'

'Nesbit & Noonan.'

'Phew. Thank goodness it's not Online. What happened to the bollard?'

'What bollard?'

'It used to be called Nesbit, Noonan & Bollard.'

'Oh. Bollard moved to Online.'

The shrilling of her mobile prompted Rosa to pull into a convenient loading bay to answer it.

'Rosa? Suki here in Online.'

Oh, *shit*. 'Oh, hi, Suki! How are you?'

'Fine, yeah yeah yeah.' Rosa couldn't work out whether the brusque response was directed at her or at someone else in the studio. 'Busy. How are you fixed for the rest of the week? Are you available?'

'Absolutely.'

'OK. Maybe you'd give Roydon a buzz?' Roydon Sneyde was the freelance producer who supervised the recording of CD-rom gigs. 'He's got a mega session to organize – at least six files to be recorded starting tomorrow.'

Shit. Recording CD-roms was earth-shatteringly *boring*: Rosa had once found herself recording the word 'pumpkin' forty-seven times. ('Don't ask me why!' she said to anyone who appeared puzzled by this. 'I don't have a clue how the system works. I just do as I'm told.') Sometimes she reeled out of that tiny recording booth with a raging headache and a sore throat, and once her brains had been so badly scrambled by the multitude of meaningless words she'd had to intone that she'd almost crashed the car.

'It's possible there'll be another project next week. Can you keep next Wednesday, Thursday and Friday free for him? He should be able to confirm those dates by the end of today.'

Double shit. It was Calypso's birthday next Thursday, and she was having a glitzy party. Rosa would have to forgo it. She'd never be able for a mega session with Roydon Sneyde and Julian Bollard on a hangover. 'Absolutely. I'll give Roydon a ring later. I'm running late for a booking right now.'

'Don't leave it too late, will you?'

'No, no. I'll phone him before five.' Why had the girl asked her that question? There was absolutely no point in it. A pecking-order thing, Rosa thought resignedly. 'Thanks, Suki. Bye.'

'Yeah, yeah. Bye.'

Rosa stuck her phone back in her bag and started doing mental gymnastics. Six files would take between sixteen and eighteen hours. It was Monday now – that meant she'd be working every day this week. Roydon restricted his CD-rom recording sessions to around four hours because he got migraines if he tried to string them out any longer, and this suited Rosa fine. But Roydon liked to work afternoons, which meant that it would be a challenge farming Lottie out after school. She pulled out of the loading bay with a sigh and an unvoiced expletive. How was she going to do it? She'd have to spend the evening phoning the Motherhood to see who might be available to help her out. *Four* afternoons this week? That was pushing the post-school networking thing to the limit – and she'd be pushing things further still if there was more stuff to be recorded next week.

'Mum?' came Lottie's voice from the back of the car. 'The man in that car's looking at you in a seriously weird way.'

Rosa slid a glance at the man in the fat Merc who was crawling along the lane parallel to hers.

He was leering unashamedly, and Rosa realized that it was because one of the buttons on her shirt had come undone, and she was exposing nearly as much tit as the bimbo in the stetson. She fumbled to do it up again, feeling cross because she knew she was flushing. The man leered even more, and she was reminded of Roydon Sneyde. Four afternoons, sixteen hours – maybe more – of being stuck with him and his sexist jokes in an airless recording studio. Ugh. What a way to earn a living. She considered Lottie's rationale behind why being a giant hamburger was an excellent job option, and she thought that actually Lottie had got it right.

'Mum?'

'Mm?'

'Will you remind me of that story again?'

'The Map Girl? No, sweetheart. I couldn't concentrate while I'm driving. And you know it's strictly for bedtime.'

'No – I didn't mean that one. I meant the one about the man at the wedding who picked you out to be my mum.'

Rosa had turned the events of the night Lottie had been conceived into a fairy tale. She had seen no point at all in telling the truth. There was still plenty of time for Lottie to find out what went on in real life, and until she was old enough to understand, Rosa wanted her daughter to believe that the world could be a wonderful place – a place where romance flourished and sex was beautiful and every baby conceived was brought forth in a joyous spirit of love. She'd even invented a name for the beautiful stranger who'd fathered her child. 'Well. You know what his name means? Emmanuel?'

'God is with us,' replied Lottie promptly.

'God is with us,' repeated Rosa. 'And he was with me the night you were conceived.'

'You were wearing a beautiful floaty dress . . .'

'And he had eyes like sapphires . . .'

'Bright blue sapphires like mine. And goldy hair like mine . . .'

'Just like yours . . .'

'But I have your mouth and nose. And from looking at you now I think I probably have your ears. They're a bit sticky-out, aren't they?'

Rosa laughed, then prompted her daughter to continue. 'And when he said goodbye?'

'And when he said goodbye he said, "Tell my daughter when she is born that I will always, always love her even though I will never know her, and call her Carlotta, because it means 'One who is all –'" What *exactly* does it mean again, Mum?'

'"One who is all that is feminine, but who rules and controls". Just like you.'

'Just like me!'

As the traffic trailed down the Rathmines Road Rosa spotted a sign in a pet-shop window that read: *Hamsters and gerbils our speciality – de luxe cages on special offer. Please feel free to come in and wander round.*

And she knew that, as soon as she had a free moment, wandering round a pet shop viewing 'de luxe' gerbil cages was exactly what she would be doing.

'The inverted commas started bickering again, and she knew that the only solution was to separate them. So she took hold of one pair and held it up by the right hand side of her face, and she took hold of the other pair and held it up by the left hand side of her face, and they finally shut up. And then she noticed her reflection in the silver tree and she thought that the inverted commas would make pretty cool earrings, along with the added bonus that it would put a halt to all that endless bickering. And that's exactly what she did.'

'Turned them into earrings?'

'Yep.'

'Cool! How did she do it?'

'I'll tell you tomorrow. I haven't worked that out yet.'

'She could glue them onto her ears with resin from the silver tree?'

'She could.' Rosa did the tucking in and cheek-kissing thing, and then said: 'Good night, baby. Sweet dreams, sleep tight – you know the rest. Love you.'

'Love you, Mummy. Love you, Mysterious One.' The Mysterious One was the new gerbil, bought that very afternoon, who was going round on its wheel. Rosa didn't think it was a terrific idea to house the cage in Lottie's room, but the child had insisted, claiming that it was the best way to 'bond' with her new pet. Rosa also found it difficult in the extreme to keep her face straight when referring to the gerbil as 'The Mysterious One'.

The dishes next. Then phone calls. Then television – if there was anything on. Then bed. Wow. What a life. She'd had confirmation from Roydon when she'd phoned him this afternoon that yes, there would be another CD-rom to be burnt next week. A 'Talking Style File', whatever that meant. This week's project was Jolly Junior Alphabet, which meant that she'd have to put on a jolly voice, which meant that she'd be jolly, jolly knackered at the end of the day because doing 'jolly' was much more knackering than doing soft-sell. But, she thought stoically as she pulled on rubber gloves, at least the money was jolly, jolly good.

She stood to make enough from the gig to see her through the next month or two. It couldn't have come at a better time. She'd got her phone bill in the post that morning along with a reminder that the fees for Lottie's Irish dancing classes were due, and an exhortation from someone she'd never heard of to 'Begin a Brand New Life of Freedom' by joining his network marketing group. She'd put the flyer in the bin, where the banner headline screamed up at her now as she scraped leftover pasta onto it.

A Brand New Life of Freedom. How seductive that sounded! Imagine being your own boss! Not having to kowtow or laugh at offensive jokes or say 'Absolutely' every time someone asked you if you were available. She cast her mind back to the time the 'absolutely' thing had first started. It had been when Lottie was a toddler, when Rosa had been living at home with her mother, Ursula, and trying to get by on waitressing and whatever bits and pieces of acting work came her way – an episode in a soap opera here, a small theatre role there, a couple of days on a film . . . And then the voiceover gigs had started, and they proved to be very lucrative. Because she had a flair for it, it meant that she could do them fast, and that saved the client money, which was, of course, what it was all about. And on the good days – the days when she would go into Nesbit & Noonan and work with people who were fun and irreverent and whom she might join for a drink in Daly's pub after a session – on those good *old* days, life was a laugh sometimes.

But things had changed. Nowadays a lot of

media people were stressed and harassed and pressurized, and they took it out on underlings like receptionists and trainee sound engineers and voiceover artists. She hadn't been subjected to such bullying behaviour since she'd been at school. 'That was – um – *crap*, to be perfectly frank,' the producer of the commercial she'd recorded today had said. 'Do it again.' *Do it again. And again. And again* were words she heard with increasing frequency in her head-phones while she was recording a gig. No-one ever seemed to say 'Please' any more. And the reason the underlings tolerated the bullying was because they knew – and the people doing the hiring *knew* that they knew – that *there was always someone else to do the job*. 'Rosa's not available? OK – we'll go with Siobhan or Paula or Grace or Becky or Paige.' And that was how 'absolutely' became one of the most frequently used words in Rosa's vocabulary.

A Brand New Life of Freedom sank under the weight of another scraping of pasta, and Rosa turned her attention to the dishes, switching on the radio as was her habit in the evening. Becky's voice, she registered automatically, extolling the virtues of a new vitamin supplement.

She slooshed water into the basin, mentally scrolling through the list of potential Lottie-minders in the Motherhood who might help her get through the next week or so. How much easier life would be in a couple of years' time when Lottie would be old enough and independent enough to stay home alone. What else would the years bring? A couple of years after being old enough and independent enough to stay home alone, Lottie would be old enough and independent enough to go clubbing. And a couple of years after that, Lottie would be old enough and independent enough to leave home, and Rosa would finally have her Brand New Life of Freedom. And as she dunked Lottie's ancient Benjamin Bunny bowl into the sudsy water, she found herself thinking that A Brand New Life of Freedom actually didn't sound that appealing any more.

'M. Muh. Mouse. N. Nuh. Nut. O. Oh. Orange. P. Puh—'

There was a snort in her headphones, and then she heard Roydon Sneyde's voice. 'There was a pop on the P.'

'Was there?' Rosa's shoulders slumped. 'Shit. Sorry. Excuse my language.'

'That's OK. Maybe it's time for a break. My brains are fried too. I'm surprised I even spotted that cock-up. Let's take ten.'

It was four o'clock. She'd been recording for two consecutive hours. She'd gone through a large bottle of Ballygowan, the senseless words on the page were dancing in front of her eyes, and the strain was beginning to tell on her voice. She set her cans down on the table beside the microphone and eased into a stretch in an attempt to get rid of some of the tension that had been accumulating in her upper back and shoulders. She could do with a massage, she thought, digging her fingers into her trapezius muscles and treating them to a little friction rub. Through the glass panel that separated the recording booth from the main body of the studio she could see Roydon and Julian Bollard, the sound engineer, watching her greedily, and as she turned towards the door of the booth she made a throwing-up kind of face.

Outside in the comparatively airy studio Roydon was helping himself to coffee from the machine. Julian was tweaking something on the Audiofile. 'Cunt of a job, this,' she heard him muttering. 'I will hit the pub with a vengeance this evening. Fancy joining me, Roydon?'

'Nah. I've some paperwork to do at home. And then I intend chilling in front of *Jackass TV*. Or a video.'

'I got *Crash* out last night. Seen it?'

'No.'

'Top film. I recommend it. You seen it, Rosa?'

Rosa had not seen it, nor did she ever want to. She knew the storyline revolved round a couple who got off on car crashes.

'The wife's away for the week, so I might

sneak in a little porn,' said Roydon. 'Preferably with a girl with very long arms feeding me pizza and giving me a blow job at the same time.'

Rosa felt the sideways look he slid at her and she automatically bared her teeth in a rictus grin – the kind favoured by monkeys when they feel threatened by the dominant male. Oh, Christ, how she hated herself for doing it! How she would love to stand up straight and say: 'Excuse me? Please do not talk like that in front of me. Call me a prude if you like, but I find that kind of spiel offensive in the extreme.' But of course she didn't. She just let the foolish grin remain stapled to her face until Roydon turned away from her, then helped herself to a mug of coffee. These coffee breaks were nearly as intolerable as the sessions themselves. Roydon and Julian combined to make an intimidatingly unassailable phalanx of male chauvinism.

She sat down on a deep couch, trying to look relaxed. Julian was muttering gansta rap, beating out a tattoo on the console as he tweaked knobs. On the couch opposite her, Roydon was lounging against the leather with his legs splayed and his paunch straining against the buttons of his Calvin Klein shirt. He'd taken off his tie and jacket at the start of the session, and Rosa could see his chest hair where it grew up nearly as far as the Adam's apple on his jowly neck. There were sweat stains under his arms. You could practically smell the testosterone. 'Well, Rosa,' he said, leering at her. 'Saw you treating yourself to a spot of shoulder massage there. Someone told me you were a certified masseuse. Is that true, or is it just wishful thinking?'

'It's true. I did a series of night classes in massage therapy.'

'Full body?'

'Yes.'

'Woo. Do you give head too? I mean Indian head *massage* of course. Ha ha ha,' went Julian, grinning at her over his shoulder.

'Ha ha ha,' echoed Roydon.

'No. That was a separate course.'

'I could do with a massage now, I'm telling you. My *gluteus maximus* has gone all stiff on me. Ha ha ha.'

'Ha ha ha.'

Oh Christ. The thought of handling the thick flesh of Roydon Sneyde's *teres minor* and *major* made Rosa feel physically sick. She looked down at her knees, feeling Roydon's eyes on her. He was clearly enjoying her discomfort.

'You're looking good, Rosa. Been away on holiday lately?'

She sent him a bright smile and said: ''Fraid not. Just taking advantage of the fine spell we've had recently. I've been doing a little sunbathing in Stephen's Green.'

He gave her a lewd wink. 'Sunbathing? Mm.'

He ran his eyes down Rosa's body suggestively, as if imagining her stretched out topless. Then: 'I had a dream about you last night,' he said.

Oh Christ! Change the subject, Rosa, quick, change the subject. 'Did *you* get a holiday yet this year, Roydon?'

He grinned. 'Yeah. Phuket in Thailand.'

'Lovely!'

'It was pretty peachy, all right. Five-star hotel, cocktails, massages, the lot. And a little bit of Thai grass on the beach, you know.' He winked again, to show her what a laid-back, radical geezer he was under the suit. 'And I had a couple of weekends in Paris and the Big Apple. Doing cultural stuff, you know? Museums, theatres. And shopping. Gotta keep the wife happy somehow. Oh – I heard a good one the other day, Julian.'

'Yeah?'

'Yeah. Why do women wear make-up and perfume?'

'OK. Why *do* women wear make-up and perfume?'

'Because they're ugly and smelly.' A belly laugh.

'Hey!' said Rosa, getting to her feet and gluing an enthusiastic expression onto her face. 'I think I'm ready to go again.'

'A. Ape. Apes. B. Baa-lamb. Baa-lambs. C. Clown. Clowns.'

'Hold it there, Rosa.' Julian's voice. 'We've hit a glitch.'

Rosa focused on the words she'd been repeating in an enthusiastic 'Now, children!' kind of voice. What a load of meaningless crap. She imagined some unfortunate infant somewhere in the world following her instructions as she urged her to: 'Click on the ape. Click on the baa-lambs. Click on the clown . . .' A. Ape. Apes. B. Baa-lamb. Baa-lambs . . . Baa, baaa, bah.

A BRAND NEW LIFE OF FREEDOM. The title of the network marketing flyer she'd dumped in the bin suddenly came into her head again, and she found herself wondering if network marketing mightn't be a better option than this alphabet hell.

And then she heard Roydon's voice in her cans again. 'OK. Next page, Rosa. Oh! Nice one! "Click on the pants you would like me to wear." How did that get in there? That's from next week's "Style File". Ha ha ha! "Click on the pants you would like me to wear." You'd better say that in your sexiest voice, Rosa!'

'Actually, Roydon,' volunteered Rosa, 'it should be trousers. Since we're re-recording for a European market.'

'Of course it's trousers,' he said. 'I know that. I just find it titillating to imagine clicking on the pants I'd like you to wear. Ha ha ha.'

Somehow she got through Wednesday and Thursday. On Friday morning disaster struck. The mother who was meant to be collecting Lottie from school rang to say her own child was sick, and she wouldn't be able to take her after all. Rosa went into a spin, rang half a dozen other mothers, and got nothing but answering machines. There was only one solution. Snooty Suki in Online would just have to resign herself to the fact that there'd be a child hanging around in reception this afternoon.

'I'm going to have to keep you out of school today, sweetheart.'

'Yay!' said Lottie.

'The downside is that you're going to have to come into Online with me this afternoon.'

'Oh, Mum! I *hate* Online.'

'I know, I know, but I've no alternative.'

Lottie scowled. 'How long for?'

'Two hours.' They'd made good progress on the files yesterday, so today's session shouldn't take as long.

Lottie's scowl got worse. 'Two *hours*? Ugh!'

'I'll buy you a Magnum afterwards,' said Rosa.

'It's netball day today. I'm going to miss it.'

'I'm sorry, Lottie, but there's *no alternative* – OK?'

The sulk intensified, and then Lottie gave her her best disingenuous look. 'Couldn't I stay here?'

'What do you mean?'

'In the flat.'

'On your own?'

'Yes.'

'No.'

'Emphatically no?'

'Emphatically no.'

Lottie scowled again. 'Why not?'

'It's against the law, for starters, and I'd be sick worrying about what might happen—'

'*What* might happen, Mum?'

'Anything. The flat might go on fire—'

'Yeah, right. I'm going to play with matches. *Mum*. Give me a break. I'm nine years old, not a baby.' Rosa could feel herself vacillating. She could tell by the look on Lottie's face that her daughter knew she was having second-thought syndrome. 'Look,' said Lottie. 'I promise I will sit here and do my homework like a good girl and then I will watch television. I will not move from this room. I will not try and light the gas for any reason; I will not answer the door to strangers; I will not do the crack cocaine I have stashed in my schoolbag.'

'Will you answer the phone?'

Lottie narrowed her eyes, considering. 'Not unless I hear it's you on the machine.'

'And why will you not answer the phone?'

'Because I'd have to say to the person on the other end that you're not here, and the person would know I was home alone and that could be tricky.'

'Right answer. Smart girl.'

'So. Will you do it? Will you let me stay here and not have to go to stinking Online?'

Rosa considered. 'Will you *promise*—'

'Mum. Re*lax*. I promise I'll be Little Miss Sensible. I'd promise *anything* to get out of going to Online.'

So would I, thought Rosa grimly, thinking of what the afternoon had in store for her. She took a deep breath and made the decision. 'OK,' she said. 'But if anything goes wrong – *anything* – you're to pick up the phone to me. I'll have my mobile powered off when I'm in the studio, but I'll leave the Online number by the phone. Just tell Suki you need to speak to me urgently, OK? Now. Done deal?'

'Done deal. And you *know* I won't need to contact you, Mum.'

Rosa tried to think of a worst-case scenario. 'What if you fall and hit your head and there's blood?'

'I'll phone an ambulance and *then* I'll phone you.'

'How did you get to be so very wise, little Lottie?'

'I inherited it from my dad. You told me he was wiser than the three wise men rolled into one and handsomer than Prince Harry, remember?'

Rosa bent down to her daughter and kissed her on the nose. 'Yes,' she said. 'I remember.'

She was well into her fourth hour of recording. It wasn't her fault that the session was taking so long – she'd been working her ass off to get the job done flawlessly and fast. The endless delays between takes were due to the fact that two high-powered suits were in attendance, and Roydon was in schmooze mode. She could see him now, smiling his oily smile and gesticulating extravagantly, doing that expansive matey thing men do when networking. Thank God it looked as if one of the suits was leaving at last. Beyond the glass window of the recording booth she saw the men shaking hands and slapping each other vigorously on the shoulder.

Come on, oh, come *on*! Rosa had been mentally urging them to get a move on for the past hour now. An opportunity had arisen to phone home during an earlier lull, and she'd been reassured that nothing earth-shattering had occurred in her absence apart from the discovery of a wasp in the kitchen. 'I hope you killed it?' Rosa had asked. 'Mum! No!' had been Lottie's response. 'I could never squish a wasp. I shooshed it out the window.'

'OK – let's go again, Rosa.' Roydon had finished his elaborate farewell ritual and flicked the talk-back switch on. He looked at his watch.

'Another twenty minutes should do it.' Rosa knew she could do it in less if there were no interruptions. She kept her fingers tightly crossed under the desk as she carefully articulated the words on the remaining pages, praying that nothing would go wrong.

'X. Xmas. Xmases. Y. Yak. Yaks. Z. Zebra. Zebras.' Yak yak yak. Click. Click. Click. Click. *Click.*' *Yes!* She was finished, and at last she was out of the booth, rooting in her bag for her mobile so that she could turn it on. The remaining client was consulting with Julian about some quibbly detail, and Roydon was laboriously filling out paperwork. 'What's your address again?' he asked Rosa.

'Oh – let me.' Rather than dictate and have to watch him slowly pen the words, she took the paper from him and quickly scribbled her name and address. Then she punched 'home' on her mobile. On the other end she heard her own voice on the answering machine, telling the caller to leave a message. 'Lottie, pick up,' she said into the phone when the beep sounded.

'Now. About next week's "Style File". How are you fixed, Rosa?' Roydon was fingering the keypad of his Palm Pilot.

Rosa didn't want to waste any more time hanging around the studio. 'Um. Can I phone you later about that, Roydon?' Then: 'Lottie? It's Mummy. Pick up.'

Roydon looked sour. 'It's more convenient for me to do it now,' he said, 'so that I can check studio availability with Julian.'

'Um. OK – sorry.' She started fumbling through her bag for her diary. 'Lottie! Lottie – will you please pick up the phone? *Lottie!* Pick up the phone at once!' She could feel sweat begin to spread under the tight sleeves of her T-shirt, and something was lurching unpleasantly in her stomach. 'Lottie? *Now* – this minute!'

'Kids. Who'd have 'em,' remarked Roydon, continuing idly to twiddle his organizer. Rosa listened hard to the silence at the other end of the phone, then pressed 'off', telling herself that Lottie must be in the loo. She'd phone again in a minute.

Julian and the client had finished their confab. The client shifted sideways on the leather sofa and patted the cushion next to him, inviting Rosa to join him. She obliged with an insincere 'thank you', and sat down beside him, trying to look relaxed.

'Julian? How's next week looking?' said Roydon.

'Let me get on to Suki about that.' Julian picked up the phone. 'Line's busy,' he said, getting to his feet. 'I'll go and check the book myself.'

'No hurry,' said Roydon as Julian ambled towards reception.

No hurry! Rosa's fingernails were digging into the palms of her hand.

Beside her the client was lounging against leather, eyeing her with interest. He cocked his head to one side. 'You did a great job there.'

'Thanks.' Rosa did her best to smile back.

'Yeah,' said Roydon. 'Rosa's a real pro. One of the best in the business. Always available, aren't you, Rosie? Always up for it.'

'Yes.' Rosa's smile was wearing thin.

The client was looking even more interested. 'Available to go for a drink, maybe?'

'Um. 'Fraid not. I've to get home to my little girl.' She saw the man's eyes move to the ringless fingers of her left hand.

'I can be pretty persuasive.' He smiled, and then his hand slid towards the slim silver phone that had started to purr at him. 'Excuse me while I take this.'

Rosa thanked God for that phone. Julian had come back with a desk diary, and he and Roydon were now comparing dates. She took the opportunity to press 'redial'. The answering machine kicked in again. 'Lottie. Carlotta. Pick up the phone.' Pause. '*Pick up the phone.*' Pause. 'Lottie. When you get this message will you be good enough to phone me on my mobile, please.' Her voice was terse, but inside she was awash with worry. She also realized she was bursting to pee.

She'd pay a visit to the loo while Julian and Roydon were aligning their agendas.

In the loo she peed, washed her hands, and then, telling herself that Lottie *must* be out of the bathroom by now, she steeled herself to press 'redial'. The same thing happened. Lottie did not come to the phone. Again she left a panicky message, and as she did her phone bleated piteously at her to tell her that she was running out of juice. Rosa was frantic now. She *had* to get out of there, had to get home.

She ran back to the studio, hoping that next week's dates would be sorted and she could skedaddle. The three men were laughing when she came through the door.

'Take it easy, Rosa,' said Roydon, when he got a load of her flushed face and anxious expression. 'We're all going to hit Daly's. Jonathan wants to buy you a drink as a reward for all your hard work.'

Rosa looked blankly at Jonathan. 'But I told you I couldn't—'

Roydon interrupted her. There was a warning note beneath the jokey timbre of his voice as he said: '*No-one* turns down the offer of a drink from a client, Rosa!' He lumbered to his feet and reached for his suit jacket. 'All right, lads! Let's call it a day!'

'Um – Roydon – what about next week?'

'I can give you those dates in the pub, love.'

131

He slung his jacket over his shoulder and hefted his briefcase. 'Shit – I've filed that invoice away. You can sign that in the pub too.'

'But—'

'Don't hassle me, Rosa.'

'I—'

Roydon took her by the arm and led her through the door, out of view of the client. His demeanour was openly threatening now. 'Look, Rosa,' he said in a very low voice. 'Jonathan wants to take you for a drink, and you are going to play ball. All right? Because if you don't, there are lots of other FVOs out there who are available for next week's gig. D'you know what I'm saying?'

Rosa nodded frantically. 'Yes, yes, yes! Of *course* I know what you're saying, but I can't, I *can't* – don't you understand? My daughter's home alone – I need to get back to her.' She knew she wasn't doing her professional profile any good by panicking like this, but she was really desperate now. Roydon's grip on her arm tightened. He was breathing heavily, he smelt fetid, and she could feel sweat on his palms. Revolted, she pulled away. 'Oh! Let *go* of me, you – you fucking *bully*!'

His cardiac arrest looked imminent. His eyes bulged, his mouth opened in a capital O, his red face flared even redder. 'How dare—' he began, but Rosa just ducked back into the studio, barely registering the uncertain expressions and slack jaws of the two men vacillating there. Roydon had followed her through, inarticulate with anger and humiliation, and she knew by the look in his eyes – that snarling look that a wounded animal turns upon its persecutor – that she would never work for Roydon Sneyde again. She'd committed a capital offence – she'd humiliated him in front of the client. But she didn't care. The only thing that mattered in her life right now was getting home to Lottie. She grabbed her bag and raced out of the studio, pressing 'redial' on her phone as she ran. There was no point. The phone was dead.

The traffic was as grim as it always was on a Friday afternoon. There were so many glitches and stumbling blocks and standstills that Rosa's panic mounted further. Her mouth was dry, her head a dizzy cavity. Her centre of gravity had gone, she felt as if she was existing in a chaotic void. She was aware that she was holding each breath she took before letting it out with a staccato rush, moving her lips in silent prayer. Oh, God. Lottie. Oh, God, please let Lottie be OK. Oh God – I'll be good. I'll believe in you again, I promise, if you'll only let Lottie be OK. Please, God, please. She's all I have. Dear God, let my baby be OK . . .

The traffic had come to a standstill again. Oh,

this was insufferable, intolerable – this was hell. She'd be quicker running. She pulled across a double yellow, and mounted a wide pavement. Her car would be towed, but she didn't care. She didn't even think to lock it, she just grabbed her bag and started running for her life, oblivious to the curious stares of passers-by and stationary motorists.

By the time she reached her apartment block Rosa was doubled over with a stitch, but she felt no pain. She rooted in her bag for her keys, dropping them twice before she could get the key in the lock. Two people were waiting by the lift door; the illuminated sign told her it was on its way up to the fifth floor. There was no way she could wait: she took the stairs to her third-floor apartment two at a time. When she arrived on the landing she fumbled with her key, but the door swung open before she could insert it fully. It was on the latch.

Rosa stepped into the apartment, and as soon as she did she knew it was empty. The television was on. Sabrina the Teenage Witch was smiling her cheekiest smile. Canned laughter filled the sitting room. Rosa automatically reached for the 'off' switch. From Lottie's room she could hear the gerbil's wheel squeaking as it turned.

'Lottie?'

Rosa moved through the sitting room into Lottie's bedroom. The child's project on Ancient

Egypt was spread out on the floor alongside a magazine open at a picture of the Pyramids. It had been partially cut out – a pair of scissors lay abandoned beside it. 'Lottie?' Rosa's voice was ragged: the sound barely registered in the empty space. Her breathing had become fast and shallow, and, aware that she was hyperventilating, she forced herself to sit down on Lottie's bedside chair and put her head between her knees. Her mind was blank, numb: a *tabula rasa*. Nothing came to her. No thoughts, no conjectures, no ideas.

Finally she stood up and moved to the sitting room like a sleepwalker. The answerphone was blinking at her, rapidly, nervously, like a frightened animal. The phone. The police. Of course. She should dial 999. She picked up the receiver, punched in the numbers, and waited for the voice to ask her which service she required. She couldn't answer. She was hyperventilating again. The voice on the other end asked the question again, more forcefully. Did she require the police? An ambulance? She didn't know. 'My daughter . . .' Rosa just managed to say '– my little girl has gone missing—'

'Mum! Hey! It's OK! Here I am!'

She wheeled round. Lottie stood wide-eyed in the doorway. Rosa froze, then all at once her mouth, her face, her entire demeanour sagged with relief. 'Oh!' she said, dropping the phone and stumbling towards her daughter. 'Oh, Lottie! Oh, God – thank you! Oh, God, oh God – oh, Lottie, where did you *go*?' The last word came out as an anguished howl as Rosa collapsed to her knees, wrapped her arms around her daughter and clutched her to her breast. Sobs convulsed her, and tears came spilling from her eyes – great big sploshy tears of relief.

Lottie looked fearful, now. She had never seen her mother so distraught. 'Mummy,' she said. 'It's OK. Everything's fine – really and truly. Please, Mummy. Please stop crying.' The little girl looked at the phone that was lying on the floor. A tinny, urgent voice was issuing from the receiver. 'And Mum,' said Lottie, uncertainly, 'don't you think you'd better answer that person who's on the phone?'

Rosa nodded mutely, but she didn't move for a while. She remained kneeling on the floor of her sitting room with her face pressed tight against her daughter's tummy. Lottie's T-shirt was saturated with tears. Her hands were gently stroking her mother's hair, but her voice was confused and upset. 'Stop, Mummy, please. Don't cry any more. Think of all the drowning fairies.'

Every tear drowns a fairy – that's what she often said to Lottie when she cried. And a spluttery laugh escaped Rosa, despite herself.

* * *

There was little to laugh at five minutes later, though. Rosa was tight-lipped and ashen with fury. 'What were you *thinking* of?' she demanded of her daughter. 'I expressly *forbade* you to set foot outside the door! Do you realize what I *went* through when you didn't pick up the phone? Have you any idea of the *torment* you put me through?' She was pacing the floor of the sitting room, gesticulating angrily. A chastened Lottie was sitting on the sofa, eyes downcast, picking at a thumbnail.

'I'm sorry, Mum, really I am. It was an emergency – I explained it all on your voice-mail, and on the answering machine. I left you a message to say—'

'You really thought that playing back messages would be high on my list of priorities when I got home to find the door swinging open and you gone?'

'I'm sorry about not locking the door. I had to put it on the latch because I couldn't find my key and I didn't have time to look for it because of the emergency—'

'And what was the nature of this "emergency"? What was so *fucking* – sorry – urgent that had you break all the promises you'd made to me?'

'Well . . .' Lottie couldn't meet her mother's eyes. Rosa never used bad language in front of her. The fact that she'd uttered the 'f' word was

137

an indication of how angry she was. 'It's all on the machine,' she said, lamely.

Rosa gave her a baleful look, then strode across the floor to the machine that was still blinking anxiously and jabbed 'playback' with an aggressive finger.

Lottie's message was the second on the tape. 'Mummy!' Her voice was wobbly with distress as it came over the speaker. 'I know you told me not to leave the flat but this is an emergency, Mummy – a real one. You see, there's a dog and he's hurt and I have to get him to the vet because no-one's *helping* him!' – here, a sob. 'So if I'm not back when you get this message I'll be in the vetin'ry surgeon's across the road. OK?'

Rosa stood frowning at the machine for a moment or two, trying to calm herself. The bleep sounded, and the automated voice parroted the usual spiel, and then she heard her own voice on the tape saying: 'Lottie, pick up.' Rosa turned the machine off, then took a steadying breath and turned to face her daughter. 'OK. Explain, please,' she said in her best stern-but-fair voice, crossing her arms.

Lottie raised big Bambi eyes to her mother, a ploy that rarely failed. The unamused expression on Rosa's face made her lower her lashes again immediately. She resumed picking at her thumbnail.

'Well, you see, I was in my room doing my

Egypt project and then suddenly I heard loud brakes – like this – "Rr-rr-rr-rr!" – and then I looked out of the window and a car had knocked down this little dog, and the car just drove on. And I could see that he was hurt because his back leg was all floppy and just dragging after him, and nobody was helping him, Mum – *nobody!* – so I just had to do it myself. You would have done it too, Mum, I promise. And Online was engaged, so I just left a load of messages and then I went out onto the street and the poor dog was whimpering and then when I stroked him he started wagging his tail, so I picked him up and carried him very gently to the vet. And he looked so sad and kind of *bewildered* – I was nearly crying – and I did try phoning you again from the vet's, Mum, honest and truly, to say there was a big queue, but I only ever got your voice mail.'

Halfway through this monologue Lottie had turned huge eyes on her mother once more. But this was no calculated 'pretty please' blink – this was the real thing. Lottie was begging, *imploring* her mother to understand.

It worked. Of course it did. 'OK,' said Rosa, when the tale had been told. 'OK. You're forgiven. But if something like this should happen ever again – God forbid – you ring Dannie in Florabundance or in her flat and explain things to her. You do not go flying off on a mission of mercy all by yourself. Is that understood?'

Lottie nodded, and then her face crumpled with distress. 'I hope he's going to be OK. He was a really nice dog.'

Rosa sat down beside Lottie on the sofa. 'What did the vet say?'

'He said that he had a broken leg, but that he could mend it. And the secretary said she'd ring the dog's owner—'

'It wasn't a stray?'

'No. He had a collar on with a phone number.'

'Well then, rest assured, sweetheart. He's going to be fine.'

'I suppose. The vet said he'd let me know. I made him promise. I gave him my name and address and phone number. He was really nice, the vet. He said that any time the Mysterious One got sick I was to bring her to him.'

'That reminds me,' said Rosa, making a face. 'The bloody Mysterious One's cage needs cleaning.'

'I'll do it!' said Lottie, jumping to her feet. Then she paused, bent down and gave her mother a kiss on the cheek. 'I'll never make you cry like that again, Mum. I promise I won't.'

The smile Rosa gave her was a little abstracted. Now that the high drama was over, more pragmatic issues had come crowding into her head. She remembered her car and wondered how much of a fine she'd have to fork out for it. She remembered that there was nothing in the fridge for supper. And then she remembered the expression on Roydon's jowly face as she'd shouldered her way past him in Online, and the thought that had occurred to her then. That little voice that had warned her that she would never work for Roydon Sneyde again.

Later that evening, just as she was finishing off Lottie's bedtime story, her doorbell rang. Dannie? she thought. Dannie often came downstairs from her fourth-floor flat at around this time of the evening with a bottle of wine. But Dannie never rang the bell – she always gave a bright ra-tat-a-tat knock. Rosa picked up the receiver on the entryphone and spoke into it. 'Who is it?' she said in a guarded voice. People occasionally rang the street bell as a prank, especially in the early hours of the morning. It was one of the many drawbacks of living in a city centre apartment.

'Is that Lottie's mother?' A man's voice.

'Yes.'

'My name is Michael Luque.' The man's voice had an accent that told her he wasn't Irish. Scottish, perhaps? 'I'm the vet from across the road.'

'Oh, yes. Is the dog all right?'

'He's fine. The owner asked me to give Lottie a cash reward. I have it here in an envelope. Will

I bring it up, or is it safe enough to put it through the letter box?'

She knew it was never a good idea to let a stranger into an apartment building, no matter how kosher they sounded. 'Oh – don't go to the trouble of coming all the way up,' she said. 'Just bung it in the letter box and I'll run down and get it later. You're very kind. Thank you.' There was a pause, then: 'Good night,' she said.

'Good night.'

Downstairs in the lobby she opened her mailbox to find an envelope with Lottie's name and address scrawled on it. There was another envelope there, too. It had obviously been dropped in by hand because it hadn't been in the mailbox when she'd checked earlier in the day. Calypso's party invite, she decided, without bothering to open it.

She went into Lottie's room. 'You asleep yet?'

'No.'

'The vet dropped this round for you.'

'What is it?'

'Open it and see.' She sat down on the edge of Lottie's bed as the sleepy child tore open her envelope. Inside was a ten-euro note, and a few brief lines written in the same hand that had penned the address. '"Dear Lottie,"' she read aloud. '"Jeeves's owner wanted you to have the enclosed as a reward." Cool! "The next time a workshop comes up, I'll let you know. Michael

Luque."' Lottie's smile mutated into a massive yawn.

'Well,' said Rosa. 'That's very generous of Jeeves's owner. He must have been delighted to get his pooch back.' She leaned against Lottie and looked at the letter over her shoulder. 'What's that about a workshop?'

'There was a poster in the vet's waiting room about a workshop in the Ark for children.' The Ark was a space in Temple Bar that specialized in children's activities. 'Michael did one last weekend, but there probably won't be another one now until the summer. He said he'd let me know when it's going to happen.'

'Is it a workshop on how to look after pets?'

'No. It's about dancing.' Lottie fell back against her pillow, and Rosa pulled the duvet up under her chin.

'Dancing?'

'Yes. It's his hobby.'

'What sort of dancing?'

'Um. I forget the name. The one where you stamp your feet.' Tap, probably, thought Rosa. 'But Roxanne says all dancing for men is poofy.' Roxanne was one of Lottie's school friends.

'And when did Roxanne give you the benefit of her politically incorrect opinion?'

'This evening when I rang her to find out about homework for Monday. She went to that last workshop in the Ark, so I told her I'd met her teacher today and she said he was a poo—um – gay.'

'Just because he dances for a hobby?'

'No.' Another wide yawn. 'She said she saw him walking down the street with his arm around another man.'

'Ah. Well. There's nothing wrong with being gay, you know. It's as legit as being heterosexual.' Rosa was well used to trotting out politically correct aphorisms. 'Now. You get to sleep. You're knackered. Night, night, sleep tight –'

'Don't let the bugs bite,' Lottie finished drowsily. 'Love you, Mummy.'

'Love you too, baby,' said Rosa, turning off the light.

In the sitting room she picked up the second envelope she'd found in her mailbox, and tore it open. It contained a photograph of a daintily heeled bootee – a lace-trimmed confection in pale blue satin of the type worn by eighteenth-century aristocrats. The back of the card told her that the bootee belonged to a collection housed by the Metropolitan Museum in New York. Calypso must have got it on her last trip to the Big Apple.

Rosa opened the card, but there was no message inside, no invitation. Just three penned Xs. How weird!

Picking up the telephone, she punched in Calypso's number.

'Dominic Forrest,' came the voice down the phone.

Shit. Rosa hated it when Dominic answered the phone. She found him a bit intimidating, and never knew what to say to him. 'Oh, hi, Dominic! Sorry to bother you. It's Rosa. Is Calypso there?'

''Fraid not, Rosa. She's gone off to the theatre.'

'Oh. Well, maybe you could help me. I got your party invitation today, and she's forgotten to fill in the details. It *is* next Thursday, isn't it?'

'Well, yes. But I don't see how you could have got an invite yet. They're all sitting here on the hall table, ready to be put into the post. She's left it till the last minute as usual. She'll probably end up e-mailing people instead.'

'Oh. That's strange. I wonder what this is, then?'

'Well, it's definitely not from Calypso. I can see an invite addressed to you right here on the top of the pile.'

'Oh. OK. I've obviously made some mistake. Well. I'll – um, I'll see you next week, then?'

'Yes. Looking forward to it. Bye, Rosa.' There hadn't been much sincerity in the 'looking forward to it', she'd noticed. The last time she'd seen Dominic had been after a girly night with Calypso when she'd been pissed and Dominic had had to drive her home when she couldn't get a taxi. Or maybe she was just being paranoid?

She looked down at the card in her hand. Who on earth had sent it? Why had she received through her door an anonymous card with a picture of a boot on it?

Suddenly, blindingly, she made sense of it. The card was from Roydon Sneyde. And the message was staring her in the face.

Chapter Four

'Shite!' Dannie had misjudged the angle of the final pearl-topped pin: its point pierced the tip of her left ring finger through the waxy green surface of the laurel leaf she was tweaking into position. Quickly, she snatched her hand away from a compact mass of creamy roses. It wouldn't do to have blood bespattering the virgin pallor of the bride's bouquet. She'd spent the best part of three hours working on the glorious confection. It would be picked up from her shop at two o'clock along with three brides-maids' posies, and then transported to the church on Stephen's Green where the wedding was to be held.

She was alone in the shop. Laura was at the dentist, and she'd given her other two assistants the rest of the afternoon off – until four o'clock, when they would be busy in the Morrison hotel working on the table arrangements for the reception. White tulips and hydrangeas. Classy stuff – but then, Dannie had established a reputation for class. After years spent working the kind of hours that gave her perpetual shadows under her eyes she had reached a place where not only could she employ a dedicated and talented staff and take time off for herself occasionally, she could also afford to turn down work. Never again would she have to cram Baby's Breath into a ceramic bootee ('Congratulations. Will that be pink or blue, sir?'), never again construct a replica Manchester United jersey from red and white carnations on Father's Day, never again work punishingly long hours on a bog-standard bouquet production line the night before Mother's Day.

She stanched the blood from the pinprick with a sheet of kitchen towel and stood back to survey her work. The bouquet was a living work of art, a poem in petals. Each of the Vendella roses was an example of Nature's astonishing symmetry – each flower was as delicate and as exquisitely wrought as a shell, or a snowflake, or a baby's ear. She'd gathered thirty of them in a nest of glossy laurel leaves and anchored each individual rose with its own gleaming, pearl-tipped pin. Dannie leaned forward and lightly ran her right hand over the blossoms. The only problem she had about creating such perfection was that it was always difficult to part with the finished product. Each arrangement she constructed – from the most modest posy to the most elaborate centrepiece – was a tour de force. She hated saying goodbye to them, and sometimes felt like clutching them to her bosom, crying 'They're mine, I tell you! *Mine!*' like a bad actor. It had never felt like that in the old days. When she'd done the baby bootees and the football kit and the production-line stuff she'd been glad to see the back of it, but now it was all she could do not to blow farewell kisses at her posies and bouquets and nosegays as they disappeared off through the shop door.

Turning away from the wedding bouquet, she reached for the order book to check what needed to be done next. A coffee bouquet – easy peasy. These were the little posies it had become fashionable to bring to a girlfriend on a lunch date: she'd come across the notion in Holland. There were two medium-priced birthday bouquets to be sorted, and the weekly delivery to the mistress of a prominent politician. Nothing too taxing, thank Christ. She could manage this without the help of the two assistants she'd deployed to the Morrison; she could even allow herself a cup of coffee before Laura came back from her dental appointment.

Ducking into the kitchenette at the back of the shop, she switched on the kettle and fished in the biscuit tin for a chocolate Hob-nob. The chocolate was melting – Laura had left the tin on the window sill in direct sunlight. Feeling chocolate stick to her fingers, Dannie crammed the biscuit into her mouth in two big bites, then went back into the shop to retrieve the kitchen towel just as the bell on the door rang. A man came in.

''Morning, ma'am,' he said.

Dannie returned the greeting as best she could, then wiped her chocolatey fingers, swallowing hard. It was a moment before she trusted herself to sound articulate. 'Sorry about that,' she said. 'Sugar craving.'

'No problem, ma'am,' he said. He stuck his hands in the pockets of his battered sheepskin jacket and let his eyes wander around the shop before returning his attention to her. For a second she debated with herself as to whether or not he was wearing coloured contacts. His irises were an unsettling shade of green, flecked with amber. And then Dannie told herself to wise up. A man like this would have no truck with anything as pansy as coloured contacts. This was a man who was – well – all *man*.

He smiled. She smiled back. It never did any harm to flirt with a male customer, and with this particular customer, it wasn't even an effort. 'I'd like a bouquet,' he said, and Dannie noticed that he pronounced the word correctly – 'boo-kay' rather than the 'bow-kay' she herself had always called them until she'd done her floristry course.

So far she had found out two things about him. He was educated, and he came from somewhere in the American Deep South.

'What had you in mind, sir?'

'Well, now.' He put his head on one side and gave her a hard look. 'You're the expert. How about I run this by you? If you could make yourself the bouquet of your dreams – price no object – from what you have here, what would you end up with?'

'Wow,' said Dannie. 'I'd have a field day. Price no object, really?' He inclined his head. 'Janey. She must be a very special lady.'

'I reckon. I've yet to find out.'

'Well, take it from one who knows. You're going the right way about courtin' her.'

'That's good to hear.'

'Let's see.' Dannie pressed her hands to her mouth as she considered the surrounding floribunda, absently licking away a lingering trace of chocolate from her thumb. 'Um. I'd go for roses. Vendellas. And a couple of oriental lilies, and orchids. And loads of white phalaenopsis. And I'd fringe the bouquet with these little chin-chins. Aren't they dotey? I'd snog any fella who gave me a present of that lot.'

Especially a fella like you, she thought. Conventionally handsome he was not. He was carrying a little too much weight, his hair was woefully unkempt, with not even lip service paid to style, and she suspected that his stubble was not designer. But this man possessed an undeniable charisma. What was it about rough-looking men with polished accents? Guy had been like that – rugged and a bit battered-looking, but with a voice that had made her and countless hundreds of other women go all woolly and weak when he reported from the latest war zone. Guy's hair had been sun-bleached, his skin wind-burnt: this fella similarly looked as if he wouldn't know Phytologie for Men or Clinique's Scruffing Lotion from a hole in the ground.

He was looking at her with amusement. 'Snog?'

'Oh. I forgot Americans don't snog.' She twinkled back at him. 'They kiss.'

'OK,' he said now. 'Go for it. Whatever it takes.'

'It'll set you back the best part of two hundred euros.'

'That's not a problem.'

'Do you want them delivered?'

'No. I'll do that myself.'

She slanted him a smile. 'Hand-delivered earns you extra Brownie points.'

He shrugged. 'I've never done this before.'

'Will you let me know if it works?'

'If you can conjure up a bouquet that'll do the trick for me, I'd be glad to.'

'You'll have to allow me a couple of hours if

you want the job done with the kind of TLC I like to lavish on my babbies.'

'Babbies?' That amused look again.

'Babies. My *creations*.' She invested the word with mock-posh. 'Are you in a hurry, sir, or can you come back later?'

'I can come back.' He leaned over a bucket of palest pink roses and inhaled their scent, then turned back to her. 'Have you any Burgundy roses in stock?'

'You're in luck.'

'Stick a few of them in, will you?'

'Surely. Um – will you be needing a card?' Dannie gestured towards the row of greeting cards that she kept displayed on the shop counter.

The man ran an index finger over the cellophane wrappers, stopping when he reached a reproduction of Gustav Klimt's *The Kiss*. 'This one,' he said, extracting it from the rack.

'Good choice, sir,' she said. 'It's my favourite too.'

He raised an eyebrow and reached into his pocket for change. 'Well,' he said. 'That's what I call serendipity.'

'Apart from that other one by him,' Dannie went on, 'the picture of the mother and child. Look.' She riffled through the cards and produced the beautiful, tender depiction of motherhood. The one that made her go weak at the knees.

'Nic Roeg got a lot of mileage out of Klimt in *Bad Timing*. Have you ever seen that movie, ma'am?'

'No. But I spoke to Mr Roeg once over the phone, in my old life.'

'And what were you in your old life?'

'I was a television researcher.'

'Uh huh? So what made you decide to become a florist?'

'I realized that I hated being a television researcher.'

'I don't blame you. I expect you had to listen to a lot of celebrities droning on about their perfect lives.'

'Ah, now. I didn't mind that so much. Generally speaking, I find people very interesting. You obviously do too.'

'What makes you say that?'

'You ask a lot of questions.'

He laughed, then dropped some coins on the counter top. 'This is for the card. I'll pay for the flowers by credit when I come to pick them up, if that suits you, ma'am.'

In situations like this Dannie normally asked for a deposit, but something told her that this man wouldn't do a runner.

'That's fine,' she said.

The man turned and ambled back through the shop, pausing momentarily to lightly rub the waxy petals of an orchid between thumb

154

and finger. 'Hey!' protested Dannie. 'Hands off!'

Quickly he withdrew his hand. 'Sorry,' he said.

'And sorry for being rude. It's just that the acid in the sweat on your fingers can damage the orchid's petals. People who grow them wear cotton gloves.'

'What a pity,' he said, and the bell above the shop door tinkled again as he opened it. 'They look as if they're designed to be touched.' A final smile, and he was gone.

For a moment or two Dannie did absolutely nothing. Then, abruptly, she pressed 'play' on the CD player and reached for the barrier cream as Vivaldi's *Four Seasons* danced over the speakers.

The bell jangled as Laura burst into the shop.

'Hi,' said Dannie. 'What a dramatic entrance. Was the dentist that bad?'

'The dentist was fine,' said Laura. 'But was that who I think it was coming out of the shop?'

'What do you mean?'

'That guy that just came out of the shop. Was he Jethro Palmer?'

'Jethro Palmer? The film director? I dunno. I wouldn't have a clue what he looks like.'

'I saw him in *Hello!* last week.' An aspirant media star, Laura was addicted to magazines: every week she forked out a small fortune for *Hello!* and *OK!* and *heat* and *VIP*. 'It *was* him. I'm almost *certain* it was him.' She dived towards the window to see if she could catch a glimpse of the man's retreating back. 'It's got to be – I read somewhere that he was due in Dublin soon to direct some new blockbuster. Jesus, Dannie, is he *sexy*! I saw him being interviewed by Mariella Frostrup once. She couldn't stop flirting with him.'

'He's not that good-looking.' Dannie was inspecting her Burgundy roses.

Her assistant sent her a cynical look. 'Good looks have nothing to do with sex appeal, Dannie. He is what I would describe as an überdude.'

'An überdude?'

'Like – the ultimate man. Rich, sexy, intelligent, GSOH. And I bet he's a fantastic ride.'

Dannie laughed.

'Feck it!' said Laura with feeling. 'I'm devastated I missed him. What did he want?'

'A very special bouquet for a very special lady.' Dannie listed the details.

'Wow,' said Laura. 'It's probably for Jeanne Renaud. She's the romantic lead in the film. What's the delivery address?'

'He's picking it up himself later.'

'*Yes!* I'll get a chance to meet him.' Laura's jubilant smile faded almost immediately. 'Oh, no. I'd rather I didn't, come to think of it.'

'Oh? Why's that?'

'Because if he doesn't fall on his knees and say:

"Hey, Laura! You are the most beautiful woman I have ever seen. Please star in my next film and marry me at once," I don't think I'll be able to stand the disappointment.'

Dannie threw the tube of barrier cream across to her assistant. 'Will you commission me to do your bridal bouquet?' she said.

Laura grabbed the tube of cream with a deft hand and started to unscrew it. 'Sure,' she said, with a film-starrish toss of her head. 'And I'll allow you to design the corsage that I'll wear to the Oscars too.'

Laughing, Dannie turned up the volume on Vivaldi, and then both women were silent for a long time, intent on the business of creating a floricultural *chef-d'oeuvre*.

It was getting close to six. Dannie should have closed up shop half an hour ago. She checked her watch again, then looked towards the gorgeous confection of roses and orchids and camellia leaves that she had spent so much time and effort constructing earlier in the day. Shite. The bastard might have phoned to say he'd changed his mind. She'd clearly made a seriously flawed character judgement earlier when she'd deferred payment.

Laura had departed ten minutes ago, bemoaning her pricked fingers and her missed bid for stardom. Dannie decided she'd give Mr

Shit-Hot Director Palmer until six. She hung around doing unnecessary jobs, doodled on the day diary, checked her watch five times in as many minutes, then phoned the girls in the Morrison to tell them she was running late. The word back on the centrepieces was good, but she should be down there herself now, to give them the once-over.

On the dot of six she gave up on him. She got her coat from the back room, jabbed off the light switches, and fished her keys out from under the counter. Just as she straightened up, the bell rang and the door to the street opened.

'Hey, there,' he said. 'Sorry I'm late. There was an accident on the freeway and the traffic was backed up for miles.'

'Well, am I glad to see you,' said Dannie. 'I wouldn't have liked to have dumped nearly two hundred euros' worth of blooms in the bin. Can we settle up quickly? I need to get somewhere fast.'

'Sure.' He extracted an envelope and his card (platinum, Dannie noticed without surprise) from a pocket and signed. *J. Palmer*. 'Thanks,' he said, and 'Thank *you*, sir,' she said. Then he pocketed his credit card, turned and strolled towards the door.

'Hey,' Dannie called after him, picking up the envelope he'd abandoned on the counter top. 'Mr Palmer, sir! You forgot this!' The doorbell tinkled. 'And your flowers! Jesus, Mary and Joseph! Don't forget to take your flowers!'

He turned in the doorway. In the dimness of the shop she couldn't read his expression, but his voice when he spoke sounded amused.

'Take a look at the envelope,' he said. Then the door swung to and he was gone.

What? What the hell was all that about? wondered Dannie. She looked down at the envelope, turned it over, and read – in the same hand that had scrawled the signature on the credit card slip – these words: 'For You.'

'For me?' she said aloud, stupidly, turning the card over again as if expecting to see another name written somewhere, or an address. 'For *me*?' she said again. Then, with cautious fingers, as if anticipating that the envelope might contain something dicey, she pulled it open. Inside she found the card bearing the reproduction of the Klimt. *The Kiss.* When she opened it she read, in J. Palmer's distinctive handwriting:

Dear Lady in the Flower Shop,

Presenting you with the bouquet of your dreams is, I know, a gesture so mock-heroic as to verge on the tacky (and somehow unfitting for a sad bastard hitting middle age). But there you have it. I've acted on impulse. I enclose a card with my phone number, and I hope very much that I might hear from you. You may consign my

159

card to the trash, of course, but please keep the flowers.

With very warm wishes,
Jethro Palmer

PS: If you are interested in having dinner with me some evening at a restaurant of your choice, I would be more than happy to make a reservation.

Dannie read the letter twice. On the second reading, when she came to the words '*a gesture so mock-heroic as to verge on the tacky*', she found herself smiling. She relocated her key, shrugged into her coat and gathered the sheaf of fabulous blossoms in her arms. Then she slipped the card into her pocket and shut up shop.

After she'd finished in the Morrison, Dannie picked up the makings of dinner from a Temple Bar deli and headed for home. She toyed with the idea of inviting Rosa up for a glass of wine and a gossip, and then thought better of it. She wasn't sure that she was ready to confide in anyone about Jethro Palmer just yet. She wasn't even sure what she should do. She'd have to call him, obviously, to say thank you for his insanely extravagant gesture, but – dinner?

In the five years since Guy, Dannie had run scared of men. She hadn't had very many liaisons – a couple of indulgent one-night stands and a more prolonged affair that seemed to have potential: but she had backed out of that one when the individual involved started insisting on commitment. She was still combustible. She'd had her fingers so badly burnt by Guy that there was no way she was going to allow some other relationships pyromaniac the opportunity of getting under her skin with a box of matches and a length of cordite.

She took out Jethro Palmer's card again. What did his handwriting say about him? It was slanted, kind of italic. He'd used a fountain pen – always a good sign. It was a strong hand, without the over-elaboration that indicated egotism or the jaggedness that signified neuroses. And as closely as she scrutinized it, she could see nothing that might betray deviousness. Jethro Palmer's handwriting was quite unlike her politician customer's – the sleeveen with the mistress. *His* expensive pen (not a fountain) scratched in a style that dripped duplicity.

Her empty wineglass was ready for a refill. Dutch courage was sometimes useful in situations like this. She sloshed in some red, took a gulp, then reached for the phone.

'Jethro Palmer.'

'Mr Palmer, hello. It's Dannie Moore here.'

'I beg your pardon, ma'am. Who's calling?'

She remembered that he couldn't know her name. What had he called her in his letter? *The*

Lady in the Flower Shop. 'Um. The lady in the flower shop,' she said.

'Hey! It's you! Can I call you back? I'm stuck in a meeting here.'

'Oh. Surely.'

'Give me your number.'

She did so.

'We'll talk later. Thanks for calling.'

Dannie put the phone down, feeling strange. His voice in her ear had given her a very nice feeling indeed. '*Stuck in a meeting*.' She wondered what it must be like to be involved in a meeting to discuss a big-budget movie project. Creative types in expensive bohemian threads, swapping ideas and 'think-tanking'. Skinny girls in Prada taking notes and sending e-mails. Maybe a diva movie actress having a crisis, being consoled with Valium or Xanax or promises of meatier scenes and more flattering costumes. And there would be Jethro at the helm: authoritative, relaxed, issuing orders in the kind of voice that didn't have to raise itself to be obeyed. It was an intriguing picture.

What had Laura called him? An überdude. Christ, a man like him could have *anyone*! He could have Julia Roberts! He could have Cameron Diaz! And for the life of her, Dannie just couldn't understand how someone like Jethro Palmer could possibly be interested in someone like her.

The wine bottle was almost empty. Dannie stuck a cork in it and resumed brushing her teeth. It was nearly midnight, the phone hadn't rung all evening, and she had to be up at half-past five. She was just about to put the cordless back on its base when it rang. Racing into the bathroom with it, she sluiced, spat, then took a deep breath and pressed 'talk'.

'Hello?'

'Hi. Sorry again. That's twice I've cut it fine with you. I'm sure you're on your way to bed.'

'No,' she lied. 'I was reading.'

'So you can talk?'

'I can.'

'Good.' There was a smile in his voice; he sounded relaxed. She pictured him in some five-star hotel bedroom, reclining on a vast bed, maybe, with a glass of something.

'Well. I suppose the first thing I should know is your name. I didn't take it in when you told me earlier.'

'It's Dannie. Dannie Moore. And I don't know how to thank you for the flowers. They're beautiful. But sure, you saw them yourself.' Dannie moved back into the sitting room, where the bouquet was resplendent in her favourite chinoiserie vase on the mantelpiece. She sat down on her big sofa with its piles of squishy sequined cushions.

'So my attention-seeking behaviour worked?'

'Yeah,' she said with a laugh. 'I suppose it did.'

'Good. It was a risk worth taking, then. I have never done anything quite so quixotic in my life.'

'What on earth made you? Do it, I mean?'

'I'd been wandering around for hours, recceing locations, watching people. I love people-watching. It's part of my job. I direct films for a living.'

'I know you do.'

'Well, this morning I was stopped in my tracks, literally. By you.'

Dannie sucked in her breath, then tried to turn the sound into a disparaging laugh. 'Yeah. I must have looked dead traffic-stopping in my jeans and T-shirt.'

'It wasn't the clothes. It was your demeanour. I watched you from the other side of the road, and for ten whole minutes I was, well – "transfixed" is the only word to describe how I felt. You were so entirely absorbed in what you were doing, I felt like a voyeur.'

'And that's exactly what you were.'

'*Touché*, ma'am! But the fact that you were so sublimely unaware that you were being observed lent you the best kind of beauty.'

'Go away! And what kind might that be?'

'The unselfconscious kind. That's why I asked you to include the Burgundy roses in your bouquet. You know what they're symbolic of?'

'Burgundy roses? In the language of flowers, d'you mean?'

'Yes.'

'Well, I couldn't tell you off the top of my head. I'd need to get my book out.' Dannie kept a book in the shop that told her what each of her flowers symbolized. Most people knew the obvious ones – red roses for love, white lilies for death, and so on, but some of them were quite obscure. It always amused her to stick a few yellow lilies in the bouquets she did for the politician, because yellow lilies symbolized false-hood. 'How would you know a thing like that?'

'One of the actors in the film I'm directing makes a reference to Burgundy roses. They represent "unselfconscious beauty".'

'One of the *actors*? Sure who'd trust a man who came out with guff like that?'

Jethro laughed. 'He's a villain. A Don Juan type.'

'And does the actress fall for it?'

'She does.'

'Get away! What an eejit!'

That laugh again. Then: 'You know who you reminded me of? When I was watching you earlier? Juliette Binoche. You have that same artless quality she has.'

'Juliette *Binoche*? Janey mackers, are you mad?'

'Janey mackers?'

'Oh – it's an Irish expression that means – well,

165

actually I haven't really a clue what it means. It – um – denotes surprise.' Dannie settled deeper into her cushions and stretched her legs so that her bare heels were resting on the arm of the sofa. The silk of her kimono parted and slid away, exposing her thighs.

'Well, you have that same quality Binoche has. In spades. When I approached you I half expected to hear a French accent. I was very pleasantly surprised by your soft Irish brogue.'

'My mother was Italian.'

'That explains the Continental looks. Watching you working, assembling that bouquet, was very –' there was a pause while he searched for the word '– affecting.'

She raised an incredulous eyebrow. 'Well. That's a first. I've never been called affecting before.'

'It's a term I'm not often tempted to use. Maybe once in a while, when I get a genuinely moving performance from an actor. And let me tell you, ma'am, that's a rare enough thing.'

For some reason, she understood that he was referring not to his actors, but to her. *A rare enough thing*. God, it felt good to be described that way! Dannie wedged the phone between her jaw and her collarbone and tucked an arm behind her head.

'Well. Thanks for the lovely compliment,' she said. She was never sure what to say when someone complimented her, but she'd read somewhere that it was cooler to acknowledge compliments than not.

'I like to think that I can tell a lot about people by observing them,' he said.

'Well, then. Here's a challenge for you. What kind of person am I?'

'You're fragile. I think you're probably more vulnerable than you'd like to appear. You have a sussedness about you, but a lot of that's veneer. You're creative, but efficient with it. You're a closet romantic. You're sensual. You have secrets.'

'And this in-depth character assessment is based on the ten short minutes you spent watching me through a window?' Dannie had uncorked the wine bottle, and was draining the remains of the red into her glass.

'Not all of it. The sensual bit I got from the way you relished licking chocolate off your fingers.'

Oh! Dannie set the bottle back down on the coffee table, then took a sip of wine. 'Well,' she said. 'You clearly know a lot more about me than I know about you.'

'I don't know enough yet. I'd like to know more. I'd like to know some of your secrets.'

'They're pretty closely guarded, I can tell you. You'd have your work cut out to uncover them.'

'I'm not afraid of hard work. It gets results.'

There was a pause. Dannie shifted a little as

she raised the wineglass to her lips, and felt silk slither again against her thigh. 'Mr Palmer?'

'Don't call me that, Dannie. My name is Jethro.'

He was right. Any formality between them was redundant now. 'Jethro.' She liked the way the name sounded on her tongue. 'Are you *plámásing* me?'

That smile was in his voice again. 'Plamawsing? What's plamawsing?'

She laughed at his execrable attempt at an Irish accent. 'It's another Irish expression. It means "flattering". Or "oiling up" somebody.'

'What makes you think I'd want to oil you up?'

Jesus! Dannie felt her face flare, but if Jethro Palmer was aware of the sexual nature of the innuendo he gave no indication. 'I don't know,' she said slowly. She drained her glass and set it down. The small thud it made as it met the surface of the table sounded like a punctuation mark: a full stop. Christ. What on earth was she doing, flirting over the phone like this with a complete stranger? It was time to call closure on this conversation. She drew herself up, folded her legs underneath her and pulled her robe more tightly around her.

'You think I'm the kind of man who routinely buys strange women flowers and pays them lavish compliments?'

'I don't know. I don't know you.'

'Do you think you might want to?'

She bit her lip. 'I don't know,' she said again. 'Maybe.'

'Dinner?'

Oh, Janey. No. 'Um. Ohhkaay.'

'Tomorrow?'

She'd heard about the Rules. She knew she should demur, invent a prior engagement. But Dannie had never been into playing silly relationship games.

'Tomorrow would be grand.'

'Somewhere in town?'

She'd want to avoid anywhere she'd be likely to run into a friend. Out of town would be better. 'No. How about Bistro na Mara?' she said. 'It's in Dun Laoghaire, on the seafront.'

'Sounds good. I'll pick you up. Where are you?'

'Pick me up at the shop,' she said. 'I'll be working late tomorrow.' It wasn't true, but Dannie didn't want him coming up to her flat.

'OK. Seven o'clock?'

'Seven's cool.'

'Till tomorrow, then. Good night, Dannie.'

'Good night, Jethro.'

'Oh, by the way? Remember what you said in the shop today, when I ordered the flowers? *Am* I going the right way about courting you? Or is it too soon to tell?' There was a smile in his voice.

She smiled back. 'It's *way* too soon to tell,'

she said. And then she put the phone down.

She remained lying on her sofa for some minutes afterwards, contemplating. That was the third untruth she'd told in the course of that phone call, she realized. Because Dannie suspected – rather apprehensively – that Jethro Palmer was actually courting her all too well.

The following evening when he rolled up outside the shop in a chauffeur-driven Merc she told herself not to be surprised. It stood to reason that a shit-hot movie director would travel with a driver. She let herself out of the shop, and started to pull the shutters down. They jammed – something they did on a fairly predictable basis.

'Allow me,' said Jethro, finishing the job for her. Then he stood back and they looked at each other. 'You smell of your flower shop,' he said.

'Well, that's not the worst thing you could say to a girl.' Actually, she smelt of Yves Saint-Laurent's Nu. She'd discovered it a couple of years ago when Brown Thomas had sent her a flyer which bore the legend: 'Nu defines a new Saint-Laurent woman: mysterious, complex and always in control, she is an enigmatic seductress who chooses not to reveal all of her secrets at once.' Dannie prided herself on never falling for ads, but she'd found the copy on this one irresistible. She loved the idea of being mysterious, complex and in control. She'd laid her soul bare to that gobshite Guy Fairbrother, and she didn't intend to reveal too much of it in a hurry to anyone ever again.

Jethro indicated for her to precede him into the car, the door of which was being held open by the chauffeur. 'Thank you,' she said, trying to look as if she climbed into the back of a limousine every other day.

'One of the perks,' Jethro said, sliding into the seat beside her, then leaning forward to exchange some words with the driver.

Dannie took the opportunity to study his profile. His reddish blond hair tufted thickly and untidily over his collar, there was a scar on his temple and a fresh nick just above his upper lip where he'd cut himself shaving. The skin around his jawline was beginning to sag, he had five o'clock shadow, and he smelt of almonds. She reminded herself of what Laura had said about him yesterday. *Good looks have nothing to do with sex appeal* . . .

Jethro finished his exchange with the driver, then settled back against the leather upholstery. 'Well, here we are,' he said. And then he said: 'Oh. What an uncool thing to say. I should have come up with something a little more memorable on a first date, shouldn't I?' A discreet chirrup sounded from his pocket, and he looked apologetic as he extracted his phone.

'Forgive me,' he said, checking out the display. 'I really do need to take this.'

'No problem.' Dannie turned to look out through the tinted windows as the car slid through traffic. It was a rather pleasant feeling, she decided, being able to observe passers-by while remaining unobserved herself. She remembered how Jethro had told her that he'd observed her through her shop window yesterday, and compared her to Juliette Binoche. She'd been so secretly thrilled by the compliment that she'd tried to do her hair tonight the way Juliette Binoche had worn hers in *Chocolat*. Beside her, Jethro was talking into his phone in a low, urgent voice.

'Hell,' he said finally. 'If I'm the only person she'll discuss it with, then put me on to her.'

There was a hiatus before he spoke again, and this time his tone bore no trace of its former pissed-offness. It was soothing, reassuring, verging on the avuncular.

'Hello, sweetheart. Yes, I heard. I'm sorry I couldn't be there for you, darlin' – get it all off your chest now. Yeah. Uh huh. Uh huh. Oh, baby, of course I understand. I know it's difficult – but I can understand the impulse that made him do it. You're just so gorgeous, sweetheart – sometimes I don't think you realize exactly just *how* gorgeous you are, or the effect you're bound to have on a – um – a *callow* youth like him. Yeah.

I'll talk to him about it. Tomorrow. That's a promise. The rushes are fantastic. You look beautiful. Trust me. Let me give you some advice, Jeanne – pretend he's someone else. I'll let you in on a secret. A very famous actress once confided in me that bed scenes weren't nearly as difficult when she tried that trick. No, I'm sworn to secrecy.' A low laugh. 'Absolutely. No problem. Till tomorrow then, angel. Take it easy.' Another laugh: low, sexy, like treacle.

How wonderful it must be to have someone talk to you in such reassuring tones! thought Dannie. The only man who'd ever talked to her that way had been her eldest brother, Joe. The others had always just slagged her. She must give Joe a ring some time soon, she decided – find out how he was getting on with the biography he was writing. He'd taken a sabbatical from the Sunday broadsheet he worked for in order to concentrate on the book. She should ring her father, too – maybe suggest visiting the farm in Connemara for a weekend. Except she hated talking to her father over the phone. He was such a taciturn individual that even she – who had once made a living eliciting information from people – had to rack her brains to think of anything to say to him. Their conversations were always full of embarrassing silences.

Embarrassing silences clearly had no place in Jethro's scheme of things. 'Good night, darlin',' he was saying now. 'Everything's gonna be AOK.'

He slid his phone back into his pocket. 'Sorry about that. An insecure actress seeking re-assurance is about as urgent as it gets, believe me.' He smiled at her. 'You told me yesterday that orchid growers have to wear cotton gloves. Film directors have to wear kid ones, to smooth the ruffled petals of the delicate plants they handle. Actors have such fragile egos they need kid-gloving twenty-four, seven.'

'You're obviously very good at it. You've a great telephone manner,' said Dannie, suddenly thinking of the way he'd talked to her on the phone last night. She felt awkward now when she recalled how easily she'd flirted with him. The wine had helped to weaken her defences – she would have to be careful not to drink so much this evening. 'I love that accent. Where are you from?'

'Atlanta, Georgia.'

She'd read somewhere that Atlanta was the last bastion in the world of male chivalry. 'So you'd be a typical Southern gent?'

'I like to think so, ma'am. I was reared to revere womenfolk, and I'm a great believer in good old-fashioned manners.'

Well, at least that meant he'd be unlikely to make a move on her on a first date. The last guy she'd been out with had been extremely pissed off indeed when she hadn't invited him up to her flat after he'd left her home.

'Sister Agatha was always on at us at school about manners,' she observed. 'I thought they were a load of crap until I got my job as a researcher, and then I realized how important they are.'

'You were educated by nuns?'

'Yes. I was a convent girl.'

She waited for the slightly salacious response this information generally elicited, but it didn't come. Instead he enquired politely: 'And where were you educated?'

'In Kylemore Abbey, in Connemara.'

'Hey! I know the joint. I recced it as a possible location for *Don Juan's Double*.'

'*Don Juan's Double*?'

'The film I'm here to direct. We recced a lot of castles and abbeys and suchlike.' The phone in his pocket chirruped again. He extracted it and depressed the 'off' button. Dannie felt enormously chuffed that talking to her was higher on his agenda than talking to some Hollywood hotshot. 'You must feel very privileged to have been brought up in such a special part of the world.'

'Yes. I suppose it *was* a privilege. I get homesick for the West of Ireland, sometimes. Where do you live, Jethro?'

'I've houses in LA and Gozo.'

'Gozo? Where's that?'

'It's a tiny island off the coast of Malta. I have

175

a villa by the sea. Sadly, I don't get to spend as much time there as I'd like. Most of my time's spent in hotel rooms just about everywhere in the world. My work takes me to some very far-flung outreaches. I've even filmed in Tasmania.'

And then Dannie remembered how Guy had used to finish his dispatches with the words: 'Guy Fairbrother, northern Afghanistan', or 'Guy Fairbrother, eastern Angola', or 'Guy Fairbrother, west Belfast'. Guy had been a citizen of the world, too. She thought of the last time she'd seen him. It hadn't been on television. It had been in a photograph in the *Guardian*, at some media event, where he'd been receiving an award. He'd been in standard award-winner pose, holding the trophy in one hand. But there'd been another trophy in the picture. Standing next to him, linking his arm cosily and looking up at him with big baby-blue eyes, had been a little blond socialite famed for her gossip slot on a breakfast television show. Guy, who'd always looked askance at Dannie if he'd found her reading anything less weighty than *Newsweek*, had thrown her over for a bimbo dressed in bum-cleft-revealing Julien Macdonald. The sense of betrayal she'd felt had been so staggering that she'd spent half the day crying under her duvet before pulling herself together and attempting to re-establish control over her life.

She took a deep breath now, and banished

Guy from her brain. She *was* doing it. She *had* re-established control over her life. Hey! Here she was in a chauffeur-driven Merc with an über-dude de luxe on her way to a fancy restaurant! She had her own business and she was her own boss and she was mistress of her own destiny.

Beside her, she noticed Jethro run his eyes briefly and appraisingly down her form.

'Elegant get-up,' he remarked. At home earlier that evening she had cast off the jeans she normally wore for work and exchanged them for a simple, soft grey sheath. She loved the way it felt against her skin. 'Cashmere?' he asked.

'Yeah.'

'Mind if I touch?' He put out a hand and rubbed a thumb down her arm. Her sleeves were three-quarter length. When his thumb finally made contact with her bare skin he withdrew his hand, but the fleeting touch had been enough to make the hair on her forearm stand up like a cat rubbed the wrong way. Except, of course, in her case those tell-tale hairs were evidence that she'd been rubbed the *right* way. Uh-oh, she thought, wondering if he'd noticed.

'So. Tell me some of your secrets,' said Jethro.

She found his smile disturbingly seductive. And all of a sudden Dannie wasn't quite so sure about the control thing. Or her destiny.

177

Chapter Five

Calypso made an excuse to visit the studio during Leo's first week of filming, on the pretext of wanting to consult with Jethro about some of the secondary casting. She hadn't heard from Leo at all since the encounter in her office, and she was suffering from what could only be described as withdrawal symptoms. She sat for a while on the sidelines of the studio floor, observing his behaviour on the set, taking in the air of easy camaraderie he adopted around the rest of the cast and crew, marking with approval the respect with which he deferred to his director, and clocking with awful, gut-wrenching jealousy the rapport he'd established with his cute French co-star, Jeanne Renaud. The actress was unmistakably smitten with him.

In the busy canteen at lunchtime she watched him fetch coffee for Jeanne, and tried not to look as he laughed and bantered in French with her.

She knew Jeanne rarely condescended to eat lunch in the canteen, preferring to have it brought to her in her dressing room. The fact that she'd emulated the laidback attitude towards film-set hierarchy that Leo had adopted was a real indication of the effect he'd had on her.

Calypso was running very late. She had a hair appointment scheduled for half-past two. It was now ten past one, and it would take her for ever and a day to get back into town. But she *had* to see Leo before she went, *had* to have some contact with him, however fleeting, *had* to know that they might see each other again.

Finally, thankfully, people started to disperse: the starlet was called away to make-up, and Leo's black eyes met hers at last. He sent her a smile that made her turn to mush, and then he set his cup down on the table and strolled over to where Jethro was taking leave of her.

'Thanks for finding the time to get out here, Calypso,' Jethro was saying as Leo joined them.

She assumed a jaunty demeanour. 'No problem. I wanted to make sure my protégé had settled in. How are you getting on, Leo?' She was amazed at how normal she sounded. 'I've been hearing terrific things about you from Jethro.'

'I'm getting on fine, thanks. Having fun. Not sure about the gear, though. My mates will give me a really hard time when they hear that I'm poncing about in riding boots and a billowy shirt.'

'You look great, Leo,' said Calypso. It was a ludicrous understatement. The Regency garb made him look like a Mills & Boon fantasy made flesh.

He reached down under his redingote to adjust himself. 'Thanks. But these breeches are seriously uncomfortable.'

Jethro laughed. 'You can lose the breeches tomorrow. You'll be spending all day in bed with your co-star.'

'On a closed set, I hope,' said Calypso.

Jethro nodded. 'For sure. Cast and crew only.'

'I've no objection to Calypso being there,' said Leo, with a bland smile.

'Oh. Um, actually, I'm going to be up to my eyes all week. I won't be able to make it out here,' said Calypso

'Well, you know you're always welcome, ma'am.' Jethro turned to Leo. 'Incidentally, you'll go easy on Jeanne, won't you?'

Leo sent him a questioning look.

'She had a run-in last week with the actor who played her first lover. Although I can't see you having the same problems, somehow.'

'What happened?' asked Leo.

'The individual in question got a bit over-enthusiastic. Overstepped the mark during an intimate scene. She was very distressed.'

'*Pauvre petite*.' Leo's brow furrowed moment-arily in concern. Then: 'Is that a problem you encounter on a regular basis?' he asked curiously.

'Actors getting a bo—' Jethro stopped in mid-word and turned to Calypso. 'I beg your pardon, ma'am. I should, of course, say actors becoming "sexually aroused".'

'That's OK, Jethro. You needn't run shy of talking boy talk round me. I got a pretty good idea of men's-room-speak when I eavesdropped in the cubicle of a Gents once. I think the word you wanted was "boner".'

Leo turned to Calypso with a surprised smile. 'Woah. A Palmerston Princess talking dirty? You stop that, naughty girl.' He took hold of her wrist and administered a couple of mock slaps before turning back to Jethro. 'Well? *Do* many actors have problems with boners?'

Jethro shrugged. 'It doesn't happen often. Or if it does, they manage to conceal it pretty well. You'd sure have a problem in those pants, Leo.'

Leo laughed. 'Better put saltpetre in my tea, in that case.' He was still holding Calypso by the wrist. She mirrored his smile with an effort.

Jethro registered the empty canteen and looked at his watch. 'Gotta get back on the floor. You finished for the day, Leo?'

'No. I've a pick-up scheduled for later.'

'I warned you there'd be a lot of hanging

around, man.' He biffed Leo on the shoulder (Why did men do that? Calypso found herself wondering absently. A pecking-order thing, she supposed), and kissed her on the cheek. 'Bye, Calypso. I'll see you this evening. I found a terrific birthday present for you, incidentally. Sheer serendipity.'

'Oh, how nice! I love getting presents. What is it?'

He tapped his nose with a finger. 'It's a surprise. By the way, is it cool if I bring a mutual friend along to your party?'

'A mutual friend?'

'Another surprise.'

'Well, of course it's cool. Bye, Jethro.'

Leo watched Jethro move towards the canteen door, and then he turned to Calypso. 'I have a present for you too,' he said. 'It's in my dressing room. Come with me and I'll give it to you.' His eyes were wicked, black and bantering.

'I can't,' said Calypso, aware that she was faltering – and that he knew it, too. 'I really can't right now.'

'Oh, come, Calypso. Do come.'

'I have a hair appointment.'

'A hair appointment? How redundant is that? Your hair looks gorgeous. *You* look gorgeous.' He gave her an appreciative smile, looked her up and down, then took a backward step towards the canteen door. Because he was still holding her wrist, Calypso was forced to move with him. 'Come on.' He moved again, a couple of steps this time, and Calypso teetered after him. His smile was so engaging that she found herself laughing, and then his fingers slid between hers and they were swinging hands as they made for the exit. Calypso was relieved that the canteen was empty. The High Queen of Casting hooking up with one of her discoveries? Un*heard* of!

When he reached the door, he held it open for her and the look he gave her as she slid past him made her feel weak again. 'How did you know it was my birthday?' she asked, trying to sound conversational as they moved down the corridor.

'Iseult mentioned your birth date that time I read out horoscopes in your office.'

'Oh!'

He laughed at the horrified look she shot him. 'Have no fear, Calypso. She was discreet enough not to disclose the year. Your age is still a state secret.' She didn't much like the reference to her age, but still – how sweet of him to remember her birth date!

They had reached the door of his dressing room. Again he stood back to let her precede him, then shut the door behind him. She saw him turn the key in the lock, extract it and slide it into his pocket.

'May I come?' he said. 'To your party. Or do

my plebeian origins rule me out? I understand you move in very celebrated circles.'

Oh, God! She should dream up some excuse to put him off. She *couldn't* have him in her house! But then, she really, really didn't want to run the risk of offending him, either . . . She shrugged, trying to appear offhand. 'It's really just family and close friends,' she lied. 'But you can come if you like.'

He gave her a contemplative look, then crossed the room, sat down on the day bed and took a gift-wrapped package from a drawer in the bedside table. 'Come here, then, Calypso,' he said, patting the mattress. 'Come here and unwrap your present.'

She moved to join him, feeling that now familiar ache of lust begin to rise in her. The knot on the ribbon was stubborn: it refused to yield, and her fingers were more than usually feeble.

She finally managed it. Inside, wrapped in tissue paper, was a silver bangle of the type worn by Egyptian slaves. It was perfectly plain, apart from the smoothly bossed edges.

'Oh, Leo! You shouldn't have! It's absolutely beautiful!'

'It's rather elegant, isn't it? Try it on.'

Shaking her head in wonder, murmuring more thanks, she slid the bangle onto her wrist.

'No,' said Leo, reaching out and unbuttoning

the cuff of her shirt. 'It should be worn higher, on the upper arm.' He pushed her sleeve up, and she felt goosebumps rise where the cool metal rubbed against her skin. She looked at the bangle, and then she looked back at him. 'I've something else for you,' he said. 'What do think it is?'

His expression was so meaningful that no answer was necessary. Calypso smiled a little uncertainly, then leaned towards him, tentatively proffering her mouth. Leo took her chin between thumb and forefinger, then lowered his face to hers and slid the very tip of his tongue between her parted lips.

She felt blissfully passive, blissfully compliant, blissfully *soft* as she closed her eyes and allowed him to explore her mouth. This he did lightly, unhurriedly, and with such casual expertise that Calypso knew that he had kissed a great many women before. A leisurely hand moved to her back, between her shoulder blades. She felt it travel to the nape of her neck and up through her hair, and then he cupped the back of her head, exerting just enough pressure to show her who was boss. His other hand moved to the buttons on her blouse, and as he undid the top one and then the next and the next, she felt softer and softer and ever more compliant . . .

And then the phone on the wall by the bed jangled.

Leo paused in his perusal of her geography, and Calypso's eyes opened at once. She saw him give a resigned sigh, then a shrug as he reached for the receiver. 'Yeah?' he said. 'Hell. Tell her I'm sorry. I'll be right there.' He put the phone down and looked at her. 'They want me in wardrobe. You proved so very distracting, you sexy bitch, that I forgot I was meant to have a fitting after lunch.'

Calypso bit down hard on her lip, looking away. She knew she looked flushed and muzzy and awfully vulnerable with desire. To cover her confusion, she started to fumble with the buttons on her shirt.

'Allow me.' As his hands moved to redo the buttons for her, he took the opportunity to caress the silk over her breasts. 'Beautiful,' he murmured. 'Perfect. When oh when, Calypso O'Kelly, will I get to see them naked?'

'Maybe –' she said, taking a huge risk '– maybe we can arrange to meet somewhere private?'

He gave her an interested look. 'You mean somewhere private where I can get to see your naked breasts?'

'Um. Yes.'

'Touch them?'

'Yes.' Her voice was very small now.

'Anything else?'

'Yes.' The word emerged as a whisper.

He looked at her thoughtfully. 'Your husband's away a lot, isn't he?'

'Yes.' Oh, God! She couldn't allow Leo to come to her house! She flailed around for an alternative. 'I could book a room, somewhere discreet.'

He smiled. 'Discreet. What a namby-pamby word that is. It reminds me of that film with that pair of stiff-upper-lipped British twats falling in love on a railway platform. What was that called?'

'*Brief Encounter*.' It was one of her favourite films of all time.

'*Brief Encounter*? Sounds like the title of a bad porn film.' Leo finished doing up her buttons, then stood up and held out a hand for her to help her to her feet. As Calypso rose, there was no mistaking the bulge of the erection he was nursing under his riding breeches. He smiled at her reaction. 'See what you're after going and doing, you naughty thing,' he said. 'I might have serious problems if that very pretty girl in wardrobe wants to measure my inside leg.' He reached for a bottle of Volvic on the bed-side table and unscrewed the top. His eyes were wicked, his smile urbane as he raised the bottle to her in a mock toast and said: 'Here's to our next encounter, then, Ms O'Kelly. May it prove not to be quite so brief as this one was. I want to take my time getting to know you.'

Calypso's smile was uncertain. She was feeling

very shaken. 'Will you let me out now, please?' she said.

He strolled to the door and leaned against it, not once breaking eye contact. 'The key's in my pocket,' he said. 'Why don't you try letting yourself out?'

Hardly daring to keep her eyes on his, she moved towards him, stopping when she was about a foot away. Then she looked down and bit her lip.

'Hey. Who *is* this shrinking violet? This can't be the same woman I heard talking boy talk ten minutes ago?' There was a smile in his voice. 'Come on, darling – don't be shy. You know you want to.' He reached out a hand, took hold of hers, and drew her closer to him. Then he guided her hand to where his pocket was located, next to his hip bone. 'That's right, princess,' he coaxed. 'Feel what you're letting yourself in for.' As she slid her hand inside he made a sound low in his throat. She exerted a little pressure, saw his pupils dilate, and suddenly they were kissing again, but this time they fused with a frantic, ravening abandon, and his mouth was hard and aggressive and – and – *masterful*. After some moments – she had no idea how many – Leo finally pushed her away. 'Not here. Not now,' he said. His breath was ragged as he took the key from his pocket, unlocked the door and held it open for her.

'When?' she asked, closing her eyes and turning away, in an effort to re-establish control of her own ragged breathing. Then: 'When?' she asked again.

When she opened her eyes, Leo was looking at her, smiling. After a beat or two of contemplation, he leaned in to her and murmured in her ear. 'When you're least expecting it,' he said.

Immobilized in traffic an hour later, Calypso phoned Iseult and asked her to cancel her hair appointment. She'd blown it. And she'd blown it in more ways than one, she thought bitterly, turning the volume down on a current affairs programme. Because of her stupid obsession with Leo Devlin she was stuck here, fulminating and listening to politicians protesting too much. She changed channels. On Radio 2 the Corrs were singing smugly about being 'so young'. Calypso immediately switched back to Radio 4, but the words of the song had stuck in her head.

Was she past it? *No!* She was at that age when women were meant to be at their sexual prime! Then she thought back to the last time Dominic and she had made love and realized that, actually, her shrine hadn't been worshipped in over a week. She'd have to do something about that. She knew that one way of making sure Dominic didn't go straying was to observe the immortal rules that Jerry Hall had laid down about behaving like a chef in the kitchen, a hostess in the drawing room and a whore in the bedroom. OK – so she couldn't do much about the kitchen thing, but she was pretty damn near perfect in the other two rooms. But then she remembered that even the divine Ms Hall hadn't been able to keep her serial adulterer husband . . .

Oh, God. What if Dominic left *her*? What would become of her without him? How would she manage life as a thirty-something single-ton? She tried to shake her head free of the odious questions. She wouldn't – couldn't – con-template the answers. But the nit-picky voice continued to badger her. What if Dominic got wind of her infatuation with Leo? What if she did book a discreet hotel as she'd said she would? There was no such thing, she knew, as a discreet hotel. It was practically a contradiction in terms. Someone somewhere would bump into her – especially if she were to arrange more than one liaison – and the vanes on the gossip wind-mill would begin their inexorable turning. And while Dominic was as liberal and as easygoing as they came about loads of things, she knew that he would never, ever countenance living with an adulteress.

OK. She wasn't going to go there. She'd had enough. Enough of this Leo lunacy. Enough of this dangerous liaison. She would have to nip this affair in the bud before it blossomed into some kind of monstrous Triffid. How to do it? Simple. She would discreetly draw her protégé aside the next time she went out to the studio, take a deep breath and make it plain that nothing could come of their relationship. She remembered how Trevor Howard and Celia Johnson in the film had bade each other farewell on the railway platform, sacrificing their love in the better interest of their families. She and Leo would have to do the same. It wouldn't be easy – in fact she knew it would be hellishly tough – but she would brace herself to be stoical and do the thing he'd described as 'stiff-upper-lipped'.

And as the politicians on the radio droned on and on, Calypso replayed in front of her mind's eye that last kiss she and Leo had exchanged before she left his dressing room, and she ran her tongue along her swollen upper lip, and thought thank God, thank God, thank *God* things hadn't gone any further.

Around half-past five that afternoon she was making last-minute phone calls in her office with the handset wedged between jaw and collarbone, entering memos in her organizer and trying to gather up carrier bags at the same time. She'd attempted to salvage her day by consoling herself with retail therapy, allowing herself to be persuaded into buying a stack of unnecessary new products in her favourite beauty shop, then going on to blow a small fortune on shoes, hosiery and frivolous impulse purchases in Brown Thomas. She knew she should have spent at least a couple of hours of quality time in the office, but hell, it was her birthday. She thanked God for Iseult and Viv.

Both her assistants were in reception as she came through, Viv sending a fax, Iseult on the phone. 'Bye, Viv,' said Calypso. 'Thanks so much for covering my ass today. I truly appreciate it.'

'No problem. It's a special day for you. Enjoy your party.'

'I will.' Calypso waved her fingers at Iseult, who covered the mouthpiece of the phone and said: 'Have a lovely party!' before resuming her conversation. 'That'd be lovely,' Calypso heard her say as she negotiated her way through the door, her exit impeded by the plethora of carrier bags. 'The Octagon Bar, at seven, then. Lovely! No, it's perfect – just a hop, skip and a jump down the road from the office, you know . . .' Iseult's chirpy tones receded as the door swung shut behind Calypso.

The traffic was still unspeakable. Morning gridlock might be productive, but evening gridlock was just plain vexing, especially when there was a party to prepare for. As she watched cyclists weave their effortless way round cars, Calypso wondered if she shouldn't invest in a bike. She didn't care how undignified she would look – anything was better than negotiating this traffic chaos every evening. And if she started cycling she wouldn't need to spend so much time in the hell that was her gym. And bicycles were so much more environmentally friendly than cars. But then she registered the envious glance of a fellow motorist as she checked out Calypso's gorgeous little plum-coloured Merc and she knew instantly that she couldn't bear to replace it with a bicycle, no matter how much sense it made.

She made it home with little time to spare before her guests were due to arrive. Just over an hour in which to shower, make up, dress, and do something with her hair. A challenge! Well, she was good at challenges. 'Is Dominic in?' she asked the caterer on her way through the kitchen. There was a glorious smell of something garlicky wafting from the oven, and Jacqueline was looking her usual unflappable self as she methodically uncorked bottles of burgundy.

'Mm hm. He's upstairs,' said Jacqueline.

Calypso manoeuvred herself and her carrier bags around Jacqueline's pair of assistants, who were wielding items of catering equipment that appeared bewilderingly arcane to her un-proficient eye. Calypso was crap in the kitchen. As Dominic frequently pointed out, he hadn't married her for her culinary expertise.

'Ignore me. I'll be out of your way in a minute,' she said, grabbing a handful of macadamia nuts from a bowl, then putting them back when she remembered how packed full of calories they were. 'Everything under control here, Jacqueline?'

'No worries. You take it easy, Calypso. I'll bring you up a glass of champagne when you're through with your shower.'

'You're a doll.' Calypso took the stairs two at a time, unbuttoning her shirt as she did so. She poked her head round the door of Dominic's study to blow him a kiss. 'Hello, darling! I love you!' she sang.

'C'mere, you,' he said, unfolding himself from his swivel chair and reaching for a little packet that stood on the shelf above his desk. 'I've got something for you. Your birthday present.'

'Oh! Oh, Dominic!' Calypso stood on tiptoe and covered his face with butterfly kisses, feeling incredibly, *incredibly* glad now that she'd exchanged nothing more meaningful than a kiss with Leo in his dressing room. She couldn't have borne the guilt if things had gone any further. She gave her husband one last heartfelt smacker on the lips, and pulled away the gift wrap. A small leather box was revealed, stamped with the exclusive logo of a Bond Street jeweller.

'I got it on my last trip to London,' said Dominic, watching her carefully as she opened it. 'What do you think?'

What did she *think*? 'Oh, wow! Oh, Dominic! It's exquisite! It's the most stunningly beautiful thing I've ever seen! Oh! Oh – I don't *deserve* such a beautiful thing!' She didn't deserve this *man*, she lamented, as she unfurled a fine silver chain from its bed of velvet. Attached to the chain was a pendant – a miniature blue enamel egg embossed with roundels of cabochon emeralds. Each roundel contained a tiny fleur-de-lis, and each petal of the fleur-de-lis was represented by a faceted diamond.

'Antique,' said Dominic, taking the pendant from her and fastening the chain around her neck.

'Shit. Dare I ask the price?'

'You dare not.'

'Oh, Dominic! Give me a hint.'

'No. And it's bad manners to ask.'

'Please? Four or five figures?'

He relented. 'Nearer five,' he said.

Five figures! They both looked down at the tiny egg nestling in Calypso's cleavage. Then Dominic pulled the silk lapels of her shirt apart, cupped her breasts in his hands and bent his head to cover them with kisses. Picturing the dark eyes that had held hers as she'd been fondled in the same place earlier that same day, Calypso felt a surge of self-loathing. The emeralds and diamonds glittered between her breasts now, like a rebuke. Never again, she said to herself. She would never allow herself to succumb to the temptation of Leo Devlin ever, ever again.

Dominic finally raised his head. 'There is nothing I would rather do right now than worship at your shrine,' he said. 'But I'm going to postpone that pleasure until after everyone's gone home.'

'It'll be worth the wait. I've something very special in mind for you tonight.' She'd have to give him a bloody good blow job at the very least: not just as a way of thanking him for the fabulous jewel, but as a means of assuaging the awful, all-pervasive guilt she was feeling. Never again!

Dominic laughed. 'Go and have your shower, you sexy bitch,' he said. As she backed out of the room she realized that it was the second time that day she'd been called that.

In the shower she soaped every inch of herself, hoping she might wash her past perfidy down the plughole, still thanking God that things hadn't gone any further, thanking him for making the wardrobe girl phone Leo at such a critical moment. She felt a flush of shame now as she realized how abject she must have looked when she left the actor's dressing room, when she'd begged him to tell her when their next liaison would be. *When you're least expecting it* ... Well, she was on guard now, and determined to be a good girl.

As Calypso combed a concoction of three different Kiehl's products through her hair – hoping she might manage to pull off a 'just got out of bed' sexy, tousled look instead of the sleek style her magic-fingered stylist normally conjured – Jacqueline stuck her head round the open bathroom door. 'Champagne's up,' she said. 'Anything else you need?' Calypso piled her hair on top of her head, and padded through into the bedroom. 'No,' she said. 'I've everything I want.'

It was true, she thought, as she exchanged her damp towelling robe for her slinky silk kimono. She, Calypso O'Kelly, had everything she'd ever wanted. She was *steeped*. Wasn't she? As she fingered the chain of her latest wish-list accessory, she found herself thinking that she should have invited her mother to her party after all. She'd love to have seen the look on her face when she got a load of Dominic's five-figure birthday present. Then she made an involuntary *moue* of distaste when she thought about the blow job she'd have to administer later, in return for his generosity.

Oh, well. Whore in the bedroom, her pragmatic streak reminded her. And right now, Calypso, you'd better start thinking about being a hostess in the drawing room.

She started to rummage through her hill of

glossy carrier bags, searching for the shoes she'd bought to go with the dress she intended wearing that evening. She located the shoes easily, but the dress eluded her. Suddenly, with sickening realization, she remembered where she'd last seen it: in its dry-cleaning wrapper, hanging on the back of her office door. It was there still, a sartorial Cinderella forlornly waiting to go to the ball: her beautiful Roberto Cavalli silk chiffon.

Oh no! This was a nightmare! She had *so* wanted to wear that dress tonight! It was one of Dominic's favourites. She'd worn it on only two previous occasions, and had never received so many compliments about the way she looked, ever. Calypso ran to her wardrobe, her forehead puckered in dismay. There were other dresses she could wear, of course there were, but she had set her heart on her Roberto Cavalli. What on earth to do? Could she perhaps ask Jacqueline or one of her team to dive into a cab and retrieve it? No. There was no way they would get their heads round the tight security system that barb-wired the building. Maybe there'd be someone there still who could let them in? A cleaning lady, nightwatchman – anyone? Hell's *teeth*! A glance at her bedside clock told her the exercise would be pointless. Even if there was someone still on the premises there wasn't enough time to get all the way over there and back before eight o'clock.

Just then she was struck by a blessed brain-wave. Iseult! She'd overheard her arranging to meet someone in the Octagon Bar of the Clarence Hotel, just down the road from the office! Iseult would be obliging enough to do a favour for her – she could nip up to the office, bag a cab and deliver the dress within twenty minutes. Her date surely wouldn't mind a small blip like that? It was worth a try, anyway.

Calypso picked up the phone and punched in Iseult's mobile number. The ambient noise of a crowded bar came over the receiver when she picked up. 'Hello, Calypso! Whassup?' came her secretary's cheery voice.

'Oh, darling, darling Iseult, could you be an angel and do me an enormous favour?' begged Calypso. 'I've left my bloody dress hanging on the door of my office. Do you think you could run back and get it for me, and then grab a cab out here? It's the only way I can think of to get it – you're just down the road, aren't you?'

'Yes – I'm in the Clarence. Hang on a sec, let me just talk to someone . . .' A hiatus while more pubby noises came clattering down the line. 'It's cool, Calypso – no problem. We were just about to leave here and look for a taxi anyway. We're going to Roly's for something to eat.' Calypso smiled at the ever so faintly smug timbre. Roly's was quite a classy joint.

'Well, all I can say is – you are a star, Iseult

Morgan! You are a total star! We're the first house on the terrace. Come in and have a quick glass of champagne before you head off for dinner, why don't you? You've earned it.'

'Oh – I'd love that! Is it cool if I bring my date?'

'Of course it's cool. I'll see you in about twenty minutes?'

'We're on our way.'

Calypso zapped the 'off' switch on her phone and the 'on' switch on her CD player and performed dance steps. All was not lost! She blew a big flurry of kisses at her handsome husband as he wandered through the bedroom in the direction of the bathroom. 'What are you going to wear this evening, by the way?' he asked.

'My Roberto Cavalli?'

'Mm,' he said, nodding approval. 'That'll set off your new bauble nicely.'

Humming along to *Carmen Jones*, Calypso lined up a battery of best quality ermine make-up brushes, put on the over-the-top frilly cosmetics cap that Rosa had given her for a joke last Christmas, and started work on her face, concealing and enhancing and highlighting. She had just rubbed her ruby lips together with a satisfying *smack!* when the doorbell rang. Calling 'I'll get it!' to the catering staff, she skipped down the stairs to the front door and opened it with a flourish. 'You absolute doll!' she cried when she saw Iseult standing there with the chiffon gown draped over her arm. 'Come on in and grab a glass of fizz.'

She went to give Iseult a kiss on the cheek, and only then registered the man standing just behind her. When she did, she blanched and stumbled, almost falling down the front step in her confusion. It was Leo Devlin.

Leo took a step forward and put out a hand to stop her fall. 'Careful,' he said, with that urbane smile he was so very, very good at. She felt an intimate finger brush the crook of her elbow before he stepped back again.

'Surprise!' said bright-eyed Iseult, biting down on her lip in an effort to stem the enormous grin that threatened to engulf her face. 'You've already met my "friend"!' She turned her luminous expression towards Leo, a flower lifting its face to the sun, then looked more coyly back at Calypso. 'Leo rang late this afternoon and suggested we might have dinner some time. I broke all the rules and said "how about this evening?" at once – didn't I, Leo? I'm so uncool!'

'And I'm very glad you are,' said Leo, bestowing a warm look upon her before giving his hostess the benefit of his inscrutable smile.

Feeling like an ice sculpture, Calypso took a step back. 'Thanks for this,' she said in a tight voice, taking the dress from Iseult. 'I'll just run upstairs and change. There should be champagne in the dining room – second on the right. Help yourselves.' She blundered back up the stairs and into the bedroom. The half-empty champagne flute was still on her dressing table. Lunging for it gratefully, she knocked it back.

'Early arrivals?' asked Dominic from the bathroom.

'No. Um. It's just Iseult and – um – her date.' A champagne burp escaped her.

'Iseult? I didn't know you'd invited her.'

'I didn't. No. She was just delivering my dress. I'd left it in work.'

'What a scatty thing you are.'

'Mm.' Calypso set her glass back down, then she slid out of her robe and pulled the silk chiffon out of its plastic wrapper and over her head. She dithered as she stood in the middle of the room, absently regarding her reflection in the cheval glass. She was still wearing her frilly cosmetics cap! She pulled it off with as much force as she'd use to pull off a tacky Christmas cracker crown. How embarrassing that he had seen her in that! Her mirror image gazed back at her with enormous, desperate eyes.

Oh, God. What had she done? Why the *hell* had she allowed him into her house? But there had been no way round it – she'd extended an invitation to Iseult to come in for a drink and she could hardly back out of it. Why, why, *why* had she been so fixated on the stupid Roberto Cavalli frock? There was masses of stuff in her wardrobe that was equally stunning. Fuck. Oh, *fuck*. The situation was surreal, intolerable. Could she plead a headache, maybe – not go back downstairs? No, no, no. She'd have to join them, have to face him. But she'd make sure they got the hell out of her house before people started arriving.

For several minutes more Calypso stalled, buying time by re-tousling her hair, blotting her face with *papier poudré*, spraying herself with Chanel 19. Then she turned away from the mirror and moved towards the stairs, in her confusion almost tripping over Marilyn Monroe, who had plonked herself on one of the steps like Miss Caswell in *All About Eve*. *Fasten your seatbelts*, thought Calypso ominously, remembering Bette Davis's famous line from the film. *It's going to be a bumpy night . . .*

Downstairs she poked her head cautiously around the dining-room door, and immediately withdrew it. Leo and Iseult were sitting on a chaise longue, with their heads together. Calypso leaned back against the wall of the hall, taking deep breaths, trying to regain her equilibrium. When she finally summoned the courage to make her entrance, Leo had taken one of Iseult's hands in his and was tracing a pattern on the palm. He murmured something in her ear that made her dimple, and then he dropped a light kiss on her cheek. What on earth was he doing? Trying to make her jealous? Well, he wouldn't succeed. She would find an opportunity to get him on his own ASAP and tell him that the incident in his dressing room earlier today had been a one-off, an aberration, and that their relationship must, in future, be conducted on a purely professional footing. She felt as resolute and responsible as a Girl Guide.

'Hi!'

The star-crossed lovers looked up as Calypso strode into the room with the assured tread of the mistress of the house. Her theatrical training would come in useful this evening, she thought grimly. She saw Iseult withdraw her hand from Leo's with an embarrassed smile, then attempt to cover her confusion by taking a sip of champagne. 'Your house is fabulous, Calypso,' she said.

'Thanks.' She moved to the side table and helped herself to the champagne that Jacqueline had left in an ice bucket.

'Beautiful garden.' Leo had moved to the open French windows. 'Mind if I take a stroll?'

'Be my guest.' Calypso managed a smile.

Iseult followed him with eyes like the Andrex puppy's as he ambled out into Calypso's Zen garden. Then she turned to her employer, practically gibbering with excitement and delight and disbelief. 'Oh, Calypso! Aren't I just *so* lucky! I could hardly believe it when he rang this afternoon. When he told me who it was on the phone I said I'd put him straight through to you, and then he said no, that it was *me* he wanted to talk to. I nearly died! Isn't he just so *gorgeous*!'

Calypso didn't know what to say. She managed another tight-lipped smile, then crossed the room and looked out to where Leo was standing with his back to her, inspecting her koi. He had one hand on his hip; the other was tilting his champagne flute between languid fingers. His stance was relaxed, loose-limbed, and he looked as if he had every right in the world to be standing there in her stupid Zen garden, enjoying the last of the evening sun. He raised the glass to his lips, drank, then turned and looked at her. The look was as eloquent as it was disturbing, and the corresponding lurch of lust she felt in the pit of her stomach was so palpable it frightened her. He walked back towards her, keeping his eyes locked on hers, a sexy smile playing around his lips – until he reached the step up to the French windows. Then, quite suddenly, his focus shifted. The sexy smile was still in place, but he was no longer looking at her. He was looking at Iseult.

Calypso felt another nauseating visceral wrench, but this time the blow to her gut had nothing to do with sexual desire. It had every-thing to do with jealousy.

*   *   *

People started arriving, and still Leo and Iseult didn't leave. Every time a waitress passed them, Leo indicated for Iseult's glass to be refilled. Calypso heard her secretary say that they mustn't outstay their welcome, that they'd be late for the restaurant; and she was simply appalled to hear Leo reply that she, Calypso, had actually invited him to her birthday party earlier that day, and he was having fun now, and anyway they could always eat in Roly's another time – Saturday night, if she was free? Iseult's voice had practically quivered with happiness when she'd said yes, all right then, Saturday would be lovely, and she'd love another glass of champagne.

Calypso slid many meaningful glances at Leo, willing him to get out of there, but he remained quite unfazed. Her heart finally slid netherwards when she heard her secretary chirrup: 'Hello there, Dominic! Have you met Leo Devlin, Calypso's latest discovery?' That was her cue to dive towards the kitchen.

Jacqueline looked up from where she was sprinkling chopped basil over a plate of mozzarella canapés. 'You look very flushed, Calypso,' she observed. 'Are you all right?'

'Yes, I'm fine. I've just got a bit of a headache.' It was true. Leo Devlin was turning out to be the biggest headache she'd ever had in her life. She hung around the kitchen until she could see that she was getting on the nerves of the catering staff, and then she helped herself to a refill and hit the party again, passing an inanely smiling Iseult in the hall, who kissed her on the cheek and said: 'Oh, thank you, thank you, Calypso! This is the most brilliant party I've ever been to!' And then Iseult tottered off to the loo, still smiling to herself and humming a little song of praise.

At last she had an opportunity to get him on her own. He was standing on the far side of the drawing room, chatting easily with Jethro Palmer.

'Excuse me,' she said, laying a hand on Leo's arm. 'May I have a word in private? Sorry to tear him away, Jethro.'

'No problem. Talk to you later, Leo.'

Calypso suddenly remembered her manners. 'Oh, and Jethro? Thank you so much for the present.' There was a stack of birthday presents accumulating for her in the hall, and she'd noticed Jethro's name on a gift tag attached to a big rectangular package. 'I'm sorry – I haven't had a chance to open any of them yet.'

'You're welcome, ma'am. Happy birthday.' Jethro gave her his wonderfully old-fashioned, courteous smile, then inclined his head and backed away. Adopting her best 'gracious hostess' demeanour, Calypso said something in a clearly discernible voice about showing Leo her

Japanese carp before inveigling him ultra-casually out through the French windows and into a secluded corner of the garden.

How to put it? She cleared her throat, but before she could say anything, Leo gave her an oblique look and said: 'Sorry about dragging Iseult into this, but I hit on a rather ingenious scam. If I start dating your secretary, no-one will dream that I'm actually more interested in getting it on with the boss.'

Oh, God! This was turning into her worst nightmare!

'Leo. I'm sorry. You've got to go.'

'Why?'

'You know why.'

He gave her a contemplative look, then nodded. 'I'll go,' he said. 'Of course I'll go if you really want me to. But I'd love you to do one small thing for me first, Calypso.'

'What?'

'I love your dress.'

Calypso was fazed by the *non-sequitur*. 'Well, thank you,' she said automatically.

'I love the way your nipples are sticking out against that filmy fabric,' resumed Leo in a conversational tone. 'It's very obvious that you have no bra on. I want to see your breasts naked. Then I'll go.'

She discovered her voice. 'Leo. I can't – I—'

'There's no-one around to see.'

Calypso found herself glancing from left to right. He had it sussed.

He took a step towards her. 'Go on, darling. You promised me you'd let me see them. Such a small thing to do to make me happy. And then I'll put on my halo and leave the party.'

There was something utterly mesmeric about his voice, about his eyes. Calypso felt as deficient in free will as a member of some cult. She was like Eve in the Garden of Eden, and Leo was that smiling seductive snake. As if in a trance, she found herself raising her hands and undoing the catch that held the décolletage of her dress in place. She looked down and watched as he took hold of the gossamer lace of her straps, then drew them over her shoulders.

When she raised her eyes to his again, the look in them made her want to reach out and touch him and have him touch her too.

'How very, very beautiful you are, Calypso O'Kelly,' he said.

She stood there for a full minute – maybe more – with her breasts uncovered for his delectation before the danger of the situation kicked in and she pulled the straps back up with panicky fingers. As she fumbled with the catch she reminded herself urgently that she had a life she wanted to continue living, a privileged life with a devoted husband and influential friends, a life she wasn't prepared to risk flushing down the pan for the sake of this practised, near-irresistible, fatally attractive seducer.

'Thank you,' said Leo. 'That was a privilege. I'll go now.'

Oh God. Her *Brief Encounter* moment had come. She steeled herself to face him, then took a deep breath. 'Wait. There's something I have to say to you,' she said. Another deep breath didn't make it any easier. Just *do* it, Calypso! she told herself. 'Look. I'm sorry, Leo. This has got to stop. I shouldn't have come on to you. It was extremely indiscreet and extremely un-professional. I've never done it before, I shall never do it again, and I'm going to make sure I nip this thing in the bud now before it evolves into something that's bigger than both of us – something we're both going to regret.' The clichés trailed away. It was time for straight talk. 'I've decided that I have absolutely no intention of being unfaithful to my husband.' She tried to keep her gaze level with his, but couldn't. She looked down at where her fingers were twisting her wedding ring. 'Let's behave like sensible human beings.' Oh, God! The line was a direct quote from *Brief Encounter*!

Several moments passed before Leo spoke again. There was nothing remotely seductive, nothing mesmeric about his voice now. 'Hey. Wait a minute, Ms O'Kelly. This *is* a turn-up for the books. You're telling me you don't want to fuck me?'

She glanced to her left to see if anyone had come into the garden. 'Please can we be discreet about this?'

'*Discreet?* The way you were discretion personified just now when you got your tits out, darling? The way you were discretion personified when you practically begged me for a fuck in my dressing room earlier today? I'm confused, Calypso. Can we get this straight? Now you're actually telling me you *don't* want to ride me?'

'Yes. I mean – yes, I don't want to – you know –'

'You're a liar.'

'Oh, Jesus, Leo, I *can't*, don't you see that? It would only end in tears! I find you very attractive—'

'Attractive?' He gave a strange laugh. 'How anodyne a word is that? Don't fucking patronize me, Calypso.'

'I'm not *trying* to patronize you. I'm trying to resolve this – this situation.' It was time to make the supreme self-sacrifice. 'Look. Maybe you're going in the right direction with Iseult, Leo. She's nearer your age, she's gorgeous, she thinks you're the business – *and* she's available. If you transfer your affections elsewhere—'

'Affections?' said Leo with an even more unpleasant laugh. 'Who said anything about affections?'

'You know what I mean.'

'No. I don't think I do.'

'Whatever.' Calypso was beginning to feel very unsettled.

Leo was leaning against the wall, watching her with a horrid kind of amusement. 'Well, *well*. I hadn't taken you for a prick-teaser, darling. I had rather suspected you were a whore at heart. Do you want to know something? I don't have any regard at all for prick-teasers. They're nasty little bitches, and they deserve everything they get.' He looped a thumb in his belt, drawing attention to the erection that was straining against the tight fabric of his jeans, then added conversationally: 'Do you know what I'd like to do with this? I'd like to rub it against your nipples. And then your mouth. I'd like to see that perfect red pout smeared. And I think you'd like that too. I think that in your whore's heart you're gagging for it, Calypso O'Kelly.'

Calypso felt a tepid bead of sweat meander down her ribcage. 'Leo. I will not allow you to talk to me like that. I must ask you to leave my house now, please,' she said stiffly.

'That might be difficult,' he said, ruminatively. 'You see, I recall telling you once that I never make promises. But I've turned over a new leaf. I've decided that making promises is a good thing. Unfortunately, I've made so many of them recently that I'm not sure I'll be able to keep them all. I know I *promised* I'd leave once I'd had a gander at your tits – *love*. But I also *promised* my new friend Iseult that I'd get her another glass of champagne, and she'll be terribly disappointed if I don't deliver the goods. Maybe I should take it upstairs to her. She's intacta,' he added, carelessly. 'A little virgin. Did you know that?'

This was intolerable! It was time to call some shots, re-establish who was top cat. 'You listen to me, Leo,' she hissed. 'It would appear that you've forgotten who the boss is around here. *I* am an influential casting director. *You* are an aspiring actor. You really, really do not want to mess with me.'

'Is that so? Well, suck my dick.' Leo moved towards her and biffed her on the shoulder the way Jethro had biffed him earlier that day, and then he backed away from her, flashing her a final, taunting smile. 'You disrespect me, Calypso O'Kelly, and you're going to regret it. Sure as eggs is eggs, you're really, really going to regret it.'

And then he was gone.

Calypso was working the party: working it, she hoped, to Dominic's satisfaction. She was glad she'd listened to current affairs on the radio that morning: the man she was talking to was a diplomat. However, she was only half listening to what he was saying because she was on the alert for Leo and Iseult. She had just decided that they must have gone off without saying goodbye when she caught sight of Leo coming down the stairs. She'd had enough. She *had* to get rid of him!

'Excuse me,' she lied diplomatically to the diplomat. 'I've just seen my caterer signalling to me. I think she needs me.'

Calypso zoomed towards the stairs with as much dignity as she could muster, blowing kisses here and there, waving fingers at friends, mouthing 'Talk later!' at guests who tried to solicit her attention, but she was too late. Leo had vanished like a mirage. She bit her lip, then turned as someone touched her arm. It was Dannie Moore.

'These are for you,' she said, holding out an exquisite coffee bouquet.

'Oh, Dannie – how lovely! Thank you!' Calypso took the posy and automatically held it up to her nose. 'Did Rosa come with you? I haven't seen her yet.'

'No. The poor creature's stuck at home. She hasn't been feeling the best lately, and when her babysitter let her down at the last minute she decided it was probably just as well to stay in and take things easy. She sent this.' Dannie reached into her bag and produced a small gift-wrapped package and an envelope.

Calypso tore open the envelope and smiled

when she saw the portrait on the front of the card: a picture in felt tip of her wearing a crown – evidently the work of Lottie. Quickly she ran her eyes over the words: 'So sorry, dearest Calypso, that I can't be there tonight for your HAPPY BIRTHDAY. I'll phone you as soon as I shake this wretched cold and we'll have that girly night. Love you, Rosa. XXX. And Lottie.☺'

Calypso felt guilty at the thought of poor Rosa stuck at home with a cold. She really must get in touch. She hadn't seen her friend in weeks – not since that time she'd called to the office. 'How is she?' she asked Dannie. 'Apart from her cold, I mean. I've just realized it's been a while since I last saw her.'

'She's OK.' Calypso noticed the concerned note that had crept into Dannie's voice. 'I think she's a bit worried about money at the moment. She hasn't had any work this week. And she's not socializing.'

'She ought to find a regular babysitter and make herself get out more. That girl's always letting her down.'

'Babysitters don't come cheap.'

Of course. How thoughtless of her. Calypso determined that she would volunteer her services some evening soon, maybe take Lottie for a weekend, so that Rosa could have time to herself, for pampering or whatever. There was a fabulous masseuse in her gym that Rosa should try – Calypso had had a full body aromatherapy massage there only yesterday evening, after her Brazilian wax. And then she gave herself another mental rap on the knuckles. That massage had probably cost around eighty euros, excluding her generous tip. She hadn't even bothered to look at the total on the bill when she'd handed over her platinum card.

Something had distracted Dannie. She was smiling at someone on the other side of the room. Calypso followed the direction of her gaze to see Jethro Palmer smiling back at her. 'That's Jethro Palmer, the film director,' said Calypso.

'I know,' said Dannie. 'He's my date.'

'What? He's never!'

'Is too,' said Dannie, mock-snootily. 'We've been – seeing each other.'

'Wow. Lucky girl! He's a complete ride!'

'I know,' said Dannie, laughing.

'How did it happen?'

'It's too long and romantic a story to tell now. I'll spill the beans over a couple of bottles of wine some night soon.'

'Can't wait!'

'We're off now. Thanks so much for a lovely party.' Leo Devlin was there suddenly. Thank Jesus! At last he was going. His left arm was casually draped over Iseult's shoulders and he was wearing a polite smile. Iseult's expression was dazed and she was very flushed. Leo reached for Calypso's hand with his free one and held it lightly.

'It was fab,' said Iseult. 'And thanks for allowing us to snoop around. I *love* your house! I'm going to have a house like this one day, with a hot tub in the garden and an *en suite* dressing room like yours.'

Calypso flinched. What had Iseult been doing in her bedroom? And what did she mean by 'thanks for allowing us to snoop around'? Her apprehensive expression must have registered, because a little frown of uncertainty puckered the secretary's flawless forehead. 'It *was* OK, wasn't it? To explore? Leo did say he'd asked your permission . . .'

She felt Leo's grasp on her fingers tighten, felt a nail scratch the palm of her hand like a challenge. Calypso wriggled her fingers surreptitiously in an attempt to disengage her hand, but he refused to relinquish it. 'Sure it's cool,' she said, trying to sound careless. 'Well, good night.'

'Good night, Calypso,' he said, leaning into her and brushing her cheek with his lips.

'Good night, Calypso,' echoed Iseult. 'See you tomorrow!'

'I might be a little late,' said Calypso.

'No problem,' said cheerful Iseult. 'Me and Viv'll manage – if I don't have too chronic a hangover, that is!'

'Drink lots of water,' advised Leo. 'I'll make sure you drink at least a litre before beddy-byes like a good girl – and you'll be tucked up under the duvet before midnight.'

Her hand was finally free. Calypso watched the two beautiful young people walk away from her towards her front door, Iseult's hand clutching onto Leo's belt, Leo's arm still snaked around the slender shoulders of his brand new inamorata.

'Wow. Talk about a *dude*!' remarked a gobsmacked Dannie. 'And the girl's pretty foxy, too. They make a stunning couple, don't they?'

'Mm.'

'She works for you, I take it?'

'Yeah. She's my receptionist.'

'And who's he?'

'He's an actor. Leo Devlin. He's on Jethro's film.'

'Janey! *That's* Leo Devlin! Jethro was telling me you'd discovered some astonishing new talent. Congratulations. It must be an amazing feeling when you come across a fella who can act as well as make women go weak at the knees. Jethro says he's a demon.'

'Yes,' replied Calypso, numbly. 'I think that might be exactly what he is.'

The next morning she was not her usual sunny self. Dominic put it down to the late night, but really it was a feeling of overwhelming self-revulsion that was making her snappy and bad-tempered. How she hated herself! She hated herself for the way she'd used sex with Dominic last night as a quid pro quo, as a kind of plea-bargaining commodity, as a way of rewarding him for her birthday present, and as a means of assuaging her guilt. She'd delivered the goods with the dexterity of a professional fellatrix, all the while unable to stop thinking about Leo Devlin.

You disrespect me, Calypso O'Kelly, and you're going to regret it. The words came back to her with the kind of echo effect you get in spooky films. Fuck him! What kind of respect had he ever shown *her*! None. But the truly vile thing was that she found the arrantly disrespectful way he treated her incredibly, disturbingly thrilling. When he'd told her last night what he wanted to do to her, how he'd wanted to smear her lipstick, she had felt an appalled fascination. She hated herself for feeling that way, and she hated Leo Devlin even more for making her feel that way.

She was squeezing fresh oranges as venomously as if they were Leo's testicles when Dominic wandered into the kitchen, on a quest for coffee. 'You got some terrific birthday presents, baby,' he remarked. 'I've just been looking at the stack of goodies in the drawing room. Who gave you the daguerreotype?'

'Jethro. He found it in an antique shop in Francis Street. Beautiful, isn't it?' Jethro hadn't exaggerated when he'd told Calypso that he'd found her a perfect present. The framed Victorian daguerreotype depicted the Goddess Calypso all alone on her Mediterranean island, lamenting her abandonment by her lover, Odysseus.

'Mm. Daguerreotypes in that kind of nick are worth quite a lot now – although it's not really our taste. I can't see where in the house we could hang it. Maybe your dressing room? It won't work anywhere else. What's all this?' asked Dominic, indicating a pile of forgotten belongings that Jacqueline had assembled on the granite top of the kitchen island.

'Stuff people left behind. It's like a lost bloody property office in here. Somebody even left a Patek Philippe wristwatch behind. Talk about *temps perdus*. Sorry. Not the best pun ever.' Dominic laughed and nuzzled her neck. She didn't want him to. It made her feel even more wretchedly guilty. She broke away from him and dumped squeezed-out oranges in the waste disposal. 'I mean, how am I supposed to know what belongs to whom?' She started to riffle through the pile. 'A make-up bag, a cigarette lighter, a Filofax – at least that has a name on it, it's Jane Taylor's – a mobile phone – hey!' she said, holding up a dinky little top-of-the-range

Nokia – 'Someone's got good taste! It's the same as mine! A pen, sunglasses, a stash of hash. Ha! I bet that's Roman's. He was seriously out of it last night.'

'He can't have been the only one who was out of it,' remarked Dominic. 'Look what I found in the bedroom.' He slid a hand into the pocket of his bathrobe and held up a pretty, rosebud-trimmed bra. 'Not yours, I suspect, darling – unless you've suddenly gone up several cup sizes?'

Calypso shook her head wordlessly.

Dominic wandered over to the swingbin and dropped the lacy confection into it. 'Well,' he said. 'I wonder who was trashed enough to make out in our bedroom last night?'

Chapter Six

Rosa's babysitter *had* been available on the night of Calypso's party. And Rosa hadn't been so unwell that she couldn't have managed to get herself over to her friend's des res for a glass or two of champagne and some gourmet canapés. The truth was that Rosa had decided she was too scared to go to the party. She adored Calypso, and felt bad about not being there to celebrate her birthday with her, but Dominic and Calypso moved in such vertiginously elevated social circles that Rosa felt dizzy just thinking about them. Any time she'd gone to one of Calypso's cocktail parties or brunches or barbecues or dinner parties in the past, she'd always felt small, stupid and insignificant. Especially the dinner parties. She shuddered when she remembered the last one. There had been luminaries there that night from the film and theatre and art world, people who knew about wine and politics, whose idea of small talk was what was currently showing at the Tate Modern or the National Theatre, and whose conversations were peppered with references to dear friends such as Mick and Jerry, Damien and Tracey, Nicole, Bono and Bob (de Niro). To someone whose idea of bedtime reading these days was nothing more demanding than *heat* magazine, these kinds of social occasion were akin to boot camp.

Rosa had painted a mental picture of herself at Calypso's soirée hemmed into a corner, surrounded by people who were all chattering madly to each other and not to her, decked out in her Next sale little black dress and clutching one of Calypso's designer champagne flutes as if she were a drowning person and the bubbles in the glass were keeping her afloat. She knew that she would drink too much, as she always did when she was nervous, and Dominic would end up calling a cab for her and she'd lose her key and have to ring the doorbell for the babysitter to let her in.

So instead of going to Calypso's party, Rosa had stayed in and drunk a bottle of wine all by herself. The empty bottle was still there on the table the next morning while Rosa threw breakfast together for Lottie.

'What does vin doo patron mean, Mum?' asked Lottie, examining the label. Lottie read everything. Backs of cereal packets, newspaper advertisements for B&Q, the 'Nutritional Value' copy on the Mysterious One's gerbil feed. Rosa had once come across her reading an article in a women's magazine that she had stupidly left lying around about how to pleasure a man in bed. 'Men are crap, Mum, aren't they?' Lottie had said conversationally. 'Imagine them wanting to put their willies in ladies' mouths –' At this, Rosa had smartly pulled the magazine out of her daughter's grasp. 'Why do they want to do that?'

'Because it feels nice, I suppose,' Rosa had said, dumping the magazine in the bin.

'It wouldn't feel nice if the lady bit them. I think men are stupid. If I were a man I'd never put my willy in—'

'OK, sweetheart. Let's talk about something else. Look – there's a special offer for a Tony Tigercam on Frosties!'

Now Rosa said: '*Vin du patron*? Well, it means "Wine of the Boss". The *patron* is the head of the vineyard in France where they grow the grapes to make the wine.'

'So it's really special wine then, if it's for the boss?'

Rosa smiled. 'Well, no. Not really. It's not an expensive vintage wine, or anything. Another way of describing it is *vin ordinaire*. That means "ordinary wine". I couldn't afford posh vintage stuff, Lotta.'

' "One litre",' read Lottie. ' "A robust full-bodied red". Why does this wine have a screw top, Mum? The wine that Calypso and Dannie bring has corks always, doesn't it?'

'Well, some wines come with corks, some with screw tops. Nowadays, wine even comes in boxes—'

'*Boxes?* That's daft. How does it—'

'Lottie – we're running late. I don't have time to explain now. I'll buy one today and show you how it works, OK? Now, hurry up and get your schoolbag. And don't forget you've Irish dancing today, so pack your shoes. Here's your lunch box. Tuna sandwiches OK?' Lottie made a resigned face. 'And you've got a mini Edam –' This time the child made a 'yeuch' face '– which you *will eat*, Carlotta. Understood? You are a growing girl who needs her calcium. And there's an apple and a Penguin.'

After she'd got the school run out of the way, the first thing Rosa did on her return to the apartment was to check her answering machine in case someone from an agency had left a message. The red eye of the machine met hers unblinkingly. No messages. Ow. That was the fifth day in a row that she'd come home to find her answering machine mute. She reached into her handbag for her mobile, to see if she'd missed a call. There was no envelope icon displayed.

Rosa bit her lip. She'd had no voiceover work for a week now. It didn't surprise her that Roydon Sneyde hadn't booked her for another CD-rom session. That little money-spinner was no longer a runner, for obvious reasons. What did surprise her was that she had had no calls from other studios or agencies. It sometimes happened that there was a lull in voiceover work – some weeks she'd be rushed off her feet trying to fit in sessions, some weeks she'd be glad of a couple of badly paid demo gigs – but since her career as a voiceover artist had taken off, she had never had an entire week go by without a single booking.

There was nothing else for it. She would have to pick up the phone today and ring round agencies to tout. She *hated* doing this, but hey – life was full of shite things to do, and you sometimes just had to grit your teeth and get on with it. It was still only half-past nine, she reminded herself. If she made a few calls, by midday she might have half a dozen gigs lined up for next week. But she wouldn't start making those calls just yet. Instead, she set about tidying the flat, trying to convince herself that it was important to have a clutter-free environment before she picked up the phone.

She cleared Lottie's breakfast dishes off the table, and the cereal packet and the empty tin of tuna, and the wine bottle. It joined the other half-dozen or so empties that she kept meaning to bring to the recycling bin near Lottie's school. She'd have to be careful that the other mothers didn't see her when she dumped them. She didn't want them thinking she was a lush!

Rosa hadn't meant to drink an entire bottle last night. She'd just wanted a glass or two to help her unwind after a hectic day, the way Calypso often did. Except when Calypso had a seriously hectic day she opened a bottle of champagne. Calypso's fridge was permanently stocked with champagne in the event of such an emergency, and Calypso had her fair share of the hectic days that were the fate of the stressed working woman. A reasonable little voice reminded her that her day yesterday *hadn't* actually been that hectic. *Oh, shut up*, she told the voice, before admitting to herself that the day hadn't been stressful at all, really – apart from the bogging traffic on the school run – and it certainly hadn't been stressful enough to justify consuming an entire bottle of wine on her own. *Excuse me?* said the voice. *Did you say* a bottle? *A bottle of wine is actually 75 centilitres. You drank an entire* litre *of wine last night, Rosa Elliot, and the recommended maximum weekly alcohol intake for women is no more than—*

Oh – shut *up*! Rosa told the voice, turning on the radio to drown it out. She remembered what she'd said to Lottie this morning about wine that came in boxes. Maybe she should start buying that kind? Much more convenient than lugging home heavy bottles that she kept forgetting to take to the recycling bin. Yes. She'd definitely look out for a wine box when she did the supermarket shop before picking Lottie up from school. *Clever you!* said the voice in her head. *That way you won't have as clear an idea of exactly how much of the stuff you've consumed at the end of the evening!* Oh – shut up, you nasty, niggling *nag*!

And now the flat was sorted and she had to make the phone calls. Rosa took a deep breath and booted up her geriatric computer to access her address book.

Does your ironing pile resemble Everest? she heard coming from the radio in the kitchen. It was Conor Mullen's smooth voice. The cursor on the screen was still in endless flickering 'pause' mode. *Will your next wash load be the straw that breaks the camel's back?* Conor asked her. *New Quik Press from Farrell & Farrell, blah blah blah . . .*

Oh. She'd just remembered that her ironing pile actually *did* resemble Everest. There was masses of Lottie's school stuff – gym gear as well as uniform – that she'd need to get out of the way before Monday. She'd better do some of it now – she didn't want to spend the entire weekend slaving over an ironing board. She'd defer the phone calls for a little longer.

You're procrastinating . . .

Shut *up*!

She'd just finished the last shirt when the phone rang. At last! She picked up the receiver and did her best voiceover voice: low, husky, sexy. It was amazing how alluring you could make nine syllables sound. 'Hello? Rosa Elliot speaking.'

'Rosa? Hello there – it's Dannie.'

Rosa tried not to sound disappointed. 'Oh, Dannie! Hi – how are things?'

'Grand. It's Friday, I'm leaving Laura to it, and I'm on the doss for the rest of the day. How's about some lunch?'

'Lunch?' She glanced at her watch. It was ten to one. She'd be mad to start phoning agencies now: everyone would be heading out to lunch themselves. The idea of lunch with Dannie was very seductive – they hadn't done it in ages, and she could find out how Calypso's party had gone last night. 'I'd love that. Where?'

'Fallon's?'

'Fallon's it is. See you in ten minutes.'

Rosa found herself humming the obnoxiously catchy tune from that Quik Press commercial as she slung garments on hangers and stowed the ironing board back in its cupboard. She shut down the dozy PC, tucked her mobile in her bag and grabbed her jacket, sticking her tongue out at the dead-eyed answering machine before swinging out of the flat.

Dannie was in Fallon's pub already, ensconced in the snug. She looked so radiant that Rosa hated herself for the stab of jealousy she felt. When was the last time *she* had looked radiant?

'Hi. How'd you manage to get the snug?' she asked, joining radiant Dannie on the lumpy banquette.

'There was a couple leaving just as I arrived. I grabbed it off them.' Dannie gave Rosa a kiss on the cheek. 'How are you, mavourneen? Feeling better?'

'Better?'

'You weren't well yesterday.'

'Oh. Yes. Much better, thanks.' Rosa had forgotten about the fibs she'd told in order to get out of going to Calypso's. 'How was the party?'

'Deadly. Full of real famous people. I ate too much, got fluthered on champagne and left my phone behind. Calypso said she'd drop it in to me later this evening on her way home from work, so I said I'd cook something for us. Will you come?'

'I'd love that.' One of the great pluses for Rosa about visiting Dannie in the evening was that, because they lived in the same apartment block, she didn't need to bother with a babysitter. 'You're not seeing your new man tonight, then?' she asked.

Dannie made a face. 'No. He's off to London for the weekend.'

'I'm dying to meet him.'

'Ladies? What can I get you?' Seamus the proprietor leaned on the counter and gave his twinkly smile.

'A salad sandwich for me, please, Seamus,' said Dannie. 'And I'll have a glass of white wine to go with it.'

'Same for me.' Twinkly Seamus saluted them, then went to fill their order.

'God, I love this pub. 'When I think of the pretentious joints I used to frequent in London. Janey! All clattery and "aren't-we-so-important-and-trendy"! I don't know how I stuck the feckin' place for so long.' She turned back to Rosa. 'So, girl. Tell me all your news.'

Rosa took a deep breath. 'Well,' she began.

By the time they'd finished their lunch, Rosa had filled Dannie in on her treatment at the hands of Roydon Sneyde and the grim, gig-free week she'd just been through; and Dannie had commiserated and tried to be upbeat and positive, assuring Rosa that things were bound to look up soon. She hadn't dwelt over-long on her shiny new relationship and the hopes she had for it because she didn't want to seem like a jammy bitch in the face of poor Rosa's glumness. Her single-word response to Rosa's enquiry as to what Jethro Palmer was like had been simply: 'überdude'.

Halfway through lunch Rosa's phone rang, and she practically ransacked her bag to get to it before it rang off. 'I'm just nipping to the loo,' Dannie mouthed at her as Rosa dashed to the door to take her phone call away from the ambient din. She also mouthed 'Mind our places' to Seamus, indicating their wineglasses and sandwiches. It was risky to leave the snug unattended – not because someone was likely to do a bunk with their lunches, but because it was the most coveted corner of the pub, and some unprincipled type might try and annex it on them.

In the loo, Dannie indulged in a little reflection. She knew that the reason she'd been reluctant to volunteer information to Rosa about the new man in her life wasn't simply because she didn't want to look smug. It went deeper than that. She and Rosa rarely kept secrets from each other. They enjoyed dissecting and analysing relationships – their own and other women's – and that naturally extended to soap opera and celebrity relationships as well. It was a girl thing, after all. But this time Dannie knew that she had fought shy of opening up too much about Jethro Palmer because she was still trying to make sense of him herself.

The truth was that Dannie had fallen for Jethro fatally, and very, very fast. They hadn't gone to bed on their first date, nor on the second

– even though Dannie had worn her most beautiful underwear on that occasion. On their third night out (three in a row!) they had gone back to her flat – the first time she had *ever* invited a man into her *sanctum sanctorum* – and rode each other's brains out. That was the only way to describe it. She had never experienced such – what was the word? – such *synergy* with any man before – not even with Guy.

Afterwards he had left her lying on the length of embroidered velvet that was draped over her bed, and he'd wrapped a towel around his waist and wandered round the room, making a running commentary on the surprising things he was discovering about Dannie Moore. He'd studied the books on her bedside table and scrutinized the artwork on her walls, he'd run the palms of his hands over furniture and fabrics – as if reading her in Braille – and he'd un-stoppered her bottle of Nu and inhaled her scent. He'd frowned at the residual suits in her wardrobe – relics from the bad old days that she still had occasion to wear if she was doing the flowers for a major function – and he'd raised an approving eyebrow at her lovely cobwebby knits, and then he had slid her beautiful antique kimono off its padded hanger, held it in his arms, and rubbed his cheek against it like a big feline. A big, rugged lion.

And Dannie had let him. Jethro Palmer had

slid into her personal space as subtly and un-expectedly as a cat burglar, and she had done nothing – nothing at all – to stop him. He had penetrated all her defences and unveiled all her disguises, and left her psyche as exposed and vulnerable as her naked body as she'd lounged against velvet, watching him. And, well – wow! Surrendering to him made her feel so *sexy*!

When he lifted the lid on the carved Indian chest that contained her lingerie, the little, frothy, frilly things she'd indulged herself in since she'd forsaken her old life, her London life, he'd sucked in his breath, and smiled. Then he'd delved both his big hands into its sandal-wood interior as though he'd come across a treasure trove, and ransacked the silken contents. 'Now I know all your secrets,' he'd said, before unwinding the towel from around his waist and joining her on the expanse of embroidered velvet.

Dannie almost couldn't bear to recall what happened next. It did strange kind of snaky things to her insides.

When she returned from the loo, Rosa was back in the snug with two fresh miniatures of wine in front of her.

'Oh,' said Dannie. 'Are we having another?'

'My treat,' said Rosa brightly, as she unscrewed the metal cap.

'You've no gigs this afternoon, then, I take it?'

'No. That call was from an actress friend.' Rosa's voice was tight. 'She's just got into voiceover work. She wanted to know what the rate for a thirty-second telly commercial would be.'

'How much is it?'

'A lot of money.' Rosa swigged back a mouthful of wine and set the glass back down on the table with an emphatic thud. 'Fuck it, Dannie. She was doing a chocolate bar commercial, for Faulkes & Benson. That's *my* territory. Faulkes & Benson *always* use me for that kind of soft-sell stuff – I can do it in my sleep. Why didn't they phone *me* about it?'

Dannie made a dubious face. 'Beats me, sweetheart.'

Rosa picked up the metal cap of her miniature and started twisting it between her fingers. 'Maybe they think I'm too ubiquitous. Maybe I've hit saturation point. Maybe the listeners are fed up with hearing my voice over and over again. You've no idea how often people come up to me and say: "Heard you on the radio today!" as if it's a good thing. Maybe it's not. Maybe it's a bad thing. Ow.' Rosa put a finger to her mouth and sucked. The jagged metal edge of the bottle top had given her a paper cut. 'Shit, Dannie. I wonder should I ring them, or would that just make me look too desperate? What do you think?'

'Here.' Dannie reached into her bag and handed Rosa a tissue to stanch the blood that was beading on her index finger. Then she leaned against the back of the banquette and took a sip of her wine, looking thoughtful. 'Might there be someone new on board who doesn't know your stuff?'

Rosa brightened. 'Well, yes. That's a possibility. Agencies are always changing their staff – headhunting and all that. Maybe I should send them another demo CD.' She slugged more wine. 'Oh, fuck it, Dannie! Insecurity's such a killer. What a stupid, stupid job for a single parent to have!'

Dannie gave her a sympathetic look. 'I know you hate doing it, acushla, but maybe it's time to start making phone calls?'

'Yeah.' Rosa acknowledged the advice with a grimace. 'I was going to do it this morning, and then the ironing pile gave me a great excuse not to. And another bloody thing I'm going to have to do is ring round all the agencies' accounts departments and ask them to send out the cheques that are overdue. I *really* hate doing that, Dannie. If anything, grovelling to accounts is even worse than brown-nosing producers.'

'It's a weird one that, isn't it? I've often wondered why asking for money that's yours by rights is so squirm-makingly embarrassing.'

'Tell me about it. There's a woman in the

accounts department in the Definite Article, and I swear you'd think by the way she treats you that the money actually belongs to *her* personally. She uses that "cheque in the post" lie all the time – I practically hyperventilate every time I have to pick the phone up to her.'

'It really is torture for you, isn't it, God love you? A phobia, even.'

Rosa nodded. 'Sometimes I wonder if I'm the only person in the world who suffers from it. I know loads of voiceover artists who pick up the phone at the drop of a hat, and socialize in Daly's with producers after recording sessions, and take them out to lunch and do all that schmoozy stuff. I'm completely in awe of them. If I took someone out to lunch I'd just sit there and stew with worry in case they found out how boring I was.'

'Excuse me? I'm having lunch with you, and I haven't yawned once.'

'Yeah, but you love me, and love means never yawning at your mate even when she's in major Moaning Mary mode.' Rosa gave Dannie a look of assessment. 'You truly *are* a mate, you know, Dannie. You're such a good mate that I bet you'd even make those phone calls for me if you could.'

'Well now, there's a thought. Shouldn't your *agent* be making those phone calls for you?

'No. She doesn't handle my voiceover work – I can't afford the luxury. She'd cream 15 per cent off, and that adds up to quite a lot. Fifteen per cent covers all the perks I can manage – like Lottie's dance classes and gymnastics and summer camps. Anyway, sometimes I'm too scared to even pick up the phone to *her*.'

'Are you serious?'

'Mm. I always think she's too busy with all her more lucrative clients to be bothering with me. I think the last thing she negotiated for me was that awful film that starred a giant squirrel. Although, come to think of it, working with that squirrel was a lot more fun than working with Roydon Sneyde.'

Dannie laughed, then reached out and squeezed Rosa's hand. 'You listen to me, sweetheart. You mustn't allow yourself to get too depressed about all this. I'm sure it's just one of those temporary blips all businesses go through – really I am – but maybe you should think about investigating a different line of work if things don't pick up soon. Didn't you do a load of courses once? I seem to remember you told me you'd a diploma in computer studies?'

'Oh, Jesus, Dannie, it's so long since I did that course that my computer skills would be Neanderthal compared to someone fresh out of college.' She reached for her wine, then said suddenly: 'D'you know something? I don't think I can bear my own crapness any more.'

'You are *not* crap, Rosa Elliot! How dare you

say that about yourself!' Rosa just shugged her shoulders and gave Dannie a rueful smile. 'And d'you how I know you're not crap?' persisted Dannie. 'You have reared a lovely, healthy well-adjusted nine-year-old all by yourself. Crap people rear crap kids, and by no stretch of the imagination could anyone ever describe Lottie as crap.'

There was a pause. Then Rosa shrugged. 'You're right. I should count my blessings instead of being Moaning Mary – and you should write one of those positive-thinking self-help books, Dannie Moore.' She took another sip of her wine. It had mellowed her. She found she wasn't feeling quite so scared of things as she had earlier that day. She went to pour the remains of her miniature into her glass, then realized that the bottle was empty. Oh! She'd forgotten she'd emptied it. Her glass was nearly depleted. She'd dearly love another one, but something made her fight shy of suggesting it to Dannie. Anyway, if she had another she'd be over the limit, and she still had the school run to do.

The school run! Rosa clapped her hands over her mouth. Shit! She'd forgotten that school was closing early today for a staff meeting! Lottie would at this minute be standing at the school gate wondering what on earth had become of her mother. She grabbed her bag and jumped to her feet. 'Dannie – I have to dash,' she said.

'Sorry about this. I'd completely forgotten that Lottie's out of school early today, and I'm late already.'

'Oh! Be off with you then, Rosa! I'll see you later.'

'Later?'

'Yes. Dinner at my gaff, remember?'

'Oh, great. I'll look forward to that.'

Sonia O'Sullivan might have envied the speed with which Rosa went racing out of the pub door and down the road to the apartment block car park. And lucky, lucky Dannie Moore sat back in the comfort of the snug in Fallon's feeling happy as Larry. Happier.

The mouth of the lollipop lady from hell was more pursed than Rosa had ever seen it when she finally pulled up outside the school gates. Oh shit. She was in for it. Should she just open the door, let Lottie in and then zoom off like a getaway driver? All she needed now was a lecture. But she'd be in the lollipop lady's black books for ever if she didn't thank her for staying on to keep an eye on Lottie, and all mothers know how important it is to keep the lollipop lady sweet.

'Hi!' she effused as she got out of the car. The lollipop lady didn't say anything. She didn't need to. Her look was more eloquent than the longest of lectures. And from the expression on her daughter's face, *she* was in a snit with her, too. A double whammy! Great. 'I'm *so* sorry I'm late,' said Rosa. 'Thank you *so* much for staying on – I really appreciate it.'

The lollipop lady looked pointedly at her watch, and her mouth disappeared completely. Then she turned on her heel and stalked off across the tarmacked playground, wielding her lollipop like a spear carrier in some epic tragedy.

'Oh, shit, darling. I'm so sorry!' Rosa bent down to embrace Lottie, who looked majorly pissed off. Rosa couldn't blame her. Anyone would be feeling grim after being stuck for the best part of half an hour with witchy Lolly.

'Pooh! You stink of wine and pub smells.'

'Oh, yikes, do I? I went to Fallon's for lunch with Dannie.' She opened the back passenger seat for Lottie, thinking that if Lottie had smelt wine and pub smells off her, Lolly probably had too, and word would soon be all over the school like a computer virus that she was an unfit mother. She'd have to buy Lolly a box of Roses to re-ingratiate herself. Hell! Why was life all about pleasing other people? She wouldn't expect anyone to give *her* a box of bloody Roses if they'd put her nose out of joint. She pulled away from the kerb and took a left.

'Where are we going?' demanded Lottie.

'The supermarket.'

'Oh, *no*! First of all I have to stand for ages

listening to Lolly's moaning while you shoot the breeze with Dannie, and now I have to go to the poxy supermarket! I hate my life. It sucks!'

Rosa had had enough. 'Oh, shut up, Lottie! I've had a tough day too, you know. D'you think I spent the entire morning "shooting the breeze" with Dannie? No, I didn't. I spent the morning slaving over a pile of ironing – most of which, incidentally, was yours.' She didn't mention the fact that she'd also spent most of the morning in a lather over her finances.

The supermarket was full of ratty-looking, bad-tempered people. She sent Lottie off with her own basket and instructed her to get eggs, milk, cheese, yoghurt and Frosties. She knew she shouldn't really allow Frosties, but getting out of the house in the morning was bad enough some-times without Lottie moaning about having to eat good-for-her, macramé-type cereal on top of everything else. Rosa wandered listlessly along the aisles, mentally ticking off her shopping list. She'd do some kind of pasta for Lottie's evening meal tonight, and a salad. She was glad that Dannie had invited her up to her flat for supper – it would be nice to have somebody put food in front of her for a change, and Dannie was a terrific cook.

She helped herself to tomatoes and red peppers and lettuce and fruit, then rounded the corner of an aisle to where the bread was stocked. A bloke with his back to her was helping himself leisurely to items from a shelf, blithely unaware of the fact that his trolley was blocking her passage. She stood there waiting for him to notice her, but he was too busy scanning the biscuit section. Rosa watched as he helped himself to a packet of custard creams and another of jam tarts. He was just reaching for a tray of fairy cakes when he became aware of her eyes on him. She noticed his hand hover, waver, then lunge for a packet of pricey demerara all-butter shortbread.

'Excuse me,' said Rosa.

'Oh – sorry,' he said, in a strange, strangled accent, hastily moving the trolley out of her way.

Rosa checked out the contents of his trolley with an oblique eye on her way past to the bread section. Uh-oh. Steak-and-kidney pies, corned beef, picnic ham and Bisto gravy granules. She'd read something in a magazine once about finding romance in supermarkets. You were supposed to fill your trolley with sexy food like wine and cream, exotic fruit and vegetables, and dead expensive olive oil in bottles that looked as if they belonged on a market stall in Tuscany. This bloke obviously wasn't on the make. Rosa tossed a loaf of wholemeal brown into her trolley and carried on.

Cotton wool, loo roll, soap. Then round the corner to the household section. There was Mr

Fairy Cakes again, helping himself to Mr Sheen and Swiffers dusters. She noticed that the contents of his trolley had been augmented by marrowfat peas, Smash instant potatoes, own-brand fish fingers, and sliced pan. Loser.

Stopping off in the off-licence section, Rosa scanned the shelves for something half decent to bring to Dannie's. She went for a bottle of Chilean Sauvignon Blanc, and turned to the selection of cheaper wines for her own tippling pleasure. She opted for her usual litre of *vin du patron*, and when she saw it was on special offer, opted for another two litres. Then she remembered that she'd promised to show Lottie how a wine box worked, and she slung a box of not very special Chardonnay into her trolley as well.

Turning the corner of an aisle, she spotted Lottie in the dairy section, clutching her Frosties and talking animatedly to a stranger. Feeling cross that she was infringing the never-talk-to-strangers rule, Rosa rolled her trolley up the aisle as if it was a chariot. The stranger was Mr Fairy Cakes.

'Hi, Mum!' carolled Lottie. 'Look who I've met. This is Michael Luque, the vet from across the road.'

'Oh, hi.' Rosa didn't bother with an overly bright smile. The anaesthetic effect of her lunchtime wine was beginning to wear off, and the supermarket Muzak was getting on her nerves. 'Nice to meet you.'

'Yeah.'

Lottie was always going on about how cool Michael Luque was, but Rosa couldn't see much to recommend him. He was one of those people who look as if they're trying too hard to be cool. He wasn't much to write home about in the looks department, either. His nose was too big, he had a perma-tan, lank black hair and shifty eyes. She saw his eyes shift to the contents of her trolley, and she wished she hadn't helped herself to so much wine. Well, fuck it! Why should she care what he thought of her! And what did *he* have in his bloody trolley? Alongside the other items of dubious nutritional value there now nestled tinned fruit cocktail, Shape low-fat spread, Angel Delight and goldfish food. Cool? *Not*.

'Well, come on, Lottie. Let's get out of here.' She treated Michael Luque to a peremptory smile which he barely returned, and manoeuvred her trolley towards the checkout. As sod's law dictated, she found herself in the queue that never moves. When she eventually got to the front of it, she realized that she was twenty cents short of the total amount. Shit! Twenty piddling cents! Something would have to go back. The milk. She could pick up a carton later in the local Londis. Rosa sent Lottie running back with the milk just as Michael

Luque joined the queue next to her – the one Rosa *should* have joined, the one that was whizzing along. They nodded stiffly at each other, and made small talk about the weather as Rosa stuffed her shopping into bags.

Michael had added more items to his trolley – pre-wrapped sirloin steak, garlic, and black and white pudding – and now he was counting out euros and cents from a little tasselled felt purse. Rosa remembered that Lottie had told her he was gay, and found herself automatically chastising herself for her political incorrectness. He had every right to be gay and have a gay kind of purse.

They continued to pack their bags with their backs to each other, and then Michael wheeled his laden trolley to the counter where cigarettes and Lottery tickets were on sale. Rosa observed him from the corner of her eye, curious as to what other supermarket dating game *faux pas* he was going to make. She watched him hand over a lot of euros for a carton of Silk Cut and some scratch cards, and mentally awarded him a load more points in the *faux pas* stakes. She remembered how Dannie had described Jethro Palmer as being an überdude. To her mind, anyone who bought scratch cards was an überloser.

Lottie finally arrived back from returning the milk, and at last they were out of there, retrieving their coin from the trolley chain gang before loading the boot. The queue to get out of the car park was endless. And as Rosa sat there, feeling dog-tired after her mini-binge, depleted now of alcohol-induced endorphins, all her worries came flooding back. Lottie was right, she thought. Life sucked.

Later that afternoon, after she'd unpacked the shopping, she knew that she couldn't put off making the dreaded phone calls any longer.

She dialled the first number on her list, and asked to be put through to accounts. 'Sorry,' came the answer. 'Lisa only works mornings. Try again on Monday.' Number two, then. 'May I ask who's calling?' was the response this time, before she was put on hold. The laidback on-hold music went on for ages. It was some kind of esoteric-sounding jazz. The longer Rosa listened to it, the more she despised Faulkes & Benson. *We are so radical*, the music seemed to be saying to her in a kind of DART-y accent. *We are an* advertising *agency. We are movers and shakers. We have cool jazz on our on-hold facility, not that crappy electronic stuff* . . . 'Hello?' The inhuman voice of the receptionist came back on. 'I'm afraid Antoinette's out of the office at the moment.'

'OK. Thanks anyway.' Rosa put the phone down, feeling quite grateful Antoinette had been out of the office. She wrote 'Ring back on Monday' by the number on the list.

Now it was time for the Definite Article. This was the scariest one, the one she'd been putting off till last. Maybe she should make herself a cup of tea first. 'Lottie?' she called into the child's bedroom, where the Egypt project now covered the entire floor. 'Do you want a cup of tea?'

'No.'

'No *thanks*,' Rosa automatically corrected her. Oh! Why *bother*?

In the kitchen, she opened the door of the cupboard where she kept her dry goods. As she took the packet from the shelf, her eyes fell on the box of Chardonnay she'd purchased earlier. She looked at the packet of tea in her hands. Then she looked at the wine box. Tea. Wine. Tea. *Wine*. At half-past four in the afternoon? At half-past four in the afternoon from hell, she reminded herself. She still had that mega-scary phone call to make. A little Dutch courage wouldn't go amiss.

Rosa opened another cupboard and reached for a wineglass. Then her hand swerved towards a mug on a lower shelf. She didn't want Lottie to see – she wouldn't understand the Dutch courage principle. She struggled with the un-familiar mechanics of the wine box's pouring system, reopening her paper cut in the process. When it was poured, she took an experimental taste. The stuff was tepid, but still quite drink-able, she decided. She sloshed another couple of centilitres into her mug before returning to the sitting room, sipping as she went. Then she picked up the phone and punched in the third number on the list.

'Good afternoon. The Definite Article,' came the receptionist's crisp tones.

'Hello. May I speak to Angela in accounts, please?'

'May I ask who's calling?'

'It's Rosa Elliot here.'

'And you're calling from . . . ?'

'Um. I'm calling from home.' Oh *fuck*! What a totally dorky thing to say! Elaborate, Rosa, elaborate! 'I'm um – I'm a voiceover artist,' Rosa mumbled. A voiceover artist who was dorkily inarticulate, she thought, as a wave of chronic self-loathing swept through her.

'One moment, please.'

If she'd wanted to say anything else she wouldn't have been able to, because Miss Crisp Tones had put her on hold. She took a couple of swigs of wine as she listened to the Definite Article's music. Albinoni. So what was the message this time? *We are an advertising agency with taste. We are classy. We play baroque music on our on-hold facility*. Yeah, thought Rosa sneerily, but that Albinoni piece is *so* overused. Couldn't you have come up with something a little more recherché?

'Hello?' Good old Crisp Tones was back at last.

'I'm afraid Angela is on another call. Can you phone back later or will you hold?'

'I'll hold,' said Rosa firmly. Now that she'd actually plucked up the courage to make the call, she was damned if she was going to back down. If she put the phone down now, she wouldn't pick it up again until Monday, and she didn't want this burdensome chore hanging over her head like a ghoul all weekend.

She drained her mug and wandered back into the kitchen for a refill. *Encore un petit verre – mais non! Une petite* tasse – ha ha! – *du bon vin blanc* wouldn't do any harm. In for a penny and all that jazz. Albinoni soared in her ear, and she sang along as the wine splashed merrily into her mug. 'La la la la la laaaa la. La la la la la laaaaaaa la.' Singalonga-Albinoni on the Definite Article's on-hold phoney! Phoney being the operative word for all those advertising arseholes. Well, no. That wasn't fair of her. Some of them were OK. Nick, the chief copywriter from the Definite Article, was a sweet bloke. And Angie from Reflex was dead kosher. But that was about it. The rest were too riddled with stress to bother about being nice to needy voiceover artists. They saved their charm school skills for the client.

This Chardonnay wasn't half bad, she decided, as she replaced the wine box on the shelf beside the bottle of Sauvignon Blanc that she'd bought to take to Dannie's tonight. Ten euros it had cost her. But then, it wouldn't do to bring *déclassé* stuff to Dannie. No sirree. Calypso and Dannie drank wine that had *corks*. No screwtop or wine box shite for *them*.

'Hello?' came a voice in her ear, giving her a fright.

'Angela!'

'No, I'm afraid Angela's still on that call. Do you still want to hold?'

No, no, *no*! 'Yes, please,' she said meekly.

Five peak-rate minutes of listening to Albinoni (and another mug of Chardonnay) later, Angela deigned to take her call. 'Oh yeah, hi, Rosa. That cheque is in the post.'

'Um, sorry, Angela, but you said that last week.'

'Oh, did I. Hang on a sec. I'll just check.' More music assaulted Rosa's left eardrum before Angela's horrible voice came over the receiver again. 'Oh yeah, you're right, it's here. Will I put it in the post or will you come and pick it up yourself.' Why did Angela appear never to use question marks? And why did Rosa feel as if she were some teeny tiny crawly creature in the pecking order of the universe, and that Angela was a big fat hen?

'I'll come and pick it up myself this afternoon.'

'Oh yeah, well, you'd better hurry: we'll be closing the office soon. I'll leave an envelope at reception.'

'No problem, Angela,' she ingratiated, hating herself. 'I'm just a short walk from where you are. Talk to you later. Thanks. Bye.'

When Rosa put the phone down her palms were damp with sweat. She swigged back the remains of her wine and rinsed the mug quickly under the tap, then poked her head round Lottie's door. Lottie was cutting out a picture of the Sphinx from a Sunday supplement colour ad for the Egyptian tourist board. There was a big photograph of Tutankhamun stuck up on her wall, next to her Westlife poster. Lottie nodded at it and said: 'Tutankhamun's a ride, Mum, isn't he?'

'Yeah. Now, listen, you. I'm dashing out for half an hour. You'll be OK? The same rules as last time apply – and *don't even think* of leaving this apartment. Even if a team of the cutest puppies in the world with bows in their hair get squashed by a steamroller outside the front door you are *not* to go to their rescue.'

'Mum, you're horrible,' retorted Lottie equably. 'What if the fire alarm goes off? Do I just sit here and ignore it?'

'Lottie, on occasions like this your wisecracks can be bloody irritating. Just do as you're told for once without having to question my authority, OK? I'll be back soon.'

Rosa grabbed her jacket and raced down the stairs, not bothering with the lift. If she cut across Stephen's Green she could be at the Definite Article in around fifteen minutes.

She made it. By the time she got there she was breathless and sweaty, but she made it. The girl behind the desk looked up as Rosa blundered into reception. 'Good afternoon,' said Miss Crisp Tones. 'How may I help you?' She wore a polite lipsticked smile and Prada, and even though the Prada was probably fake on her receptionist's salary, she wore it very well.

'Good afternoon. I'm Rosa Elliot. Angela said she'd leave an envelope for me in reception.'

'I don't think there's anything here.' Crisp Tones looked through a neat pile of stuff on her desk. 'No. I'll phone up to her for you. Take a seat.'

'Thank you.' Rosa sank into one of those massive sofas that upmarket joints seem to consider mandatory – the kind that swallow you whole. She wondered what was the point of them. They were difficult to sit in without looking as if you were slouching, and they were impossible to rise elegantly from without practically pulling a leg muscle. It was a one-upmanship thing, she decided. The bigger the sofa, the more kudos it conferred on your business. She had a mental image of a row of massive sofas with big-swinging-dick types like Roydon Sneyde floundering around on them, trying unsuccessfully to get up like Pozzo in *Waiting for*

Godot, and she sniggered out loud. Crisp Tones shot her a curious look, then returned her attention to the phone. 'Hello?' she said into the receiver. 'Angela? There's a –' she covered the mouthpiece with a French-manicured hand – 'I'm sorry? I've forgotten your name?'

The impulse to snigger had vanished into the ether. 'Rosa Elliot.'

'A Rosa Elliot here for you.' A beat, then Crispie put down the receiver. 'She'll be with you in a moment,' she said, then looked up with a smile as two men strolled into reception. Rosa knew one of them: it was Nick, the copywriter she liked, who used her a lot.

She wished she'd made more of an effort with her appearance – not because she fancied Nick, but because appearances were important in the superficial world of advertising. She always took care to make sure that she was smartly dressed and made up before a recording session. A little touch of kookiness was permissible because she was an 'artist', but today she wasn't looking kooky: just disreputable. She hadn't even brushed her hair, or spritzed herself with scent, or brushed her teeth. She wished she had Tic-Tacs or something in her bag to mask the wine on her breath. And the presence of Prada-clad Crisp Tones only served to accentuate her shabbiness.

The two men stood doing matey men stuff for

a minute or two before the one she didn't know left, and Nick finally registered her presence. 'Rosa!' he said, with genuine astonishment. 'What are you doing here?'

'Hi, Nick. I'm here to pick up a cheque.' She hated having to admit it, it smacked so of desperation, but she could think of no excuse.

'No, I mean, what are you doing here in Dublin?'

Nick took a step towards her and she felt at a disadvantage, swamped by big, squishy cushions. She tried to sit up a bit straighter. 'What am I doing in Dublin?' she repeated stupidly. 'I – well – I *live* in Dublin, Nick.'

'So there's no truth in that story then?'

'What story?'

Nick flung himself down on the couch beside her, and Rosa felt herself bounce. 'There's a rumour doing the rounds that you'd suddenly gone all New Agey and moved to the country to work in aromatherapy.'

What? 'What?'

'Yeah – you know. As a masseuse.'

'I'm sorry, Nick? Are you sending me up?'

'No! Scout's honour! Someone told me that you'd got sick of living in the city and that you'd taken yourself and your daughter off to the wilds of Donegal or somewhere.'

'But that's – that's bonkers, Nick! Who on earth told you that?'

'I can't remember. Someone in Daly's, I think. I wish I'd known it wasn't true. I could have used you on a gig today.'

Shit! How had this utterly bizarre rumour *started*?

'Oh, well,' said Nick, stretching out a wrist and looking at his watch. 'You win some, you lose some. I'd offer to buy you a pint, Rosabelle, but I've a plane to catch. I'm on a mission to buy an apartment. Wish me luck.'

'An apartment?' she parroted. Shock had rendered her brain-dead.

'Yes. In London.' He leaned towards her and hissed in a mock-conspiratorial tone: 'I've been *headhunted*! By *Saatchi's*! Next week's my last week here.'

'Oh, *no*! Oh, no, I mean, I don't mean it that way!' she corrected herself quickly. 'I mean that it's great you've been headhunted, but it's not great for me. I've got more work from you than from anyone, Nick.'

'Don't worry, sweetie-pie. I'll put in a word with my replacement.'

'Oh, will you? Oh, thank you, thank you, Nick!' she gushed, gratitude making her effusive. 'Who's taking over from you?'

'Roydon Sneyde,' said Nick, plonking a kiss on her cheek and hoisting himself to his feet. 'I'd better run or I'll miss my flight. Take care, baby.' He saluted her with a grin, slung his jacket over his shoulder, and then he was gone.

The next five minutes were hazy. Rosa made her way out of reception and down a corridor to the loo, where she sat with her head in her hands, disoriented and dizzy with dread, trying to make sense of what had just happened.

For some reason an image flashed across her mind's eye with dazzling clarity – an illustration from a book of fairy stories she'd had as a child. The girl in the story had let drop a precious heirloom – a blue bowl – and the artist had captured with uncanny accuracy the horror on the child's face as she gazed wide-eyed and aghast, hands covering her mouth, at where the bowl lay in scattered fragments around her bare feet. That was how Rosa felt now. The blue bowl of her life had been shattered into pieces so myriad it could never be mended. It had been snatched from her by a vindictive hand and hurled to the ground and the shards had been ground underfoot and spat upon.

She pictured him now, the author of her ruin, Roydon Sneyde, spreading the vile rumour of her decampment to Donegal in the hothouse atmosphere of Daly's where it would spread as efficiently and destructively as the Ebola thing. She pictured the malicious delight he would have taken as he embroidered his lies, painting a picture of a young mother, concerned for her child's well-being, forsaking the city for the countryside and a new life as a New Agey aromatherapy masseuse. It was preposterous, *preposterous*! But it was plausible. She wouldn't be the first single mother she knew who had made a similar decision to downshift, and most people in the business were aware that she practised massage – she'd given enough freebie neck-rubs in her time to stressed-out advertising executives.

She knew she should be full of rage against Roydon Sneyde, she knew she should be fired up and blazing and full of determination to hit back at him at once and do something dramatic to reclaim her life, like dashing down to Daly's this minute and denouncing his vile fabrications, or picking up the phone and confronting him. But she felt too weary, too distraught, too *defeated* to take any kind of positive action right now. Hell. She pulled her head away from her hands and shook it. She'd think about all this monstrous crap that had hijacked her life over the weekend. Something constructive was bound to come to her when she felt calmer, and she could start trying to put her world back in order on Monday. In the meantime, she couldn't stay any longer whimpering and cringing in the Definite Article loo. She had to get back to Lottie.

She passed by her reflection in the mirror as she moved towards the door and pulled it open. Christ, she looked terrible! Grey of face, tousled of hair, haggard as – well – haggard as a hag. She'd have to do something about that next week. Get her highlights done for starters. *That'll set you back a load of euros* said that horrid little voice in her head, that voice that was persistently invading her thoughts these days, and that she kept trying unsuccessfully to stifle. Oh, fuck off, she said to the voice, letting the door fall shut behind her, then realizing that she'd spoken the words out loud. She was going mad now, as well as everything else. 'I'm going mad, mad, fucking fucking mad,' she said, as she rounded the corner and careered into someone who had just come down the stairs and was, like her, heading for reception. It was horrible Angela from accounts. She looked rather taken aback, and Rosa could tell that it wasn't the collision that had shocked her so much as Rosa's appearance, and the fact that she'd been muttering to herself.

'Oh, sorry, Angela. Hi. How's it going.' Angela's habit of not using question marks must be catching, she thought, and she gave a mirthless smile.

'Oh, hello, Rosa. Here's your cheque.' The accountant handed her an envelope with the Definite Article logo on it, then turned in to reception. Rosa was aware that there was a bunch of people in there now – the staff getting ready to hit Daly's or the comfortable driver's seats of the Beamers and Saabs that would transport them smoothly to their residences in Dalkey or Dublin 6. She saw a copywriter among them for whom she'd done some work a couple of months ago, and wondered if she should remind him of her existence, but she wasn't up to schmoozing. She'd have to write it off as a missed opportunity. 'Have a good weekend,' Angela threw at her over her shoulder.

'Thanks. Same to you. Bye,' Rosa intoned, stuffing the envelope in her bag, then trailing out of the front door of the agency and down the steps to the street. As she reached the bottom, it struck her that the last time she'd picked up a cheque from the Definite Article, it had been made out for the wrong amount. She'd better make sure that they hadn't done it again. She tore open the envelope and scanned the cheque. Yeah, wow – amazing and well done, Angela, she thought. You got the sums right this time, but you forgot to get the fucking thing counter-signed. She trudged back up to the door and pressed the bell. The receptionist buzzed her in without bothering to use the intercom. I could be an axe murderer, for all Miss Crisp Tones knows, she thought rattily as she pushed the door open and moved towards reception. I could have a Kalashnikov on me, or an AK47, or a Luger and—

Her ratty thoughts came to an abrupt end.

'I could definitely smell alcohol off her

breath,' Miss Crisp Tones was saying in crisp tones.

'She looked awful,' said someone else. 'It's just as well there were no clients around – she'd really have lowered the tone of the joint.'

'Well, at least I've got her off my back now. I won't get another of her griping bloody phone calls for at least another month.' Angela put on a posh, singsongy parody of Rosa's voice. '*You still owe me for that radio commercial I did for Piggie Pork Pies last month!*'

Angela was smirking and Crisp Tones was tittering when Rosa stomped through the door. The smirk faded and the tittering petered out. An appalled silence fell amongst the assembled admen as Rosa held out the envelope and said: 'Would you be so kind as to get your enormous fat arse back up those stairs now, Angela, and ask your dickhead brain-dead boss to countersign this cheque?'

Chapter Seven

'Agent Provocateur,' instructed Dannie down the phone, with a smile. 'It's on Pont Street, not far from Harrods. Oh, you're such a hero, Jethro Palmer! I know it won't be easy for you to go into a shop that specializes in frilly knickers.'

'Damn right. You'll owe me bigtime for this, Dannie.'

'In that case, dear heart, I suggest that you ask the sales assistant for something that's easy to rip off with your teeth.'

He laughed. 'Get real, Dannie! I'm not asking those gals anything. What size should I look for?'

'Size 12 knickers and 34b bra.'

'12 knickers. 34b bra. I can't believe I'm doing this.'

'And you're definitely back on Monday?'

'Yes, ma'am.'

'Will you come straight here?'

'Much as I'd love to, I can't. I've to hit the

studio first. I should be through around seven.'

'I'll cook something for you.'

'I'll take you somewhere if you like.'

'No. I don't mind cooking again. In fact, I'd really enjoy that, Jethro.'

'Well, in that case I will accept your invitation with pleasure. Panties, 12. Bra, 34 – 34 – what was it you said again?'

'34b.'

'I'd better put it in my organizer. This is ridiculous. I can't believe I'm entering a dame's vital statistics alongside all the big budget figures for my movie.' But she could hear the smile in his voice. 'Here's my PA, now. I gotta go, Dannie. Enjoy your evening in with your girlfriends.'

Dannie was still wearing a half-wit's smile as she put the phone down and turned her attention to the pasta sauce on the hob. It had been great *craic* to take the afternoon off, to have a pub lunch with Rosa, wander into town and stock up on fresh grub for tonight and to browse through bookshops and boutiques and the lingerie department in Brown Thomas. Luckily, she hadn't felt tempted to splash out on anything. If Jethro was as good as his word, he'd come off the flight on Monday laden with Agent Provocateur carrier bags. He'd made her promise to model the purchases for him. The force of the sexual *frisson* she experienced at the prospect almost made her knees go.

Dannie twisted her hair into a knot on the top of her head, uncorked a bottle of wine, and swayed a little to the rhythm of the Buena Vista Social Club. She couldn't remember the last time she'd felt so happy! Her new fella was a man in a million. Flowers, dinner, and now lingerie! What could she buy him as a pressie in return? She'd never known what to buy for Guy on special occasions, but then Guy had very much 'eschewed materialism', as he'd put it. And then she remembered a gorgeous new coffee-table book on classic movies that she'd seen in a bookshop on Grafton Street that afternoon, and she knew it would be perfect. She'd nip in during her lunch break on Monday and buy it for him. She might even inscribe the flyleaf. Or was that getting too intimate? What would she write? To darling Jethro? To dear Jethro? To Jethro, the best ride ever? On second thoughts, she decided she'd leave the flyleaf blank.

He had asked her if she'd stay over at his hotel one night next weekend. He was staying in a suite in one of the most luxurious hotels in Dublin, the Hamilton, and Dannie was dying to check out the ambience of their bedrooms. She definitely intended spending Sunday morning having a leisurely breakfast in bed.

The doorbell rang. There was a knock at the door: it must be Rosa.

'Rosa-belle!' sang Dannie, letting her in.

'Thank *you*! Sauvignon Blanc – lovely!' She took Rosa's gift of wine and slid it into her fridge. 'Red OK for you?'

'Sure.'

'Well, sit down, mavourneen, have a drink and let me regale you with stories about my wonderful new man!' Since her phone call, Dannie had wanted to talk the hind legs off someone about Jethro. She wanted to share her happiness.

Rosa took a glass of red, and sat down by the fire Dannie had lit earlier. It was so comfortable here. So comfortable and so bohemian and so – so *perfect*. As perfect as Calypso's gaff, really, though in a very different way. She took a gulp of wine and managed a smile. 'Tell me all,' she said.

Dannie was grinding pepper into her sauce. She turned to Rosa with a big smile. 'Well, I'm cooking for him on Monday night, and on Saturday I'm going to stay over in his suite at the Hamilton! *Yes!* Breakfast and the Sunday news-papers in bed!' She was about to make a reference to rampant, glorious sex, but some-thing about the expression on Rosa's face told her not to go too overboard.

'The Hamilton? Cool,' said Rosa. 'Remember to bring your swimming togs.'

'There's a pool?'

'Yes. A really beautiful one.' Rosa had swum

there one afternoon with Calypso, who was a member of the very exclusive, very bijou gym – the Sybaris – that was located in the basement of the hotel. They had treadmills with little matt black tellies at the end of each one so that the keep-fit merchants could watch Sky News or MTV as they ran, and there was a beauty salon where Calypso went for her facials and treatments, and there was a steam room and a Jacuzzi and a sauna, and a relaxation area where newspapers and magazines were fanned out on a big glass table, and where a fruit bowl was piled high with grapes and nectarines and strawberries, and a pitcher of freshly squeezed orange juice was topped up every hour. Beauty products and towels were provided gratis in the changing rooms: big soft fluffy white bath towels with the Sybaris logo embroidered on them. Calypso had helped herself to three after her swim – one to dry her body, one to dry her hair and one to use as a mat, and then she had blithely slung the lot into the laundry basket. 'Calypso!' Rosa had chided her. 'Three towels! That's dead environmentally unfriendly.' And Calypso had balked, and looked guilty. 'You're right, Rosa. I will make myself manage with just two in future.' And Rosa thought with loathing of the awful frugality that prompted her to get as much usage out of her towels as possible before she consigned them to the laundry.

Now she thought of Dannie cavorting in the pool with her sexy new lover, and for the second time that day she hated herself for the spasm of jealousy Dannie's happiness afforded her.

'How's Lottie?' queried Dannie as she continued doing things culinary.

'She's fine. She was in a bit of a snit with me for leaving her this evening, but she cheered up when I told her she could watch a video. I'll go down and do her bedtime story later. God, that smells good, Dannie. What is it?'

'It's a kind of makey-uppy thing. I like pretending I'm Nigella Lawson when I sling something like this together.' I'll do that on Monday evening too, she thought dreamily. I'll do that suggestive finger-licking thing, and I'll throw my head back while I suck strands of pasta into my mouth, and I'll make those sexy, appreciative purring noises . . . Oh, *yes*! And I'll do something with chocolate for pudding . . .

The street doorbell rang. Dannie pressed the intercom to let Calypso up, then she topped up wineglasses and fetched another from the cupboard.

Calypso breezed through the door swinging expensive carrier bags and wearing her usual air of casual glamour. Inside, she was feeling anything *but* casual. On her way to Dannie's she'd received a text message from Leo. The message had fazed her badly: she couldn't decide whether it meant 'Lots Of Love' or 'Laughing Out Loud'. She hadn't texted him back.

'Hi, Dannie, hi, Rosa,' she said now, plonking kisses on their cheeks. 'Here you go, Dannie,' she added, handing over a classy-looking Bordeaux.

'You shouldn't have, Calypso. You're the one doing me the favour after all, returning my phone.'

'I'd better let you have it now in case I forget. Look! We have the same ones,' she said, producing them from her floppy suede satchel and setting them on the table. Rosa couldn't help noticing that both her friends had the latest must-have Nokias. Her own phone was neolithic by comparison.

'How do we tell the difference?'

'Easy.' Calypso tapped buttons and accessed her last message. *LOL. Leo.* 'This one's mine,' she said crisply, pressing 'erase message'.

Dannie tucked her phone into her pocket, then turned back to the stove.

'How've you been, Rosa mia?' asked Calypso. 'And how's my angelic godchild? I must go down to her later and steal a kiss. I've brought her a present.' She held up a carrier bag. BT2 – the most upmarket kids' clothes shop in town. 'I couldn't resist it – take a look!'

It was a little circular felt skirt trimmed with

velvet. It was exquisite. Rosa took the garment from Calypso and held it at arm's length. 'Oh, Calypso – you shouldn't have!'

'I wish you two would stop telling me what I should and shouldn't do,' shrugged Calypso.

'No – I mean, you *really* shouldn't have,' said Rosa. 'I've just got a load of the price.'

'Nosy Parker. Give me that!' Calypso snatched the skirt back from Rosa and bit through the plastic on the price tag before returning the garment to the carrier bag. She sat down beside Rosa on Dannie's couch. 'You still look a bit peaky, sweetie-pie,' she said. 'Haven't you shaken that cold yet? I was so sorry you missed the party last night. You would have met Dannie's new man – or have you met him already?'

Rosa shook her head. 'Haven't had the pleasure yet.'

'He's something else, the same Mr Palmer,' said Calypso, shooting Dannie a sly look. 'He looks pretty damn sexy wearing nothing but a towel around his waist.'

Dannie turned round from the stove, open-mouthed. 'What did you just say?'

Calypso sent her a cat-like smile. 'You heard.' Then she laughed. 'I saw him in the gym in the Hamilton the other evening. He'd come in for a steam and a massage. I'd discourage him from having too many massages there, Dannie. The masseuse is a stunner. Maybe you should suggest that he goes to Rosa instead.'

'I'd be cheaper, too,' said Rosa. 'I'm sure they charge an arm and a leg in that joint.' She gave a pallid smile. 'Sorry. Bad massage joke. Can I have some more wine, Dannie?' Dannie was folding tagliatelle into a pan of bubbling water. Rosa saw the sideways look she gave her as she ambled over to the counter to refill her glass. Neither Dannie's nor Calypso's needed refilling yet. 'I know I'm knocking it back a bit, but I've actually had a bitch of a day.' She tried to sound flippant, but the catch in her voice betrayed her.

'Oh, Rosa! What's happened?'

She put the bottle back down on the counter, took a deep breath and said: 'I committed professional hara-kiri this afternoon.'

'What? What do you mean?' Calypso reached out a hand and drew her back down beside her on the couch. Her concern was so palpable that Rosa felt even more tearful. 'What happened, Rosa?'

Dannie moved across from the kitchen area and sat down opposite them. 'Tell us all about it, sweetheart.'

And Rosa did. She told them everything. She told them about the humiliating phone calls and the vile receptionist and horrible Angela. She even told them how, before her final sortie into reception, she'd been thinking about guns. Now she gave a feeble, spluttery laugh as she told her friends that she had taken aim with arrant recklessness, and shot herself very accurately in the foot.

'The Definite Article's not the only agency in town,' soothed Calypso. 'You've a wonderful voice, Rosa! Why don't you ring round and tell everyone you've ever worked for that there's some vicious rumour going round town that you've taken yourself off the voiceover circuit, and that there simply isn't a word of truth in it?'

'You don't understand, Calypso. I *hate* making phone calls to agencies. Some of the receptionists have a brilliant knack of making you feel about the size of a flea when they find out that you're a mere voiceover artist and not some shit-hot client, and then my confidence just flies out the window.'

'You could send e-mails,' observed Dannie, reasonably.

'Or you could write,' enthused Calypso. 'I know it's more time-consuming, but it's so much more personal. People love to get handwritten notes these days. Use a fountain pen, and get some of that lovely handmade paper they have in the Pen Shop—'

'E-mail's cheaper,' Dannie quickly pointed out.

'It's no *good*!' Rosa took a big swig of red. 'Don't you see that it's not just Roydon Sneyde's stupid rumour! What I did this afternoon will be

271

all round town by Monday morning. I am in deep doo-doo, girls. You don't talk to *anyone* in accounts the way I talked to Angela. You don't barge into an upmarket reception area looking like a vagrant. And you never *ever* call the MD of a top advertising agency a brain-dead dickhead.' There was dead silence for a couple of seconds, and then Rosa started to laugh. Beside her Calypso bit her lip and exchanged glances with Dannie, and suddenly she was laughing too.

Dannie smiled. 'A brain-dead dickhead doesn't quite make sense, don't you know?' she mused. 'After all, don't most men *think* with their dicks?'

Now there was no holding back. The three of them laughed and laughed until tears were streaming down their faces. 'Oh, Rosa!' gasped Calypso. 'I'd love to have got a load of that Angela woman's expression when you told her to take her enormous arse back upstairs! Oh, you brave, brave girl!' She flung her arms around her friend's shoulders and gave her a big kiss on the cheek.

'I'm not sure I *was* brave, actually,' said Rosa. 'Just very, very stupid. It was the most foolhardy thing I've ever done in my life.' She drained her glass and held it out. 'May I have some more wine, please?'

'Of course you can,' said Dannie, peeling the foil off Calypso's Bordeaux. 'And it's about time you had some food to go with it. Grub's up. Sit down and help yourselves to salad.'

As Rosa drew up a chair to the table she found herself thinking how lucky she was to have two such good friends. She was feeling so much better now that she'd offloaded to them. A problem shared is a problem halved – isn't that what they said? It was true. Friends could help. Good friends really could help. Good friends, and good wine. 'It's weird, Dannie, isn't it?' she said. 'I mean, just this afternoon I was sitting in the pub with you, talking about what skills I had to fall back on – and now I suddenly find myself in a position where I really *am* going to have to fall back on them.'

'What do you mean?' asked Calypso.

'I mean, my dear chum, that I am going to have to start looking for some kind of a job pretty pronto.'

Dannie was doling pasta out onto plates, looking thoughtful. 'You have your massage certification, don't you?' she said. 'Couldn't you set yourself up working from home in a small way until this whole thing's blown over? In a few months people will have forgotten all about it, and in the meantime you could work from home as a massage therapist.'

Rosa looked dubious. 'I'm not sure. People often get the wrong idea, don't they? I mean, have you ever seen the small ads in *In Dublin*

273

magazine? I don't want a load of creepy dirty-raincoat types banging on my door.'

'You could put word out amongst friends, and make sure that everyone you see has references. That way you could keep it hidden from the tax-man too.'

'Dannie! That's not like you! You're usually so honest and above board about that sort of thing.'

'I know, sweetheart – but I've seen how you've had to contend with the kind of flak that women in your situation get. You know – the fact that you get virtually nothing from the social services—'

'*Nothing?*' interrupted Calypso. 'But you're a single parent. You must be able to claim something!'

Rosa shrugged. 'I may be a single parent, but I have an income.'

'But it's wildly erratic!'

'It's still an income. And I own my own home. I can claim bugger all, really.'

'Don't you get a children's allowance?'

Rosa raised an eyebrow at her. 'A hundred and seventeen euros a month?'

Calypso looked aghast. 'A hundred and seventeen euros a month? Hell's teeth! What do they expect you to buy with that?'

'They expect you to *buy* nothing. They just expect you to *get* by. That's why so many people lie and try to buck the system.' Rosa gave a great big, heartfelt sigh. 'It seems so unfair sometimes. I've been paying the taxman religiously for years.'

'That's what I mean,' said Dannie. 'Isn't it about time you got something back? Nobody need know you're working from home.'

'No. It's too dodgy,' put in Calypso with decision. 'No matter how kosher the connection, she'd still be letting strangers into her apartment.'

'I suppose,' conceded Dannie. 'It was thick of me to think of it, really. I was just trying to come up with some way of Rosa earning a few bob.'

'But,' said Calypso, retrieving her phone from her bag, 'I think I might have a better idea. Let me make a phone call.'

'Your dinner will get cold!' scolded Dannie.

'This will only take a minute.' Calypso pressed buttons. 'The Sybaris, please,' she said, giving Rosa a mysterious wink. 'Hello! It's Calypso O'Kelly here! Fine, thank you! And you? Good! Is Miriam free to talk? Thank you. I will.' Calypso put her hand over the mouthpiece. 'Hee hee,' she said. 'Sometimes I'm such a genius I impress even myself.'

'What is going *on*?' asked Rosa.

'You'll soon see! Miriam! Hello, honeybun. Yes, thank you. Now, listen to me. Have you found anyone yet? Yeah. Will you see someone I can wholly recommend? Absolutely kosher – letters after her name and everything. Yes indeed – loads of times. Tomorrow? Hang on—' she covered the mouthpiece again. 'How are you fixed tomorrow? Are you free?' she hissed at Rosa.

'Well, yes. Theoretically. If I can find someone to mind Lottie—'

'I'll mind her.' Calypso returned her attention to the phone. 'What time, Miriam? One thirty? Brilliant. Thank you – you are a star. See you soon. Bye!'

'Let us in on it, why don't you?' Dannie passed Rosa a lump of Parmesan and a grater.

'I have set up an interview for you,' announced Calypso, 'with Miriam Jerome, the beautician in the Sybaris.' She unfolded her napkin with a flourish.

'What's the Sybaris?' asked Dannie.

'It's the spa in the Hamilton hotel I was telling you about,' Rosa told her. 'Where you're going to be doing mermaid antics with lover boy on Sunday.' She turned back to Calypso. 'Why have you set up an interview for me?'

'Because Miriam has been run off her feet and is desperate for some back-up—'

'Wait – wait a second, Calypso. I'm a certified masseuse, not a certified beautician.'

'That's exactly what she's after. Apparently a visiting contingent of some American networking outfit have all received – as their annual productivity reward, no less – a package of three nights B&B at the Hamilton, with one massage included. They're arriving next week. Miriam's desperate. She can only accommodate one person at a time in the salon, so loads of guests will need to have their massages done in their rooms. She's lined one other girl up, but she needs someone else. And she told me that she could do with a back-up anyway – someone who could come in and do piecemeal work for her when she's oversubscribed.'

'Jayz, Rosa,' said Dannie. 'Piecemeal! This sounds dead-on! A bit like the way you do your voiceover work.'

'You're right.' Rosa looked thoughtful. 'Piecemeal's perfect. The thing is,' she said, hitting upon the spanner in the works that she knew was bound to be there somewhere, 'what if I have to turn round to this Miriam and say –' Rosa put on a singsong moany voice – ' "I'm sorry – I can't work for you today. I can't get a minder for my daughter." She's not going to take too kindly to that, is she?'

'Isn't Lottie old enough now to stay at home on her own?' asked Calypso.

'Absolutely not,' said Rosa, remembering the fateful events of the Day of Jeeves the Dog. 'Not for extended periods, anyway. And I don't want her being a latchkey kid.'

'I'll tell you what,' said Dannie. 'Train her to get the bus. Do the run with her a couple of times over the course of this weekend. Then, if you're called off to work, she can come into the shop and I'll keep an eye on her until you're finished.'

'I can't allow—'

'I wouldn't mind, honest!' Dannie intercepted Rosa. 'She won't get in the way. I'll fix up a corner for her in the back room and she can do her homework there.'

Rosa was uncertain. Everything was happening so fast that she was finding it hard to readjust. Her mother had always told her to embrace change, but this new set of circumstances was so scary . . . She knew Calypso and Dannie were observing her with keen anticipation, and she found herself wishing they hadn't picked her up and brushed her down so efficiently – she wasn't sure she could match their dynamism. Now, if things went wrong, she'd only have herself to blame. She took a sip of wine to buy time, casting around furiously to see if she could find any more spanners, but there was no sign of one. 'Well.' Rosa heaved a sigh. 'Well, well, well. All I can say is that you are two swell gals!' She raised her glass. 'Here's to your beauty and brains!'

'Here's to your new job!' corrected Calypso, chinking her glass against Rosa's.

'Calypso! I haven't even got through the interview stage yet.'

'Pshaw. I have no doubts that you will, Ms certified ITEC massage person.'

'Oh! Yikes. I've just thought of something.' Rosa adopted an expression of extreme trepidation.

'What is it?' asked Dannie.

'What if Roydon Sneyde's a member of your gym? I'd rather massage a crateload of slugs than massage him.'

'You could always do a Bobbitt and cut off his head,' suggested Dannie.

'But thingummyjig Bobbitt cut off her husband's dick,' said Calypso, looking perplexed.

'So you get my point then,' deadpanned Dannie. And for the second time that evening the three of them were rendered inarticulate by laughter.

The dishes had been cleared away, and Rosa was idly leafing through an *OK!* magazine that she'd purloined from one of Calypso's carrier bags. She'd noticed a stack of other glossies in there: *Hello!*, *Vogue*, *Elle*, *Marie-Claire*, and Condé Nast's *Traveller*, and had caught herself doing hateful sums again. She could feed Lottie for a week with what Calypso spent on magazines.

'How do you find time to get through so many magazines?' she asked, abstractedly noticing that she had pronounced the word 'magazheen'.

'I don't, really,' said Calypso. 'I just can't resist buying them. Then, when I get them home I flick through them and think, "oh I must get round to reading such-and-such an article", and I set it aside, and by the time the next *Marie-Claire* or whatever has hit the news-stands I still haven't read whatever it was I meant to read. I'm a total sucker for magazines. I feel horribly guilty when I trash them. I really must start recycling them.'

'You could recycle them to me,' said Rosa, who was having trouble focusing on the small print of a soap opera star's wedding. 'Unemployed single parents can't afford to buy magazheens.' Ooh, she thought. Am I sounding bitter and twisted here? And then she thought that, fuck it, she didn't care if she sounded bitter and twisted. She had every reason to be.

'Oh! All right. I'll do that,' said Calypso in the bright tone she used to disguise the guilt she inevitably felt when she compared her lifestyle with Rosa's. 'I've a pile of last month's at home that you can have. Remind me to give them to you tomorrow when you drop Lottie over. Oh – and I'll tell you what else I have. A big pile of chick fic that I was going to send to the Oxfam shop. I'll let you have those, too.'

Rosa curled her lip and squinted at Calypso. 'Ooh. Thanks so much, Lady Bountiful,' she said. 'I'm not a fucking charity case, you know.'

Ow! Calypso was wondering what was the best way to respond to this when her phone told her peremptorily that she had a new message. Glad of the distraction, she accessed it at once. She'd always found it difficult to handle Rosa when she was pissed, and Rosa got pissed so *easily*. Calypso prided herself that she could handle her drink. Occasionally she would match Dominic drink for drink just for the hell of it. She felt a rush of adrenalin when she saw that the text message was from Leo. Then: 'Oh!' she said. The horror must have shown in her expression, because Dannie immediately said: 'Bad news?'

'No – no,' stammered Calypso, executing a quick and extremely unconvincing cover-up. 'It's – um – just about something I forgot to do.' She turned the phone off and shoved it back in her bag, but the words that had appeared on the tiny screen still danced tauntingly across her mind's eye. *I'm fucking ur tasty little sec tonite. LOL.* Abruptly, she got to her feet. 'I'm going to have to go. Sorry.' She didn't have to go, but she was so upset and disturbed by the message that to sit here drinking wine and trying to be sociable was impossible. She gathered up the carrier bags, slung her satchel over her shoulder, and kissed her friends goodbye. 'You should get an early night, sweetheart,' she advised Rosa. 'Don't forget you've an interview tomorrow. I'll call you in the morning.'

Rosa felt guilty about being so mean earlier. Calypso really did look shaken. 'Are you sure you're OK?' she asked, with an expression of overdone solicitude. 'Nothing awful's happened to dear Dominic?'

'No, no – it's nothing. Honestly.' Calypso was backing towards the door.

'Don't forget your magazine,' said Rosa, holding out *OK!*

'It's all right – you keep it. And tell Lottie I'm sorry not to have been able to give her her present myself, but I'll see her tomorrow.'

'Tomorrow?' echoed Rosa in a puzzled voice.

'Calypso's looking after her while you do your interview,' Dannie reminded her discreetly, waving her fingers at Calypso who was disappearing round the door.

'Oh, yes! Oh – my interview. I'll drink to that. Cheers!' Rosa went to pour more wine into her glass, and peered at the bottle belligerently when she realized it was empty. 'Dammit. Shall we open another one, Dannie?'

Dannie shrugged apologetically. 'Sorry. I don't have any more,' she lied. The wine rack in her cupboard was laden with bottles, but she knew it was imperative to get Rosa to bed. She staged a yawn and looked at her watch. 'Holy God! Is it that time already? I'll have to hunt you, Rosa. I've an early start tomorrow.'

'I thought you didn't work Saturdays? C'mon,

Dannie. Let's celebrate my new job. I'll run downstairs and get a bottle.'

Dannie was going to have to be firm. 'Rosa, you've had enough. And Calypso was right. You should have an early night. You want to be on the ball for that interview.'

'Interview, schminterview. And Calypso's always bloody right. D'you know that – oops. Phone.' With difficulty, Rosa fished a bleating mobile out of her bag. 'Hello? Oh! Lottie! My baby! No, don't worry – Mummy's fine. Oh! Your story!' Rosa looked stricken. 'OK. Yes – I'm coming. Two minutes, angel.' Rosa stood up from the table and held onto the back of the chair. Then: 'Oh. Oh, Dannie,' she said, looking completely disorientated. 'Could you—'

Dannie took Rosa's bag from her and put her arm round her waist, encouraging Rosa to hook an arm over her shoulders. Together they left the apartment and took the lift to Rosa's floor. Even though it was only one storey down, Dannie didn't want to risk negotiating stairs. When they reached the flat, Dannie looked for keys in Rosa's bag, then inserted them in the locks.

'Sh!' said Rosa, holding a dramatic finger to her lips. 'Don't want to wake Lottie!'

They made stumbling progress towards Rosa's bedroom door. Dannie could see light coming from Lottie's door: she hoped the child would not emerge from her room until she had Rosa sorted out.

'Mum! Is that you?' called Lottie.

'Yes, indeedy!' Dannie answered for her, keeping her voice light and chipper. 'And it's me, Dannie, too. I'm just helping get your mammy to bed – she's not feeling too well. I didn't realize my cooking was *that* bad!'

Dannie manhandled Rosa into the room and onto the bed.

'No,' Rosa murmured, 'no bed. Have to tell Lottie her story, have—'

Dannie crouched down so that her face was on a level with her friend's. 'Rosa. Listen to me. Leave it.'

Rosa stuck her bottom lip out mutinously. She was having a great deal of trouble focusing on Dannie's face. Who was this person who was telling her what she could and could not do? How dare they interfere with her child and—

'Rosa!' Dannie's tone was a peremptory hiss. *'You must not let Lottie see you in this state. D'you understand? You mustn't upset her.'*

An expression of confusion flickered across Rosa's face, and suddenly, yes, she *did* understand. She allowed herself to be persuaded back against the pillows. She could feel someone's hands fumbling with the straps on her shoes – whose hands? Dannie's of course. 'Dannie?'

'Yes, mavourneen?'

Rosa could feel tears start to burn her eyes. 'Thank you, Dannie.'

'It's OK, mavourneen, *de nada*. Sure, you'd do the same for me.' And as Dannie backed away from the bed, she could see by the light coming in from the corridor the great tears that were starting to course down Rosa's cheeks.

Lottie was standing in the doorway, wearing Barbie pyjamas and holding onto the paw of her much-loved threadbare teddy. Dannie wondered how much the child had seen.

'Is Mum very sick, Dannie?' she asked. 'Does she need a doctor?'

'No, mavourneen. She just needs some rest. She had a busy day today and the bold thing didn't have enough to eat, and that's why the big feed of pasta I gave her didn't go down too well. Come here to me.' Dannie took the child by the hand that wasn't holding the teddy's paw and led her back to her bedroom.

'Oh. Oh, Dannie, I feel awful now.' Dannie felt a tug at her heart when she registered the anxious expression on Lottie's upturned face. 'I gave out to her when she was late picking me up from school. Poor Mum. I didn't know she wasn't feeling well.'

'She'll be right as rain tomorrow. I'll tell you what. I'll come down in the morning and make breakfast – how's that for an offer?'

'Pancakes?' Lottie brightened.

'Pancakes is a great idea. Now – whoosh! Under the duvet you go. There's a good girl.' Dannie pulled the duvet up to the child's chin. 'Now. How's about a story?'

Lottie considered, then shook her head with decision. 'No. I don't mean to offend you, Dannie, but Mum's in the middle of this really brilliant story at the moment, and another story would only get in the way of it, d'you know what I mean?'

'Mm. I think so.' Dannie smiled down at the pale little face. 'Nobody tells stories like your mam. I've heard her sometimes when I've been in the sitting room. Sometimes I've even tiptoed down the corridor to listen better. She should write them down some day, those stories.'

'Yes, she should,' agreed Lottie. 'And then she could be a millionaire like J. K. Rowling.' Another uncertain look crossed Lottie's face. 'Are you *sure* she's going to be all right?' she asked.

'Absolutely,' said Dannie. 'But because you're still a wee bit anxious, this could be a good thing to do. Where's your mobile phone?'

'Um. Over there somewhere.' Lottie indicated a pile of junk with a vague hand.

Dannie finally located the phone in one of Lottie's Irish dancing shoes. 'My number's on here, isn't it?' she asked.

'Yep.'

'Under M for Moore, or D for Dannie?'

'Both. You're under F for Florabundance, too. Mum put loads of numbers in when I got my phone. All my friends' mums' numbers are on there too.'

Dannie was impressed by the network of numbers she saw as she scrolled down the screen. So that was how mothers did it! It was evidence of an astonishing level of mutual support. 'OK. Here I am,' she said, when she'd accessed her home number. 'Now, look. I've dialled it. That means that if you have any worries at all, all you have to do is hit "redial" and I'll be downstairs in a jiffy.'

'Cool! Thanks, Dannie,' said Lottie, taking the phone and setting it on her pillow. Dannie noticed that the pillowcase was torn. Lottie held out her arms for a kiss, and Dannie snuggled up to her, inhaling her lovely child's scent and making growly noises. 'And Ted, too,' commanded Lottie, when they'd disengaged. Ted got similar treatment.

'Now. You've got your night light, and your mobile phone, and I'll leave the light on in the hall and in the kitchen just in case, so you'll be safe as houses and snug as a bug in a rug.'

'Why do they say that? "Safe as houses". Why isn't it "Safe as flats"? They're much safer. I heard it on the telly.'

'You're right. So did I,' said Dannie, who had

never heard any such thing. 'Flats are *much* safer than houses.' She gave the little girl one last kiss, then backed out of the room on soundless feet. 'Good night, Lottie. Love you.'

'Good night, Dannie. I love you too. And don't forget about the pancakes.'

'The pancakes,' said Dannie, 'are a solemn promise.'

She moved around the apartment, switching off lamps and making sure that nothing was plugged in that shouldn't be, and then she went back to Rosa's room. Rosa was lying on her back in exactly the same position as when Dannie had left her. The tears were drying on her cheeks, forming a trail of salty residue. Dannie tiptoed across the room, and as she tucked the duvet more snugly round Rosa's comatose form she was struck by how young she looked in repose – a child really, not much older than Lottie. She was on the verge of leaving when she realized that Rosa was saying something in a low voice. She leaned closer in to her, the better to hear.

'*She was walking through a prairie where the strangest birds she had ever seen were grazing,*' murmured Rosa. '*The map told her that this was the prairie of the semi-detached Phoenixes, and she knew that these weird creatures must be them. They were fearsome-looking, with big beaks and angry eyes, and they were stomping clumsily around in pairs, linked together with golden chains at the ankles. And then,*' *suddenly, out of the blue, flames went shooting out from one of the birds' bums, and she heard it squawk with embarrassment: "Oh! Pardon me!"'* Here Rosa went off into a peal of giggles, which within seconds had turned into a light, rhythmic snore.

Very quietly, Dannie left the room.

Upstairs, she surveyed the ruins of her meal. The pasta dishes were stacked in the sink, and there were the remains of cheese, and wine-glasses still on the table. She should really get the dishes out of the way, she thought, but she was feeling so bloody *tired* now! And she'd have to forgo her Saturday-morning lie-in and set an alarm so that she could get down to Rosa's flat and sort her out. She made sure that the spare key to Rosa's flat was hanging by the door where it should be, then took a second look at the detritus. Shite. She'd leave the tidying up. All she wanted to do now was sit down with a glass of wine and watch something mindless on the telly.

She cleared the empties off the table – they'd got through three bottles, she saw, most of it having been put away by Rosa – then uncorked a bottle of red from her stash, before settling down on the sofa with her zapper and *OK!* magazine. There was nothing worth watching on the telly. Even the Discovery Channel was crap tonight – another one of those awful things about tornadoes. She couldn't understand how people *watched* stuff like that, had never been able to tune in to the mindset of viewers who actually enjoyed watching the awful misery of human lives collapsing and victims weeping as houses and businesses were swept away into oblivion. She zapped the misery off and turned her attention to *OK!* That might be more uplifting.

The feature on the soap star's wedding didn't interest her – she'd had it up to here with soap stars. She turned the page and found more wedding coverage, and still more on the next page *and* the next. Finally she came to the last picture – which was of the soap star and her new husband (her third, according to a caption) careering off in a sports car to their honeymoon destination (Mauritius) with their friends and family grinning madly and waving goodbye. She turned the page to find an advertisement for Dolmio pasta sauces.

What she saw on the page opposite the pasta made a muscle in her gut go into spasm. '*Our Baby Joy!*' she read. She didn't bother to read on: it was the picture below the headline that had arrested her. There was a half-page colour photograph of the 'It' girl she'd seen in the *Guardian* with Guy some time ago. She was beaming to camera, her fingers with their peony pink-polished nails fanned out prettily over her swollen belly, and on the ring finger of her left hand she sported a fabulous jewel. Also splayed over her belly were the big, protective hands of her partner, who was embracing the pretty blonde from behind. His chin rested on her shoulder, his ruggedly handsome face was creased into a sexy smile, and his blue eyes were made more attractive still by the laughter lines that surrounded them – and that were a little more pronounced than the last time she'd seen him. It was Guy Fairbrother.

Calypso had walked from Dannie's flat. She hadn't bothered with a taxi, despite all the carrier bags. She wanted to walk and walk. When she became aware that her calf muscles were beginning to give her grief (never a good idea to walk much more than half a mile in Versace heels), she decided to stop at the Hamilton hotel for a restorative drink.

She ordered a large Remy Martin and sat in a corner nursing it, welcoming the heat of the liquid in her belly like an antidote to some stomach ailment. She was feeling distinctly bilious. Her stomach was churning in a way that she suspected might herald the beginnings of an ulcer. Calypso had never had an ulcer before in her life. What was happening to her?

She knocked back the brandy in small, rapid sips, then looked at her watch. It was late. She wanted to get back to Dominic. Her gorgeous, beloved Dominic. Maybe she'd suggest they share a hot tub together before bed? She felt the need to be cosseted and held, and there was no better place for that than the soothing warm water of the tub.

She got her stuff together, walked with aching feet out to the vestibule and asked the doorman to hail her a cab. Within minutes she was comfortably ensconced in the back of a people carrier, being whisked off to one of the most desirable homes in Dublin. She felt calmer, now. The brandy had helped; her biliousness had almost gone.

The intrusive sound of her phone made her jump and stiffen. She sat motionless for a minute, taking short, shallow breaths, regarding the urban landscape beyond the window with unseeing eyes. When she unclenched her fists and went to take the phone from her bag there were marks on her palms where her nails had been digging. She took a deep breath. Maybe she should just erase the message without viewing it? But what if it wasn't from Leo? What if it was from Dominic, or one of her true friends? She pressed a button. It was from Leo. Again, she hesitated. *Erase it. Erase it. Erase it,* her instinct urged her over and over. But what if it said something like: 'Don't worry! I was only messing about Iseult!' She shut her eyes and depressed 'read' with her thumb. When she opened her eyes she saw the following words, vividly displayed against the luminous green background: *God, was she good! Fingerlickingly fucking fabulous! A little plump guineafowl of a plat du jour! Care to join us for dessert, Ms O'Kelly?*

Calypso's hands flew to her mouth. She wasn't just feeling bilious any more. She was feeling positively nauseous.

Chapter Eight

The next morning Dannie was awoken from a bad dream by the persistent sound of her alarm. She hadn't been able to get to sleep for hours, and in the end had had to resort to a homeopathic sleeping tablet. She hated taking them because they made her feel so dozy the next day, but last night she had been so beleaguered by demons that oblivion was something devoutly to be wished for.

The knowledge that Guy had conceived a child with some blond bimbo of an 'It' girl had caused her the kind of searing anguish she had only experienced once before: on the night he'd sent her the fax that had ended their relationship. Last night she had hunched weeping over her laptop until nearly four o'clock in the morning, writing him a letter crammed with profanities and abuse.

The feature in *OK!* had been full of quotes

from Pelagia Brookes, the 'It' girl, waxing lyrical about Guy and their baby. 'He's going to make a wonderful father!' she'd gushed. 'He may look like a tough guy on the outside, but underneath he's just a big pussy cat!' No, he's not, thought Dannie. He's just a big feckin' bastard.

With a huge effort, she hauled herself out of bed. She was glad she'd made the promise to Lottie about the pancakes. If she hadn't had a reason to get out of bed this morning she'd probably have stayed there all day with the duvet over her head, the way she'd done after seeing that picture in the *Guardian*.

In the sitting room, Guy and Pelagia Brookes smiled up at her from the pages of *OK!* She picked the magazine up gingerly, as if contact with it might contaminate her. As she banished the evidence of Guy's betrayal to the bin, her eyes fell on one of Pelagia's more memorable quotes under a photograph of her lounging on a bed wearing a clingy, filmy thing that showed off her beautiful belly and her abundance of cleavage to perfection. 'I'm going to be an old-fashioned stay-at-home kind of wife, but I'm not going to let him off the hook when it comes to nappy-changing duties! I imagine nappy-changing might be daunting for even a hardened war correspondent like Guy Fairbrother!' Jaysus! Whatever attractions Pelagia may have held for Guy, it couldn't be her sense of humour, decided Dannie. She took great pleasure in scraping the remains of last night's dinner over Pelagia's picture.

So. The glib pronouncement she'd come out with yesterday was true. All men *did* think with their dicks. To judge from the photographs, Pelagia was not long out of her teens. Well, Guy Fairbrother! What a scoop! To have escaped from the clutches of a needy thirty-something career woman desperate for a baby, and to have landed in the soft lap of a peachy, fecund, biddable wifeen! Good old Guy must be the envy of all his bastard forty-something friends.

On the table in the sitting room, her laptop had shut itself down. She booted it up, accessed the bin where she'd dumped Guy's letter last night and pressed 'delete'. *Are you sure you want to delete 'Dear Gobshite from Hell'?* the computer asked her. She was sure. She didn't want to reread the poison that had come pouring out of her heart onto the screen in those agonizing hours before dawn.

Funnily enough, as she clicked smartly on 'yes', she had the really rather satisfying impression that she was finally deleting Guy from her life as well. All the spleen she'd vented in the letter must have had a cleansing effect, like colonic irrigation. Yes! Fuck the bastard. It was time to forget him, time to move on. Sure – wasn't there a new man in her life now that she was mad about? And *what* a man! Guy Fairbrother might consider himself to be an ultra-desirable überdude, she thought sneerily. Well, sorry, Guy, but they don't come much more über or desirable than Jethro shit-hot director Palmer!

She had a quick, ridiculous image of her and Jethro at the première of his epic movie, strolling hand in hand along a strip of cordoned-off red carpet, surrounded by paparazzi. Ha! What if a picture like *that* appeared in *Hello!* or *OK!* That would show that bastard war correspondent from hell just how well she was surviving without him. She banished the image back to Doolally land where it belonged, because she knew that even in the unlikely event of her fantasy coming true, Guy would never see the picture, because he never read *Hello!* or *OK!* Huh! She bet that pretty little Pelagia read nothing more demanding than gossip columns, though – if, Dannie thought even more sneerily, the bimbo bridelet could read at all . . .

'Rosa? Rosa?' She felt a hand on her shoulder, gently shaking her. It was her mother, telling her it was time to get up, time to go to school. No! She didn't want to go to school today! She was so comfy and warm in bed, and besides, she realized, she wasn't well. She had a headache, and a dry throat. She couldn't go to school if she wasn't well . . .

'Rosa!' The voice was more insistent now, and it wasn't her mother's voice, it was – she opened her eyes and gazed dully at the face that owned the voice until it came into focus. It was Dannie. And she, Rosa, wasn't a little girl. She was a grown-up with responsibilities and a lot of problems, and a nine-year-old daughter to look after.

'Hi,' she croaked.

'Hi,' said Dannie back.

Rosa shut her eyes again. She swallowed. There was a vile taste in her mouth. 'Oh, fuck,' she said. 'I'm so sorry.'

'It's OK.'

'Is Lottie awake?'

'Not yet. I'm just going to make us some breakfast and then I'll rouse her.'

Rosa drew in a deep breath, as if by doing so she could magic energy from somewhere, and then she sat up very slowly. 'I'm sorry,' she said again. 'Was I awful?'

'No, acushla,' answered Dannie, truthfully. 'You were just very sad.'

'Oh!' Rosa looked at her friend with stricken eyes. 'I think I'd rather have been awful.'

'I know. The truth hurts, sometimes, doesn't it?' A slightly awkward silence fell, then Dannie leaned forward and took her friend's hand. 'Oh, Rosa! You must promise me – for Lottie's sake – you mustn't ever do that again. *Ever*.'

'I know I mustn't.' Rosa nodded. 'It was just

that yesterday was such a bitch of a day . . .' She cleared her throat, then blinked a bit. 'What did you tell Lottie?'

'I said that you were sick. I blamed my cooking.'

Rosa managed a wan smile. 'You are a true chum, Dannie. I don't know what I'd do without you. And Calypso.' The smile disappeared. 'Oh! Calypso! I've to see her today for some reason, haven't I? Something to do with books . . . ?'

'Um. This is the bad news. You've an interview at 1.30.'

'An interview? Oh fuck! Oh, yes, of course! The Sybaris. Oh, Jesus, Dannie – how am I going to pull this one off?'

'You'll do it. You'll need some nutrition first, though, to set you up. I'm on breakfast detail. Look. I brought you some pink grapefruit juice.' Dannie nodded towards a glass on the bedside table. 'And Solpadeine.'

'Thank you, thank you, thank you.' Rosa took the glass of grapefruit juice and drained it. 'Christ, that was good. But I'm not sure I could manage anything solid.'

'You are having breakfast, Ms Elliot. You need food in your belly. I promised Lottie pancakes.'

'Eugh! Oh, Jesus, Dannie, no. Don't make me eat pancakes, please.'

'Oh, all right then. But I'm going to boil you an egg. And you might manage some toast?'

'I'll try. You're being so good to me, Dannie – but oh, *God*, I feel wretched!' She reached for the Solpadeine.

'Give the drugs ten minutes to kick in, then go and wake your babba.' Dannie stood up from her hunkered position. 'I'll put the kettle on. D'you want coffee or tea?'

'Tea, please,' said Rosa meekly.

After Dannie had gone, she lay on in bed for some minutes, not wanting to think about last night, and knowing she had to. How much had she drunk? Which glass of wine had toppled her over the edge? She remembered sharing her sorrows and then having a laugh with Dannie and Calypso, and then the evening became full of blank bits. Calypso was there, and then gone suddenly, and she remembered that Calypso had seemed upset for some reason. Oh, fuck! Was it something Rosa had said to her? Did she owe her an apology? Then she recalled being in bed, and Dannie's face, and the words that had come out of Dannie's mouth. *You must not allow Lottie to see you in this state. Do you understand? You mustn't upset her . . .*

Lottie. She wanted to see her baby, hold her in her arms. Shaking her head to try and rid herself of hateful thoughts, Rosa dived into the bathroom, showered, washed her hair and cleaned her teeth. She was going to have to do a bloody good job with her make-up today, she thought as she peered at her reflection in the mirror over the basin.

Lottie's room was in a total state, but she wouldn't give out to her today. Rosa leaned over her child's bed and smiled at her drowsy miracle. Her daughter's face – usually rather pale – was flushed and rosy with sleep. Her eyelashes fanned out across round cheeks, her ears were more perfect than shells, her rosebud mouth too kissable to resist. Rosa didn't resist it. 'Wake up, sleeping beauty,' she said in her sweetest, lowest voice. 'It's Mummy here. Mummy, who loves you.'

Calypso woke up feeling wretched. She lay beside her sleeping husband for a while, thinking hard. What Leo had done to her last night was abominable. How dare he harass her by sending her stupid text messages? How dare he – how *dare* he seduce her secretary? She remembered what he'd said to her at her party, about Iseult being a virgin still, and the thought of what Leo might do to her frightened her. Iseult was such a naïve little thing, really – she was incredibly vulnerable. And then she remembered Dannie's remarks at the party – *They make a stunning couple, don't they?* – and the tug of jealousy she felt frightened her almost as much as the notion of Leo deflowering her secretary.

Change the subject, change the subject, *change*

the subject. Calypso screwed her eyes tight shut for an instant, then turned her head on the pillow and studied Dominic's profile. How patrician he was. She knew that loads of her girlfriends fancied the arse off Dominic and would probably jump if he gave the slightest indication that he might be interested in a bit on the side. Loads of her girlfriends were jealous of her. She knew that for a fact, and she didn't give two hoots, because she, Calypso O'Kelly, was the cat who'd got the cream! Wasn't she?

Sometimes Calypso wished she had a girlfriend as lucky as she was, so that she could share her happiness with someone. She'd love to be able to come out with stuff like: Hey! Guess what! I've just been asked to cast the new Neil Jordan film, and I'm going to spend a fortune in the Brown Thomas designer room today, and then I'm going out to lunch with some mega-rich celebrities, and then I'm going to book our annual Christmas holiday in Bali, and then I have to go to a funky exhibition opening, and then I'm going out to dinner in Le Blazon with my gorgeous husband. What are *you* doing today?

Somehow, she didn't think she'd ever find a friend that she could talk to like that. And it was doubly tragic that, of all her friends, it was her best friend to whom she could least afford to confess her happiness.

And then it occurred to her with a stab of

vindictive delight that actually, yes, there *was* a person she could call this very morning and have that conversation with. That person was her mother. She hadn't spoken to Jessica for ages – it was about time she gave her a bell. Calypso narrowed her eyes, weighing pros against cons. Did she dare? The last time she'd plucked up the nerve to speak to her mother she'd thought she was feeling strong, but when she'd put the phone down she'd dissolved into such floods of tears that she'd been practically unable to walk. Dominic had helped her upstairs and tucked her into bed with a hot-water bottle. Darling Dominic! She turned to look at him again, smiling at her good fortune to be married to this tower of strength, and then she stretched and yawned and squirmed like a cat.

Still half asleep, Dominic turned his head and looked at his wife through half-shut eyes. 'Oh, fuck,' he said. 'You're so fucking beautiful. Do you know that?'

'No, no! Shut up!' she said, covering her face with her hands.

But Dominic pulled them away. 'Come here,' he said.

And some minutes later, as her husband was thrusting himself into her, an image of Leo fucking her, thrusting into her the way Dominic now was, came unbidden into her head and, try as she might, she could not banish it.

* * *

'Hello.' Rosa was standing on Calypso's doorstep, looking abashed. 'I'm really truly sorry if I said anything to offend you last night.'

'Oh, shut up and come in, Rosa. You've already apologized over the phone. We all say things we don't mean when we're –' Rosa flashed Calypso a glance that warned her to be circumspect '– when we're feeling a bit under the weather,' she amended. 'Hello, darling Lottie! Kiss me at once!'

Lottie obliged. 'Thank you for the skirt!' she sang. 'Look! I'm wearing it!' She peeled off her coat.

'Hey! It looks wonderful on you. I knew it would. Do a twirl.' Lottie obliged again. 'Oh, little Carlotta Elliot – you do the best twirls of anyone I know. When you grow up you could be a supermodel.'

Lottie gave her a scathing look. 'No way! I'm not going to allow myself to be exploited. I'm going to be President.'

Calypso laughed. 'Way to go, Lottie! You certainly do live up to your name, don't you? Run it by me again?'

Lottie had it off pat, now. She cleared her throat before declaiming: ' "One who is all that is feminine, but who rules and controls." '

'You're that all right, darling girl!'

'What does "Calypso" mean?' asked Lottie.

'Let me tell you exactly who Calypso was,' said Dominic, who had just come into the hall from the kitchen. He hunkered down so that his face was on a level with Lottie's. 'Calypso was a beautiful sea nymph, a goddess who seduced the great Greek hero Odysseus and kept him captive in her far-away island kingdom for years until he tired of her embraces, and Zeus ordered her to let him go. I have a book all about it in my study. Do you want me to find it so you can read about their adventures?'

'Yeah. Cool,' said Lottie. 'I love adventure stories. My mum tells me a brilliant one every night. She could be the new J. K. Rowling, you know.'

'Tell her to write her story down,' said Dominic. 'I have friends in high places in the publishing world.' He stood up and looked at Rosa. 'My osteopath has just signed a three-book deal with a major publishing house in London. He's been writing thrillers in his spare time. Maybe you should give it a bash, Rosa.'

'I wish I *had* spare time,' said Rosa, with a self-deprecating shrug.

'Well! Imagine if J. K. Rowling had had that kind of defeatist attitude,' said Dominic. Oh! Why did he always make her feel so *pathetic*? 'Come with me, little Lottie,' he said now, leading the way into his study, 'and I will find the book for you. I think by some extraordinary coincidence that there may be Rolos in here too – that is, if Rolos are OK by your mum?'

Rosa nodded. 'They're OK. Thanks, Dominic.'

'Coffee's made, sweetheart,' he said over his shoulder to his wife.

Something about the look they exchanged made Rosa certain that they'd had sex this morning. Sex! It had been so long since she'd had sex that she'd forgotten what it felt like. Sometimes she wondered if she'd ever have sex with anyone ever again in her life. Calypso certainly had a post-coital look about her. Her mane of Jemima Khan-esque hair was gloriously tousled, her lips were bee-stung, and she was still in her kimono.

'Have you time for a coffee before you go?'

Rosa shook her head. 'I'd love one, but I want to get there early. Make a good impression.'

'You're right. There's no need to be nervous, you know. Miriam's a perfect honeybun. How are you feeling, by the way – after last night?'

'Not half as ropy as I felt first thing this morning. Dannie was a trouper. And you're a star for setting this whole thing up, Calypso, and for taking Lottie.'

'No problem.' Calypso yawned and stretched languorously before moving to a massive vase of arum lilies that stood on the hall table and removing a stem that looked a bit droopy. 'I'd better give

Florabundance a ring and ask them to send round more flowers. These are a bit tired-looking. Sometimes they don't last the whole week if I forget to top up the level of the water –' Calypso broke off, and Rosa could tell that she was regretting this reference to her weekly flower deliveries. How Rosa wished the money thing wasn't a problem! How she wished that Calypso didn't always have to be on guard around her, feeling guilty every time she let slip some reference to her great good fortune.

'I'd better go,' she said, leaning forward and kissing Calypso on the cheek. 'Thanks for everything, Calypso, you star. I'll see you later.'

She turned and walked down the Zen pathway, but before she'd made it to the gate, her friend was at her shoulder again. 'Here!' she said, pressing a tiny package into her hand. 'I nearly forgot.'

'What is it?' asked Rosa curiously, unwrapping tissue paper. Then she smiled. She took the tiny object between finger and thumb and examined it. It was the kind of little ornament you get on charm bracelets – a representation in gold of the theatrical masks of comedy and tragedy.

'It was my grandmother's,' said Calypso, smiling. 'For luck.'

Rosa smiled back, and then she slid the miniature talisman into her pocket and moved on down the pathway, hoping it was taking her in the direction of some not-too-far-in-the-distant-future happiness.

Calypso had been right. Miriam *was* a honeybun. She was a pretty, dark-skinned girl, with eyes so candid they verged on the disconcerting, and she had a great laugh. She had shrugged a coat on over her beautician's pale pink uniform when Rosa had arrived at the Sybaris, and taken her to the coffee shop across the way to conduct the interview over a cappuccino. Once there, the first thing she'd done had been to take hold of Rosa's hand to assess her grip. 'I'm glad to see short nails and no rings,' she said, producing a phial of oil from her pocket and handing it across the table. 'Give me a quick hand massage,' she challenged. 'I like to see if I can learn anything new from another practitioner.' Rosa could tell it was a tactful ploy of Miriam's to ascertain whether or not she had what it takes.

She poured a small amount of oil onto her palm, rubbed her hands together to warm them, and took hold of Miriam's left hand while the girl watched her carefully. Miriam kept up a murmured running commentary while Rosa worked. 'Effleurage . . . Good. Friction . . . Interlace fingers . . . Mobilize and stretch . . . Good.'

After she had gently stretched and eased each finger, Rosa performed a small twisting motion, scooping out any bad karma that might have accumulated in the joints, and throwing it away from her, towards the light that streamed in through the window of the café.

'Hey! You do that thing too!' said Miriam. 'I approve! Not everybody does that. Good. And the palm, now. Good . . . Good . . . Final effleurage. Great. Now show me your certification.'

Rosa wiped her hands on a paper napkin and produced the ITEC cert. that she'd spent half an hour rummaging through her bureau to locate earlier that morning.

Miriam scanned the sheet of paper. 'ITEC. Kosher. This is to certify . . . blah, blah, blah. OK.' She raised her eyes and gave Rosa the benefit of her beautiful candid gaze. 'The job's yours.'

'What?'

'The job's yours.'

'Well!' Rosa was completely taken aback. 'You certainly don't beat about the bush—'

'What's the point? I never bullshit. I like you. I like your eyes. They tell me you have integrity, and that's important. Plus, you've got the touch, Rosa. You could have all kinds of impressive initials on your cert., and still cut no ice with me.'

'But – don't I have to meet the manager, or someone else – well –'

'More in authority?' Miriam gave her an

amused look. 'You *will* meet them, later. But if I say you're kosher, Rosa, they'll take my word for it. They value my opinion, they need someone in a hurry – and they're even more eager to keep me happy since I was headhunted.'

'Oh?'

'Yeah. A resort in Antigua offered me the managership of their salon.'

'*Antigua?* What on earth persuaded you to stay on in Dublin?'

'I like my job here. I like my regular client base. And I'm in love with a Dub.' Her smile said it all. 'When can you start?' she asked.

'Whenever you like. Oh, Miriam, thank you so much! I'm so glad Calypso made that phone call.'

'That was a character reference in itself. Calypso wouldn't have recommended you if she didn't know you were good. Now. What do you need to know? Money, obviously. It's forty euros an hour. More for a full body massage, but the hotel takes a cut. If you're as good as your word and can come in at the drop of a hat we can negotiate the cut downwards. Does that sound OK?'

'That's cool,' said Rosa, not allowing herself to think of the kind of money her CD-rom work had afforded her.

'There'll be tips as well, of course, and I'll kit you out with a uniform. Get a load of what you'll be wearing every day from now on.' Miriam struck a pose. 'Da dah!'

Rosa smiled. 'Could be worse. Could be lime green. *So* not my colour.'

'You'll know to wear sensible shoes. Scholls or whatever. A minimum of make-up – the wealthy older broads don't like competition. Discretion is mandatory. No gossiping to *anyone* about the celebs who stay here – and some of them are pretty stellar. Gossip's a firing offence. And remember to keep all the buttons on your uniform done up. Not an excess inch of cleavage or thigh is to be displayed, otherwise you could be sending out the wrong signals to our male clients.'

'Oh. You mean, they might expect more than just a massage?'

'Damn right.'

'It's an occupational hazard, I suppose. Do men come on to you a lot?'

Miriam shrugged. 'Not really. Most of the clientele is sophisticated enough not to expect sex for sale in a five-star hotel. Some of them try it on, but as soon as you make it quite clear that it's not on the menu, they back off. If things get really serious, you can always call the manager. I had to do that quite recently, actually. It was a really horrible experience.'

'What happened?'

Miriam shook her head. 'I shouldn't tell. It might put you off!'

'Oh, go on. You should fill me in on the pitfalls as well. Forewarned is forearmed, and all that.'

'OK.' Miriam leaned her elbows on the table and looked around to make sure no-one was ear-wigging. 'Well. This American geezer had booked himself in for a full body massage. It was weird – you can usually tell the jerks who are going to be a problem, but this guy seemed OK. We chatted about the usual things, you know – was it his first time in Ireland, how did he find the weather, the people, the traffic, blah, blah, blah. And then he starts telling me how gorgeous I am, and did I ever think of getting into the movies, and how he could arrange for me to get work on his film as an extra.'

'He's in the movies?'

'Yeah. He's a director. He's working on some epic that's being filmed out in Ardmore Studios. So naturally I was quite flattered – I've always fancied the idea of being in the movies – so I said yeah, I was interested. And then he tells me he's going to be filming a brothel scene next week, and he tells me how great I'd look in one of those corsets like Nicole Kidman wore in *Moulin Rouge*, and I started to hear warning bells. I'm working away on his upper thigh at this stage, and I can tell he's getting aroused. So I try and ignore it for a while because sometimes the trouser snake loses interest when it's made perfectly clear that nothing's going to happen.

And then he comes right out and tells me that if I give him a "relief" massage he'd make it worth my while. So I just told him that we weren't that kind of a joint, and that if he came out with any more suggestions like that, I'd call the manager. And then, when I was working away on his thigh, he let out a grunt, and then he grabbed my hand and held it against his dick.'

Rosa covered her mouth with her hands. 'Ew, Miriam! Gross! What did you do?'

'Man, I was out of there like a bat out of hell. Went straight to the manager and reported it, and said I would not continue.'

'Did the manager sort it?'

'Yeah. They're diplomatic wizards. Of course the geezer claimed I had over-reacted, but I'm telling you something, Rosa, I will not go near that slimeball again.'

'What's *with* men like that? Is it some kind of a power thing?'

'I guess. They'd never dream of getting away with that sort of behaviour with anyone else. They just expect a pretty girl in a beautician's uniform to put out at the drop of a hat – especially when she's offered a part in a movie.'

'Is he still staying in the hotel?'

'Yeah. A few of the stars are staying here too – you'll probably get a call from Jeanne Renaud.'

'I hope I don't get a call from him.'

'I don't think he'd chance his arm again. He's

tried to book me since, but I told management there's no way I'd go near him. It hasn't put him off trying, though. He came down to me one day with a huge box of handmade chocolates, and spun this spiel about how I was the most accomplished masseuse he'd ever visited, and wouldn't I forget the "unfortunate incident", and reconsider. You should have seen the look he gave me when I said no. Scary.'

'But, Miriam – that's harassment. Can't you report him for that?'

'Oh, what's the point? I just get on with it. *He's* the sad bastard, not me. I *have* a life. A bloody good one.' Miriam gave a big, self-satisfied smile, waved at the waitress to bring the bill, and produced her purse.

'Let me get this,' said Rosa, picking up her bag.

'Not at all. This is my shot. You can get me again.'

'Well, thank you.'

While Miriam settled the bill, Rosa visited the loo. She didn't need to pee – she just wanted to wash her hands. She soaped them twice and then rinsed them thoroughly, murmuring 'Discard! Discard!' to herself as she sluiced water over her wrists and forearms. Cleansing and discarding bad karma was an important part of the massage ritual for her. But she wasn't concentrating very hard right now. Something was niggling at her: an unpleasant little thought.

Miriam had her coat on when Rosa emerged from the loo. 'Now, come and meet the rest of the happy campers in the Sybaris,' she said.

'It must be great working there,' replied Rosa, shrugging her own coat on. 'It's so luxurious.' Rosa pictured herself moving around the Sybaris kitted out in her pale pink uniform and Dr Scholl sandals, carrying piles of fluffy white towels for her glamorous clientele.

'Mm. But remember you won't be working in the Sybaris itself. You'll be visiting clients in their rooms. Do you have your own massage plinth, by the way?'

'Yes.'

'Portable?'

'Mm hm.'

'Another plus! You don't mind bringing it with you, occasionally, do you? We could use a spare one when we're busy.'

'Sure,' said Rosa, absently. She was finding it difficult to let go of the thought that had taken a nagging hold of her. 'Miriam? You know the client you were telling me about? The sleaze merchant?'

'Yeah?'

'What was his name?'

Miriam raised an eyebrow and tapped her nose with an index finger. 'Remember what I told you earlier? I am paid to keep my lip well zipped, Rosa.'

But as Rosa followed Miriam's trim figure across the road and down the steps to the Sybaris, she found herself adding things up and coming to an extremely unpleasant conclusion. The sleazebag Miriam had told her about could only be Jethro Palmer.

Chapter Nine

Calypso hadn't heard from Leo since he'd sent her those vile text messages on Friday night. Late on the following Monday afternoon he came to her office.

Iseult had been on cloud nine all day after a weekend spent with her new boyfriend. She had floated round the office like something out of a frothy romantic comedy. She'd been more painfully upbeat than ever: she didn't speak – she *sang*; she didn't walk if she could dance; she took to humming endlessly some frightful aria that she called 'their' song. And now Calypso heard her secretary's squeal of delight as Leo announced himself over the speaker. Instantly she left the reception area where she'd been about to get into her coat, dived into the sanctuary of her office and shut the door.

Some minutes later, Iseult's voice came through the speaker on her desk. 'Leo's here to see you, boss!' she trilled. Calypso didn't have time to dream up an excuse not to let him through, because the door opened and in he ambled.

'Hello, Calypso,' he said, not bothering to shut the door, then sitting down opposite her without waiting to be asked. 'That was an absolutely super-dooper party last week. I've come to take you out for a drink to say thank you.'

'I've got an engagement,' she lied. 'I can't get out of it.'

'Yes, you can. Iseult told me you were on your way home to watch *Coronation Street*. I don't call that a pressing engagement. Come for a drink with me. We've a lot to talk about, you and I.'

Iseult came through the door with a Post-It note for Calypso. 'Do go, Calypso,' she said. 'I'll wrap up here. And – oh! Yikes! I nearly forgot to tell you. Dominic rang from London to say that he's had to postpone his flight. He'll be taking the red-eye tomorrow instead.'

'Thanks, Iseult,' she said, wishing that her secretary hadn't let slip the information that her husband was out of town.

Iseult handed her the Post-It and whisked out of the room, sending Leo a radiant smile over her shoulder.

'Come on, Calypso. Let's go get that drink.' Leo stood up and held out a hand to her. Numbly, she took it, reminding herself that all she was doing was going for a drink with a client.

In the Octagon, he ordered champagne for her and a pint of Guinness for himself. Then he lounged back on the banquette and looked at her.

'What do you want to talk about?' she asked him curtly.

'I have a proposition to make to you, Ms O'Kelly,' he said.

'Shoot.'

'Before I make it, I want to tell you about the lovely weekend I spent with your secretary. Do you want to know what we got up to?'

'Not especially.'

'I'll tell you anyway. I want to come clean, because I told you a fib. Naughty, naughty me! I texted you on Friday that I'd fucked her. That was a little joke. The truth is, I didn't fuck Iseult on Friday. I fucked Jeanne Renaud. But Jeanne was going back to see her boyfriend in France the next day, so I rang Iseult and asked if she'd like to go out on a date. Jolly dee, she was free, so on Saturday evening we went to the movies, and then for something to eat. I dropped her home in a taxi, and we had a little snog in the back seat. I will confess that I could not resist having a grope of her glorious titties, but that's as far as it went.'

'Leo. I don't think I want to hear this,' said

319

Calypso tersely. 'Your love life is of exceptionally marginal interest to me.'

'I beg to differ, Calypso. I think it might be of *considerable* interest to you. To continue. On Sunday Iseult borrowed her daddy's car, and I drove her out to the country for a walk. It was a *beautiful* day yesterday, and we did the kind of stuff couples do in films – all that romantic video interlude crap, you know? Holding hands, swatting each other playfully, blah, blah, blah. The little lambs that were frolicking in the fields were nearly as frisky as Iseult was when I chased her into the woods and stole another kiss. She allowed me another grope, and I showed admirable restraint by continuing to confine myself to her tits.' He gave Calypso an assessing look, and then said: 'Now. This is where my proposition comes into play. I told you once I reckoned I could have Iseult Morgan. And I don't just reckon – I *know* I could. I could phone her this minute and she would come running. I don't think she'd even mind missing *Coronation Street* for an opportunity of being shafted by me.'

'Jesus! You're unspeakable!'

'Yes, I am,' he replied equably. 'I was born without a conscience. I am capable of doing *quite* unspeakable things to that girl. I am capable of doing to her all the things that you secretly want me to do to you. And afterwards I will drop her in the trash, and laugh when she begs me to take her back. I will do all these things and more. I will destroy that pretty little poppet, princess. Unless ... And I'm confident that, as a concerned and responsible boss, you'll want to know what that "Unless" is.'

Calypso was watching him with a fascinated repugnance. 'What?'

'I will back off Iseult if you give yourself to me. You see, I want to possess you entirely, Ms O'Kelly. I want to fuck you in a thousand different ways, each more depraved and lurid than the last. I want to make you come and come and come again when you think you can't come any more. *I want to smear your lipstick, Calypso.*'

Oh, *Jesus*!

'What do you say? Is it a deal?'

'Dear God – this is preposterous, Leo! You can't mean this—'

'Oh yes, I can, Calypso. You know I can.' He took a swig of his pint and regarded her over the rim before setting it down and wiping his mouth with the back of his hand. 'And you're hot to trot, sweetheart.'

'How dare you!'

'I *dare*, Calypso, because I suspect I *know* you. Shall I tell you some of the things I suspect I know about you? I suspect that you give excellent head because it's a good way of keeping hubby happy. I suspect that you fantasize about me when hubby fucks you. And I also suspect that you're soaking wet. I'll check that out in the privacy of the taxi.'

'What? What are you talking about?'

'The taxi we're taking back to my gaff. Finish your drink and we'll go.'

It wasn't knocking back her champagne that made the course of events over the next half-hour hazy. Leo was right. Calypso was so muzzy with sexual arousal that she almost came when he put his hand between her legs in the taxi and said: 'I told you so.'

In his friend's flat, Leo shut the door and looked at Calypso hard for a moment or two. 'Lucky lady. You're in for the most mind-blowing fuck of your life. I think you'd better brace yourself, darling.'

He strode towards her, grabbed her by the wrists, thrust her down so that her face was pressed hard against the arm of the sofa, and forced up her skirt. Pulling her panties aside, he rolled on a condom and entered her roughly, with no preamble, no soft words.

And suddenly, to her incredulous, appalled horror, Calypso found herself crooning with pleasure. Moaning and crooning, she urged him on as he fucked her hard and rhythmically to an exquisite, racking, tumultuous climax – a climax so beyond intense it made her nerve endings fizz and her skin sing. And as he came and she heard that luxurious growl low in his throat, she felt a surge of joyful gratification that she had been responsible for inducing it. Such gratification that when he'd finished she traced the curve of his cruel mouth and found herself murmuring: 'Thank you. Thank you. Oh, thank you so much, darling.'

She stayed there for several hours. They took their time to discover each other, and she was glad to see that she afforded Leo almost as much pleasure as he did her. She remembered something a famous rock chick had once said in an interview about a new lover, something along the lines of: 'The first time we went to bed he did at least five things to me that I'd always thought were illegal.' Leo was similarly revelatory, alternating cruelty with kindness, praise with scorn. Sometimes he'd be brutal with her, laughing low in his throat when he saw how fervently she responded to a bit of rough, and muttering something guttural when she came. Other times he treated her with such languorous, sensuous expertise that she felt svelte and lissom and deliciously malleable under his touch, as if she were being sampled by an epicure. He would run appreciative hands and eyes over every inch of her body, and taste every inch of it, too, treating her to the tantalizing expertise of his tongue. He even tasted her toes, and didn't seem to notice how ugly her feet were. One minute he'd lavish her with terms of endearment, the next he'd shower her with unspeakable insults. He called her angel and whore, bitch princess and yum-yum tart. He called her baby sweetheart and lady love and honey and poppet and *poule de luxe*.

'There's nothing sexier in the world than watching a woman come,' he said, when she'd re-entered the stratosphere. She was lying in his arms, slick with sweat and limp with post-coital lethargy. 'I have to compliment you on your performance, princess. You come beautifully.'

'It wasn't a performance,' she said, with mild indignation. 'I couldn't fake that.'

'I know,' he said. 'I'm a connoisseur.' She felt even more miffed now, when she thought of all the women he must be able to compare her with, and then she told herself to wise up. What was the point of getting het up over his other women? It wasn't as if they had a *relationship*. Or did they? She felt strangely comfortable to be with him now that all the preliminary pussy-footing and protesting of the past few weeks was out of the way.

'I must remember to get more condoms,' he said, slinging an empty sachet into the waste-paper basket. 'You might start carrying them too, Calypso, to be on the safe side.'

Well! The arrogance of the man! What made him think she was going to behave like some kind of slapper, carrying condoms around with her on the off chance that he might fancy a ride? She gave him a supercilious look, but then remembered that she was no longer in denial, and there was no point in pretending any more.

'Unless of course,' he continued, studying her expression with amused eyes, 'you don't *want* me to fuck you again.'

He was looking down at her with what could only be described as an awful *knowingness*. And now Calypso knew what he knew. She knew that she was his plaything, his instrument; he was a maestro who knew exactly which stops to pull and which keys to press to make her sing. He could look straight into her heart and see the shame there, and the wretched swollen libido. He could read her like sheet music and play her like a cello.

And then he did something so incredible with his fingers that Calypso found herself saying: 'Oh! Oh, God, yes!'

'Yes, what? Say it.'

'Yes, I do.'

'You do? What do you want me to do?'

'I want you to . . . to . . . Oh! God!'

'To *what*? *Say it!*'

'I want you to fuck me again!'

'Good girl. You're learning fast,' he said, sliding a finger inside her. 'I'll have you talking filthier than an Amsterdam whore at this rate. You're going to learn words from me that you never knew existed, Calypso O'Kelly. I'll have you begging me to fuck you. And I will. Again and again. I like fucking princesses. And you're about as close to royalty as they get, aren't you, darling?'

Calypso was on the verge again.

'I can tell you like what I'm doing with my fingers. Don't you?'

'Yes. Oh – God – yes!'

Leo smiled down at her, then, abruptly, he withdrew his hand, slapped her flank and swung himself off the bed. 'Now, put your clothes back on, dearie. You've a home to get to before dawn comes up. We don't want rumours being circulated by any early-bird residents of Palmerston Terrace that you stayed out all night when hubby was away.'

She didn't want him to stop doing what he'd been doing to her! She didn't deserve to be deprived of another climax! She'd been so good, so compliant! She was on the verge of saying 'Please, Leo', then caught herself on. She, Calypso O'Kelly, High Queen of Casting, in begging mode? Well, no! She didn't *think* so . . .

Face flaming, she slid her legs over the side of

the bed. Leo dumped her discarded clothes in a heap beside her, then slid on a pair of loose cotton pyjama bottoms and made himself comfortable on a club chair, leaning back and swinging his legs up onto a side table. Lounging bare-chested he looked sexier than she'd ever seen him. He watched as she stepped into her panties and shimmied her hips to shuck them up, and then he said: 'The next time I see you, I want no VPL.'

'What are you talking about?'

'In future, you leave your knickers off when you're with me. And wear skirts. Always. I want access to all areas. Have you ever fucked in a public place?'

'No!'

'You'll enjoy it. It's wicked. The next time I fuck you, I'll do it somewhere dangerous. You'll never want sex in a safe place again. Danger's a very, very potent drug, Calypso.'

He smiled at the uncertain look in her eyes, then threw back his head and laughed out loud. Oh God, how she hated it when he laughed like that! 'Lordie, Lord! How I'm going to enjoy educating you, darling! Don't you know, there are thousands of ways of managing an al fresco fuck *discreetly* – to use one of your favourite words. I fucked a chick standing up at a rock concert once. No-one was any the wiser. Apart from the chick, of course.'

She finished dressing quickly. Leo got to his feet to show her to the door. Before he opened it, he gave her a chaste kiss on her forehead. 'May I make a suggestion?' he enquired.

'What?' she said testily.

'I very humbly suggest,' he said, not sounding humble at all, 'that you take a shower before your hubby gets in off the red-eye, princess. You smell like a bitch on heat.'

Thenceforth with Leo, that's exactly how she felt. She was always available, always up for it; and because Dominic was away a great deal, opportunities for them to fuck each other senseless were manifold. Calypso took to removing her panties any time she knew an encounter with Leo was imminent, stowing the undergarments in the glove compartment of her car. It made her feel incredibly aroused when she caught him eyeing her across a crowded room, checking her ass for the non-existent panty line, knowing that he'd soon find some excuse to get her on her own and lift her skirt.

The locations for their trysts varied from his dressing room at the studio (when Jeanne Renaud – with whom he was now officially involved – wasn't around), to her office, to the toilets of clubs and restaurants, to public car parks after dark. Leo had been right. Calypso found the element of danger in these encounters a huge turn-on. In restaurants they would sit side by side so that he could access her under cover of the tablecloth; in public parks she would surreptitiously slide her hand under a strategically placed coat or jacket in order to pleasure him. Once he took her up against a wall in a back alley, and they were both turned on beyond belief when they realized that a man in a nearby car was getting off on them. Occasionally they'd spend time in his apartment, but increasingly they found the thrill of sex in public places more potent.

Leo had promised Calypso that he'd drop Iseult as gently as he could. He'd done it over the course of a weekend. The following Monday the secretary had called in sick. On Tuesday she'd trailed into work looking like a drooping plant, with red eyes and a runny nose, and of course it hadn't been a cold that had kept her away from work the previous day, it had been grief. Since then, Iseult's demeanour had altered beyond all recognition. She was no longer the sunny girl that people loved to chat up on the phone, and around whose desk crash-helmeted couriers constantly lingered. The plot of the romantic comedy she'd lived for barely a week had taken a totally unexpected twist and had plunged without warning into blackest tragedy.

Calypso felt unconscionably guilty. She

couldn't bear to see her secretary so miserably heartbroken. And she imagined how betrayed Iseult would feel if she knew that her own boss was now fucking the man with whom she'd been so besotted. But then, she reasoned – using all her powers of self-persuasion – Iseult would have been even more miserably heartbroken if Leo had done as he'd threatened. After all, if she, Calypso, hadn't agreed to be his mistress he'd have robbed Iseult of her virginity; he'd have corrupted and depraved and humiliated her – and then he would have dumped her. That would have been infinitely worse.

Thus Calypso O'Kelly justified her shameless, shameful behaviour.

She was having a quiet night in. She stuck the top back on the tube of her Dead Sea Mud face pack, poured herself a glass of chilled Meursault and wandered into her home office to check her e-mail. She loved this space. *Irish Interiors* magazine had done a feature on her 'Favourite Room', and she had chosen this one because it made her feel like a proper grown-up. The photograph had shown her reclining on her imported Italian chaise-longue looking beautiful in her pristine white *peignoir* – the very one she was wearing now – pretending to be leafing through a pile of actors' mugshots.

Dominic was away on business again. She

missed him, and she was going to send him an e-mail to tell him exactly how much. She logged on, and deleted with distaste the numerous invitations to visit explicit porn sites that had accumulated in her mailbox. She'd been getting a lot of those lately. They made her feel *contaminated*, somehow, and she wondered with a shudder about the minds of the sad, sad individuals who felt the need to post them. She now deleted anonymous mail without bothering to check out what it contained – she wanted to whoosh that repugnant vileness out of her beautiful, rarefied life. The only anonymous stuff that interested her were the numerous invitations to feel 'Young and Healthier' by investing in growth hormones. The prospect of reversing the 'ravaging effects of ageing without diet or exercise' held infinite appeal for her.

Several work-related messages were waiting for her. Fiddle-de-dee. It was Saturday night. She wasn't going to access those. Saturday night was a work-free zone. A friend had phoned earlier to ask if she fancied going to see the new Hugh Leonard play at the Abbey, but going to the theatre was work as far as she was concerned. She even had a big envelope full of theatre tickets to send to her accountant: for her, theatre tickets were tax deductible. No. Tonight she wanted to forget about work, to enjoy her peace and quiet, to drink her Meursault and relax in a bath and drift around her beautiful house in her lovely *peignoir* with something classical playing in the background.

Darling, she typed with two fingers. *You've only been gone a few hours, and I miss you already. I wish you'd been here to see the expression on the cat's face when she saw me in my Dead Sea Mud face pack. Her eyes went all wide and her mouth went into a little O of surprise. No exageration!* (Contrary to what her English teacher at school had predicted, Calypso's spelling hadn't posed a stumbling block in her life's flight path.) *I'm staying in tonight. I've just poured myself a glass of Meursault (the shockingly expensive one – don't scold!). Anyway I think you'll agree that I deserve a reward for discovering the hottest new Irish talent in years. I was talking to Jethro earlier. He has just finished editing a ten-minute segment, and he says Leo is going to be stratisphericly stellar! Hee hee! Clever me for discovering him!* On review, she decided to erase the reference to Leo. It made her feel uncomfortably duplicitous referring to her lover in an e-mail to her husband. Instead she decided to pen some white lies she knew Dominic would find gratifying. *I'm going to run myself a bath now, and light some candles and think of you as I soap myself. Hell's teeth, darling – I'm feeling sexy already! I'd better turn those taps on quick (they're not the only things that are going to get turned on, as if you couldn't guess . . .). Love you, love you, love you,* C. XXX

The bit about feeling sexy was true. At this comparatively late stage in her life she'd discovered the delights of masturbation for the first time. However, she'd been a bit economical with the truth when she'd told her husband she'd be thinking about him in the bath. It was always Leo's face she saw in her mind's eye when she got off on her increasingly depraved fantasies.

Calypso pressed 'send', and as she did, she saw that new mail had arrived as she'd been typing. The message description read: *Feeling Horny?* With a 'tch' of irritation she was just about to send it packing when the name of the sender caught her attention. It was from Leo. How did he know that she was feeling horny? was her first thought; her second was: Oh God oh God oh God. He was going to start sending her e-mail now, as well as the indelicate text messages he'd taken to firing off. How on earth had he got her address? She'd have to put a stop to this at once. She'd e-mail him back and tell him to watch his lip. With an indignant thumb, she clicked on the mouse.

Check out this web site, angel. If you're feeling horny it might be just your cup of tea. Or, in your case, 'glass of Chablis' is doubtless more appropriate. By the way – ever messed about with handcuffs? L. XXX

Under the black mud of her face pack, Calypso's face had flushed a bright scarlet. Her fingers fumbled for the 'delete' button. *Ever messed about with handcuffs?* vanished into the ether.

After her bath, in the sanctuary of her beautiful white bedroom, she creamed her face and neck and brushed her hair with a proper bristle brush before going to bed with her book. She was on the verge of settling down to sleep when Dominic phoned. He wanted to ask Calypso how she'd enjoyed her bath earlier.

'Mm, darling,' she said. 'It was pretty gorgeous, but it would have been even more gorgeous if you'd been there in the flesh instead of in my fantasies . . .' She spent quite a long time cooing and purring to him. Calypso had become so adept at phone sex that she could easily have got a job on a chat line. When she finally settled back against her puffy white pillows to sleep, she found herself wondering about the web site Leo had recommended.

She woke some hours later, flushed and jittery. The flush was from the mother and father of an orgasm, and the jitteriness was from an awful sense of doomy dismay. The bastard had started invading her dreams.

She was giving him a lift back from the studio one evening. Calypso was feeling so woozy with post-orgasmic bliss that she wasn't sure she should be driving. Leo was leafing through a script she had in the car – a movie she was casting that featured a lot of adventure with a bit of romance thrown in for good measure. It was to start shooting in the West of Ireland in a couple of months' time.

'There's a part for me in this,' said Leo.

'Oh? Which one?'

'The lead, of course. Dakota.'

'No, darling. You're not right for it.'

'Why not?'

'I want somebody fresh-faced and wholesome for Dakota. A younger version of Brad Pitt.'

'I could do fresh-faced. Look.'

He gave her such an ingenuous smile that she laughed. 'Leo, I know you're a terrific actor, but I'm thinking blond here—'

'Ever heard of Clairol, sweetheart?'

She laughed again. 'Blue eyes?'

'Coloured contacts.'

'Leo – it's just not you.'

'Well. How unadventurous is that? You told me once that casting was all about using the imagination, and here you are now, entrenched in typecasting groove. I'm disappointed in you, Calypso.' He leafed through a few more pages. 'Hey – Dakota gets to drive an Aston Martin. I've always wanted to do that. And he packs a mean pistol. That means I could learn to shoot. I've always wanted to do that too.'

She sent him an indulgent smile. Under his mean and moody façade, Leo was just a boy like all the rest.

'Oh, go on, Calypso,' he cajoled. 'At least let me meet the director.'

She stopped at traffic lights and turned to face him.

'Go on,' he said again.

Calypso considered. This was the first time in their relationship that the power balance had shifted. Leo was the one who usually called the shots, now it was her turn. She kinda liked the feeling. 'OK,' she said. 'I'll organize a lunch with him when he's over next month.'

'Good girl.' Leo leafed through more pages. 'Who's playing the female lead? Do you know yet?'

'I was thinking of Sophie Burke. But I understand she can be a bit of a diva.'

'Cast her anyway. She's pretty damn sexy. I saw her on the cover of *GQ* recently.'

'Think you could handle a diva?'

'Damn right I could. Oh – yes! I like it!'

'Like what?'

'On page ninety-two I get to ride the arse off her.'

Calypso smiled again and raised her eyes to heaven.

Leo slung the script onto the back seat. 'By the way,' he said. 'I've three free days in a row coming up.'

'Lucky you,' she said. 'You've been working very hard. You could do with a break.'

'An added stroke of good fortune,' he continued, 'is that they happen to coincide with your hubby's next trip to London. I think it's about time you had a little holiday, Calypso, don't you? Why don't you pack your Vuitton weekend bag – or is it Mulberry? – and a case of champagne into the boot of your car and come and spend three fun-filled days in my flat? Bring your reddest lippy. The tartiest one you have.'

Leo had started insisting that she apply lipstick before he'd condescend to have sex with her, and he derived enormous gratification from watching her put it on. He also derived enormous gratification from smearing it, and watching the way she'd weep with self-loathing afterwards. He'd fuck her relentlessly then, levelling unspeakably vile accusations at her as he did so, warning her that unless she talked equally salaciously back at him he would kick her out of his bed. She acquiesced every time.

In the driver's seat, Calypso dithered.

'What's wrong?' said Leo. 'Scared that hubby might come back unexpectedly and find that wifelet's flown the coop?'

'Shut up, Leo.' She couldn't handle the disparaging way he often talked about Dominic. She knew that her husband hadn't the first, faintest idea in the world about her carryings-on

337

with Leo and that if he ever did find out, a tragedy of epic proportions would ensue. Of all the risks they'd taken to date, by far the one that appalled her most was the risk of Dominic finding out about them. Spending three days with Leo would be the riskiest thing she'd done yet.

'I'll have to think about it,' she said.

'Why?'

'I'd have to dream up some excuse for being away from the house.'

'Why don't you tell him you're going off on a girly weekend?'

'I dunno. I hate subterfuge –' She shot him a cross look as he flung back his head and crowed. 'And then there's the cat –'

'The what? The *cat*? Sorry, darling. The offer's off.'

'What do you mean?'

'If the welfare of your cat is of greater concern to you than my sexual gratification, you can forget about it.'

'Oh, no, Leo – please! I didn't mean that, I'm just worried about—'

'I said forget it.'

The power balance had shifted again. 'I'm sorry,' she said. 'Honestly I am. Please – I'd love to come. I'll sort things out, really I will.' They slid through the traffic lights into gridlock. Calypso laid a hand on his thigh and gave him a look of entreaty.

He looked her up and down, and his lip curled a little. 'All right. I'll reissue the invite. Jesus, Calypso. You really are abject, aren't you?'

She shrugged. 'I'm getting used to feeling abject these days. You do a mean line in humiliation, Leo. Why do you take such delight in it?'

'There's such a thing as quid pro quo, Calypso. You enjoy being humiliated.'

She forced a little laugh. 'I suppose I do.' She was aware as she uttered the words that any vestigial defences she had were now gone for ever. 'It's something I don't understand about myself.' Calypso didn't much want to dwell on it. She suspected that if she did she'd be forced to confront things about herself she mightn't be able to handle. 'But I wouldn't allow anyone else to treat me the way you do, Leo.'

'Not even hubby?'

'No. And he wouldn't want to treat me that way. He has too much respect for me.'

'Of course. You're his goddess.'

'Yes. I am. It's funny, isn't it, how I can be two such completely different people to two such completely different men? To Dominic I'm a goddess, to you I'm a whore. He worships at my shrine, you defile it.'

'He "worships at your shrine". Jesus! Does he really call it that?'

'No,' lied Calypso. She didn't want to hear the

mocking things Leo would come out with about Dominic if she told him the truth.

Abruptly Leo turned to her and narrowed his eyes. Then he smiled. 'Hitch up your skirt,' he said.

Glad of the change of subject, Calypso smiled back at him, then did as he asked, wriggling her bum and stretching out her legs.

'Hitch it up more,' commanded Leo, running the tip of his tongue lightly along his lips.

She obliged without demurring, raising the hem to the very top of her thighs.

'More,' he said. 'Hoist it right up round your waist.'

Again she did as she was told, her breath coming a little faster in anticipation of what Leo was going to do to her. But he didn't touch her. He just continued to lounge back in the passenger seat. Then he smiled a slow, slow smile. 'Oh, wow, princess,' he said. 'You just made that geezer's day.'

Calypso followed the direction of Leo's gaze. There, to her right, in the passenger seat of an articulated truck, a man was looking down at her Brazilian-waxed lap with an expression of slavish, gobsmacked lust. And instead of feeling shame, Calypso just felt an overwhelming desire for Leo to slide his hand between her thighs and touch her there.

* * *

On the appointed day, she brought a picnic to his flat so that they wouldn't have to leave their love nest. She brought quails' eggs and caviare and champagne and chocolate. And cash for the cocaine Leo had said he would score. After he'd inflicted a little pain, and smeared her lipstick, and done things to her that she'd once have found beyond degrading, he cracked the second bottle, cut some lines, and rolled a joint. Finally they slumped back in each other's arms in a wrecked, abandoned stupor.

'Well, sweetie-pie,' he said, looking at her through half-shut eyes. 'You *have* learned a lot in the past few weeks, haven't you? An able and willing pupil – a veritable teacher's pet.'

'Thank you. I was never that at school. A girl called Grace Moynihan was the pet. Most of the teachers hated me.'

'Because you were academically challenged?'

'No. I worked bloody hard, actually. It was because I was pretty. The women teachers were jealous, and the men couldn't handle me. I used to give them erections, deliberately.'

Leo laughed. 'How?'

'The usual methods. Standing too close, exposing too much leg, leaving too many buttons undone on my shirt, that kind of thing. My girlfriends used to egg me on. They loved seeing the history teacher especially trying to hide his crotch. He was a total walkover.'

He turned his head to face her on the pillow and smiled at her. 'I'd love to get a load of you in school uniform. Do you still have it?'

'No,' she lied. In fact, Dominic asked her to wear it sometimes when he was pissed. He'd sit her on his knee and pretend to give her an art history lesson, leafing through the raunchier sections of the *Erotica Universalis*. Calypso often wondered about men. She supposed Dannie had had it spot-on that time when she'd spouted that cliché about them all thinking with their dicks.

'Do all men think with their dicks, Leo?' she asked, preparing herself for some put-down.

'Of course,' he said. 'That's why the world is the fucked-up mess it is. If my father hadn't thought with his dick, I'd never have had the misfortune to be part of it.'

'Part of what?'

'Part of the fucked-up mess that is this world, dimbo.'

'Leo. I am not a stupid person. Why do you always treat me as if I'm an idiot?'

'I don't treat you like an idiot. I treat you like a whore.'

She bridled. 'I'm not a whore, either.'

'All women are whores.'

'*All* women? Even your mother?' As soon as the words left her lips she regretted them. It was a rash and stupid thing to have said – she knew

342

that the mother thing was a sacrosanct subject for most men.

He narrowed his eyes and looked at her appraisingly for a long time. Calypso got the impression that he was calculating how much truth he could trust her with. Then he said: 'My mother was forced into whoredom by my father.'

It was the first time Leo had ever volunteered anything to her about his family background, apart from the fact that he'd been poor. Trusting she wasn't chancing her arm, she pressed on, 'How do you mean, *forced* into whoredom?'

'Economic necessity, sweetie-pie. Ever heard of it?'

'You're saying it was the only way she could make ends meet?'

'Got it in one. Apart from scrubbing floors, of course. She eked out a living doing that too. As you can imagine, neither career option was especially well paid. But then she'd had no careers guidance at school.' He took a toke of the joint and exhaled luxuriously. 'I know all about hard-working whores, Calypso. I come from a long line of them. And I must say it's a real eye-opener to meet a woman like you who embraces whoredom as a leisure activity rather than as a desperate, last-ditch attempt to earn a livelihood.'

Oh! Calypso quickly changed the subject.

'What did your father do?' she asked, refilling their glasses.

He paused again, considering. 'My father was, I believe, a High Court judge or some such luminary in the legal profession. My mother never told me exactly who he was – she just hinted.'

'I take it they weren't married.'

He took another toke and handed her the joint. 'You take it absolutely for read, my dear, that they weren't married. She scrubbed his floors for him. He simply took it for granted that – as her employer – sex was one of the perks.'

Calypso was aghast. 'But that kind of thing went out in Victorian times! Didn't she know her rights? Couldn't she have reported him to the authorities?'

Leo gave her a pitying look. 'Get real, Calypso. The only "right" my mother might have been made aware of would have been *droit du seigneur*.' He shot her an amused look. 'Oh, sorry. You probably don't know what that means.' Of course she didn't! '*Droit du seigneur* is an ancient French expression that refers to the right of a feudal lord to roger his subordinate females. Come to think of it, you'd probably enjoy that.'

Because she was so fascinated by his life story she let the remark pass without comment. 'Whose looks d'you think you inherited?' she asked, blowing out smoke. 'Your mother's or your father's?'

'My mother was dark, like me. She was of Romany descent. I haven't a clue what jolly old Pater looked like.'

Calypso had a mental picture of Leo's mother, a Carmen lookalike scraping by on her meagre earnings, obliged to submit to some despotic aristocratic type.

'What Mills & Boon scenario is wafting through your pretty head, Calypso?' Damn his eyes! He'd tuned in with uncanny accuracy! 'You're thinking my life story's wildly romantic, aren't you, darling? I won't be so dastardly as to disabuse you.'

'No,' she lied. 'I'm actually wondering how the authorities would have responded if she *had* reported him.'

He laughed out loud. 'You really think they'd have taken her word against his, those "*authorities*" to whom you so quaintly refer? You think anyone would have *dared* to prosecute him? Calypso darling, mark this. This is the kind of stuff that goes on all the time in the real world out there. The one that you have chosen not to inhabit.'

'I know you think I'm naïve. I just find it really shocking.'

'More shocking still is the very real fact that my mother would have lost her job if she hadn't obliged him. But then, she lost it anyway when she became pregnant.'

'Christ! What a *bastard* your father must have been!'

'I'm surprised it surprises you. Aren't all men supposed to be bastards? *I* certainly am, in every sense of the word. And there are quite a few.' He took the joint from her and gave her a look of lazy enquiry. 'Do you know what the *OED* definition of the word "bastard" is?' he asked.

'No.'

'*No?* I'm amazed. I would have thought that the *OED* would be your bedtime reading of choice.'

'Ha ha.'

He kissed her on the nose. 'Bastard, my darling, not only means born out of wedlock and illegitimate. It also means unauthorized, hybrid and counterfeit.'

'All those things? So. Jethro was right when he called you a highly educated son-of-a-bitch.'

'Right on both counts. I'm highly educated, *and* I'm the son of a bitch.'

'Don't be horrible, Leo. Your mother was just deeply unfortunate.'

'All women are bitches, just as all women are whores,' he said in a matter-of-fact tone. 'Anyway, the word "bitch" doesn't have the

346

same connotations it once had. You love it when I call you that, don't you, bitch?'

'No. Yes. I don't know.' The joint had made Calypso feel very fuzzy round the edges. 'Where did you end up studying?' she asked him.

'Trinity. I won a scholarship.'

'What subject?'

'Solo English.'

'Really? I'm impressed. No wonder you know so many big words.'

'What kind of education's that for the real world?'

'A more privileged education than your mum had.' Calypso's own mother had scoffed at her when she'd announced her intention of going to Trinity to do theatre studies. She picked up her glass and drained the remains of her champagne before putting it down again very carefully on the bedside table. She wasn't sure how to ask the next, very obvious question that was lurking in her brain. She didn't need to. He asked it for her.

'You want to know why, despite my education, I ended up working as a "lowly" carpenter, don't you? Let me tell you, Calypso. Carpentry is a fine and honest trade that affords me a great deal of creative satisfaction. And remember this: one of the biggest stars in the world was a dab hand at carpentry before he found his true vocation.'

'Harrison Ford?'

'Jesus Christ.' He flicked ash onto her bare belly, then handed over the joint and asked with very deliberate casualness, 'Incidentally, how many cleaning ladies have you been through in your career as a chatelaine?'

Ah! She drew herself up in the bed, wrapped her arms around her shins and looked at him levelly. 'I see now,' she said slowly. 'When you make love to—'

He put a finger to her lips.

'Sorry. When you *fuck* me,' she amended, 'you're getting revenge for the way your mother was treated. A kind of vic- vic – oh! What's that word?' The hash had made her worse than dopey now. She'd need another line to clear her head.

'Victory?'

'No, no! It's a word to describe the kind of revenge you're getting! Vic – vic – it means kind of at a remove . . .'

'Vicarious?'

'Yes! That's it. You're getting vicarious revenge, isn't that it?'

Leo shrugged. 'The idea had never occurred to me. I'm just lucky to have found a princess who likes being fucked by a bit of rough. I bet you'll really get off now on the fact that romantic Romany blood flows through my veins.'

'Come on, Leo. You've got to give my theory some credence,' she said loftily. 'I'm a symbol of everything you despise. *Ergo*, by shafting me you're shafting an entire ethos.'

'My, my! Aren't we perspicacious! Dear old Dr Freud *would* be impressed.'

She gave up. Crawling towards him on the bed, she kissed Leo's contemptuous mouth.

'Ah,' he said. 'What a clever, clever girl you are to have done the right thing.'

'What right thing?'

'You've shut up and kissed me, you fool.'

'Poor, poor Leo,' she said into his mouth. 'No wonder you're so full of bile and hatred.'

'I am?'

'Yes. Well, towards people like Dominic and me, anyway.'

'Poor, poor you. Poor little rich girl.'

'Mm. Poor, poor little me.' She slid against him, feeling more than usually naked, wanting his arms around her for reassurance and feeling absurdly grateful when he obliged.

They lay in silence for some minutes. It was a companionable silence, Calypso decided – as if they were each lost in their own individual thoughts. Then: 'Are we going to fall in love, Leo, do you think?' she asked.

'Christ, no. Are you mad? That would be disastrous. Anyway, what makes you think I could ever fall in love with a chick with such hideously ugly feet?' He gave her his usual black bantering look, and kissed her nose again.

Calypso smiled back and snuggled closer to him. He was protesting too much – she knew he was. She suspected that Leo Devlin was a lot more vulnerable than he'd led her to believe. Poor Leo had erected so many defences around himself! He'd had to – of course he'd had to – for sheer self-preservation. But she knew she was infiltrating those defences, winning his trust. He wouldn't have opened up and told her all that stuff about his past if he didn't trust her. She felt a genuine warmth towards him now – a peculiar *tenderness*, she supposed it was. 'I want to make you happy, Leo,' she said. 'Tell me how I can make you happy.'

He made himself comfortable against a pile of pillows, reclining like a pasha. 'You know what to do,' he said. 'Princess.'

Feeling pathetically grateful that she could afford him the pleasure he wanted, Calypso dropped a trail of little kisses along Leo's sternum and down his belly before taking him in her mouth and proceeding to do the one thing she knew she was very, very good at.

Much, much later, Leo took a shower. Calypso had wound a bed sheet around herself (she'd seen Jeanne Renaud do it in a film) and was pottering in the living area, organizing food. She set plates on the table and arranged cutlery and the candles and crystal that she'd brought, and then she sat down to wait for Leo, feeling strangely homey and comfortable in his space. It was a bit like playing Mummies and Daddies, she decided, that game she'd loved so much as a little girl – although she hadn't often had a chance to play it. Some of her friends hadn't been able to get their heads around her interpretation of the rules.

His flat was looking a bit scruffy. Men were so crap at keeping things tidy! Organizational ability was Calypso's only housewifely virtue – one that she also brought to bear in her work. Like most 'glamorous' jobs, casting was one per cent inspiration, 99 per cent hard graft. Her files were meticulous.

Humming to herself, she idly got to her feet again and ran her eyes along the books that were ranked haphazardly on Leo's shelves, resisting the impulse to align them in a slightly more orderly state. They were an eclectic bunch: there were books on art and culture, erotica and poetry, philosophy and politics, biography and history, with a great preponderance of literary works. Were they his, or did they belong to the friend who owned the apartment? Pulling one out at random, she opened it and saw that it was the property of Dublin University Library. Bad boy, Leo – stealing library books! She was careful to put it back exactly where she'd found it.

Calypso continued her humming while she ran her finger along miscellaneous spines, pausing here and there to check titles before finally drawing out an antique volume whose tooled leather and gilt edges caught her attention. She was curious to see whether the owner had written his name on the title page. The book she'd selected was Dostoevsky's *Crime and Punishment*, and it was clearly quite an early edition. Except, when she opened it, she saw to her dismay that pages had been torn out, and there were notes scribbled in the margins. What a shame to spoil such a rarity!

Turning her attention to the title page, she read the following handwritten words: *For my dear young friend Leo, as a token of my appreciation. Gordon DeLapp.* The handwriting was neat, slanted – almost Victorian copperplate. On the opposite page was a mass of scribbled graffiti. Except, on closer inspection, she saw that it wasn't graffiti. Leo's name was reproduced on the cream vellum in countless styles of rather juvenile handwriting that ranged from dramatic quasi-italic to an indecipherable schoolboy squiggle. How sweet! Sweeter still, Leo hadn't confined himself to his given name. He'd signed it in varying permutations. *Leo Devlin. Leo DeLapp. Leo DeLapp-Devlin.* The fledgling actor trying out his future stage name!

She remembered having done that herself when she was in her early teens and determined to embark on a career as an actress. She'd spent hours trying out different signatures, each more flamboyant and flowery than the last. Her lips curved in a smile as she pictured a much younger Leo tracing the loops and curls of his trademark signature, tongue stuck out in concentration, fantasizing and dreaming about that far-off day when someone might ask for his autograph . . .

'What are you doing?' He was standing in the doorway, lounging against the jamb with a towel wrapped around his waist, watching her.

'Oh! You gave me a fright! I was just looking at some of your books.'

Leo watched her, smiling with his mouth. 'Don't ever snoop around me, Calypso,' he said.

'I wasn't snooping. I promise!'

'I think you were. I think you were being a nosy, snoopy little girl. And you know what happens to nosy, snoopy little girls, don't you? They get punished. Drop the sheet.'

'What?'

'The sheet you've wrapped round you. Lose it.'

Calypso did as he told her, slowly unwinding the sheet and feeling gorgeously, agonizingly vulnerable as Leo ran calculating eyes over her naked body. For an eternity he just stood there, head tilted to one side, scrutinizing her. Finally she held her arms out, smiling at him invitingly – and suddenly his expression changed. He crossed the room in one swift movement and grabbed her by the hair, jerking her head backwards and forcing her to the floor. 'Why do you do it? Why do you make me do it?' His voice was fierce as he turned her over and bludgeoned himself into the place between her buttocks.

The pain made her cry out.

'Shut up!' he said, and again – when a whimper escaped her – '*Shut up!*' He covered her mouth with his hand, then climaxed almost immediately. After he came she heard his voice again, and the anguish that was in it. 'Oh, God! *Why do you make me do it?*'

Calypso tumbled out of a taxi two days later. She crawled up the stairs of her elegant house, ran a very hot bath and lay there with her eyes closed, trying not to remember what had occurred in the past seventy hours. Not remembering wasn't proving to be too difficult – her recollection of events was cloudy and vestigial from the drugs she'd used. There'd been too many drugs, too much sex. *Way* too much sex.

And still she wanted more.

In her fabulous bathroom, Calypso squeezed her eyes tight, tighter shut still, and then she slid further into the bath until the perfumed water covered her beautiful burning face, craving the oblivion she knew would elude her as long as she was still in thrall, as long as she continued to play slave to her despotic, dancing-eyed, demon lover.

Chapter Ten

Rosa enjoyed working at the Hamilton hotel. She knew how surroundings could affect your mood, and the Hamilton was a stunningly beautiful place. A vast dilapidated Victorian mansion had been gutted to create the hotel, and the building that had been allowed to fall into a grim state of disrepair was now restored to its original architectural glory. A garden had been planted at the rear, where statuary posed and fountains played. In fine weather guests sat out at wrought-iron tables, having afternoon tea al fresco, or drinking champagne.

Rosa never entered the reception rooms, which she knew were full of antique furniture and original art by some of Ireland's most celebrated painters, but sometimes she passed by the great open doors or the floor-to-ceiling windows and caught glimpses of how the other half lived – the movers and shakers of the Irish political and art worlds, the cognoscenti, the privileged. Calypso's crowd. Once she'd seen Calypso herself chatting to a prominent politician, being offered champagne and canapés from one of the silver trays that were borne by the discreet, liveried staff who circled the room, and she'd smiled to herself because she knew that politics bored Calypso silly.

Miriam had surreptitiously pointed out the director who'd harassed her early one morning while he was taking a swim, and Rosa had disliked him on sight. A smooth gobshite, she'd thought, as she'd watched him posing on the poolside before diving in and doing showy-off laps. She wondered how on earth a savvy gal like Dannie could have fallen for that smarmy trick of his he'd used to turn her head, the time he'd bought her flowers. And she wondered how Dannie would feel if she knew that her lover had sexually propositioned a vulnerable female. He never asked for massages now, and Rosa knew it was because management had made it plain to him that it was one of the hotel perks he'd forfeited for having disregarded the rules first time round.

Rosa worked hard, she was punctual, and – best of all from Miriam's point of view – she was available. Miriam soon learned that any time she picked up the phone to Rosa and asked if she could run across Stephen's Green and oblige a visiting celebrity with a massage in their room, the automatic response would be 'Absolutely'. And Rosa was discretion personified. No amount of cajoling and pleading from nosy Calypso would dislodge the smallest crumb of gossip from Rosa's zipped lips about any of the juicier goings-on in the joint.

One afternoon Rosa went into Florabundance to pick up Lottie. She was dog tired today; she'd been performing massages 'back to back' – as she ironically put it – since she'd dropped Lottie off to school that morning. But at least that meant she'd earned a tidy amount. Last week had been dismal financially.

'Hey, Rosa!' Dannie's assistant Laura was sitting on a high stool at the counter, working on a wreath constructed entirely from ethereal-looking gypsophila. 'Dannie and Lottie are in the back room. Your mum's here, Lottie!' she called.

'Hi, Mum!' Lottie called back.

'How's it going?' A shiny-eyed Dannie emerged from the back room, wiping her hands on a cloth. Dannie was always shiny-eyed these days, and Rosa knew it was because of awful Jethro Palmer. Sometimes, when she heard Dannie mention that she was going out to dinner or the theatre with her new man, she wondered if she should let her know the truth about Mr Slimeball Palmer. She always decided against it. Who was she to interfere? On a few occasions

Dannie had asked Rosa to join her and Jethro on one of their outings, but Rosa had always made some excuse. She couldn't bear to sit across a table from that man, knowing what she knew about him. She felt full of righteous indignation when she contrasted the way he treated Dannie with the way he'd treated Miriam.

'Hi,' replied Rosa now. 'I'm fine. Everything OK here?'

'Mm hm. Lottie's working away back there. She's starting on a new project – about film-making. I told her Jethro'd be glad to help out.'

Rosa didn't much like the idea of Jethro coming into contact with her daughter, but she couldn't let Dannie know that.

'He's taking me out to Brittas Bay tomorrow for a picnic,' Dannie continued. 'I asked Lottie if she'd like to come along after her gymnastics class.'

'Oh. That's really sweet of you, Dannie, but Lottie's got a sleepover to go to.'

'No, I haven't,' came Lottie's imperious voice from the back room. 'The sleepover's been cancelled. Roxanne has tonsillitis.'

It was a *fait accompli*, then. 'Oh. Well, in that case, I'm sure she'd love to go.'

'What about you, Rosa? Do you fancy a day on the beach?'

'I'd actually fancy a *month* on a beach, but I can't come, I'm afraid. I've masses to do.'

'And what might that be?'

'Well – I'm sky-diving in the morning, having a cookery lesson with Darina Allen at lunchtime, going to a tea dance in the afternoon and working out with my personal trainer in the evening before dashing off to the opera. Hah! Fooled you.' Rosa flung her arms wide in an expansively theatrical gesture. 'I'm actually doing housework and accounts! Da dah!'

'Does anyone want a cup of tea? I'm just going to make some.' Laura had slid down off her stool and was tweaking her gypsophila wreath. 'Pretty thing!' she said, putting her head on one side and admiring her handiwork.

'No tea, for me, thanks, Laura. I'd better get Lottie home.'

'Guess where Dannie's going for supper tonight? Les Frères Jacques!' Laura slid Dannie a sideways look and put on a singsongy voice. 'With her überdude film director boyfriend.'

'D'you want to come, Rosa? Oh, come on! Ring your babysitter and see if she's free. I'm dying for you to meet Jethro, so it'll be my treat.'

Rosa sensed at once that the invitation had been impulsively blurted, out of pity. She knew that Dannie would be feeling guilty at the idea of her friend trailing home after a hard day's slog and having to organize supper for Lottie while she swanned down to a posh restaurant to be waited on. 'No. No, thanks all the same,' she said quickly, looking away. 'Lottie!' she called. 'Come on. It's time we went home.'

Something had altered in the dynamic between the two women. There was an awkwardness in the air now. Rosa cast around for something to say. 'Jethro's movie's wrapping soon, isn't it?' she asked, carefully straightening a branch of willow that she'd tilted with her elbow.

According to Miriam, filming on the big budget epic was nearly finished, and then Jethro would be gone from Dannie's life. It was Dannie's turn now to look uncomfortable. Rosa knew that neither she nor Jethro had brought up the subject of what would happen to their relationship after filming was over: it was way too thorny a topic.

'Yeah. The wrap party's tomorrow night. The *craic*'ll be mighty.' Dannie's voice rang with false brightness. She reached for a peony rose that had passed its best-before date and started to pluck off its petals.

'Will I bring my swim togs to the beach tomorrow, Dannie?' Lottie had finally emerged from the back room and was struggling to get her arms through the shoulder straps of her schoolbag.

'Of course, mavourneen.'

'Will Jethro pick me up in a limo?'

Dannie laughed. 'Arra, no! I'm meeting him at the hotel.'

'Bum,' said Lottie. 'I'd love to get into a limo outside our flats. The neighbours would all stare. I'll bring a notebook too, will I? So I can write down the answers to all the questions I want to ask him. D'you think he could get me some autographs?'

'If you ask him nicely.'

'Here – let me take that.' Rosa unhooked the heavy schoolbag from the child's shoulders. 'Crikey! Why do you have to carry so much *stuff*, Lottie? Goodbye, Dannie. Bye, Laura. Thanks for doing the needful. Say thank you, Carlotta.'

'She's no trouble,' said Laura. 'I'm going to teach her how to make a coffee bouquet some day soon, aren't I, Lottie?'

'Yup. And I'm going to give it to my mum because she's the best.'

'You babe!' Rosa bent over her daughter's head, smoothed her hair and gave her a kiss. When she straightened up, Dannie was wearing the most peculiar expression. If Rosa hadn't known better, she could have sworn that it was envy.

Dannie resumed plucking petals. 'Bye, then, Rosa. I'll pick Lottie up around eleven tomorrow morning. And we'll have her back to you by seven – I'll be wanting to get myself dickied up for the party.'

'Enjoy it. And enjoy yourself tonight. And thanks again for everything.'

Rosa and Lottie walked home hand in hand, Rosa listening distractedly to Lottie's running commentary on the day's events. God, she was tired this evening! She welcomed the fact that tomorrow her day would be a Lottie-free zone. She'd get all her chores out of the way and then she might treat herself to a movie, or she could stay in with a video and a glass of – a cup of tea.

Every evening now, when she went to make herself a pot of tea, the wine box on the shelf looked at her invitingly and Rosa ignored it resolutely. She hadn't poured herself a glass since that awful night in Dannie's over two months earlier.

Dannie collected Lottie the following morning and they walked through Stephen's Green to the Hamilton hotel. It was a glorious, joyous late spring day, and Dannie felt blissed out at the prospect of chilling on a beach with her fella and this small pal who was skipping along beside her.

In the Hamilton they asked the receptionist to tell Mr Palmer they'd arrived, then moved into the drawing room to wait for him. Lottie was agog at the poshness of it all. She inspected the paintings, tried all the sofas, and opened the cupboards of antique sideboards when there was no-one looking. 'Hey, Dannie,' she said. 'Wouldn't it be cool to bring in one of those fake dog turds – you know, the kind you get in joke shops – and put it in one of the cupboards? Can you imagine the expression on the person's face when they opened the cupboard door and got a load of what was in there?'

Dannie laughed. Being with Lottie was a great excuse to be juvenile. Since Guy, she'd found that being juvenile could sometimes be a blessed release, and she'd been delighted to discover that Jethro had an unexpectedly silly side to him.

'Yeah. A fake dog turd would be great *craic*,' she said. 'Or fake puke.'

'Hey, Dannie?' Lottie flung herself down beside Dannie on the sofa. 'What's the pool like in the Sybaris? Calypso's taking me some time next week. My mum says it's dead posh.'

'I don't know, mavourneen. I've never used it.' Whenever Dannie had visited Jethro in the hotel, they'd spent all their time in bed in his suite upstairs. Jethro really, *really* valued his leisure time because he had so little of it, and Dannie was incredibly chuffed that he seemed to want to spend all of it in bed with her. The downside of their relationship was that he worked such punishingly long hours that they never had much time for fun stuff like messing around in swimming pools.

Today was a real bonus. Only the second unit was working, on something Jethro referred to as 'pick-ups'. The rest of the cast and crew had wrapped. Jethro could have – and probably should have – been tying up a load of loose ends on the production side of things, but because his days with Dannie were numbered, he'd decided that if he wanted to skive off, he was the boss and no-one could stop him.

Now she felt giddy and light hearted as she reclined against the back of the luxurious sofa, one arm slung lightly around Lottie's shoulders. 'You know another brilliant thing you could do in here? You could put a whoopee cushion under one of the cushions on the couches. Janey, I'd love to do that!'

'Yeah, and then the Taoiseach or a big film star might come in and sit on it.'

'What are you two tee-heeing about?' Jethro came up behind them and bent down to kiss Dannie on the cheek.

'We're tee-heeing about really silly stuff,' said Dannie, smiling up at him. 'We're in a very silly humour. Oh, I forgot – you two haven't met. Jethro Palmer, Carlotta Elliot. Lottie, Jethro.'

Jethro scooped up Lottie's hand. '*Enchanté, mademoiselle*,' he said, executing a formal bow. 'I may say that it is a real pleasure to be able to escort two such lovely ladies to the beach today. I instructed the hotel to prepare a hamper full of goodies for us, and our car is waiting outside.'

'A limo?' asked Lottie excitedly.

'Not a limo,' said Jethro, leading the way

through the vestibule. 'It's something even better.'

It *was* even better. Outside the Hamilton hotel was parked the prettiest, silliest car that either Lottie or Dannie had ever seen. It was a powder-blue Karmann Ghia, with a darker blue soft top, a dark blue leather interior, and a white wheel trim.

'Oh!' said Dannie. 'It's dotey! Kind of like Noddy's car, only blue! Did you hire it for the day?'

'No,' said Jethro. 'I bought it. For you.'

'What?'

'I bought it for you, Dannie Moore.'

'Way to go, Dannie! Cool!' Lottie ran down the steps of the hotel to inspect the car, and Dannie turned to Jethro with incredulity plainly scrawled across her face.

'I can't accept this!' she said.

'Of course you can,' he returned smoothly, taking her hand and pressing a set of car keys into her palm. 'And if you don't accept it, I shall present it instead to the first person who comes round that corner. I mean it, Ms Moore.'

Something about his expression told her he *did* mean it. 'But – but *why*, Jethro?'

'Because it's got your name written all over it. Hell, that car's got more personality than most of the movie stars I've worked with. And you'll look sensational driving it.'

Dannie gazed at him in dumbstruck astonishment, and then she threw her arms around this extraordinary man whom she had been astute and lucky enough to allow into her life, and she kissed him and kissed him and kissed him while the liveried doorman looked on, smiling uncertainly at this demonstration of affection on the steps of his hotel. It was as if he wasn't sure whether he should ask the lovers to be a little more discreet, or whether he should cheer them on.

Dannie drove them out to Brittas with the soft top down and Lou Reed's 'Perfect Day' playing. On the driver's seat – as well as the Lou Reed cassette – she had found a silk scarf and a pair of movie-star sunglasses. 'Put them on,' Jethro had instructed her, and he'd helped her arrange the scarf in the style favoured by Italian film stars in the fifties, enveloping her hair and neck, and knotting it at the nape so that the filmy ends of the scarf flew out behind her in the breeze. They kept fluttering backwards into Lottie's face, making her cross, but Dannie was oblivious to the crossness because an image had come into her mind of the beautiful Italian mother she'd never known. This, she thought, was how Daniella might have looked all those years ago when, as a teenager, she'd hitch-hiked through Connemara and met up with the man she would marry.

It was a brilliant day – one of those days that her grandmother had used to refer to as 'pet' days. Wicklow was looking especially pretty, as if the county had known that this was a special occasion and had made an effort to push the boat out. Birds sang as joyously as the ones in Disney cartoons, the foliage on the trees gleamed greener than Patrick's Day, and a bright golden sun shone in a *Teletubbies* sky. And – wonders might never cease – people in cars were actually *smiling*!

When they reached the beach, Jethro swung the picnic hamper out of the boot of the car, which, to Lottie's amazement, was under the bonnet.

'I will confess that opening a trunk that's located at the front of a car – especially a car as girly as this – makes me feel like some kind of a pervert,' said Jethro in an undertone to Dannie as he pulled the bonnet back down. 'It feels a little as if I'm lifting a lady's skirt.'

'And that's something you're very good at,' returned Dannie with a smile.

'What are we having?' asked Lottie, eyeing the hotel hamper with suspicion. 'I suppose it'll be all posh hotel-type stuff like cucumber sandwiches and Bath Olivers –' Lottie didn't know what Bath Olivers were but posh characters in books were always eating them. She also couldn't imagine anything quite so dull as cucumber sandwiches '– and those tiny little eggs that birds that begin with a q lay, and – um – caviare. D'you know what caviare really is, Jethro? I found this out recently. It's only a load of old fish eggs.'

'Well, sorry to let you down, Lottie.' He threw open the lid of the hamper with the aplomb of a showman. 'No cucumber sandwiches, caviare or quails' eggs for you today. Come and have a look.'

Lottie peered into the wicker interior, and a big smile spread over her face. 'Wicked!' she exclaimed. Inside was an assortment of sand-wiches, Pringles, pink marshmallow pigs, chocolate fingers and Coke. 'This is the best picnic I've ever been on!'

Jethro gave a smile at Dannie's appalled expression. 'Don't worry,' he said. 'There's a load of old fish eggs for you, and some more grown-up stuff in the cool box. I asked them to pack ours separately.'

'Well, Janey – that's a relief. So this might turn out to be the best picnic I've ever been on, too?'

It was. After they'd eaten they played a game of Donkey with a ball that Jethro had stopped off earlier to buy, and then they had a sandcastle-building competition. Dannie's sandcastle – decorated with shells and seaweed and sea pinks – was easily the most beautiful, but they deemed Lottie to be the winner because she had devised a killer moat with a drawbridge that worked.

Jethro had attempted to construct a castle with turrets at each corner, but it just ended up looking like a sheep that had been left on its back with its legs sticking up in the air, and they laughed and laughed at it so hard that they ended up with tears streaming down their faces.

'I wish the Mysterious One was here,' Lottie announced as she attempted for the umpteenth time to fill her moat with water. She had spent nearly ten minutes running to and from the water's edge, fetching water in a discarded Volvic bottle, and every time she sloshed the water into the moat it had filtered away into the sand by the time she got back with the next bottleful.

'Who's the Mysterious One?' asked Jethro. He was wearing denim cut-offs and was lounging on the picnic rug looking pretty bloody irresistible, Dannie thought, even with his hint of middle-aged spread. If Lottie hadn't been with them, she'd have snogged him there and then.

'The Mysterious One,' Lottie informed him, 'is my gerbil.'

Dannie slid a sideways glance at Jethro. To his credit, he betrayed not a hint of mirth. He just kept his eyes fixed with intense interest on Lottie. 'They're fascinating animals, gerbils,' he said. 'I must meet this Mysterious One some day. I kept a gerbil myself, as a child.'

'Oh? What was it called?'

'The Lone Ranger.'

Dannie resisted with difficulty the impulse to guffaw. She *loved* the idea of Jethro as a boy with a gerbil as insanely monikered as Lottie's!

'Good name for an only gerbil,' said Lottie.

'Only gerbil?'

'Yeah, you know, like "only child". I'm an "only child".' She manipulated her drawbridge into the 'up' position. 'And the Mysterious One's an "only gerbil". I bet if she was here I could train her to use this drawbridge. She's highly intelligent, you know.'

'The Lone Ranger was pretty bright, too.'

'Bum,' said Lottie, as the last traces of water disappeared. 'The water's never going to stay put. I'm going swimming. Will you come, Dannie?'

'Of course.' Dannie had on the prettiest bikini under her jeans. It was a forties-style ruched confection, with a discreet ruffled trim along the bra that couldn't help but draw attention to her cleavage. She was dying to show it off to Jethro. 'Come on, lazy-arse!' she said, stripping off her T-shirt and shimmying out of her jeans. She extended a hand to him where he lay on the beach, leaning back on his elbows and looking up at her with eyes so appreciative they made her feel horny. She could tell by the bulge at his crotch that he was feeling the same way. 'I've a strong suspicion you could do with an energetic swim in very cold water, Mr Palmer,' she added, raising an eyebrow as she pulled him to his feet, and started racing down the beach.

'Last one in's a smelly pig!' shouted Lottie, and the shout became a shrill squeal as she hit the water.

Beside her, Dannie heard Jethro's sharp intake of breath as he made contact with the icy sea. 'Oh, *shit!*' he exclaimed, before hurling himself into the waves and swimming strongly horizon-wards.

Dannie and Lottie watched him go. 'Hee hee! He's just like Roadrunner!' observed Lottie, splashing up water vigorously with her feet.

'It *is* bloody freezing,' observed Dannie. 'He's probably used to swimming in heated pools.'

'Then he's a wimp. Let's do duck dives,' suggested Lottie, taking a deep breath and going for it.

Dannie hadn't done a duck dive in years. She performed a series of inelegant dives, spluttering and laughing every time she came to the surface.

Jethro had swum a distance of about a hundred metres before he finally turned round and did a fast crawl back to the shore. He passed Dannie and Lottie, who were now competing to see who could stay down the longest, and Dannie could just make out some gibbered expletives as he zoomed past.

'Did you spend your entire swim effing and blinding?' she asked him when she joined him on the beach some time later.

'Pretty well,' he admitted. 'I have never swum in such scrotum-tighteningly freezing water in my entire life.'

'Careful,' warned Dannie as Lottie drew abreast. She knew the same child would be intrigued to find out exactly what a scrotum was. 'I suppose you're used to swimming off *tropical* beaches, Mr Poncy Palmer.'

'Less of the ponce, if you please, Ms Ballsy Moore. I will have you know that I can list the following among my macho credentials.' He struck a mock-heroic stance and cleared his throat with aplomb. 'I ski to professional level, I climb mountains and I have a black belt in karate.'

'Cool!' said Lottie.

Dannie gave him a sceptical look.

'All true,' he said. 'I'll prove it to you by taking you climbing in the Grand Canyon some time. It'll blow your mind, my dear.'

Oh!

'As a special treat my godmother's taking me swimming in the Sybaris next week, Jethro,' said Lottie. 'I could meet you there for a duck-diving competition, if you like.'

'Alas, Lottie, I will not be available next week for duck-diving competitions. And I would not be able to dip so much as a toe in the Sybaris pool even if I *were* available.'

'Oh? Why not?'

'I suffer from a condition known as contact irritant dermatitis.'

'Contact *what*?'

'Well, to put it simply, I have an allergy to chlorine. Even a whiff of the stuff brings me out in a rash. I have to confine all my swimming to beaches.'

'Of the tropical variety, naturally.' Dannie smiled at him.

'Naturally.' He smiled back.

'Are you really, really rich, Jethro?'

'Yes, Lottie. I am.'

'A millionaire?'

'Yup.'

'Hey! That is *beyond* cool! I have a real millionaire film director to interview for my project!'

'If you want to interview Jethro, you'd better get on with it, Lottie,' advised Dannie, stretching herself out on the picnic rug. 'We can't stay on here much longer. I told your mam we'd have you back by seven.'

'We could phone and say we'll be late.'

'No can do, sweetheart. We've a party to get to this evening.'

Lottie made a face, and then she fetched her pen and notebook from her swimming bag and started quizzing Jethro about the world of film, while Dannie lay on her tummy in the sun and drowsed. Their voices receded into an ambient drone – not at all unpleasant – the child's high reedy voice in *contrappunto* to Jethro's drawly Southern growl.

Dannie was still thinking about what Jethro had said. *I'll take you climbing in the Grand Canyon some time* ... It was the first time he had ever referred to a future in which Dannie Moore might feature. She pictured herself in some far-away time and place, lying in the sun after a picnic with Jethro and their own little girl, listening to father and daughter chatting like equals. He would make a brilliant father: he would spoil their girleen rotten. Where would they be? By the Grand Canyon? She saw herself from a great height now, stretched out against the red earth of Colorado, while beside her Jethro and ... and ... *Paloma!* – she'd always loved the name Paloma! – played Cat's Cradle or Paper, Stone, Scissors, and laughed the way Lottie had laughed earlier at Jethro's bonkers sandcastle.

Dannie felt like languor personified when he woke her some time later by dropping a little trail of kisses down her spine. She turned over to see his face blocking out the last of the low-slung evening sun, and she felt a wrench in her gut when she realized how dear and familiar it had become to her. Tomorrow he'd be gone. 'You have goosebumps,' he said. 'It's getting cold. It's time to go home.'

Lottie was knackered by the time they hit the road, and cold now, too. Dannie wrapped her in the picnic rug and drove back, still trying to feel languid, not allowing herself to think about tomorrow. Jethro kept his hand on her thigh the entire way. She'd never felt more like a Smug Married in her life. The cassette he'd given her had played itself round on a loop, and 'Perfect Day' had come on again. Dannie sang along, mindful of how pertinent the lyrics were. It *had* been a perfect day, and Jethro Palmer had masterminded it. He was so clever he'd even chosen the right music. He was an *exceptionally* clever man. Intelligent, manly, talented, devastatingly sexy . . . Guy had been all those things, too, she thought, and then wished she hadn't. The memory of Guy and his duplicity had sent a cloud scudding across the blue sky perfection of her day. Perhaps the day had been *too* perfect? She was superstitious about stuff like that – she wished there was something made of wood in the car that she could touch for luck, but she made do with crossing the fingers of her left hand as she manipulated the gears. At the next traffic light a single magpie stood sentinel. No, no, no . . .

She cast around for something to distract her.

'Did you really have a gerbil called the Lone Ranger?' she asked Jethro.

Beside her in the passenger seat he turned to face her, an expression of amused cynicism on his face. 'What a gullible gal you are,' he said. 'Of course I didn't. I actually had a Dobermann called Fang. I was just playing along with Lottie, telling her what she wanted to hear. There's no harm in that.'

'Oh.' Dannie felt silly, but she also felt something else. She actually felt a bit disappointed that Jethro had had a Dobermann called Fang and not a gerbil called the Lone Ranger. The gerbil story had suggested to her that underneath the rugged macho exterior, Jethro was in touch with his caring, feminine side. Over the speakers, 'Perfect Day' came to its bittersweet conclusion.

When they reached her apartment block, Jethro took the wheel. They had decided that, until Dannie could organize a space in the car park of her apartment block, the Karmann Ghia should remain in the parking lot of the Hamilton hotel. She knew that if she left it on the street some gouger would inflict serious damage on the soft top with a sharp object.

She let herself and Lottie in through the main door, and they turned to wave Jethro off.

'Thanks, Jethro! That was the best afternoon I've had in ages,' sang Lottie.

'You're welcome, Mademoiselle Elliot. We must do it again next time I'm in Ireland.'

Next time he's in Ireland! Dannie registered the words with glee.

'Bye, Jethro,' she said now, trying not to let her glee show too much. 'Will I meet you at the hotel before we hit the party?'

'Yes. Do that. By the way, I don't much relish the idea of buffet-party food, do you?'

Dannie thought about it. 'Not a lot,' she said.

'In that case, we'll have something delicious to eat from room service before we go.'

The look he gave her invited a collusive smile back. Releasing the handbrake, he indicated right and then turned back to them. 'I must say I feel like a right nancy boy driving this poofy car. My street cred will be in tatters if anyone spots me between here and the Hamilton.' And he blew her a farewell kiss as he took off down the street.

'Are you going to marry him?' asked Lottie as they waited for the lift.

'Ah, now – don't be daft, Lottie!'

'It's not daft. He likes you. I can tell. And you like him. Have you had sex with him yet?'

'*Lottie!* The cheek of you, the nosy creature!'

'You have, haven't you? Maybe you'll have a baby.'

The lift arrived with a ping! and they got in. Dannie bent down until her face was on a level with Lottie's. 'I am now officially nipping this conversation in the bud, OK?'

'OK,' said Lottie equably. 'D'you know something? I wish Mum had a boyfriend like Jethro. I'm going to try and find her one. I'd hoped that vet might have been a boyfriend for her, but he's a poof.'

'Hey, now! That's a very politically incorrect word.'

'Jethro just used it.'

'That doesn't mean you're allowed to.'

'It's not fair. Olds are allowed to do loads of things that us kids can't.'

'What are olds?'

'Grown-ups.'

'Janey mackers, child! Couldn't you use the more respectful "adults"? And who's this vet you mentioned?'

'He has a place across the road. I'm going to have to take the Mysterious One to him soon. She's got a cough. Don't tell Mum, because I don't think she'd approve, but I drop in and see him sometimes on a Saturday when he's not too busy, on my way back from gymnastics. He lets me stroke the animals that aren't too sick.'

'He sounds nice.'

'Yeah. He is. He's very kind.'

They got out of the lift and walked down the corridor to Rosa's apartment. Rosa answered the door, looking distracted. 'Jethro not with you?' was the first thing she said.

Dannie felt embarrassed. She realized that she didn't particularly want to come clean about Jethro's over-the-top, wonderfully romantic gesture, and reveal that he'd gone whizzing off in the glamorous car he'd presented her with that morning. But Lottie did. She launched into the story with gusto.

'So he's driven it back to the Hamilton until Dannie can organize parking for it here,' she finished. 'And then she can take us out for rides in it! It's the best fun! Apart from her headscarf whacking me in the face all the time, that is. And we could go back to Brittas – could we, Dannie? Oh – it was a totally brilliant day, Mum! I wish you'd come with us.'

During Lottie's monologue, Dannie had been studying Rosa carefully. There was something wrong. Rosa was only half listening, Dannie could tell. She was definitely abstracted: something had happened to upset her. Lottie got the vibe too. She stopped abruptly, and then said: 'What's wrong, Mum?'

'Oh – nothing. Nothing.'

'The Mysterious One's OK, is she? Has something happened to her?'

'No, no, she's fine, Lottie. Coughing a bit, that's all.'

'Oh! I'd better go and check on her!' Lottie

tumbled into her room to make sure that the Mysterious One wasn't languishing like Garbo in *Camille*.

'There *is* something wrong, Rosa. What is it?' asked Dannie.

'I – there's something I have to tell you, Dannie, and I don't know how. Come into the kitchen and I'll put the kettle on.'

Dannie followed Rosa and sat down at the kitchen table. Rosa filled the kettle and switched it on, but remained standing by the worktop with her back to her. 'What's up, Rosa?' she asked again.

Rosa took a deep breath, then went for it in a rush. 'It's about Jethro Palmer, Dannie. I ran into Miriam from the Sybaris this afternoon. She told me something really horrible about him.'

Rosa turned to look at her friend and, on seeing the expression on her face, Dannie felt something inside her fragment. It was the same sensation she'd experienced when she'd come across the picture of Guy Fairbrother and his pregnant child bride. She knew that whatever news she was going to hear would be shocking, and that it would be unbearable. So she steeled herself and said: 'Tell me, Rosa.'

Rosa forced herself to meet Dannie's eyes square on. 'Jethro Palmer sexually assaulted one of the chambermaids in the Hamilton hotel early today,' she said.

* * *

Rosa had been cleaning out the Mysterious One's cage earlier that afternoon when she realized she'd run out of Dettol. She had just nipped out to the local Londis to get a bottle of the stuff and a few other things when she'd seen Miriam passing by on her bicycle.

'Hey! Miriam!'

'Rosa!' Miriam applied the brake too fast and skidded past her. Rosa ran to where she'd pulled the bike up onto the verge of the road. 'I'm in a mad dash!' rushed Miriam. 'I shouldn't stop – I'm late for my Reiki class.'. She glanced at her watch. 'But there's just time to fill you in on the latest. Did you hear what that jerk-off's done now? The bloke who asked me for a hand job?'

'No. What?'

'He lured one of the Filipino chambermaids into his room early this morning and sexually assaulted her.'

Rosa's eyes widened with shock, and her hands went automatically to her mouth. '*No!*'

'Yes,' Miriam assured her, with an emphatic nod of her head. 'The poor girl was so terrified that she didn't tell anyone about it until after lunch, when she broke down in front of the housekeeper.'

'Oh, no, Miriam! Did he – did he rape her?'

'No. He forced her to strip, then made her masturbate him.'

'Oh, *God*!'

'I imagine he thought she'd never have the nerve to report him – and she nearly didn't. He very nearly got away with it.'

'Oh, Christ, Miriam. What's going to happen?'

'I haven't a clue. Depends on whether or not she decides to press charges.' Miriam scooped up a pedal with her left foot, preparing to glide off into the traffic.

'Miriam!' Rosa laid a hand on her arm to detain her. 'You're *sure* this happened? You're positive it's not just a rumour?'

'Absolutely. Why?'

Should she tell Miriam? She didn't feel quite comfortable with the idea of entering into a discussion about Dannie's private life with someone who didn't even know her. But this was important. 'A friend of mine is involved with him,' she confessed.

'What? You mean – she's having an affair with him?'

'Yes.'

'He's bad news, Rosa. Tell her to get out fast.'

'You think that's the best thing to do?'

'Absolutely. Tell her to write him off and find herself a man who doesn't include sexually harassing subordinates amongst his hobbies.' Again, Miriam prepared to move off. 'Unfortunately, it might not prove to be that easy to find such a paragon. The world is chock-full of men who think with their cocks.'

Rosa bit her lip as she contemplated the consequences of telling Dannie. 'Oh, God. I can't do it. Oh, God. You're right. I *must* do it.'

'I really have to dash, Rosa.' Miriam was looking over her shoulder for a break in the traffic. 'I'll see you next week.'

'Yeah, yeah – Monday,' said Rosa abstractedly. 'Bye, Miriam.'

In Londis she helped herself to Dettol and Tampax and milk and went to join the queue with Miriam's words still echoing in her head. *The world is chock-full of men who think with their cocks* . . . Dannie herself had come out with almost the same phrase only a few months ago, when she'd first started seeing Jethro. Oh, God! Although Dannie never talked about it, Rosa suspected that she had gone through a rough time with some dickhead in her past life, in London. Now she was being shafted again.

As she handed a tenner to the girl at the cash desk and waited for her change, Rosa's stomach went porridgey at the prospect of having to re-acquaint her friend with the 'All Men are Bastards' ethic. Dannie was going to be devastated.

Dannie had taken the news very calmly indeed. Then she'd thanked Rosa for being upfront with her, and gone up to her own apartment and sat there like a hollow thing for a long time, feeling as if all the happiness she'd ever known had been sucked out of her. What pained her most was that she'd allowed herself to be taken for a major sucker – not just once in her life, but twice. First Guy, now Jethro.

Guy may have betrayed her, but at least he hadn't bullshitted her. This time she'd allowed herself to be seduced with flamboyant gestures – flowers, compliments, candlelit dinners, extravagant gifts: the classic way to a first-class bimbo's heart, she thought bitterly. She remembered what he'd said the first time they spoke on the phone, when she had thanked him for the flowers: *I have never done anything quite so quixotic in my life* . . . How many times had he come out with that line before, how many other blinkered Bettys had bought it? It made her feel sick just to think about it.

Rosa had spared her none of the details about Jethro's goings-on in the Hamilton because Dannie had insisted that she be spared nothing. She wanted no obfuscations, no half-truths: she was determined to know the full extent of her betrayal this time round because she wanted to use every last nugget of knowledge to fuel her hatred for this man who had spent the past three months manipulating her so cynically and so expertly. So *cruelly*! For a second a real searing pain flared up in her heart, and she wanted to cry out loud as she recalled how perfect today had been. And other things made her want to weep too: how delighted they'd been at the start of their relationship, for instance, when they'd discovered silly things about each other that they had in common, such as a partiality for coconut Liquorice Allsorts or their unhip predilection for tomato ketchup; she remembered how he had explored her bedroom, naked but for a towel, getting to the very heart of her in a way no other man had ever done; and the way they'd laughed and laughed today on the beach at his stupid sheep-shaped sandcastle.

How had she got him so wrong? Jesus! She'd even misinterpreted his handwriting – she'd seen no treachery there. Now more stuff from the past came flooding back, and she saw it all in a new, revealing light. The way he'd spoken to Jeanne Renaud on the phone the first time he'd taken her to dinner – how he'd flattered the actress and smoothed her ruffled petals and told her what she'd wanted to hear. He'd even described himself as an expert at 'kid-gloving'. For 'kid-gloving', read 'conning'. That was the precise word for what he'd done to her. This consummate con-artist had kid-gloved, conned, and then shafted her. Now she remembered the way he'd looked at her earlier today when he'd commented on her gullibility. How could she have lost sight of the fact that manipulating people was his *job*? How had she allowed herself to become his puppet? How was it possible that she, Dannie Moore, who'd worked so hard to acquire invulnerability and who prided herself on her not unreasonable intelligence, how had *she* fallen for the kind of flattery even a severely cerebrally challenged bimbette might see through?

The sudden electronic jangle of the phone rattled her so badly she jumped to her feet. She stood motionless in the middle of the floor until the answering machine picked up. The usual bleeping noises ensued, then Jethro's voice slid over the speaker. Now that she'd unmasked the two-faced bastard, even his voice sounded different. It made her almost want to cover her ears with her hands. How had she *ever* thought it sexy? She'd compared it to treacle once, and treacle it was. Tacky, cloying, unctuous.

'Dannie – hi. I've to sort something here in the hotel . . . um . . . personal stuff? – so I'm going to have to ask you not to stop by here this evening. It's a better idea if you just head straight to the party, and I'll join you as soon as I can. Calypso will be there to keep you company. Sorry about this. Life gets complicated when you least want it to. Oh – by the way, maybe we should stay at your place tonight? I'm getting kinda tired of anonymous hotel living. See you later, Dannie. Bye.'

387

You bloody bet it didn't suit him to have her stop by the hotel! He'd probably been kicked out of the joint on his ear. The bastard! The fucking, fucking bastard! He was still persisting in stringing her along like the malleable sucker she'd been up until now! She heard his voice in her head again, uttering the words she'd heard only an hour ago: *just playing along with Lottie, telling her what she wanted to hear ... There's no harm in that.* Yes, there *was* harm in it. He had hurt her, Dannie, horribly. He'd deceived her, humiliated her and abused her.

Her reflection was studying her from the mirror on the wall opposite. Did she want revenge? she asked herself. No. What was the point? Tomorrow he'd be gone out of her life for ever. She would never see him again. What *did* she want, then? the reflection demanded. Well, she definitely knew the answer to that. She didn't want any reminders in the form of tacky souvenirs.

Dannie marched into her bedroom. Methodically she sorted her underclothes into two piles – the stuff Jethro had given her, and the stuff she'd bought herself. Then she took the frothy gift items into the sitting room, set them in the grate, doused them with methylated spirits and put a match to them.

What else? The car. She winced when she thought of her stonking gullibility there. The little Karmann Ghia had clearly been hired for the occasion – there was a car-hire firm in Dublin that specialized in classic cars for weddings and promotions and suchlike. Oh, *Christ* – what an abject sucker she was!

She picked up the phone and speed-dialled in the number of the Hamilton hotel. 'Good evening,' she said when the receptionist picked up. 'Could you please convey a message to Mr Jethro Palmer, who is currently staying in the Fitzmorris suite? Could you tell him that Ms Dannie Moore no longer requires the car. No, that's all. Ms Moore no longer requires the car. He will understand. Thank you.'

And then Dannie sat down on the floor of her exotic boudoir and cried her heart out.

Chapter Eleven

For the first time in her life, Calypso didn't feel like going to a party. The film had wrapped, and it was time for everyone to really let their hair down. But Calypso didn't want to let her hair down. In fact, she decided, she'd wear it up this evening in the elegant chignon that Dominic told her made her look like an ice-queen. Because tonight, more than ever, Calypso O'Kelly needed her ice-queen defences around her.

Since spending three days in Leo's company, she had discovered something very scary. She had discovered that her feelings about Leo Devlin were no longer driven simply by lust. In fact, Calypso was very scared indeed that she was either falling desperately in love with him, or that something in her was addicted to him. She was even more scared that if she went to the party tonight she might not be able to resist having a crazy, spontaneous fuck with him in some sordid car park or alleyway, and yet again run the fearful risk of discovery.

Her nerves jangled every time she thought about the risks she'd taken, the wanton recklessness she had displayed. In the time that had elapsed since her debauched weekend she had effectively blocked a lot of stuff from her consciousness. But what she *hadn't* been able to block was the way Leo had responded to her after he'd violated her. She had clung to him, abject with humiliation and self-loathing, and he had stroked her hair and whispered sweet nothings in her ear and told her that everything was OK, that there was nothing wrong with a little healthy sexual experimentation and that – there, there – Calypso was a good girl. He'd run a bath and lit candles and soaped her and fed her with the canapés she'd brought, and towelled her dry afterwards, and made her laugh. And then he'd made love to her with more than usual tenderness, gazing into her eyes as he coaxed her to her climax. And the day she'd left his flat she found herself wondering twenty-four, seven about when she might see him again.

What frightened Calypso most about her feelings for Leo was that she had jeopardized the thing she valued most in her life: her very nearly perfect marriage. She, Calypso O'Kelly, was the most happily married woman she knew (apart from the sex), and to have risked injecting bad blood into her alliance with her beloved Dominic was an indication of how insane her behaviour was becoming. Now she wished to high, high heaven that Dominic was there to escort her this evening. If she had Dominic by her side she need have no fear that she'd allow herself to fall under the influence of the awful, irresistible voodoo that Leo worked on her. But Dominic was in London again, wining and dining some famous painter.

He phoned while she was having her bath.

'Oh, Dominic! I wish you were here!'

'Where are you?'

'I'm in the bath.'

'I wish I were there too. What's up with you? You sound a little glum.'

'I really don't feel like going to this party on my own.'

'You'll feel fine once you've had a glass of champagne.'

'I'm having one. It's not doing any good.'

'Why don't you just opt out if you're not feeling up to it?'

'That would be a very professionally incorrect thing to do, darling. I have to say goodbye to Jethro and the producers and put out feelers about what's in the pipeline. It's *networking* for me, Dominic, not really a party at all.'

She heard him sigh down the line. 'You used to love wrap parties. Maybe you should think about getting out, Calypso.'

'Getting out of what?'

'The business. It's not as if we need the money, and you don't seem to be getting the same kind of enjoyment from it as you used to. It's not right that you should suffer the kind of stress you've obviously been suffering from the past couple of months.'

'Have I? Been stressed, that is? I don't think I'm suffering from any more stress than usual.'

'Well, something's wrong. You're not as upbeat about life as you used to be. And it's taking its toll on you physically, too. You've been losing weight – you have a kind of gaunt look about you these days. Where's the golden girl I married disappeared to?' Oh! Oh, God! He'd said it in a jokey voice, but the observation still flooded her with panic. 'I'll tell you what. I'll bring you back a present from London to cheer you up.'

'Oh, will you, Dominic?' She quickly adopted the bright, girlish tone she knew appealed to him. 'What is it? Have you got it yet?'

'It's a surprise.'

'Oh, goodie! I love getting surprises! Thank you, darling! I'm dying to see you. What time will you be back on Tuesday evening?'

'The plane gets in at half-past ten. I should be home by midnight.'

'I'll be in bed.' She invested the sentence with a disingenuous suggestiveness.

'I know. The timing's perfect. I shall start peeling my suit off the minute I get through the front door. D'you know something, Calypso O'Kelly? Any time I'm away from you, I get a hard-on when I think about you.'

'What a lovely compliment! Have you got one now?'

'Of course. I've been nursing it since you told me you were lying in the bath drinking champagne, you cock-teasing bitch.'

Calypso laughed low in her throat. 'Save it for Tuesday night,' she said.

'A physical impossibility, angel. I have to go. I'm running late for Daniel and Madeleine.'

'Enjoy dinner, darling! See you on Tuesday.'

'Looking forward to it already. And do try and enjoy your party.'

Calypso pressed 'end call' and put the receiver down on the mosaic edge of her bath. Dominic's phone call had seriously disturbed her. She remembered what Leo had said to her all those months ago before her birthday party. *Have no fear, Calypso . . . Your age is still a state secret.* She wasn't a golden girl any more. The gilded goddess Dominic had married was beginning to show signs of wear and tear.

She looked around the bathroom shelves at all the magical lotions and potions that promised her eternal youth. Had they been lying? Were the halcyon days of her beauty over? 'Radiance Revealing Serum' read the copy on one product. Ouch! Maybe she had no radiance left to reveal. Was she going to end up like some old Hollywood diva, investing massive amounts of money and energy on the cosmetic equivalent of facial scaffolding? Would she have to start getting up earlier and earlier in the morning simply to accommodate her beauty routine? The thought filled her with dread.

She pulled the plug and got out of the bath, not caring to look in the full-length mirror until she'd shrugged on her towelling robe. She didn't want to see any saggy bits or cellulite. Then she wandered into her walk-in wardrobe, telling herself to think about something else – such as what to wear tonight.

Hm. Nothing too sexy. Something spare and elegant. Heels, of course: the higher the better. She riffled along the rail and selected a tunic in clingy white silk jersey. Underwear was a no-no in a dress like that, but that didn't matter because it was ankle-length. Dominic loved this dress because he said it made her look more than ever like a Greek goddess. And that's how she wanted to feel tonight – elevated, remote, and powerful as the goddess whose name she bore.

She zapped 'play' on the radio, hoping that

some easy listening might lighten her mood. The tune that came on was that ancient Cliff Richard number 'The Young Ones'. She zapped it off again immediately, hating those young ones. Awful reports had been reaching her recently of lovey-dovey behaviour on the set between Leo and his nubile co-star Jeanne Renaud. Their astonishing sexual chemistry had by all accounts translated beautifully onto film. People were saying that such extraordinary on-screen synergy hadn't been seen since Burton and Taylor. Yet another disincentive for Calypso to attend this odious wrap party. She was dreading witnessing the couple together. She didn't think she could handle the searing jealousy she knew she was bound to feel.

She switched on the lights that surrounded her dressing-table mirror and opened the drawer that contained her most effective weapons. Methodically, expertly, Calypso O'Kelly proceeded to put on the armour she felt most comfortable wearing. Her make-up.

She looked the part, but she certainly didn't feel it. Even the fact that a man did a classic double-take and nearly walked into a lamp-post as Calypso emerged sleekly from the taxi did nothing to reassure her. She hummed as she made her way up the steps of the nightclub in a vain attempt to persuade herself that she was feeling happy and confident. It didn't work, and Calypso suddenly realized that she hadn't felt happy or confident for ages.

Dominic was right. She *had* changed recently. She'd noticed that the little stammer that had plagued her in her childhood was starting to recur. It was as if she'd lost control over her life . . . How *could* she? She, who had prided herself so on having wrested control from the producers and the directors and the designers and the agents and the script editors and all the other despots who breathed down actors' necks! She remembered the heady blast of liberation she'd experienced on that memorable occasion when she'd made her decision to forsake acting for casting, the life-enhancing revelation that power was control and control *self*-empowerment. What had happened to her since? Leo Devlin, that's what. She'd relinquished control of her life to her lover.

She handed her wrap to the cloakroom attendant and took a deep breath. The party was kicking already. Calypso had deliberately decided to arrive late because it meant she wouldn't have to spend so much time there. In fact, she realized as she looked round, preparing to schmooze, she really needn't have bothered coming. The executive producer was clearly pissed, and there was no sign of Jethro. Even the second unit director didn't seem to have turned up, and of this Calypso was glad, because he had a nauseating habit of looking at her tits instead of her eyes when he was talking to her.

The minute she walked through the door all eyes were on her. She hoped it was because she'd put so much effort into the way she looked, but knew it was actually because the joint was coming down with actors, all of whom were desperately sending vibes in her direction. She was being bombarded with subliminal messages. *Over here, Calypso! Calypso, look at me! Listen to the way I laugh, Calypso! It's flagrant! It's sexy!* Some of them opted for what she knew they thought was a more subtle approach, ostentatiously avoiding eye contact and half turning their backs to her; the message here was: *Yeah, we know you are an all-powerful casting director goddess-type, but that cuts no ice with us. We are so cool that you'll be bound to notice us sooner or later, and then you'll realize how profoundly interesting we are.*

Oh, fuck you all, anyway! Calypso thought dispiritedly as she headed to the bar for Dutch courage. I've been there, I've done that, and at least I don't have to wear the fucking T-shirt any more.

Wishing more and more that she hadn't come, she tapped her fingers impatiently on the counter as she waited for the bartender to bring her drink. Scanning the room, she wondered where Dannie and Jethro were. It was typical of her luck that the only two people she felt like talking to either hadn't arrived yet, or else they'd seen sense and had left early to bonk each other's brains out.

There was no sign of Leo, either, or of pretty little Jeanne Renaud, and she didn't know whether to be relieved or disappointed. She didn't know what to think any more. She had just taken the first sip of her drink and stapled a smile to her face, mentally preparing to work the room, when a tone on her phone alerted her to a text message. She recognized the number immediately. *Erase it*, said the voice of reason. But as was Calypso's wont, she completely ignored the voice of reason and pressed 'read message'. *Good girl*, she read. *No VPL*.

Calypso turned back to the bar in order to conceal her expression. Stupid boy! How dare he send her a message like that – especially when she was here in High Queen of Casting mode! She took a sip of wine, then another, and shifted her centre of balance from foot to foot, feeling the skin on her inner thighs rub together as she did so. Her phone shouted at her again. This time the display read: *I want 2 tuch ur arse*.

Oh! He was obviously in one of his awful laddish moods. She hated it when he was like this. Should she text him back? Tell him to shut up and leave her alone? Or was it more dignified simply to ignore his juvenile messages? She dithered, and drank more wine, and waited for the next message to come through. *Turn round*, it read. She found herself doing as she was told. Her eyes scanned the crowd from left to right, and from right to left, but she couldn't see him.

Bee beep! *Up here*. She looked up.

He was on the balcony, leaning against the railing, watching her with that lethal look. *Oh God!* More than ever, Calypso didn't know what to think. Leo raised his glass at her, then returned his attention to his phone.

Calypso turned back to the bar. Unwisely she downed the rest of her wine in a series of rapid sips, then indicated to the barman to bring her another. Her heart was beating itself to death against the bars of her ribcage when she accessed the next message. *Downstairs. Second door on left*.

'Calypso! Hi!' Oh no. It was Pamela, Jethro's PA, a woman who talked the hind legs off not just donkeys, but horses, cows and mules as well, and who never, ever took the hint. She *couldn't* get stuck in a conversation with her now, she just couldn't! She cast a glance upwards, to the balcony. Leo was gone.

'How are things?' Pamela was saying now. 'I'm really glad I ran into you, Calypso, because—'

'I'm sorry, Pamela. We'll have to catch up some other time. I think I'm actually about to throw up.' Calypso turned away abruptly and navigated her way across the room, hearing an astonished 'Oh! Can I get you something?' rising above the ambient chatter.

Downstairs. Second door on left.

Downstairs was a service corridor. There was no-one around. The sound of her heels on the concrete floor bounced off the ceiling and walls and reverberated in her ears. The rhythm she made as she walked went like this: *Don't be stupid, don't be stupid, don't be stupid . . .*

The second door on the left led to a staff loo. She remembered how she'd mentioned to Iseult once that Dominic had proposed to her when she got locked in a hotel loo. It had been in a men's loo that she'd made that life-changing decision to quit acting. She'd had some of the most mind-blowing sex of her life with Leo in an assortment of loos. What was it about her life that so many of her most vivid memories were to do with loos?

She sat down on the seat to wait, and checked the time on her phone. It was 9.52. What would Dominic be doing now? she wondered. Sitting in some elegant restaurant making intellectual chit-chat with an international painter and his beautiful, intelligent wife. He wouldn't in his wildest dreams imagine that his own wife was at that minute sitting on a lavatory in a hotel waiting for a serial Lothario to come and slip her a length. And it wasn't even a posh loo, with carpets and bowls of pot-pourri and individual hand towels like they had in the Hamilton. It was a bog standard, not particularly clean staff toilet. What was she *doing* here? And why wasn't he coming? She checked the time again. Nine fifty-six. Four minutes had passed. He must have got held up, bumped into someone he couldn't avoid talking to, she decided. She'd give him till ten o'clock.

Well, five past, then. Five past came and went. OK. So. That was that. The bastard had been having her on. He'd been playing one of his stupid little pranks. Just as she was about to text him a scathing message telling him that she would never, ever have sex with him again, she heard footsteps coming down the corridor. Well, thank you very much, Leo, she thought crossly. You've actually deigned to show up at last. Getting to her feet, she smoothed the skirt of her dress over her hips and adopted what she hoped was a dignified stance.

The door opened. 'Oh,' said the kitchen porter who stood there. 'Excuse me, madam.'

Calypso tried to wipe the appalled expression off her face. 'Oh! Um – no p-problem,' she said. 'I've just finished, anyway.' Oh *fuck*!

'For future reference, madam, the Ladies is upstairs on the first-floor corridor. This is the staff toilet.'

'Oh! Thanks very much! Enjoy your – um – evening.'

Calypso reeled out of the loo and up the stairs as if she were being pursued by a flock of pterodactyls.

In the Ladies on the first floor she dived into a cubicle and stood there for a moment or two, jiggling with anxiety. She had to get out of there. She would have to sneak down the stairs and find the back way out – she didn't want to run into *anyone*, she just wanted to flee to the haven of her perfect home and husband. But her husband wasn't *at* home, she remembered, wanting to weep. She sat down on the loo seat with her head slumped in her hands, and tried to gather her thoughts without whimpering.

What was wrong with her? What would the partygoers think if they could see her now? Would any of those people in the room downstairs believe that she, Calypso O'Kelly, could descend to such a level of depravity that had her gagging for a root in a nightclub toilet? An image of Leo smearing her lipstick rose to the surface of her consciousness, and she swiftly blasted it back into the murky depths. It could never, ever happen again.

Something occurred to her suddenly. Maybe she was suffering from sex addiction. Such a condition did exist, she knew. Michael Douglas had been a sex addict before he'd been reformed by Catherine Zeta Jones. Maybe she should seek psychiatric help? But no – then she'd have to confront stuff about herself and spill secrets, and she really didn't want to do that. Other people did that – the kind of people who didn't have perfect lives. The last thing people with perfect lives needed to do was see a psychiatrist, for Christ's sake.

Calypso shook her head and slumped a bit more as she wimped and dithered, but, aware that she would have to emerge some time from her loo sanctuary and try sneaking out the back way, she finally sat up straight and forced herself back into goddess mode with a Trojan effort.

Hey, hang about. What was she *thinking* of? *Sneaking* out the back way? Never! *Never!* She, Calypso O'Kelly, didn't sneak – she *strode*. She didn't *flee*, she confronted things. She was a mover, she reminded herself. A mover, a shaker, and a society-column headline-maker. This was the pits, and Calypso O'Kelly most certainly did *not* belong in the pits. She couldn't allow that fucker Leo Devlin to make her feel like some harried hedgerow animal.

Calypso sat up even straighter and assumed her most autocratic expression, even though there was no-one to see her. She would make sure her hair and make-up were still perfect, and then she'd go back down and rejoin the party and scintillate. She'd show that bastard that he hadn't the power to faze her. How dare he! How *dare* he show her such appalling disrespect! *She* was the one who should be calling the shots in this relationship. She had *discovered* him, he was her *creature*, and he would fucking well toe the line from now on. From now on their relationship would function on a strictly professional basis. There would be absolutely no more sex. Leo Devlin would want to be careful! Directors and producers *listened* to her. They valued her judgement and respected her opinion. If he continued to diss her in this way, she could clip the wings on his fledgling film career pretty damn smartly. She could end it with just six little words. *He's not right for the part.*

The cooling-off period would start from tomorrow, she decided. She'd investigate the call-barring service on her mobile network. He'd soon get the message when he realized that she was no longer taking his calls or receiving his laddish text messages. Hah! She smiled as she pictured Leo begging to be put through to her on the office phone. He'd probably come grovelling with a smarmy letter when Iseult kept saying 'Sorry, Leo. Calypso's not available.'

Calypso's not available. She liked the sound of that.

A twittering had impinged upon her consciousness. On the other side of the loo door, girl talk was going on. Lost in her fantasy, she'd chosen to ignore it until three words made her stiffen.

'Leo's so *sexy*!' A girly giggle. Calypso's ears felt larger than life, as if they belonged to some nosy cartoon character.

'Yes. 'E 'as the most beautiful – how you call it in your English slang? – cock. Like a Rodin masterpiece.' Excuse me? The puny cocks sculpted by Rodin bore *no* relation to Leo's. 'And 'e make love like an artist – so beautiful! With candles and music – always music! Mozart, Beethoven, Ravel.'

The speaker was Jeanne Renaud. Calypso wondered what Jeanne would say if she knew that her artful lover had spent three days in bed with Calypso O'Kelly, messing about with handcuffs and indulging in acts of depravity.

'And the compliments 'e pay me! 'E compare me sometimes to a painting by Ingres, sometimes to a painting by Goya.'

Leo had clearly refrained from comparing the lovely Jeanne to a painting by Picasso. Calypso thought of the compliments he'd paid *her* in the past. *Yum yum tart, up for it bitch, down and dirty little whore* was a fairly representative sample. And then she remembered the uncharacteristic tenderness he'd demonstrated the time he'd gazed into her eyes as he'd made love to her – and he *had* 'made love' to her that time, he hadn't simply 'fucked' her –

406

and the yearning she felt for him frightened her.

'And last night, as we lay in each other's arms, 'e told me—'

Calypso didn't want to hear what he'd told Jeanne last night as she lay in his arms. She took a deep breath, slid the bolt on the cubicle door, and stalked out, trusting that her goddess persona was intact.

'Hi, Jeanne! Girls!' she greeted the little coterie of actresses, and they twittered in response.

''Allo, Calypso,' cooed Jeanne. ''Ow lovely you look tonight in your Grecian gown!'

'Thanks, Jeanne. You look pretty gorgeous yourself.' The actress did look gorgeous, in a little frothy chiffon number. Calypso couldn't stop herself checking her rival out for VPL, and felt gutted when she saw there was none.

Stalking to the mirror, she inspected the damage. She reapplied lipstick, blotted her shiny face with *papier poudré*, and spritzed herself lightly with Chanel 19. In the background she was aware of all the actresses being aware of her, prinking themselves prettily and clearly thanking their lucky stars that they'd chanced to be in the loo at the same time as Calypso O'Kelly. Somehow 'Discovered in a hotel loo' didn't have quite the same ring to it as Lana Turner being discovered on a high stool in Schwab's ice-cream parlour.

One actress was hovering beside her, pretending to check her eye make-up. 'Um, Ms O'Kelly? May I take this opportunity—'

Beep beep! Hooray! Saved by text alert! 'Excuse me,' said Calypso, bestowing a smile on the grateful little girl. 'I have to access this. It's urgent.'

Here we go, a stoical part of her thought, as she prepared herself for punishment.

He didn't disappoint her. Leo's latest message read thus: *If u c my tart tel her I'm looking 4 her. Cud do with a decent ride. Haven't had one in ages! LOL, Leo XXX.*

Calypso pressed 'erase' with an angry thumb, then pretended to dial a number so as to discourage the needy actress from engaging her in conversation. 'Hello,' she said to nobody as she exited the loo. 'Yes, yes, that sounds good.'

Back downstairs, raging with humiliation, Calypso marched up to the bar and demanded a drink. The dozy klutz of a bartender took for ever to bring it. Standing there seething, beating a tattoo on the counter with her immaculately lacquered nails, she heard an elaborately accented voice come from behind her. 'Giff me a visky, ginger ale on the side, and don't be stingy, baby!' Another actress airing her audition piece! She wished they'd all fuck off and leave her alone. She wished Dominic was there. She wished she'd never come to this dismal excuse for a party.

Grabbing her drink, she surveyed the joint for a face she could talk to. Over by the door, Leo was now snogging Jeanne Renaud. Everybody was pissed. Wrap parties were notoriously *Hey! Free bar! Let's all drink as much as we can and get completely rat-faced!* type occasions. Oh! Was there *no-one* here she could talk to?

There! At last! Jethro Palmer! He was standing in the crowd, nursing a drink and looking as lost as Calypso felt. She snaked through the hordes and dived at him as if he was a lifebelt, and she a drowning woman.

'Jethro! Hello! I'm so happy to see you. I feel so vulnerable!'

'Vulnerable? You? You're the most powerful woman in the room.'

'You forget that I've enemies here. All those freeloading actors I've never cast. Where's Dannie?'

'I was going to ask you that very same question. I was meant to meet her here. Haven't you seen her?'

'No. You've only just arrived, I take it?'

'Yeah. I know it's late, but I had to pour oil on some troubled waters back at the hotel.'

'Oh?'

'Yeah. The second unit director was guilty of a misdemeanour. I think it's all blown over, but I certainly won't be using him on a film again.'

'What happened?'

'Let's just say that there are some lines in life you don't overstep, and he took a step too far. I have no truck with men who sexually harass women.'

'Oh. He tried it on with a member of the hotel staff?'

'He did.'

'Rosa told me that that was one of the occupational hazards of working in a hotel. I must say I never liked that geezer. He had a smarmy manner, and he never took his eyes off my tits.'

Jethro's eyes went to her cleavage, but it didn't give her the same creepy feeling as when the slimeball had done it. Jethro actually made her feel *good* when he smiled and said: 'I can't say I blame him, ma'am.' Oh! Lucky, lucky Dannie, to have landed the last gentleman on earth! Apart from Dominic, of course.

'Well, thank you kindly, Mr Palmer.' Calypso looked at her watch. 'I'm out of here at last. I can't hack this joint any more. Say hello to Dannie from me when you find her.'

'Will do. If you need to contact me by phone, by the way, use this number.' He took a card from his pocket. 'It's my address in Gozo.'

'Gozo? You have a place in Gozo?'

'Yeah. I've a villa there I can work from. I just

installed a screening room with editing facilities.'
Jethro kissed her cheek. 'You must come and
visit some time. You do know, don't you, that
according to legend Gozo is the island where the
Goddess Calypso kept Odysseus captive?'

Calypso remembered the daguerreotype that
Jethro had given her for her birthday, the one
that depicted Calypso all alone on her
Mediterranean isle, pining for her lost love.
'Maybe I will come,' she said. 'I could do with a
holiday.'

A loud laugh came from over by the door, and
heads turned. It was the insufferable Leo.
Calypso turned back to Jethro. 'I'm off. Enjoy
Gozo.'

'I'll do that. So long, Calypso. It was mighty
fine working with you.' He bent down and kissed
her cheek.

'Likewise. You're a true gent, Jethro. I hope
we can work together again.' She kissed him
back, then turned away, dreading the fact that
she'd have to pass Leo in the doorway on the
way out.

The centre of a little cluster of chattering
people, he was lounging against the jamb,
chatting up some vacuous-looking ingénue.
Jeanne Renaud was shining like the star she was,
busily signing an autograph for a bedazzled
fan.

'You should have a look at Stanislavski's *An*

Actor Prepares,' Leo was saying. 'It was written ages ago, but it's a classic well worth reading. Oh, hello, Calypso.'

'Leo,' she said smoothly as she slid past him, wishing she could spit in his face.

'Is that Calypso O'Kelly, the casting director?' she heard the ingénue squeak. 'Oh, introduce me, please!' Calypso would have been out of there like a bullet from a Luger, but Leo's hand lashed out and grabbed her wrist before she could pull the trigger. Her impulse was to turn and lash back, but people were watching. She couldn't run the risk of looking undignified.

'Calypso, this is Marjory Mellick, an actress. We were just trading techniques. Marjory's very into Stanislavski. As am I, of course. There's nothing like living a role to invest it with authenticity.'

Marjory nodded and simpered and extended a hand. 'Calypso. Delighted to meet you.'

Calypso took the proffered hand with her free one. Her left was still locked in Leo's grasp. She shot him a look, and immediately wished she hadn't. It was virtually impossible to stop looking at him once you'd started, impossible to disengage from those dangerous eyes.

'Did you use Stanislavski's method this time round?' she heard Marjory ask.

'Absolutely.'

'What kind of character were you playing?'

'Actually, the character's not unlike the role I played in the Thespus production of *Les Liaisons Dangereuses* – the Comte de Valmont.'

'Valmont?' breathed Marjory. 'Oh, wow. That has to be the sexiest role ever written. What were the similarities?'

'Well, like Valmont, the character in *Don Juan's Double* is a serial seducer of women – that's the best way of describing him, isn't it, Calypso?' His grip on her wrist tightened. 'He's utterly depraved – until, of course, he meets the gal who redeems him, as played by my real-life inamorata, Jeanne Renaud.'

'And how did you research the role?' Marjory gave him a mock-coy look from underneath her lashes.

'I fucked every woman who was up for it,' said Leo.

'Oh!' For a moment Marjory looked like a guppy out of water, gobsmacked and floundering. Then she made a go of regaining her cool so heroic as to be worthy of an Oscar nomination. Maybe this girl had something after all? thought Calypso abstractedly, subtly trying to extract herself from Leo's grip. She should find out who her agent was.

'Yup. Find 'em, fool 'em, frig 'em and forget 'em – that just about encapsulates the research I did on this role.'

'Well, hey – that's putting it bluntly, Leo. Were

there – um – *many* who were up for it?' *Could I be next in line?* read the subtext.

'A surprising number were. You'd be amazed at how gullible the most unlikely-seeming people can be.' He looked directly at Calypso. 'I even spent three days in bed with a married woman, making her fall in love with me.'

'Oh? How intriguing!' That coy look from Marjory again. 'How did you manage to bamboozle her?'

'Easy-peasy. The oldest trick in the book. I fed her an elaborate tissue of lies about my deprived childhood and the stupid bitch fell for it, hook, line and sinker.'

Calypso felt as if she'd been punched in the stomach. Somewhere far away she heard Marjory titter.

She could have dissolved into a puddle of tears. She could have reeled out of the party like a tragic Greek heroine pursued by Furies. She could have hit him a dig like some punch-drunk flyweight. But she knew that Leo was expecting her to do all or any of those things. He had manipulated this situation in order to goad a reaction from her – he *wanted* to see her publicly humiliated. So she made a supreme effort. Drawing herself up to her full regal height, Calypso looked him unflinchingly in the eye and smiled before leaning in to him and brushing his ear with her lips. 'You are the saddest, sickest fuck I have ever met, Leo Devlin,' she murmured, before kissing his cheek. Then she turned on her high, high heel and stalked through the door.

When she hit the street she was hyperventilating.

Chapter Twelve

Rosa hurried through heaving Temple Bar. She wanted to get to the Ark, the kids' cultural centre in Eustace Street, where Lottie was attending a dance workshop with her friend Roxanne. She'd been invited to stay in Roxanne's parents' weekend cottage in Wicklow for two weeks, to stave off the boredom that invariably settled in after the initial euphoria of the first days of the summer holidays had worn off. Rosa dreaded the summer months. Trying to figure out what to do with Lottie while she was working was more taxing than the *Irish Times* cryptic crossword. Hooray for Sonia, linchpin of the Motherhood, who had come to her rescue and suggested that her husband Will pick the girls up from the Ark and cart them off to the country.

After Lottie had seen a poster for the dance workshop in the window of the vet's, Rosa had booked her and Roxanne in for this Saturday afternoon. The minute she had left Lottie off at the Ark, she had raced home to catch an old film on the telly (Joan Crawford in *Mildred Pierce* – it always made her weep buckets), and only then discovered that most of her daughter's essential kit was lying dumped on her bedroom floor. Lottie had been rooting in the bag Rosa had packed for her, and she had obviously pulled out all the important stuff and forgotten to put it back in again. Now Rosa was racing back down the cobbled streets of Temple Bar with a carrier bag containing Harry Potter PJs, Harry Potter toothbrush, Harry Potter hairbrush, Harry Potter facecloth and several changes of underwear (Harry Potter and Barbie).

Despite the hassle of this last-minute rescue dash with the Harry Potter merchandise, Rosa was feeling light-hearted: had been all week. Work had been less demanding than usual. That was usually not such a good thing because it meant her earnings were down, but this week a superstar diva staying in the hotel had taken a real shine to her and had tipped her a fifty-euro note every time she'd had a massage. She hadn't done it in a condescending way either, she'd just said: 'You deserve it. You work hard. Why not use it to have a little fun?'

Fun. There was a real fun buzz in Temple Bar this afternoon. Rosa passed a group of girls outside a hip boutique. Decked out in pretty-pretty frocks, they were admiring the slogan-emblazoned T-shirts in the window and giggling like – well, like girls. Probably a hen party over from the UK.

It had been so long since *she* had done any partying, any giggling! Perhaps she should phone Calypso and see if she was on for going clubbing tonight? Or they could book somewhere not too madly expensive to eat. There were loads of joints in Temple Bar where they could get tapas or sushi or Tex-Mex. Have a couple of glasses of wine. She was due a treat – she hadn't had a drink in ages. Then there was that film on at the IFC that she'd read rave reviews for – she was dying to see it.

The automatic doors of the Ark slid open and Rosa found herself in the kid-friendly foyer. Helen, the administrator of the centre, was at reception. She knew Rosa because her actress sister was an old friend.

'Hey! You're early,' said Helen, looking at her watch. 'The workshop hasn't finished yet.'

'I thought it finished at five,' said Rosa.

'Nope. Half-past.'

'Dammit. Can I leave a bag of stuff with you to give to Lottie, Helen?'

'Sure you can.'

From the theatre space came a burst of children's laughter.

'Sounds like fun,' remarked Rosa.

'Have you half an hour to spare? Why don't you sneak upstairs onto the balcony and have a gawk at what's going on? Michael – the guy who's taking the workshop – is sex on legs.'

'Michael *Luque*?' Hel*lo*? Mr Fairy Cakes the vet? Rosa had seen him a few times in the local Londis. She still found him rather brusque and stand-offish, with a self-consciously world weary air that made her want to laugh when she thought of his goldfish food and his Angel Delight and his scratch cards and his gay purse. Nobody – but *nobody* – could find a man who had a penchant for Angel Delight sexy.

'Yeah. Go on. Enjoy,' Helen urged her. 'I'd be up there myself with my eyes out on stalks if I didn't have to work.'

'Well, I will then. I'd love to get a load of Lottie cutting capers. Thanks, Helen.'

Rosa negotiated the steel staircase, aware of the mounting racket that was issuing from the theatre space. Out on the balcony, a din assaulted her ears – a staccato, rhythmic, drumming din. She recognized it immediately as the thrilling sound of heels on hard wood. Below her a bunch of children were stamping their small feet, laboriously trying to emulate the steps of the dance that Michael Luque was demonstrating. Oh, wow! This wasn't a tap class, as

Rosa had somehow mistakenly inferred. This was flamenco.

Well! *This* Michael bore no resemblance to the surly, silent geezer Lottie had introduced her to. He was wearing the kind of loose black trousers favoured by Dean Martin in those fifties films, teamed with a plain white shirt that was neither too tight nor too Flatley-esque, and he'd had a good haircut. His arms were raised above his head as he executed the steps with effortless precision, his hands clapping a rhythm that conjured a weird kind of primitive sensation in her. 'One, two, *three*, four, five, *six*, seven, *eight*, nine, *ten*, eleven, *twelve*. O. . .K. Very good.' The arhythmic clatter of feet gradually stumbled to a halt, like a train running out of steam. Rosa could see Lottie's flushed face, spread with a wide smile, laughing at her own breathlessness. 'Now,' resumed Michael. 'I want you to do the clapping with me. The *palmas*.' Some of the kids looked at each other, and laughed and squirmed a bit. 'Come on,' coaxed Michael. 'Flamenco isn't shy – it's *bold*! You lot have to believe you're beautiful – you've to believe you're the most beautiful young people in Ireland! Look at Gabriella. Copy the way she stands.' For the first time Rosa became aware of a woman and a male guitarist who were seated downstage right. The woman got to her feet, stepped into the playing space, and struck an arrogant pose. 'See?' said

Michael. 'A beautiful, open chest, a beautiful, slender waist, a beautiful smile. That's really, really important!'

The woman called Gabriella wasn't conventionally beautiful, but the minute she'd assumed her stance she had *become* beautiful.

'Try doing the *palmas* for Gabriella. Lick your hands first – like this. It stops them stinging and it makes them have a better sound. Come on, Rachel.' He took hold of a small girl's hands and, as he clapped her palms together for her, the other kids followed suit while Gabriella demonstrated dance steps, hoisting her long black skirts up above her knees and holding them tightly around her hips in order to display the elegance of her legs and the articulation of her feet in their plain black, stack-heeled shoes.

As the guitarist matched the rhythm of the dancer and the clapping of the children, Rosa found herself automatically tapping her feet to the beat that Michael was co-ordinating, encouraging the children to stamp their feet now as well as clap. 'Heel, heel, flat, flat, heel, heel,' he shouted over the din. 'Ay! *Olé!* That's it! You see, when you do something good, you shout "*Olé!*" In Scotland it's "hoots", in Ireland it's "begorrah"—'

'No, it isn't!' laughed Lottie. 'Only an eejit would say "begorrah". We've been saying *Olé* in Ireland for yonks.'

The children were loosening up, obviously enjoying the liberating feeling of stamping, clapping and shouting *Olé!* They were having real fun now, relating to each other and smiling. Behind the smiles was a fierce concentration when Michael leaned towards them and issued instructions in a low voice.

Rosa saw that he was enjoying this every bit as much as they were. Michael Luque was clearly more comfortable in the company of children than adults. This assured, smiling dancer couldn't be more different to the reticent individual Lottie had introduced her to in Tesco's, the man who avoided Rosa's eyes when she passed him on the street, and who stonewalled her when she said hello. He was moving from child to child now, clicking his fingers, humming along to the guitarist – 'da dum, da *dum*!' – taking the children's hands and bending towards them, looking into their eyes. One little girl he approached wore an anxious expression. 'Hey!' he said. 'No shy girls! We're flamenco dancers – big and bold and beautiful and strong! You're far too quiet for a flamenco dancer! Shout at me, Deborah! *Olé!* Hey! Lottie! *Olé!*'

'*Olé!*' shouted Lottie with abandon, stamping the floor with the balls of her feet, then the heels, and managing to keep to the rhythm. Rosa was impressed. She herself had always suffered from a chronic lack of co-ordination; had never been able to master even the most basic steps of any of the dances she'd been taught during her theatre studies course. She identified easily with another child in the group who was stomping around randomly with a baffled, embarrassed expression on her face.

'*Olé!*' The guitarist and the dancer finished simultaneously with a flourish. Michael turned to the class and said, 'Splendid flamenco dancers! Now, please thank your guitarist, Ramón, and please thank the beautiful Gabriella.'

'Thank you,' intoned the children in that awful sheepish manner that children adopt when asked to repeat something. Michael assumed an expression of disgust.

'No, no!' he scolded them. 'What do you say when you find something is good? You say . . .'

'*Olé!*' shouted the children, and Michael laughed. Gabriella and the guitarist applauded them.

'That's better! Now run along, the lot of you, and show your parents how beautiful and brave and strong you are.'

The workshop was over. As Rosa slid out of her seat and went back down the stairs she remembered something W. C. Fields had once said. *Never work with kids or animals*. Evidently, in Michael Luque's case, the reverse applied. Kids and animals were what he was good at.

In the foyer Lottie was practising her flamenco steps with Roxanne. When she saw her mother she tap-tapped over to her with a big smile. 'Look, Mum! Beautiful, brave and strong! See how my arms are like eagles' wings – and look! My hands are like a waterfall!' Lottie waggled her fingers at her. 'What are you doing here?'

'Arms like eagles' wings, hands like a waterfall, and a brain like a sieve. Look what you forgot, you great twit.' Rosa held the bag of overnight gear out to Lottie.

'Oops! Sorry, Mum.' Lottie started dancing again. 'Will rang Roxanne to say he'd be a bit late. You can go on and we'll stay here and do flamenco.'

'No, Carlotta. I will not "go on" anywhere. I'm staying here to be sure that Will *does* arrive.' Will was not the most reliable bloke on the face of the planet, Rosa had previously learned to her cost. He'd sent Lottie back from his and Sonia's town house in a taxi once, because Sonia was at an evening class and he was too out-of-it to drive the child home himself. The idea of Lottie in a cab with a strange man had made Rosa go stiff with horror. Now she felt a flutter of apprehension. 'Lottie? Sonia's going to Wicklow too, isn't she?'

'Yeah, Mum. 'Course she is. We're picking her up on the way.'

The flutter disappeared into the ether. Sonia was kosher as they came.

'I'll still hang on here till Will comes, in case there's a problem.'

'Oh. OK then. Da-dum, da *dum*!' Lottie flamenco-ed back to Roxanne.

From the open door of the theatre, Rosa heard a stirring 'thrumm' of guitar strings, and a low laugh. She edged towards the door to take a look. The guitarist was beating a light rhythm on the wooden belly of the instrument. In the half-darkness two silhouettes were poised in arrogant, confrontational stance. The guitar sounded again, and the woman began to move, to dance flamenco. She was all hips and breasts and fluid, eloquent fingers: eroticism personi-fied. But there was nothing tacky or subordinate about this eroticism – it was a celebration of joyous physicality, an affirmation of supreme womanly confidence. The sinuous movement of her arms was both seductive and proudly magisterial, fiery yet elegant.

As she strutted with sexy authority, Michael too began to move, and as soon as he did, Rosa's jaw hit the deck. He positively exuded virility. It was apparent in the thrust of his jaw, the angle of his shoulder, the twist of his arm, the jut of his hip. Rosa stared at the plane of his back, the definition of his muscles under the white cotton that clung to his skin, the sheer streamlined, sweaty *animality* of him. One minute he was a matador, wielding an invisible cloak, taunting and provocative, the next he was all sleek, dangerous beast, his upraised arms a graphic representation of the horns of a bull. Helen had been right after all. When Mr Fairy Cakes danced he *was* sex on legs.

The pair danced on, dictating the rhythm to the guitarist, who matched their passionate, staccato steps. Rosa found herself moving her hips in time to the music, seduced by its gutsy charisma. The thrum of the guitar came faster, louder, the heels of the dancers clattering more loquaciously than castanets as they circled each other with glittering eyes. Then, with one last defiant cry of *olé!* and one last autocratic stamp, the dancers struck a theatrical pose, the dance was over, and the three collaborators in this virtuoso display resumed a relaxed, everyday demeanour.

Beside her she heard an intake of breath, and Rosa realized that Helen had been watching the couple over her shoulder. 'Wow,' she breathed. 'This stuff's macho-er than a matador. Who'd have thought Michael had it in him? He's such a gentle man.'

'You know him?'

'Mm hm. I'd been at him for ages to do a workshop for us. He wasn't keen initially because he hadn't done any dancing for years, but the first one went down so well with the kids that he approached me himself about doing another one when he heard Gabriella and Ramón were coming to Dublin.'

'Ramón's the guitarist?'

'Yes. He and Gabriella are Michael's cousins.'

'So he's Spanish?'

'Well. Second generation. He's actually Glaswegian. His grandad left Spain during Franco. How did you hear about our workshop, incidentally? Are you on our mailing list?'

'No – but I should be. Stick me on, Helen, will you? It was Lottie who found out about the workshop. She saw the poster in his surgery window.'

'He lives near you, doesn't he?'

'Yeah. It's funny. Any time I pass him on the street he pretends not to see me, so I've deliber-ately started saying hello to him so that he *has* to acknowledge me. He looked very put out when I first did it, and now I think he crosses the road deliberately when he sees me coming. I always thought he was a prize jerk.'

Helen shook her head. 'Michael? No. He's just painfully shy.'

Just then Lottie and Roxanne came tip-tapping up, followed by Will, Roxanne's father. 'Hey, Rosa,' he said. 'We're ready to roll.'

'Oh, Will – let me have your number in Wicklow.' Rosa located the pen and notebook she always kept in her bag so that she could jot down any ideas that came to her for Lottie's bedtime story. Making sure that the book was open on a page that had none of her scribbles on it, she handed it over. She found the notion of anyone reading her stuff highly embarrassing.

As Will jotted down the phone number, Rosa cast a sidelong glance into the theatre space where Helen had joined the flamenco trio and was laughing at some remark of Ramón's. Michael was laughing too. He slapped his cousin on the back, then enveloped him in his arms.

Lottie nudged Rosa. 'See, Mum?'

'See what?'

Lottie pulled on her mother's arm and stood on tiptoe so that she could whisper in her ear. 'I *told* you he was gay.'

'Don't be ridiculous, Carlotta. Continental men hug and kiss each other all the time – especially when they're related. It's only uptight Irish men who don't. I think it's great.'

'Yeah,' said Will, handing back the notebook. 'Irish men are so out of touch with their inner child. C'mon, you kids. Let's go hug some trees. *Slán*, Rosa.'

Oh! How did Sonia *stick* him, Rosa wondered. She hoped Sonia would be encouraging the kids to *climb* the trees in Wicklow, not bloody *hug* them.

'Bye, Will. Bye, Roxanne. Have fun.' Rosa

bent down to kiss Lottie goodbye. 'Love you, baby girl. Be good.'

'Love you too,' said the child, kissing her back. 'Don't forget to feed the Mysterious One.'

'*And* I'll end up cleaning out her quarters, again. You were meant to do that days ago.'

'Oops! Sorry! Bye!' Lottie gave her a guilty grin and was gone.

Rosa waved her fingers at her daughter, then turned and looked uncertainly towards where Helen was still chatting easily with the flamenco artistes. She waved her over, and Rosa crossed the floor feeling self-conscious. 'Michael,' Helen said, when she reached them. 'This is Rosa Elliot. Rosa, Michael . . .'

'Uh. Yeah. We've kind of met,' he mumbled. She shook his hand anyway, and he gave her a smile. The uncertainty of this smile was at total variance with the kind of smiles she'd seen him exchange with Gabriella when they'd danced earlier.

'Rosa, Gabriella; Rosa, Ramón.' More hand-shaking. Then Helen looked at her watch and said: 'I'm closing up shop. Can I buy you guys a drink? I bet you'd murder one after that session.'

'Thank you,' said Ramón. Michael said, 'Yes please, Helen,' and Gabriella said: 'I'd love one, but I'm meeting some people at six o'clock, and it's nearly that now.' She unzipped a holdall, pulled out an assortment of street clothes and proceeded to discard her dance threads.

Rosa felt a bit uncomfortable. She didn't know whether to stay or go – she hadn't been included in the invitation. She glanced at her watch, then started to sidle towards the exit. 'Um. Thank you for the workshop,' she said.

'You're not going, are you?' Helen looked surprised. 'Come and join us.'

'Oh. Thanks. I'd like that.' Rosa sang a little song inwardly. She turned towards Michael to say something, anything, but he was moving away from her, unfastening the buckle on his belt. He noticed her noticing, and gave her that uncertain smile again. 'Excuse me for a minute,' he said. 'Unlike my exhibitionist cousin, I prefer to change in the dressing rooms.'

'How did you learn to dance?' asked Rosa an hour and a bit later. They were in the Octagon Bar of the Clarence Hotel, and, being a Saturday, it was fairly jammed. Ramón had just put two fresh drinks down in front of her and Michael, and had disappeared back to the bar to chat up some girl he'd met. Helen had made her excuses and left ten minutes ago.

Michael took a long drink from his pint and wiped the back of his mouth with his hand. 'I had the best teacher going,' he said.

'Oh? Who?'

'My da. His name was Rodriguez Luque.' He pronounced 'Rodriguez' with a burr. Rosa giggled. 'What's so funny?' he asked.

'Oh – it's just the way you said his name. "Rodriguez". It sounded kind of strange in your Glasgow accent.'

Michael looked askance at her, then resumed. 'He – my da – was taught by my grandfather, who, I'm sorry to say, didn't have an amusing Glaswegian accent. He was quite famous in his time, in Spain, my grandad. His name was Federico Luque.'

'What made him decide to move to Glasgow?'

'You may not know this, but Spanish politics were very unstable in those days. My grandparents decided to quit the country when Franco started his bullyboy tactics.'

'I do know it, actually,' she said, with a small attempt at hauteur. 'I used to be an intelligent, educated person once upon a time, believe it or not.'

'Oh, I'm sure you still are, Rosa.'

Michael took a swig of his pint and set it down, and then he picked it up again and took another drink. One of those conversational vacuums that spring up between people who are just getting to know each other was starting to spread. Rosa didn't find it uncomfortable – the wine had made her feel nicely laid back – but Michael clearly did. 'Uh. What do you for a living, Rosa?' he asked finally.

She longed to be able to say: 'I'm an actress who specializes in voiceover work.' Instead she said: 'I'm a single parent who massages wealthy clients for a living. Oh!' She reached out and touched his thigh, then wished she hadn't and withdrew her hand immediately. 'That sounds awful! I don't mean that in the way it sounds! But really, I am. I mean, that's what I do.' Rosa took a sip of her wine, aware that he was watching her with new interest. Aha! Men's eyes always got all gleamy when they discovered that she practised massage. She lowered her lashes, then shot him an oblique look. 'I'll do you one day if you like.'

'Oh! That's very kind of you. Thanks.'

'You're welcome.'

'It must be very hard work.'

'It is. Backbreakingly hard.' Another little giggle, another little sip. 'Mm. This Chardonnay's delicious. Delicious!'

Another silence. Michael finally cleared his throat and came up with a new conversational gambit.

'Lottie's a great kid, isn't she?'

'Yes. She is. I *adore* my daughter.' Rosa shifted on the banquette beside Michael and crossed her legs. She saw his eyes go momentarily to where her skirt had ridden a little higher up her thighs, and she felt a flash of pleasure. Hooray! What luck that she should be wearing a skirt! 'Do you think she could be a dancer? She does Irish dancing, too, you know,' she said, trying to look grave. 'I was quite impressed when I saw her dancing today.'

Michael considered. 'Aye. I do. She has a natural talent. Has she ever taken ballet classes?'

'She did when she was younger, but I disencouraged her.' Oh. Should it be 'discouraged'?

'Why?'

'Her teacher was a vile snob.'

'I'm not surprised she wasn't fired up, then. Um.' He shifted in his seat and then blurted: 'I'll have a go at teaching her, if you like.'

'What! You would?'

'I would, yeah.' He looked away from her, and she could see that his face had gone very red. 'But could I ask you for something in return?'

'Sure.'

'I'll teach Lottie flamenco once a week in return for a massage once a week.'

She narrowed suspicious eyes at him. 'I don't do relief.'

'Rosa,' he said gently. 'Catch yourself on. I'm not asking for a bloody "relief" massage.'

'I'm sure you're perfectly capable of doing that for yourself.' Rosa giggled again. That surprised her. She didn't often 'giggle'.

Michael went even redder. 'What I would

really like,' he continued, 'is a back massage once in a while. I suffer from a dodgy back, and my doctor's recommended either massage or chiropractic.'

'Well,' said Rosa, fishing in her bag for one of the cards the Hamilton hotel had had printed for her. 'It's a deal. Give me a bell any time. Here's my card.' She handed it over to him, and as he reached out for it, the rolled-up sleeve of his white shirt slid up further, exposing his tanned forearm. 'Have you been away on holiday?' she said conversationally. 'You've a great tan.'

'No, I haven't been away yet this year. I just tan really easily.'

So it wasn't a perma-tan! 'I suppose it's your Spanish blood.'

'Yeah,' he said vaguely. He was staring at something or someone by the bar. Rosa's eyes followed the direction of his gaze.

'There she is,' he said. 'The woman in the flower shop. You know her, don't you? I've often see you pick Lottie up from there.' He turned eager eyes back to Rosa. 'Maybe you'd introduce me? I've always wanted to talk to her, but I've never had a chance.'

Rosa felt like a party balloon that had just been punctured. What a wuss she was! What a total, fucking, wussy loser! Here she'd been, flirting away with this sweet, shy man who made Michael

Flatley look like a Morris dancer when it was patently obvious he wasn't in the slightest bit interested in her – and now, to make matters worse, one of her best friends walks into the joint and his face lights up like a Christmas tree . . .

'Sure I will.' She got awkwardly to her feet and stapled an artificial smile on to her face as she negotiated her way to the bar. Introduce them, she told herself. Introduce them, then back off, get out, and get real.

'Dannie?' she said, laying a hand on her friend's shoulder. 'Hi! There's someone over here I'd love you to meet.'

It was Dannie's first night out without Jethro. She hadn't felt like going anywhere, but her brother had phoned earlier that day to say that he was spending some time in Dublin, and how about getting together? She was glad when he'd refused her offer to put him up. She didn't think she could hack the idea of sharing her space with anyone right now, not after the Jethro Palmer shambles.

She had tried to persuade herself that she was better off without Jethro. She'd received no communication from him before he'd left the country, bar three e-mails. The message in the first one read '?', the second one read '??', and the third one '???'. Dannie hadn't bothered to reply.

As she'd got ready to go out this evening she had noticed something new about her appearance in the bathroom mirror. There was a wary expression in her eyes, and a new and unattractive twist to her mouth. Dannie had read somewhere that you get the face you deserve by the time you're forty, and she had seen a similar look on the faces of disillusioned women everywhere. It was the look habitually worn by the 'All Men are Bastards' brigade, and it made her wonder if anything would happen over the course of the next half-dozen years to alter it, or if the wind had changed for good and she was stuck with 'bitter and twisted' for the rest of her life.

Now, as she sat on a high stool at the bar in the Clarence hotel waiting for her brother Joe and her drink to arrive, she made an effort. She sat as erect as she could, she made eye contact with a man on the other side of the room who regularly spent a lot of money in her shop, sending him a bright smile for good measure, She wanted to convey the impression that she was a confident woman with a healthy measure of self-esteem, not a gullible wretch whom men habitually shafted.

'Dannie?' She heard a voice at her shoulder, and turned to find Rosa there. 'Hi! There's someone over here I'd love you to meet.'

'Rosa!' Dannie leaned forward and kissed her

on the cheek. The last time she'd seen her friend was when she'd been compelled to make the grim disclosure about Jethro, that shit-hot shit of a director, and she knew that poor Rosa was probably still feeling bad about having been the messenger. 'How's it going? You look great.' In fact, Rosa looked a little droopy, Dannie thought, and was sporting a mascara smudge under her left eye.

'Oh, thanks. So do you,' came the automatic response. 'How are things?'

'Ach. I'm grand. Bearing up.' Dannie gave a mock-heroic smile.

'Are you meeting someone here?'

'Mm. My brother – he's up in Dublin for a couple of weeks, and the lucky article's decided to lay his hat here in the Clarence.'

'Your favourite brother? The journalist?'

'Yeah. He's on a year's sabbatical from the day job. He's working on a biography of some oul senator, and he's up to do research in the National Library.'

'And he's staying *here*? Is he really rich?'

'No. He's just *flaithiúlacht*. He'll probably run out of money and end up sleeping on my futon. Who is is that you want me to meet?'

'Well, actually, it's more that the Who wants to meet you. He's seen you in the flower shop and taken a shine.'

Dannie gave an ironic bark of a laugh. 'Ah,

Jaysus, Rosa! Spare me from going down that road again!'

Rosa slid onto the stool beside Dannie and adopted a confidential tone. 'Remember I told you Lottie was going to a tap-dance workshop?'

'Yeah?'

'Well, it turns out I'd got it wrong – it wasn't tap after all. It's flamenco, and he's the teacher. He's the dark-haired bloke sitting over there with a pint in front of him. I know he doesn't look like much, but you should see him when he dances. Oh, God!' Rosa sounded despondent. 'I'd love him.'

Dannie was just about to remind Rosa that All Men are Bastards when a tall, slightly over-weight man descended on Dannie, flung an arm around her shoulders and kissed her smackingly on the cheek.

'Yeuch, you kissed me, Joe – you big slobber!' said Dannie, energetically wiping the kiss off her cheek. But then she couldn't resist grabbing him and giving him a big hug. 'Oh – it's brilliant to see you! It really is!' It *was* brilliant to see him, she realized. Big, breezy Joe always succeeded in cheering her up. She let him go, mock punched his arm, and performed introductions. 'Joe, this is Rosa. Rosa, my brother Joe.'

'Nice to meet you.' Joe turned to Rosa and looking lingeringly into her eyes.

'Joe,' warned Dannie. 'This girl is my friend. Hands off.'

'Sure, divil a bit. I can tell I'm not her type. Am I right?'

Rosa gave a silly flirty little laugh, and Dannie said. 'We're moving over there, where it's more comfortable.' She indicated the banquette where Michael was sitting. 'Rosa wants me to meet her friend.'

'I'll join you. Let me order first.' He turned to the bartender. 'What are you having, Rosa?'

Rosa had intended leaving after she'd finished the glass of wine that Ramón had bought for her, but she wanted something to lift her spirits now that she knew Michael Luque wasn't interested in her. She'd stay for one more. 'I'll have a glass of white wine, please, Joe. Thanks.'

Rosa and Dannie moved back through the crowded bar and Rosa sat down beside Michael. Dannie slid into one of the comfortable leather club chairs opposite and smiled at him. Rosa's heart wrenched as Michael returned the smile, leaning forward. How did Dannie do it? How did people just fall for her in the blinking of an eye? She supposed it was because Dannie was so open and friendly and attractive and confident and had such – such – what was that French word? It eluded her. It meant 'vivacity'. Oh, what *was* it? The damn word had escaped out of her brain just like that plume of fizz escaping from a bottle of champagne the barman was opening. And she'd used to be an intelligent, educated person once upon a time . . . How sad.

Dannie was looking at her expectantly. Oh! She'd forgotten that she needed to make the introductions. 'Um. Dannie Moore, this is Michael Luque. He was teaching Lottie flamenco earlier.'

'Flamenco?' Dannie bestowed the gift of her smile on him again. 'I'm impressed. You're really a flamenco dancer?'

'Well, not full-time. It's just something I have a gift for, that I inherited from my da and from his father before him. There's been flamenco dancers in my family for generations.'

My God! Words were positively flowing out of Michael, now! Rosa remembered the hiatuses that had peppered their conversation earlier, and she decided to throw in the towel there and then. There was quite clearly no point in competing with Dannie. Michael was smitten already.

'Your drink, Rosa.' Joe lowered himself into the seat opposite her, and set down her glass of wine. He introduced himself to Michael, then: 'Here's to your bright eyes, Dannie!' he said. 'It's a grand thing to see my one and only baby sis again after all this time.' He raised his pint in a toast to her, and Michael mirrored his move.

'To Dannie,' said Rosa, trying to sound more

enthusiastic than she felt. Bloody Dannie with her bright eyes and her *élan*. Hey! She'd remembered the word! *Elan*. A perfect way to describe Dannie Moore. Rosa took a sip of wine, and another, then set her glass down on the table with a decisive clunk. Stop it! she told herself. Just stop it. Stop being so bloody begrudging and horrible. After all, Dannie deserved a go with a guy like Michael Luque after what she'd been through with Jethro Slimeball Palmer. She, Rosa, should be glad that Michael seemed to be a regular bloke and not a bastard. *A gentle man* – that was how Helen had described him. Anyway, what made her think that Michael would be interested in someone like her – a knackered single parent whose brain cells were fizzing away out of her head into the ether?

Joe extracted a packet of cigarettes from his pocket, and she saw Dannie give him a cross look.

'I thought you'd given up.'

'I have. I just find holding the packet reassuring. Are there any other nicotine addicts here?'

'Not me,' said Rosa, and she saw Michael shake his head. He must have kicked the habit since she'd seen him buying multi-pack Silk Cut in Tesco's. Now Joe smiled at her, leaned forward and engaged her in eye contact. He was the kind of man who had damn sexy eyes, and he knew how to use them. 'Rosa,' he said. 'Tell me about yourself.'

'What?' she said, just resisting the impulse to look round to check that he wasn't directing the remark to someone else called Rosa who was sitting directly behind her.

'Tell me about yourself,' he said again. 'You're a grand-looking girl. I want to hear all about you, acushla, and I want to feast my eyes on your loveliness as you do it.'

'Oh!' Rosa was dumbfounded. 'No-one's wanted to find out about me before, ever.'

'Ah, now, I'm sure that's not true.' He leaned forward a little further. 'You see, Dannie has told me about you. She said that when she first moved back to Dublin she was lucky enough to find that her apartment was just upstairs from a lovely woman with a GSOH, and she hoped that this woman would become a great pal. Could that person be you, Rosa, or does Dannie know someone else who fits this description?'

Rosa was appalled to find her eyes filling up with imminent tears. She looked away, hoping that no-one would notice, but she needn't have worried about Dannie and Michael. They were listing towards each other, obviously about to embark on a voyage of mutual discovery. She turned back to Joe, who passed a big white handkerchief across the table to her.

'Go on,' he urged gently. 'Tell us about yourself.'

And Rosa did.

Much later, it was time to go home. But Rosa didn't want to go home. She wanted to go to bed with Joe in his room in the beautiful hotel. She loved him. Joe was kind and funny and sexy and cuddly. He liked her, he was interested in her opinions, she had told him stuff about herself that she had never told anyone else. She wanted to hug him like Dannie had earlier. In the lobby – what were they doing there? – she'd asked him to kiss her, but he had declined very politely. Hey! What was wrong with wanting to go to bed with him? They didn't have to have sex, they could just cuddle. But Joe had disengaged himself from her and the next thing he had just disappeared – pouf! – like that. And Dannie was telling her that there was a taxi waiting, but Rosa had a better idea. She would ask one of the liveried staff behind the reception desk for Joe's room number, and she would go up and find him and maybe they could raid the minibar in his room, and have room service. After all, hadn't Dannie done that in a posh hotel recently? So why couldn't Rosa? But Dannie was insisting on the taxi, and that flamenco guy was helping her into the back seat – hey! Maybe she could go to bed with him! She could have sex with him – he was sex on legs when he danced. But no, she remembered – and the thought caused her such bloody awful anguish that she started to cry – he fancied bloody Dannie. And the next thing she knew was . . .

She was in her bed. It must be morning – it was light outside. She expected the light to hurt her eyes, but it didn't. When she moved, she expected to feel pain, but she didn't. It was as if all her nerve endings had been cauterized.

She was still wearing her clothes. Oh fuck. Had she fallen into bed like this herself, or had Dannie helped her? Had Michael Luque gone home in the cab with them? She seemed to remember that he'd walked away from them down the quays. Or had that been Patrick Street?

Oh! She'd propositioned Dannie's brother! Oh, God! A whimper escaped her as humiliation rose inside her like bile and that familiar feeling of self-loathing swamped her.

Pulling the duvet over her head, Rosa began to weep.

Chaper Thirteen

Two days after the wrap party, Calypso phoned Dominic in London. 'Dominic, darling, I know this is really sudden,' she said, 'but I've been thinking seriously about what you said – about being stressed, you know? – and I've decided that I'm going to take myself off for a few days. Maybe even a week.'

'Yeah? Where?'

'Jethro Palmer's recommended a hotel in Gozo. He has a villa on the island, and I can check out the mini-edit while I'm there, so it's not as if I'm skiving off work completely.'

'Hey! I think that's a damn good idea, Calypso. I really do. You deserve it – you've been working too hard. I've never known you to pay so many visits to a location as you did on this film. You'll feel better if you get some sun and swimming in. And try to take it easy on the work front. You're not to spend your entire holiday in Jethro's edit suite.'

She wasn't sure she'd go near the edit suite. She didn't think she wanted to set eyes on Leo Devlin's bastard face ever again in her life, even on celluloid.

'Have you booked your flight yet?'

'Yes. I'm leaving this evening. I've made it open-ended because I don't know when I'll be coming back.'

'I'd come with you,' said Dominic, 'if I didn't have that *vernissage* to go to in Paris tonight. Let me know when your return flight's due and I'll send a car to the airport. Where are you staying?'

'A place called Ta'Cenc. Jethro invited me to stay in his gaff, but I feel I really need time to myself to sort out my head.'

'In that case, my dear girl, will you please take my advice and leave your laptop and your mobile and any casting briefs behind? You are not to take your work away on holiday, is that understood? I know you. If you bring the tools of your trade with you, you'll spend all your time working.'

'I'll need my mobile, Dominic.'

'No mobile. Calypso, you know you are quite unable to resist answering the bloody thing.'

'What if there's an emergency?'

'Let Viv and Iseult have the number of your hotel. But tell them not to give it out to *anyone*.'

Calypso found the idea of being unavailable a most attractive one. 'OK, darling. You're a star. Enjoy your *vernissage*.'

She put the phone down feeling better already. Her husband *was* a star, her very own lucky star, worth more than a whole constellation. Oh, *God*, how she loved him! He was thoughtful, considerate, generous, caring, handsome, clever. He was perfect. How could she have been so *deranged* as to betray him with that headbanger Leo Devlin?

She couldn't bring herself to think of Leo now, couldn't bring herself to contemplate the staggering depths of the humiliation she'd suffered at his hands. To think she'd bought all that stuff about his dysfunctional childhood, to think she'd allowed herself to be used and abused by him, to think that she'd thrown caution to the winds and had had sordid sex with him in grungy locations, to think of the acts she'd performed on him . . . Oh, God! The idea filled her with such self-disgust that she thought she might get physically ill. *You'll regret it*, he'd said to her once. How loaded his words had been. Calypso O'Kelly regretted more than anything in her life the day she'd first set eyes on Leo Devlin.

She recalled what Jethro had said to her earlier on the phone, when she'd rung him with the surprise news that she was fleeing to the island home of her namesake. 'I'd be more than happy to see you, Calypso. And I suspect you'll be more than happy, too, when you see the footage I've put together. We're on to something very hot with Leo.'

Hot. So hot she'd received a searing, third-degree burn from him. She, Calypso O'Kelly, now swore before God that she would never go near Leo Devlin again.

But still – revenge is sweet, she thought. 'Jethro?' she'd asked him, scrolling down her Favourites and clicking on ebookers. 'Apropos of nothing – who wrote that stuff about revenge being sweet? There's a line in *Don Juan's Double* about it, isn't there?'

'There sure is. It's from Byron's epic *Don Juan*. The actual quote goes "Sweet is revenge — especially to women."'

Calypso smiled.

After she'd put the phone down to Jethro she'd opened the address book on her computer and located the number of a hugely successful film director.

'David?' she said. 'It's Calypso. Fine, thanks. And you? Good. Have you time to talk? Excellent. Listen. I've been thinking very long and very hard about your next project, and I've come to some fresh conclusions. I know I recommended that you see Leo Devlin with a view to him playing Dakota, but I've had a serious rethink, and I've decided that actually it's not such a good idea. No.' She listened as the director told her how much he respected her opinion, then finally, gratifyingly, asked her the question she was waiting to hear. Calypso glanced at the photograph she'd accessed on her laptop, the one that Sally Ruane had e-mailed her all those weeks ago when her life had been perfect, before Leo Devlin had sullied it. His moody face scowled at her from the screen, and Calypso scowled back as she pressed 'delete' with a categorical finger and sealed Leo Devlin's fate with just a handful of crucial words. 'He's not right for the part, David,' she said. 'And I'm determined to find someone who is. I'm right. You know I am. As soon as I get back from holiday I'm calling a casting.'

The hotel Ta'Cenc was an ideal place for Calypso's rehab. She spent her days lounging by the pool, reading and drinking cocktails between swims. She had massages and manicures and facials. She ate too much of the excellent cuisine and went for long walks and sat on cliff tops gazing out to sea. It was perfect. On the second-last evening of her stay, she took a taxi to Jethro's villa.

It was a triumph of functionalism in concrete, glass and aluminium – a whitewashed bachelor pad lapped by the blue Mediterranean. Every corner of the building opened onto the sea, giving the impression of an ocean-going yacht, for it was constructed as a series of balconies, terraces, outdoor staircases and gangways. It had been furnished in the spare minimalist style that Dominic also favoured, and Calypso was not too sophisticated to pretend that she wasn't impressed. She oohed and aahed at Jethro's Philippe Starck kitchen and his fabulous views and his fiercely modern abstract paintings, and practically swooned when he led her into his state-of-the-art screening room. Curling up on a divan she sipped at the mint julep that he conjured from behind his blue-lit bar, then waited while he threw switches and fiddled about on a console.

The lights dimmed. Calypso could feel her heart rate accelerate. And there suddenly was Leo, larger than life on the screen in front of her, smiling that cruel smile she knew so well. She sucked in her breath, and beside her she heard Jethro laugh a low laugh that said more eloquently than any words: *We've hit the jackpo*t.

She barely bothered to listen to the dialogue. She could only gaze and gaze at this mesmeric *idol*. Leo's charisma was so flagrant it was breathtaking. Whenever the camera left him, you yearned for it to return and dwell some more on that miraculous face. Jeanne was in the frame now, luscious, lissom, shameless in a chemise. She was shaking back her mane of glossy dark hair, inserting a suggestive finger between her swollen lips, looking up at Leo with challenge in those beautiful, sloe-black eyes. Leo lifted a slow hand to meet hers, and then he grabbed her hard around the wrist, wrenched her hand down to his groin, and slid his thumb into her mouth.

Oh God! He'd pulled that stunt on *her*! Calypso found herself covering her mouth with her hand. She wasn't sure that she could take this. On the screen Jeanne had thrown her head back, and was sucking hungrily on Leo's thumb. He watched her through cruel, half-closed eyes, then pulled his thumb away, grabbed her face between his hands and proceeded to devour her. Jeanne's eyes were shut; her breath was coming faster. So was Calypso's. Leo pulled at Jeanne's chemise and the actress moaned as it tore, exposing her beautiful breasts. And as she listened to Jeanne's moaning, Calypso heard again the sounds of her own pleasure, the awful gasps and the groans and the sobs and the pleas that he'd elicited from her.

Squirming on the divan, she shifted position as she watched the actors fall to the floor. Oh, God, this was intolerable! She had never felt more like a voyeur in her life. Jeanne was naked now, Leo still fully clothed as he ravished her to her climax. Then, thank Jesus, abruptly, it was over.

Jethro and Calypso sat without saying a word for a long, long moment. Jethro's denim-clad legs were stretched out in front of him, the heel of one bare foot balanced on the toes of the other. His elbows were resting on the arms of his chair, his fingers steepled under his chin. Calypso's legs were curled under her, her arms wrapped around her chest, her fingers clutching the fabric of her T-shirt. She knew her knuckles were white. She knew her face was glowing like a Belisha beacon.

Jethro was the first to break the silence. 'Then felt I like some watcher of the skies,' he said.

Calypso turned to him at a loss. 'What?' she said.

'Keats. "On First Looking into Chapman's Homer". It's all about the miracle of discovery.

> "Then felt I like some watcher of the skies
>   When a new planet swims into his ken;
> Or like stout Cortez, when with eagle eyes
>   He stared at the Pacific – and all his men
> Looked at each other with a wild surmise –
>   Silent, upon a peak in Darien."

A new planet. A new star. Congratulations, Calypso. Stout Cortez has nothing on you.'

Calypso took a thoughtful sip of her mint julep. She was feeling very strange. Part of her was very smug indeed that she had discovered this remarkable new talent, but at the same time part of her was very scared. She was Doctor Frankenstein, after all, and look what had happened to *him*. 'Maybe it's a flash in the pan,' she said. 'Maybe he's a shooting star. Maybe he'll burn himself out.' She tried not to sound too hopeful.

Jethro shot her a sceptical look. 'C'mon, Calypso. He's gonna rock the international film world and you know it.' He got to his feet and stretched. 'Let's go get some food.'

They ate alfresco on his balcony. Sardines fresh from the sea, bread fresh from the oven and salad fresh from the garden. It was a beautiful evening, dusky blue and balmy.

'I've offered the villa to Leo and Jeanne when I head back to LA,' remarked Jethro, 'so they can chill for a couple of weeks.'

Calypso tried not to think of Leo and *la belle* Jeanne mooning and spooning in Jethro's garden and skinny-dipping in his pool. She remembered the astonishing physical symmetry Jeanne had displayed in the film, and recalled the first time Leo had seen her, Calypso, naked, when he'd tasted her all over and even sucked her toes . . . Oh! Get the fuck out of my head, Leo Devlin! Change the subject, Calypso!

'Have you heard from Dannie since you left Ireland?' she asked.

Jethro looked down at the steel surface of the table and picked up his wineglass. 'Dannie Moore,' he said, 'is more mysterious than the Sphinx. I was arrogant enough to imagine that we'd established a pretty good rapport, but just as I thought our relationship was going places, she dumped me. Quite stylishly, too. "Ms Moore no longer requires the car." Jesus!' Jethro laughed, but there was little trace of mirth there. 'I guess I should have taken a look at that book about women being from Venus before I got involved with Ms Moore. I thought women liked getting presents. She seemed happy enough at the time.'

'But they do!' said Calypso. 'I mean, we do! I adore getting presents.'

Jethro shook his head. 'I dunno. Maybe she felt that she was being bought off or something. I know some people can't handle a relationship where one of the parties is considerably wealthier than the other.'

'I've never had a problem with that, either,' confessed Calypso. 'I have to admit I love the fact that I'm married to a rich man. I sometimes wonder at my luck. I have a friend who works her ass off to support her nine-year-old daughter. She's a single parent, and she doesn't have it easy. I suffer from appalling guilt sometimes, and I'd love to do more for her, but she's so kind of stubbornly *proud*!'

'I guess that's where I got it wrong with Dannie. I thought I knew her better than I did. I was preemptive.' Jethro drained his glass, then went to refill both his and Calypso's. 'Your friend – she's Lottie's mother, is she?'

'That's right. How do you know?'

'Lottie came on a picnic with me and Dannie. It was the last time we saw each other.' Calypso sensed that he was trying hard to sound un-affected. 'D'you remember I asked you if you'd seen her at the wrap party? She didn't show up.'

Calypso didn't much like being reminded of the wrap party. It had, after all, been the worst night of her life. She shivered despite the balmy air, and pulled her pashmina more closely around her.

Jethro took a sip of his wine. He was looking very pensive. 'She has a gerbil, hasn't she, that little Lottie? Called the Mysterious One?'

'That's right. What a weird thing to remember!'

'Not really. It's a pretty weird name for a gerbil. Have you any idea why she called it that?'

'Yes. She believes that behind the gerbil façade the soul of an ancient Egyptian lurks. The gerbil is actually Nefertiti or Cleopatra or some such reincarnated.'

Jethro heaved a big sigh. 'Well. That Mysterious One has got major competition.'

Calypso gave him a look of enquiry.

'Oh, yeah. *Major* competition.' He slugged back more wine. 'In the Sphinx-like form of the enigmatic Ms Dannie Moore.'

Calypso spent the last day of her holiday chatting to a charming German boy by the pool and making him fall in love with her. He was only seventeen, but he'd remember the encounter for ever.

The next day found her touching down in Dublin. There was no car waiting for her at the airport as Dominic had promised, but she wasn't really surprised. An alpha male like him had more important things on his mind than organizing transport. She took a taxi instead, and tried out her charm on the driver. Knowing how important her charm-school skills would be once her looks started to fade, she took every opportunity that came her way these days to practise them.

At home, after showering and changing, she checked e-mail in her study (Dominic had left a Dries van Noten carrier bag on her chaise longue with a glorious scarf in it – clearly her present from London), then wandered into the drawing room with the phone and punched in the office number. She wanted to make sure that everything was running smoothly. It was – they'd got along without her just fine. 'No problems at all! Everything's hunky dory!' chirruped Iseult. Calypso was glad to hear her secretary using exclamation marks again. Perhaps she'd got over being dumped by Leo at last. She told Iseult she'd be back in work on Monday, and then she accessed 'Dom. Mob.' and pressed 'call'. As she waited for him to pick up she slung her new scarf round her neck. 'Darling! Thank you! It's beautiful. I'll say an extra-special thank you this evening. I'll do delicious food and we can have it in bed.'

'Calpso – you don't do any kind of food, let alone delicious.'

'You eejit. When I say I'll do delicious food I mean I'll buy it in the Epicurean Centre.'

'Let's postpone that till tomorrow. You've two invitations to choose from this evening. Unless you're too knackered after all that travelling?'

'Me? Knackered? Fiddle-de-dee. Run the invites by me.'

'There's dinner with Jim—'

'Jim? *Jim!* Dim Sum Jim the accountant?'

'Yes,' replied Dominic.

'Oh – no, no! Please, Dominic. I couldn't bear it! I couldn't—'

'We don't have to go.'

'Oh, thank you! Thank you, Dominic. What's the other invitation?' There was a pause before he answered. 'Well?' she urged him.

'The gala performance of *Saint Joan* at the Abbey,' he said.

'Pshaw to Shaw. No no no. That's work. You know I *never* go to gala nights, ever.'

'I thought you might be interested in going to this one. Viv rang earlier to say that Leo Devlin had asked if you could swing a ticket for him.'

Something about Dominic's tone had changed.

The words appeared somehow loaded – he wasn't his usual laidback self. A warning bell went off in Calypso's head. 'What? Who? Why on earth did V-Viv ring you?'

'She actually rang your mobile this morning on the off chance that you'd be back.'

'What – what did she say?'

'She asked if Leo could come along on your invite.'

Did the arrogance of Leo Devlin have no bounds? What *possessed* the man to imagine that he could accompany her to the theatre after what he'd done to her? 'So what makes you think that I'd want to go to an opening night just for Leo's sake, Dominic? That's b-bonkers.'

'Maybe. Maybe I had a suspicion that you'd rather like to be seen in public on the arm of your latest shit-hot star. Or maybe it's because you're having an affair with him.'

Calypso sat down very suddenly on her cream sofa. She felt as if she'd been winded. There was a long pause, then: 'Ha ha ha,' she said.

'Ha ha ha,' said Dominic back. 'Your mobile was very busy while you were away, Calypso.' Her mobile! Oh God! She'd forgotten to investigate 'call-barring'. 'It was bleating text messages all the time. I accessed them in case they were urgent, but I'd rather not repeat them. Some of them are actually *un*repeatable.'

'Oh. Oh, Dominic.' Calypso started to

hyperventilate. She felt as if she'd been picked up by a giant hand and flung into some remote, scary, arid corner of the universe. She felt like a spider sucked into a vacuum cleaner. This was awful! She didn't belong here. This was where sad castaways belonged, not her, not Calypso O'Kelly! 'Oh, Dominic!' She started to cry. 'I'm – I'm sorry. I'm so sorry. I don't know why I did it, I—'

'Calypso. I see very little point in discussing this on the phone.'

So they could discuss it! At least he was prepared to discuss it. All was not lost! 'Will you come home? Now? Can we talk it through? Oh, darling, please, please come home now. I'll be able to explain things better f-face to face. Come home to me, Dominic. Please come home.'

'Calypso?'

'Yes?'

'Go fuck yourself.'

The line went dead. Calypso stared at the phone, then let it drop to the floor. She took several great, shuddering breaths, and then the tears came flooding. She pressed the palms of her hands to her face and started to sway. 'Oh God oh God oh God,' she murmured between breaths. 'Oh God oh God. What have I done? Oh God. Oh, *Dominic*! Oh, Dominic, come home! Oh, Dominic – *please* come home!' Her face was slippery now with the tears that just wouldn't stop coming. Her bottom lip was trembling, her vision was blurred: she was abject. Calypso O'Kelly was blubbing – snuffly with snot and bawling like a baby. The last time she'd blubbed like this had been when her mother had told her that Daddy wouldn't be coming home any more. The gasping breaths were interspersed with whimpers now, and then she was wailing, keening like someone bereaved, in mourning for her life, in mourning for her husband, her lover, her friend, her rock, her *champion*. She couldn't *bear* this!

Feeling as if the ground was listing beneath her feet, she made her way into the lobby and climbed the stairs, clinging to the banister as if it was a lifeline. She staggered into her bedroom and fell onto the bed, burying her face in the pillows. She lay like that for a long time, in hellish, hellish torment, howling until the pillow was saturated and she had no more tears left to cry. Even though a warm afternoon sun was streaming in on top of her, she was cold now, so cold she had to crawl in under the duvet. It couldn't warm her: she was shaking, goose-bumpy. Her eyes felt as if the lashes had been singed, she was empty and dried up as a husk, her so-recently radiant complexion was stiff with salty tears and her Christian Dior mouth was stretched downward in a mask of tragedy. She looked at the bedside clock. It was six o'clock. The time Dominic usually returned. There was a sound from downstairs. Calypso's ears flattened against her skull like a cat that hears sudden birdsong. Thank God! 'Dominic!' She sat up stiffly, aware of an ache in all her limbs. 'D-Dominic?'

Marilyn Monroe sashayed into her bedroom, and she realized that the sound she had heard had been the thwack of the cat flap.

Calypso sank down against the pillows and started to cry again.

It was dark when she woke. Beside her the cat was twitching, chasing rabbits in her sleep. The clock read half-past ten, and she could tell by the ominous silence that the house was still empty. She slid out of bed and moved towards the door, absently grabbing a pashmina and wrapping it around herself the way an old woman might wrap herself in a shawl. The image of the Goddess Calypso abandoned on her island by Odysseus gazed sympathetically at her from the daguerreotype that hung now on the wall of her dressing room.

Downstairs she opened a carton of soup and put a pan on the hob. She wasn't hungry, but she knew she needed nourishment. She opened a bottle of red wine, poured a hefty amount into a glass, and sat down at the kitchen table to take stock of things. She'd always been crap at taking stock. It seemed to her the kind of thing grown-ups did: 'Taking stock.' The very sound of the words had a pompous ring to it.

So. What was the very worst thing that could happen to her? That was obvious. Dominic could divorce her. *Oh!* OK – that was it. She'd taken enough stock and it was horrible. She wouldn't – couldn't – take any more. She took a great slug of wine – and suddenly knew she was going to throw up.

Calypso raced to the bathroom and crouched over the loo. She retched and retched so hard that tears came to her eyes, but luckily it didn't last long. Afterwards she knew that she should flush the loo and clean herself up, but she hadn't the energy. She just lay there with her head resting on her forearm like a stone, contemplating a world without Dominic. The idea was intolerable. She pictured the look on her mother's face when she broke the news of her impending divorce. Oh, God. She'd get that awful 'Told you so' look that her mother so clearly relished giving her. She imagined her passing the news on to family and friends. *I knew she'd got too big for her boots. It doesn't surprise me. I knew from day one that that marriage was doomed . . .*

Calypso's bottom lip began to shudder again. Her forehead puckered, and she knew then that if she didn't force herself into taking some kind of action, all the tears that had been building up in her inner reservoir since her last crying jag would come spurting out. She had to regain control.

A shower. That's what she needed. A nice warm shower, and then into her cashmere lounging pyjamas. Once she was warm and had some soup in her belly she'd be able to think straight, she'd be better able to devise some kind of strategy for bringing Dominic back home to her. Quickly she stripped off all her clothes and turned on the shower, making sure the dial was on its most forceful setting. She wanted to sluice all the awfulness out of her life.

She had just finished soaping herself when the phone started to ring in the kitchen. Oh! Could it be Dominic? Without bothering to turn off the water, she pushed open the door of the shower stall, and in her haste she slipped. Calypso O'Kelly hit the deck heavily in a galaxy of glittering glass, shards of shooting stars settling round her pretty head as it struck hard against the solid slate floor.

And that was how Dominic found her some twenty minutes later. Only by the time he arrived, the slate-blue slabs in the shower room were spattered vermilion with blood.

It was dark, and Daddy was never coming back. She'd brushed her hair and tied it in a ribbon and put on her prettiest dress and her new white socks with frills, but it hadn't done any good.

Daddy had taken her to see a film and they'd had popcorn, and then he'd taken her to McDonald's and he'd had coffee while she had Chicken McNuggets and Coke. And he'd kissed her goodbye in the car and told her breathlessly how beautiful she was and that it was their secret, but then he'd still said no to Mummy when she'd asked him to come in after he'd dropped her home, so Calypso had blown it yet again. And now she was lying in bed and Mummy hadn't bothered to come upstairs to the bedroom to tuck her in. But when she opened her eyes, she saw that she wasn't in her bedroom any more. This room had pastel green walls with framed Monet water lilies on, and a man was sitting beside her holding her hand. And it was . . . it was D-Dominic.

Oh, thank God. It was Dominic.

'You've been a long way away,' he said, leaning towards her. 'Thank you for coming back to me.'

The words were reassuringly familiar. Where had she heard them before? 'I'm s-sorry. I have to tell you that I love you. I love you.' She knew that it was vitally important that she said it. It was the single most urgent thing she'd ever have to say in her life.

He smiled down at her. 'I know. I love you too.' She could tell that he was trying hard not to weep. There were tears pooling in his eyes and he was biting down hard on his lip.

'You're not going to leave me?'

'No. No. Let's not talk about that now.'

Calypso went to move her hand, wanting to touch him, then realized she was hooked up to a drip. 'I'm in hospital.'

'Yes. You had a nasty fall.' His grip on her hand intensified, and she winced. 'I'm sorry. You've bruises.'

'And cuts.' She was hurting. Her face was hurting.

'Yes. They've been stitched.'

'On my face.'

'Yes. And your thighs.'

'How many stitches?'

'Thirty.'

'Altogether?'

'Thirty on your face. Fewer on your legs.'

'Thirty on my face. Was there much blood?'

He nodded. 'Yeah.' And then he slumped. Dominic laid his head on his wife's belly and started to cry. It was the first time she had ever seen him weep.

'Sh, sh,' she said, stroking his head with her free hand. 'There, there. Hush now.' She recalled now where she'd heard the words he'd said earlier, when he'd thanked her for coming back to him. They were the very last lines of *Brief Encounter*.

'Oh, God, Calypso,' he sobbed. 'Oh, God. If I'd come any later you'd have bled to death. I'd have lost you.'

'Sh, sh. I'm not going anywhere. You said I'm going to be all right. It's only cuts.'

'Yeah. Only cuts.' He straightened, then reached for a tissue from a box by the bed, and wiped his eyes. 'I'd better call the nurse now you're awake,' he said, pressing the bell.

'Thirty stitches on my face. That's some scar.'

'I got the best guy. You've got the best plastic surgeon in the business. He's cleaned you up nicely.'

'I will have scars, though?'

'Yeah. Nothing – nothing *major*. You mustn't worry, darling – they can work miracles these days.' His reassuring tone didn't convince her.

'My face is fucked, isn't it?'

'You're going to need further surgery.'

'My face is fucked.'

'Oh, darling – I know how important your looks always were to you, I know how—'

'No. No, Dominic. My looks weren't important to me. They really weren't. But they were important to you.' Tears were imminent, and she was so *tired*! Why was weeping so exhausting? 'You promise – you *promise* you won't leave me, Dominic?'

'I promise.'

'Why did you come back?'

'I couldn't not come back to you, Calypso. I tried to stay away – I even booked myself into a hotel – but I just couldn't not come back to you.'

'I'm so sorry. I'm so sorry for everything.'

'I know. I know. You can tell me about it another time.'

The tears were coming now. 'I'm so scared that you'll abandon me.'

'Trust me. Trust me. I won't abandon you, Calypso.'

'I betrayed you terribly. *Why* would you not abandon me? I behaved appallingly.'

'I love you. It's that simple. I've never loved another woman the way I love you, and I know I never will.'

'I'm so stupid.'

'You're only human.'

'Ha. Not a goddess, then.'

'Even the gods fucked up occasionally.'

She attempted a smile, but it hurt. 'My beauty's gone.'

'No, it hasn't. You're still my beautiful wife.'

'I'm so tired. I want to go to sleep again. Beauty sleep. I bet I could do with some of that. Ha. That's a joke, by the way. Will you stroke my hair for me?'

'With pleasure.'

'My roots need doing, don't they?'

'I wouldn't have a clue. They look fine to me.' The slow, measured stroking of his hand was reassuring, bringing her closer and closer to the verge of sleep.

'Will you answer something for me, Dominic?

I've always wanted to ask you this. When you first set eyes on me, what did you see? Did you see a woman or a goddess?'

'I saw neither.'

'What did you see, then?'

'I saw a golden girl,' he said. 'I saw the love of my life.'

Chapter Fourteen

Rosa had gone to work in the Hamilton hotel the day after the débâcle in the Clarence with categorically the worst hangover she had ever had in her life. She felt as if some ghoul had sneaked into her room during the night, sawn through her cranium, scooped out a big lump of her brain and then nailed her skull back on. She was glad that Lottie hadn't been around to see her: she could barely get her act together enough to get herself dressed and out of the house.

The international superstar diva had sussed that she was suffering from a hangover the moment Rosa had walked into her suite. 'I know what you need to put you right,' she'd said. And she had picked up the phone to room service and ordered two *very* large Bloody Marys to be brought to the room ASAP. 'Get that into you,' she'd ordered, and Rosa had knocked back the drink gratefully before starting her massage. It was against the rules, but it had done the trick.

That Sunday night she'd come home and picked up the phone to ring Dannie, but at the last moment her nerve had failed her. *How* could she face Dannie after the horrific events of last night? Oh, God. The humiliation! She had practically tried to drag her friend's brother off to bed! She could hardly bear to think about it, let alone ring Dannie up and have to *talk* about it. What had she turned into? Some sex-crazed nymphomaniac? And that wasn't all. Michael Luque had seen her make a complete arse of herself as well. She remembered that she'd come on to him even when it was perfectly obvious that it was Dannie he was interested in. No. There was no way she could ring Dannie.

Rosa knew that the longer she put the phone call off the more difficult it would be to make, but she didn't care. Thank God for the wine box in her kitchen cupboard. It would help keep awful reality at bay, help send her in the direction of the oblivion she craved so badly that night. She'd stumbled to bed later without bothering to clean her teeth.

The next day – Monday – had been a day off. But it wasn't a day off real life. She *had* to make a phone call to Roydon Sneyde. He still owed her for the CD-rom work she'd done for him months ago. The money was sitting in his bank account right now earning interest, and she needed it so *badly*.

The prospect made her throat constrict with nerves. She remembered how she'd made it easier on herself the last time she'd had to ring the Definite Article, by fuelling herself with Dutch courage. Maybe she could do it with a little help from her friend Wine box? She poured a large glass, swigged it back, then punched in the number with affected bravado (who – oh who – was she trying to fool?). His voicemail picked up. Shit. It would be futile to leave a message. There was nothing else for it: she'd have to try his mobile. A top-up of wine first, though, while she thought some more about how to handle the situation. Um. She wouldn't be servile, she wouldn't beg. He owed her money! She would be businesslike and polite and to the point.

'Roydon?' she said when he picked up. 'Hello! It's Rosa Elliot here. It would appear that you may not have received my statement.'

'Rosa Elliot. A blast from the past. Although I'm not sure the words "blast" and "Rosa Elliot" go together, somehow.' He yawned ostentatiously down the phone, and then said: 'What statement might you be referring to?'

'The statement for the last CD-rom gig we did.'

'And what gig was that?'

'Remember? Back in March?'

'No.'

'No? Um. What do you mean, no?'

'I mean, Rosa, that there was no such gig.'

'But – I recorded dozens of – dozens of files! I—'

'Rosa. If you'd recorded dozens of files for me I would have your signature on an invoice now, wouldn't I? I have no such invoice and no such signature. *Ergo*, there was no gig.'

'But there was! There—' Oh, God. With sick dread she remembered now that she had fled the studio on that awful day without signing anything. Without a previously signed invoice, the statement she'd sent him was null and void. 'But I have the dates in my diary! I can prove it—'

'So prove it, Rosa. Prove it in a court of law. Sue me, why don't you? You think a diary entry proves anything? Does it, fuck. Even Lord Archer couldn't get away with that.'

'You can't do this, Roydon! You can't – I mean, other proof exists. The recording itself, you can't deny—'

'I can do whatever I like, Rosiebaby. And you can go fuck yourself.'

And then Roydon Sneyde put the phone down.

Dannie had decided that keeping busy was the best way of stopping Jethro Palmer invading her head. She'd been to the movies numerous times, she'd gone to the theatre (accompanied by her big brother Joe, who had fallen asleep and snored), she'd done the flowers for three weddings in a row and come away punch drunk and reeling with exhaustion, and she'd toyed with the idea of spending this Thursday lunch break in the National Gallery. Their PR had approached her about doing the flowers for a forthcoming function, and she wanted to case the joint. However, she rejected the idea of having lunch there because she'd read somewhere that art galleries were the hunting grounds of sad singletons out looking for mates. OK. She might be a singleton, but she certainly wasn't sad. She was a singleton through choice. She never wanted to have anything to do with men again in her life. So she arranged to meet Joe for lunch instead. Her brother was probably the only man in the world who wasn't a bastard.

'How's your fortnight in the Big Smoke been?' she asked him.

'Good. I got loads done. I'm flying back on Sunday. Will you drop me to the airport?'

'What time's your flight?'

'Eight o'clock in the morning.'

'Get real, you chancer. Sunday's about the only day of the week that I can manage a lie-in. Take a Joe Maxi. Will I see you again before I go?'

'I've nothing planned for tomorrow evening.'

'Grand. I'll cook something. Maybe invite some people round. Who would you like to meet?'

'I'd like to meet that little Rosa again. She was a cutie.'

'She took a real shine to you.'

'No, she didn't. She just persuaded herself she fancied me because I found her interesting. When she was scuttered she confessed that she fancied the arse off that bloke you were talking to – what was his name again?'

'Michael. Hey, you've just given me a brilliant idea! I'll invite him for Rosa.'

'I thought you'd decided that all men are bastards. What if he breaks her heart?'

Dannie shook her head. 'No. He's kosher. I could tell.' She took a last forkful of pasta and blotted her mouth with her napkin. 'He told me a lovely story.'

'Is that girl wearing a skirt? Or is it a belt?'

'Both. Neither. Whatever. Anyway, the story was that—'

'Wow. Look at the arse on yer wan.'

'Is there any point in me going on with this story, Joe, or are you just going to ogle women's arses?'

'Sorry,' said Joe, not looking sorry at all. 'Go on.'

'Well. Apparently he's been living here in

Dublin for the past year – he's from Glasgow originally – and on the very first day he moved into the flat above the vet's practice, he spotted me locking up the shop.'

'I bet he ogled your arse.'

'Shut up. He didn't. He was dying to ask me if he could have a look around – apparently his granny in Glasgow had a sweetshop almost identical to mine in one of those old Victorian tenements – and he wanted to check out my gaff. He'd seen through the window that it was virtually unchanged, and he has this memory of sitting on the counter when he was a little boy, swinging his legs and eating those sherbet yokes with liquorice. It was dotey! He told me that he'd come into the shop a few times to talk to me, but any time he did I was never there, and he got so embarrassed at going in and never buying anything that the last time he did he bought a big bunch of flowers and gave them to the old lady who lives next door to him. Isn't that a lovely story?'

'Soppy shite. Why didn't he give the flowers to his girlfriend?'

'He doesn't have a girlfriend.'

'He must be a poof, so.'

'No, he's not a poof,' said Dannie indignantly. 'What makes you assume that just because he has no girlfriend he's a – gay? By the same token I must be a raging lezzer because I have no boyfriend. And I haven't heard *you* refer to any girlfriend lately, Mr Macho Moore.'

'That,' said Joe, giving her an oblique look, 'is because I have several.'

'Hey!' said Dannie. 'I don't believe this! My own brother is proof positive of my pet theory.'

'Which is?'

'All men are bastards, of course, you big eejit.'

The waitress arrived to clear their plates. 'Anything else?' she asked.

'I'd like another pint, please,' said Joe, giving her his irresistible smile. 'What about you, Dannie?'

'An espresso, please. And can you bring the bill?'

'Sure.'

'Pretty girl,' remarked Joe, watching the waitress's retreating rear.

'You really are a dyed-in-the-wool skirt-chaser, aren't you?'

'Yup,' said Joe complacently. He pulled a pack of Marlboro out of his pocket, extracted a fag and put it between his lips.

'You're not allowed to smoke in here.'

'I know. I'm only pretending. It gives me great comfort.'

'Are you still off them?'

'Nope. Back with a vengeance. And please don't give out to me or you'll ruin a lovely lunch.'

'Ruin it how?'

'By making me feel guilty.'

'OK,' said Dannie, without enthusiasm. She really would have loved to nag him. She didn't want her fine big hoult of a brother to end up popping his clogs from heart disease.

'So we'll change the subject, will we? How about this. When was the last time you came home to Kilrowan for a visit?'

'Now you're giving out and making *me* feel guilty. It's been a while.'

'Da would like to see you.'

'Would he? I dunno why. We never have anything to say to each other.'

'I think he wants to make amends.'

'Amends? For what?'

'For being such a shite father.'

'He wasn't a shite father. I had a grand time growing up.'

'I think he's feeling guilty. Jesus! What a load of guilt-ridden individuals we are!'

'What's *he* feeling guilty about?'

'He keeps going on about how he should have married again after Mam died, so that you could have had a mother figure. He says that growing up surrounded by boys wasn't good for you, and that that's why you've become a career woman.'

'"A career woman"! Jaysus. He sounds like *Cosmopolitan circa* nineteen seventy-something.'

'I think he's got this image of you the way you were that time we came to visit you in London, when you were still working in television. He remembers you being stressed out and wearing men's suits—'

'Men's suits! They were from Jigsaw!'

'Whatever.'

'I suppose in that case he thinks he's responsible for my turning my back on the joys of motherhood. Unlike his feckin' fecund daughters-in-law. How many grandchildren has he now?'

'Sixteen. And another one on the way.'

The corners of Dannie's mouth drooped a bit. 'Christ. If only he knew!'

Joe had been the only person Dannie had ever confided in about Guy. He had allowed her to weep on his shoulder for the duration of an entire evening. 'You never told anyone about the baby thing, did you, Joe? About Guy?' Dannie knew that her obstetrically prolific sisters-in-law were curious as to why she hadn't got round to settling down and having babies. They'd dropped big hints about it last time she'd been home for Christmas.

'Jesus, Dannie – of course I didn't. All my little sister's secrets are safe with me.'

'I know that. Sorry. I've never really doubted you. Oh – thanks.' This to the waitress, who had set her espresso in front of her and was now smiling sideways at Joe.

'Thank *you*,' said Joe, smiling back and taking his pint from her.

'You know Guy's marrying some bimbo "It" girl?' said Dannie abruptly. 'She's going to make him a daddy.'

'Oh. Shite.' Joe set his glass down on the table with a thud. He looked so pained for her that she could have hugged him. 'Oh, poor Dannie. Poor, poor wee dote.' He took her hand across the table and gave it a sympathetic squeeze. 'I'm really sorry. I know how badly you wanted a baby.'

Dannie's eyes filled with tears. 'I'll never have a baby now, Joe,' she said. 'I'm hitting that age where it gets more and more difficult to conceive. And God knows I don't want another man in my life.' An image of Jethro Palmer suddenly came into focus in her mind's eye as he had been that day on the beach when she'd thought how dear and familiar his face was, but before she could spit at him he'd disappeared again.

'Have you thought about donor sperm?'

'Yeah. And then I think about bringing a child up on my own, and I just can't hack the idea. I'd have to give up work—'

'Not permanently, Dannie.'

'Oh, Joe, if I have a baby I don't want to farm it out to a minder or a crèche. I just couldn't do it. I know some women don't have a problem with the child-care thing, but I've wanted a baby so badly that it would break my heart not to be able to give it all the love I possibly could, and that means being Mammy twenty-four, seven – at least for the first few years.'

'Couldn't you sell the business and invest the money?'

'That's a tricky one. It would break my heart to sell the business after putting so much time and effort into it. Anyway, with interest rates the way they are at the moment, I'm not sure what kind of an income I'd get from investing. Remember, most people bringing up babies have two incomes, so I might be shaky financially. And I know it's a dreadful thing to say, but I'm used to having money. I don't want to be poor, and I don't want my baby to be poor, either. I look at Rosa sometimes and I want to cry for her. She works so hard to keep Lottie happy, and she's done a brilliant job. But Rosa – well, she has no feckin' life of her own. She has no social life, no sex life, no interests. Everything she does, she does for Lottie. Sometimes I wonder what she'll do when she doesn't have Lottie any more, when Lottie grows up and leaves. Her world is so Lottie-centred that there'll be nothing to fill that vacuum. Just . . . *nothing*.'

'Sad.' Joe knocked back some Guinness. 'It's a pity. She's a lovely woman, and fun. I know she was pissed the night I met her, but I really liked her. She's bloody lucky, incidentally, to have a friend in you. Some single parents are so isolated they have no-one. I know what I'm talking about. "Research shows", and all that.'

Actually, Dannie thought, she hadn't been that much of a friend to Rosa at all lately. She'd felt a bit miffed at having to put her to bed *again* that Saturday night after she created a scene in the Clarence, and even more miffed still when Rosa hadn't phoned or called up to say thank you, so she in turn hadn't bothered phoning Rosa. She'd make up for it later, when she'd call in to invite her to supper tomorrow.

'You still haven't told me when you plan to come home, Dannie. Wouldn't you at least talk to Da on the phone?'

'Oh, Joe – he's crap on the phone. He goes all kind of stiff and tactiturn.'

'E-mail him, then.'

'E-mail? Da's on e-mail?'

'From a couple of weeks ago. He's a bit slow, but he's getting the hang of it.'

'Jayze, I've heard it all now!' Dannie leaned her elbows on the table and looked thoughtful. 'It's funny, isn't it? E-mail catching up in the homesteads of Connemara. D'you know something, Joe? When I decided to quit London, it was because I was homesick. I had this sudden vision of the Aran Islands—'

'The Aran Islands? The Aran Islands aren't home!'

'No, I know, but for some reason I've got this really clear memory of them, and that's what made me decide to come back. It's ironic, really – now I'm stuck in the heart of the metropolis. D'you remember the time you took me on a day trip there? To Inisheer? I was only about ten.'

'Yeah. And Da gave out to me for taking the car without asking. Jesus, he was a narky oul bollocks in those days.'

'He's not any more?'

'He's mellowed.'

'Maybe I will come and visit, so. But not at this time of the year. I couldn't cope with the tourists. I'll come in the autumn, when I can have Lissnakeelagh Strand all to myself. I'd love that. Every mid-term break, that's the first place I'd head for. Remember I had a little hideout in the rocks? I'd sit there, watching waves for hours and then—'

Joe sucked in his breath. 'Wow. Take a gander at your one's arse.'

'OK. That's it. I refuse to wax lyrical about my birthplace any more. It's obvious that the only thing you're interested in on the face of the planet is women's arses.'

'Sorry.'

Dannie looked at her watch. 'Janey. I don't have time to wax lyrical about anything, anyway. I should be back at work.' She knocked back her espresso and reached for the bill, but was intercepted by Joe.

'I'll get this,' he said, 'since you're cooking for me tomorrow.' He ran his eyes down the bill and extracted his credit card from his wallet. 'Do you do a lot of dinner parties?'

'Not really. Anyway I'd hardly call inviting my brother and a couple of friends round a "dinner party".'

She didn't want to think of the last time she'd cooked for someone. It had been *dîner à deux*, and her guest had been Jethro Palmer. She didn't *want* to think about it, but she couldn't help it. They'd made love in what he'd taken to calling her 'boudoir', and then she'd put an apron on over her nakedness and had gone to put the finishing touches to their meal. As she squeezed lemon juice over a dish of oysters, she had turned to find Jethro looking at her so hungrily that lust had flared again, shockingly and irresistibly. He'd taken her there and then with such spontaneous urgency that he'd ejaculated prematurely, before he could equip himself with a condom. 'Jesus Christ, Dannie,' she remembered him saying as he'd come inside her. 'Oh, Jesus Christ, I'm sorry – I can't stop myself – oh! Jesus Christ, Dannie Moore! You are the most perfect thing that's ever happened to me . . .'

'What date's today?' she asked Joe suddenly.

'The thirteenth.'

'The *thirteenth*!'

'Yes. Why?'

'No reason.' Dannie had difficulty in making her voice sound unconcerned. Deep inside she felt a little rush, a flurry of some emotion she couldn't quite decipher.

She had just realized that her period was late.

Rosa had phoned in sick, and Miriam had told her not to worry – there was no problem. Because of a baggage handlers' strike at Dublin airport, bookings in the hotel had taken a downturn and weren't expected to get back to normal until the strike was settled. She could take as long as she needed to get over her virus.

But Rosa wasn't sick. She was out of it. She had finished off the wine box in the course of the day she'd rung Roydon – surprised by how quickly it had gone down – there couldn't really be three litres in there! – and then she had gone to her local off-licence and bought another one; no, two, for good measure (she was throwing a party, she told the woman at the checkout), and a bottle of vodka. Tomato juice, too – Bloody Marys as prescribed by the superstar diva were obviously a very good idea. She had pulled a long coat on over her 'at home' threads of baggy sweatpants and T-shirt and gone the long way round to the off-licence:

she hadn't wanted Dannie to see her as she passed the flower shop. She still hadn't summoned the courage to talk to Dannie. Nor had she summoned up the energy to shower or wash her hair for days now. She knew she looked rough, but she didn't care. She was going to retreat like a hermit and blunt the razor-sharp edges of her life while she could, while Lottie was away.

She took to alternating between the off-licence and the local Londis because she didn't want people thinking she was a lush. Anyway, she reasoned, there was no harm in using alcohol for a couple of weeks as an emotional crutch when what she really needed was an emotional Zimmer frame. Once Lottie got back she'd clean up her act, she told herself, and then she'd phone her agent and ask for her advice about the Roydon Sneyde can of worms. Sally would know what to do.

One morning she got a postcard from Calypso, from Gozo – wherever that was – with a picture of her hotel on the front. Bloody bougainvillaea all over the shop, and turquoise swimming pools with sun loungers and enormous parasols. The last holiday Rosa had been on had been a week with Lottie in a three-star hotel in Westport. Lottie had loved it because there'd been a Kids' Club and she'd made loads of friends, and Rosa had enjoyed taking time out to laze and read and not have to cook, but it was at the other end of the spectrum from this joint in Gozo that Calypso was frequenting.

She was about to relegate the postcard to the bin when the phone rang. She picked it up and was surprised to hear Dominic's voice.

'Rosa? I have some bad news I'm afraid – about Calypso. She's in the Mater private – she's had an accident.'

'What? Oh! What – what's happened, Dominic?'

'She fell through the glass door of the shower. She's suffering from –' there was a catch in his voice '– she's suffering lacerations to her face and legs.'

'Oh, Jesus! Oh, poor Calypso. Oh, God. Can I – can I visit her, Dominic?'

'She isn't really up to visitors. She's to spend some time here resting. She – her face is badly cut, Rosa. She'll have to come to terms with the fact that there'll be scars—'

'Oh, *God*.' Rosa hunkered down on the floor of her sitting room. 'Oh, God, Dominic. Will it be very bad?'

'Initially. But the surgeon's been very re-assuring. He reckons he can clean her up nicely, given time. She wanted you to be the first to know.'

Rosa blinked back hot tears. 'Doesn't her mother know yet?'

'No. I'm not going to contact Jessica until Calypso's feeling stronger. She'll be a little reclusive for a while.'

'How long?'

'A couple of weeks, maybe. But she's determined to get on with her life. You know Calypso. She's a resilient creature. She'll bounce back. She'll give you a ring in a few days, let you know how she's doing.'

'Oh, Dominic, thanks so much for phoning. Tell her I'll come and see her as soon as she's able for visitors.'

'I'll do that.'

'And send her my love.'

'Sure I will. Goodbye, Rosa.'

'Bye, Dominic.'

When Rosa put the phone down her hands were shaking. She pictured Calypso lying in her pristine hospital bed with a bandaged face, and the thought of her friend's damaged beauty made her want to weep. But another awful, *awful* thought kept sliding into her head, and it was this: Rosa was actually grateful that Dominic had told her there were to be no visitors for a while. She was grateful that she hadn't had to get into the shower and wash her hair and iron her clothes and do her face and somehow get her act together so that she could go and visit her friend in the hospital. Because she wasn't ready to get her act together just yet, not even for Calypso.

She would do it, she *could* do it, but she wasn't quite ready yet.

She got heavily to her feet and went into the kitchen to visit her new chum, Wine box.

Some more days went by, and wasn't today Friday? No, Thursday. That left Friday and Saturday before Lottie was due to come home and Rosa's new life would start.

Today in the Londis shop she bought a half-bottle of vodka, a couple of cans of soup and a loaf of bread. Sliced pan – they hadn't anything else. She wasn't hungry, but she had to fuel herself with something, and soup was easy to eat. Maybe she should buy some Complan, as well. After all, she was officially an invalid, and Complan was what invalids ate. Milk and Solpadeine, too. She had the mother and father of a headache. She'd take the Solpadeine as soon as she got home, and then she'd treat herself to a nice Bloody Mary before lunch. As she queued at the checkout, she saw that this week's Lottery money was running into the millions. She helped herself to a form and filled in the panels, then asked the girl at the cash desk for three scratch cards. She scratched them as she walked home, and consigned all three to the litter bin at the bus stop, remembering how she'd once called Michael Luque an überloser when she'd seen him buying scratch cards. Hah! Who was the überloser now?

The Bloody Mary was so good she made herself another. Then lunch. Cream of tomato soup. No bread because the butter had gone rancid. Hey! She hadn't stooped so low that she was going to eat Londis sliced pan with no butter! She managed nearly a whole bowl of soup, and had wine box wine with her lunch. Ha! This was the life! She was turning into a Lady who Lunches, like her stylish friend Miss Calypso O'Kelly!

No, no, *no*! Was she becoming so bitter and twisted that she was going to start thinking bad thoughts about Calypso? How fucking *sad*. Another glass of wine and she'd feel better.

She felt sleepy after lunch. She'd have some Complan and then she'd have a little snooze. The Complan was vile, but she knew it was important to keep her strength up for when Lottie got back. She stood by the window, force-feeding herself the gooey drink, surveying the street below through grimy windows. She should wash those, she thought. That was the grim thing about living in the city centre – grime got everywhere. Grim grime. She trailed a finger along the paintwork, tracing a pattern in the dust. She'd have to get some housework done before Sunday. There was masses of ironing to be done, as usual, and the dirty laundry basket was full. She'd have to put on a wash, and that would mean even more ironing. She remembered that the sheets needed changing on both her bed and Lottie's, and as she added her empty mug to the pile of dirty dishes stashed in the sink she contemplated with dread the amount of washing and drying and putting away to be done. Maybe she'd feel better after her snooze. Have more energy.

She didn't notice the mess in her room because it was dark: she hadn't bothered to pull up the blinds this morning. The darkness was comforting, somehow, she thought as she slid under the duvet, the words of 'The Sound of Silence' thrumming lightly in her head. Rosa curled into a foetal position and laid her cheek against the daisy-patterned vest that she kept on her pillow. It was Lottie's vest – she always slept with an item of Lottie's clothing any time the child was away on a sleepover. This was the longest she'd ever spent apart from her baby. Two whole weeks!

Thinking of Lottie made Rosa feel guilty. She had toyed with the idea of giving her room a make-over while she was away – freshen up the paintwork, buy a new cheap-but-cheerful duvet cover and some new curtains and that framed print of leaping dolphins that she'd spotted in the window of a shop in Dawson Street.

But she couldn't afford to indulge her little girl right now – that framed print cost a lot of euros. Roydon fucking Sneyde had put paid to any extravagant notions she might have. Roydon Sneyde. Put paid. *Never* paid . . . Oh! How grim it must be to be him! Grim him! Grim grime. Street crime . . . Shitty city . . . Lucky Lottie to be in Wicklow . . .

She was walking barefoot somewhere by the sea. Where? The Silver Strand, of course, in Mayo, where she had used to come on holiday as a child with her parents from a very early age before she had even started going to school. They had come at unusual times of the year – staying in a beautiful hotel by a river – and had often had the beach entirely to themselves. She had it to herself now: there was no other soul to be seen on that stretch of pale sand. Waves were breaking slowly at her feet: the sea was a liquid scroll round her ankles, an aquamarine arabesque fringed with frothy white lace. Above the noise of the breaking waves she heard someone call her name, and she looked round to see her mother, Ursula. She was standing some distance away, and she was holding Lottie by the hand.

'Mum!' cried Rosa, but no sound emerged from her mouth.

Her mother was smiling and nodding. Rosa could tell she was speaking, even though her lips weren't moving. 'It's all right,' she was saying. 'I've got Lottie. She's safe with me until you're ready to take her back.'

'What do you mean?' cried Rosa. But still there came no sound. 'What do you mean, Mum? I want her now!' Rosa started to move towards her mother, but the wavelets around her ankles were impeding her. The water was thicker than treacle.

Ursula turned, still holding Lottie by the hand, and began to move away from Rosa. 'Mum! Come back! Please! Where are you taking her? I want my baby back! Give me back my Lottie!' Rosa was making Herculean efforts to run after them, but the two figures were drifting further away along the expanse of glimmering sand, and the further away they drifted, the more transparent they became, shimmering like figures walking through a heat haze, diaphanous as ghosts. Rosa cupped her hands round her mouth and yelled, yelled as loud as she could. '*Mum!*'

The shrill electronic bleat of the phone beside her bed woke her. Rosa sat up, sobbing. Without thinking, she grabbed the receiver. She needed the sound of another human voice, needed concrete evidence that she was here in her room in her apartment, talking on the telephone like a living person, needed to know that everything was all right and that what she had just experienced was only a dream.

'*Hello!*'

'Rosa?' It was Dannie's voice. 'Are you all right?'

'Dannie! Oh, hi! I'm sorry, I was asleep, I was – I'm just a bit disorientated, that's all.'

'You were asleep? Are you not well?'

'No. I'm off work with a virus.'

'Oh, Janey – you poor thing! How long have you been down with it?'

'Um. What day's today?'

'Thursday.'

'Oh, God. I dunno. About ten days.'

'Jayze, Rosa! Why didn't you call me?'

'I knew you were busy, what with your brother visiting and all that. I didn't want to be a nuisance.'

'How could you think you'd be a nuisance? I'm cross with you now, so I am. You *should* have phoned me. Is there anything I can do for you? Do you need anything?'

'No. Honestly. I'm fine.'

'I could drop in to you now—'

'*No!* No, honestly, Dannie – the place is a kip. I haven't been able to do any housework—'

'Then that's it! I'm coming round to help. I'll leave Laura to shut up the shop and I'll be there in fifteen minutes.'

Before Rosa could protest further, Dannie had put the phone down.

Oh fuck. Rosa put her head in her hands. All she wanted to do was slide back down under the duvet, but she couldn't. She'd have to whiz round the flat now and try and make it a bit less disgusting. She didn't want Dannie getting a load of the empty wine boxes and vodka bottles and unwashed glasses.

Summoning energy from somewhere, she dragged herself out of bed, went to the bathroom, stuck her toothbrush in her mouth and started to trail around the apartment, getting rid of evidence and cleaning her teeth at the same time. She would run herself a bath too. That would be a good way of getting rid of Dannie – by telling her that her bath was running cold.

Just over fifteen minutes later she had done a superficial tidy, and Dannie was knocking at the door. Rosa ran a hairbrush though her hair before answering, but it was obviously a redundant gesture because the instant Dannie saw her she sucked in her breath and said: 'Oh, poor Rosa. You look wrecked. Here.' She handed her the prettiest little bouquet of tiny tulips and hyacinths, and held up a bottle of wine. 'I don't know if you're feeling up to alcohol? I thought I'd bring it as a peace offering because I was feeling so guilty about not having been in touch for so long.'

'Oh,' said Rosa, holding the door open for Dannie to come through. 'Um, well, actually a glass of wine would be lovely. It'd make a welcome change from vile Complan.'

'Oh, Rosa! Don't tell me you've been subsisting on *Complan*? That makes me feel even guiltier.'

Dannie opened a drawer, located the corkscrew, and pulled.

Rosa got wineglasses down from the cupboard, then panicked when she realized that one of them was still wet from having been recently rinsed under the tap. She got some kitchen towel and dried it quickly. 'An old lippy mark,' she said. 'I mustn't have washed it carefully enough after the last time you were around.' Hey! That had been *clever*! Now Dannie would assume that Rosa hadn't had a drink at home for ages. She used the kitchen towel to wipe ring marks off the kitchen table before they sat down.

'Ten days off work? That's a nasty virus,' remarked Dannie, pouring. '*Sláinte.*'

'*Sláinte.*' They clinked glasses, and Rosa took a fortifying sip. 'And you shouldn't be feeling sorry for me, Dannie. There's someone we should be feeling much sorrier for. I got some really awful news about Calypso.'

'What?'

'She had an accident, fell through a shower door. There'll be scars.'

'Mother of God! When did you hear this?'

'Dominic rang –' when, exactly? She wasn't quite sure. 'Um. A couple of days ago.'

'Have you seen her?'

'No. She doesn't want visitors for a while.'

'Oh, Jesus Christ, that's desperate news, Rosa. I must send flowers. Where is she?'

'The Mater private.' Oh, God – she, Rosa, the so-called 'best friend', hadn't sent any flowers yet. She reached for her bag, which was spilling stuff onto the kitchen table. 'Will you send a bunch from me, too?' she said, finding her wallet. There was one twenty-euro note in it. That note comprised the entire contents of the wallet, apart from some small change in the purse part. But Rosa's guilt was massive. She took out the banknote and passed it over to Dannie. 'That should get her something nice, shouldn't it?'

'Indeed and it will,' said Dannie. 'And I won't charge for delivery. I'll send them out with mine first thing in the morning.' A sigh. 'Poor Calypso. That lovely face. How bad's the scarring?'

'Dominic says the surgeon's very positive.'

'And when will she be out and about?'

Oh God! Why did Dannie ask so many questions about dates that were a bit hazy in her head? 'Um. Not long, I don't think. He says she should bounce back quite well. She's always been a bit of a dynamo.'

They sat in silence for a while, brooding, and then Dannie said: 'What about you, sweetheart? When d'you think you'll be able for work?'

'Miriam told me I could have as much time as I need off. I'll probably go back on Monday. I was lucky – they haven't been busy, and Isabel was glad to cover for me: she needs the overtime. She's heading off on holiday soon.'

'Who's Isabel?'

'She's the other resident beautician.'

'And how are you feeling today?'

'Better. I should be back on my feet tomorrow. I'll take it easy for the next day or two until Lottie gets back.'

'When's she due?'

'She's being dropped back on Sunday afternoon. I spoke to her yesterday.' Rosa had a vague recollection of talking to her daughter on the phone some time during the course of the previous wine-saturated evening. 'She's having a ball. Jesus! I wish I could get her off to the country more often.'

'Maybe you should both take off somewhere. Have a break.'

Rosa wanted to say: 'A break? Chance would be a fine thing.' But she didn't. She didn't want to moan on about all her problems when they'd just had a conversation about a mutual friend who was lying with a bandaged face in a hospital bed.

Dannie put her wineglass down, then looked round the kitchen. 'Now. It's clean-up time. Where do you want me to start, and –' she sniffed the air – 'what's that lovely smell?'

'Dannie! I am not going to allow you to start skivvying in my flat. The lovely smell's Radox. I just ran a bath.'

'Have you an extension cable?'

'Yes. Why?'

'You're going to get into the bath with your glass of wine, and I'm going to set up the ironing board and get rid of that fierce pile of ironing I see in the basket. That way I can chat to you as you take it easy.'

'Dannie! You will do no such thing!'

'I bloody well will. Now strip off your clothes and get in there.'

'You're not supposed to use electrical appliances in bathrooms,' muttered Rosa.

'Well, hey! I'm a rebellious kind of chick! I like to break rules.'

Rosa knew she had no choice. When Dannie made her mind up about something she always stuck to her guns. And as she wandered through into her bedroom to undress, Rosa realized that, actually, having a glass of wine in the bath while simultaneously conducting a girly chat with her chum was a rather cheering prospect.

She walked naked into the bathroom and tested the temperature of the water with a toe. It was perfect. Rosa sank under the foam with a sigh. She was feeling pretty damn good, now. The glass of wine Dannie had poured for her had again induced that mildly euphoric state she'd experienced after lunch when she'd taken herself off for her little snooze. She wished she hadn't had that dream, though. Her memory of it was vestigial, but she knew it had been deeply disturbing.

'I forgot to mention,' said Dannie, coming into the room and setting up the ironing board, 'that I'm having my brother round for dinner tomorrow. You're on the guest list, if you're feeling up to it.'

'Oh – no, Dannie! I couldn't come. I made such a turkey of myself last time I met him!'

'He thought you were great. It was him who suggested I invite you.'

'Maybe he's changed his mind about the ride I offered him.'

Dannie laughed. 'Don't be stupid. He really liked you. And I'm inviting Michael,' she threw over her shoulder as she went to fetch the ironing basket.

'Michael?'

'The flamencoing vet from down the road.'

'Oh, no, Dannie! Not him as well,' wailed Rosa. 'He witnessed my appalling stunt too!'

'I think he fancies you.' Dannie was back with her laundry-maid props.

'That's crap, and you know it. He very obviously fancies *you*.'

'He does not. The only reason he wanted to meet me was because my shop is identical to one his granny in Glasgow had when he was a kid.' She plugged the iron into the extension cable and refilled their glasses while she waited for it to heat. 'He told me he used to eat sherbet fountains in it and listen to all the awl wans gossiping. And . . .' Dannie slid her a meaningful sideways look '. . . he also said something very interesting about you.'

'Yeah,' said Rosa suspiciously. 'What? Something along the lines of what's a gorgeous chick like you doing with a drunken tart like her?'

'No! Rosa! You've got to stop putting yourself down all the time. What he *actually* said was that he'd seen you from his window loads of times, walking down the street with Lottie, and that he'd found you – wait for it – *intriguing*. He said that a woman who could produce a child like Lottie would be a woman worth getting to know.'

'Oh!' Rosa was silent for a beat or two, pondering. She took a sip of wine. Then: 'Did he really say that?' she asked.

'He did.'

'I think that's the nicest compliment anyone's ever paid me.'

'So, now. Will you come tomorrow evening?'

'I might.' Rosa smiled up at Dannie, full of incredulous delight at what she'd just heard. Then she set her wineglass down on the edge of the bath and lifted a leg from the water to soap it.

'Ow!' said Dannie. 'Where did you get that stonking great bruise?'

Too late, Rosa dropped her leg back into the water. 'Um. I banged my shin against the coffee table,' she lied. She hadn't a clue how she'd come by the bruise, and she really wished Dannie hadn't spotted it.

Dannie ironed stoically on for another hour or so and finished the ironing pile, and Rosa prattled away in the bath and ran more hot water, and between them they finished the bottle of wine. Then Dannie went home, and Rosa was quite glad of this, because it meant she could sling on her dressing gown and pour herself another glass from her own stash of wine now that the stuff Dannie had brought was all gone. She watched telly while she ate her supper – baked beans on toast with no butter. There was nothing worth watching on tonight, but she wanted to see the Lottery results. Maybe, just *maybe*, her luck would change? She'd had such a run of bad luck recently that something good *had* to happen soon. She'd forgotten, of course, that Wednesdays and Saturdays were lottery nights. And a couple of days later she found out that the Lottery had been won by someone in Farneyhoogan.

Dannie had been quite glad to go home that evening too, because there was something she wanted to do. After she'd checked messages on her answering machine and changed into her velvet comfies, she withdrew from her handbag a purchase she'd made earlier that day in the pharmacy next door to the vet's. She'd need to study the instructions very carefully. She'd never used a pregnancy-testing kit before.

Chapter Fifteen

The kit advised Dannie to test with the first urine of the day. At six o'clock on the morning of Friday, 14 June, Dannie sat staring at the results. The lines in the little box were blue. It was official. She was pregnant.

Maybe it was a mistake. Surely these things weren't infallible? But *she* knew. Some spooky hormonal instinct told her that the kit wasn't lying, that a baby had started to grow inside her. February or March. The child would be due some time around then. If nothing went wrong she would have a little Pisces.

I'll never have a baby now, Joe ... How ironic that she should have made that pronouncement only yesterday! She recalled the conversation of the previous lunchtime, when she'd voiced her reservations about single parenthood. Those reservations had now been magicked away off into the ether. It was as if the woman who'd carped about the hardship involved in bringing up a baby single-handedly was another person. A baby! She was going to have a baby!

The knowledge made her feel as if a bubble of pure happiness was expanding inside her. She laid her hands on her flat stomach, and imagined how it might feel months from now, rounded and full of life. And then she remembered Jethro's words as he'd planted the seed that would become their child, and the bubble expanding within her burst and fragmented. *Oh! Jesus Christ, Dannie Moore! You are the most perfect thing that's ever happened to me . . .*

Rosa had cleaned up her act. She had spent the day tidying the flat and doing laundry. It was now six minutes to six. In six minutes she would reward herself for all the hard work she'd done. She would make herself an extra spicy Bloody Mary.

Hah! What will-power she had! She obviously had no problem with alcohol. That little voice that came into her head and annoyed her sometimes had been proved wrong. It had nagged at her this morning when she saw the evidence of the amount of alcohol she'd consumed last night lying around the flat. There was even an empty wineglass by her bed, the contents of which she had absolutely no recollection of drinking.

But holding out until six o'clock in the

evening was proof positive that she was not suffering from incipient alcoholism. Six o'clock was a perfectly civilized time of the day to have a drink. She remembered her grandfather had always had his pre-prandial gin and tonic at six on the dot – 'when the sun is over the yardarm,' he'd said – and *he* certainly hadn't been an alcoholic. It was a hereditary thing, after all – isn't that what they said? And there'd been no alcoholics in the Elliot family to her reasonably certain knowledge. And then the horrid niggly voice sneered at her in her head. *You're adopted, you great eejit . . .*

Shut up, shut up! She looked at the clock for the third time in as many minutes. She'd start making her Bloody Mary now, and by the time she'd finished she would be hearing the bells of St Patrick's Cathedral strike six.

She fiddled around with lemon and paprika and Tabasco, and added a tad more vodka just to make the concoction a little livelier. Ice cubes . . . ping! ping! Pity she hadn't a celery stick. The Bloody Mary that the pop diva had treated her to in the Hamilton had had a celery stick . . . Bong! There! Six o'clock!

She raised her glass in a toast to St Patrick's Cathedral, and went into her bedroom to decide what she should wear to Dannie's supper party. Could Dannie be right? she wondered. Could it be possible that Michael Luque wanted to get to know her? Oh, God. There was a problem here. If he *did* get to know her he'd find out how boring she was. Boring single parent Rosa Elliot.

Stop it, Rosa. What had Dannie said to her yesterday? *You've got to stop putting yourself down* . . . Dannie was right. It was about time she did something about her low self-esteem. She'd go into town tomorrow and look through the self-help titles in Eason's. There were hundreds of them on the shelves. There had to be something that was right for her. Dannie had lent her a book once called *The Princessa – Machiavelli for Women*, but it was mostly full of advice for women who were successful already, not for no-hopers like her. She'd need something a lot more basic, something that would encourage her to use affirmations. She'd read in a magazine about the confidence-building power of affirmations. Some people swore by them. She wondered if Calypso's self-esteem came from affirmations. She pictured Calypso standing in front of the beautiful cheval glass in her dressing room saying something like 'I am fabulous', and then she realized that Calypso wouldn't need to do that because other people did it for her all the time.

Standing there in front of her wardrobe mirror with her Bloody Mary in her hand, she tried it for herself. 'I am fabulous,' she said. It didn't work. She took another slug of her Bloody Mary and felt a tiny little tingle of fabulousness.

Bloody Marys obviously worked a damn sight better than affirmations.

OK. Back to the business in hand. Her outfit for tonight. Should she go for something stylishly simple? Her Next little black dress was quite sophisticated-looking. No. She'd never be able to pull sophistication off. Something maybe a little sexy, then? Absolutely not. Dannie had the monopoly on sexy without even trying. Even when she was wearing jeans Dannie contrived to look sexy. She'd confided in Rosa once that it was because she wore sexy underwear, and she was convinced that that did wonders for your confidence, but Rosa didn't have any sexy underwear. Something pretty, so. She'd get away with pretty. She opted for a pale pink chiffon number and high strappy shoes, hoping that nobody would spot the resemblance between her and Reese Witherspoon in *Legally Blonde*. Even though she was a brunette. Hell. So what if they did? At least then they might not entertain high hopes of getting stimulating supper-party conversation out of her.

She showered and shaved her armpits and had a little glass of wine. She'd had to buy a box of red Côtes du Rhône in the off-licence – she'd bought out all the Chardonnay. Rosa preferred white: this red wasn't much to her taste, but it was the effect that counted after all, not the taste, and red packed the same punch. Then she blow-dried her hair and plucked her eyebrows and did her make-up and had a little toppy-up glass of wine and put on her prettiest dangly earrings. It was eight o'clock. It was time to go. She sprayed herself with the Chanel 19 Calypso had given her for her last birthday. It was the scent Calypso wore herself – they'd both fallen in love with it back in their college days. The irony was not lost on her. In those days the copy for Chanel 19 had read: 'Witty, confident, devastatingly feminine'. That was Calypso to a T. So what was she, Rosa, doing even *trying*? She was nothing but an arrant impostor, a fraud in her pretty pink frock and her perfume, posturing as some kind of wannabe party girl. Get real, Rosa. You are not that pretty girl you see in the mirror. You are just a *mum*.

She sat down on the bed. She couldn't go. She couldn't go up to Dannie's beautiful flat and pretend that she was having fun, when all the time she'd be whimpering inwardly and concentrating on trying not to drink too much and worrying about what the next impossible topic of conversation might be. She hadn't read a newspaper or watched anything intellectually stimulating on the television for days – she hadn't a clue what was going on in the world. And Dannie's brother Joe was a very intelligent, informed individual.

No. She wouldn't go up there. She'd ring

Dannie and tell her that her really very useful virus had come back. She kicked off her stupid strappy heels and padded towards the kitchen to where her chum Wine box was waiting. She'd stay in with him this evening instead. He knew her too well to expect witty remarks and astute observations from her.

On her way past Lottie's bedroom she was struck by something. It was the realization that it had been a long time since she'd heard the irritating sound of the Mysterious One's wheel going round. *Oh!* She hadn't fed the gerbil in days. She scampered into the kitchen to get the packet of gerbil food, and as she rummaged in the cupboard for it, she felt panic rising.

Feeling ill suddenly, she ran into Lottie's room. The animal was in its sleeping compartment. She slid back the bolt and tentatively poked at the straw. There was a truly tragic smell – she remembered she'd promised Lottie she'd clean out the cage. She'd neglected to do it – she'd broken her promise.

The Mysterious One was curled up in its nest of stinking straw. Its eyes were shut and it was shivering. Its breath was coming very, very fast. There was no food in its dish and the water bowl was dry. Oh fuck. Oh *fuck*. The thing was clearly dying. She'd killed it. She'd murdered Lottie's beloved pet.

Rosa lifted it from its nest and laid it on a

comic on the floor. What could she do? Water first, obviously, and food. She sprinkled feed into its dish. Maybe she could encourage it to eat somehow? Then she ran to the kitchen to get cleaning products and fill the water bowl. Oh God, oh, God, oh God. Back in the bedroom she frantically set about cleaning the cage. She scrubbed it and disinfected it and replenished it with fresh straw, and then she lifted the animal back onto its bed and held a morsel of food to its tiny muzzle, gently stroking its fur and murmuring inducements to it to revive.

'Come on, little thing. Eat some of this, won't you? Come on, please? Do it for Lottie, little thing. Please do it for Lottie. She loves you so much – please get well. Please live. Please.' Big gloopy tears had welled up in her eyes and were now sploshing onto the floor of the cage. 'I don't know what she'll do if you die on her. Please, *please* get better, oh Mysterious One!'

A knock came on the door. Oh! Maybe someone who could help her? Someone who knew what to do in emergencies like this? Dannie! It would be Dannie. Dannie always knocked. Barefoot and distraught, mascara streaming down her cheeks, Rosa ran to the door and wrenched it open.

Dannie stood there, reassurance personified. 'Howrya! Can I borrow your corkscrew? Mine's gone and feckin' broken again and – Oh! Rosa! What's up?'

'Oh, Dannie – come in and see if you can help. Lottie's gerbil's very sick. I think it's dying and it's all my fault! Oh, help me, *please*!'

Dannie moved swiftly into Lottie's bedroom. She took one look at the little bundle of fur lying shaking on its bed of straw and said: 'Michael's card's on my noticeboard upstairs. I'll run up and ring him – ask him to bring any medical stuff he thinks might help.'

'Oh, God – you're so brilliant. I knew you'd think of something.'

Dannie swung out of Rosa's flat and back up the stairs. She managed to contact Michael on his mobile.

'Hi,' he said. 'I'm on my way over to your place now.'

Dannie filled him in on the Mysterious One's plight. 'D'you think you might be able to help?'

'Sure. I'll bring my bag. But from what you tell me, I don't hold out much hope. It sounds like the animal's badly dehydrated.'

He was right. By the time Michael reached Rosa's apartment Lottie's pride and joy, her real live favourite cuddly toy, the quirkily named Mysterious One, was dead.

Later, up in Dannie's apartment, Dannie poured a glass of wine for Rosa. She'd been very shaky downstairs, but Dannie had hugged her and comforted her, and she'd finally stopped crying,

511

thank God. Now Dannie was proffering advice.

'You mustn't feel guilty,' she told her. 'You mustn't blame yourself. You've been very sick – no wonder it didn't cross your mind to feed the gerbil. You had more important things to worry about, Rosa, and I know it won't be easy, but you must make that real plain to Lottie. That was a really nasty virus you had.'

For some reason, Rosa didn't appear to find Dannie's words of reassurance all that reassuring. She slid her eyes away and just looked guiltier than ever.

'Couldn't you nip out tomorrow and buy her a lookalike?' suggested Joe. 'All gerbils look pretty much the same, don't they?'

'You don't understand,' said Rosa. 'Lottie hand-picked the Mysterious One from a bunch of other gerbils because the Mysterious One was special. She said she recognized an ancient soul gazing out at her through her eyes, and knew that she'd once been some regal person in Ancient Egypt. She'd spot an impostor immediately.'

'What will you do with the, um – the corpse?' A splutter escaped Joe. 'Oh, Rosa – I'm so sorry. I don't mean to laugh, and I know it's not funny at all, but it just seems so bonkers, referring to the "corpse" of a dead gerbil.'

Rosa managed a wan smile.

'I could have it incinerated for you, if you like,' volunteered Michael.

She shook her head. 'No. I think it's important for Lottie to see her, and to have the opportunity of giving her a proper funeral. I know it seems absurd—'

'It doesn't,' put in Michael. 'It doesn't seem absurd at all. I'll come to the funeral.'

'So will I,' said Dannie, moving to the stove and checking her sauce. 'Where will you have it?'

'Oh. That's going to be a problem. I can't very well bury her in a public park, can I?'

'I'll drive you out to the country,' said Michael. 'We could do a proper funeral, with tea and cake in a hotel afterwards. Make it a really meaning-ful occasion for Lottie.'

'Is it her first bereavement?' asked Joe.

'Yeah. She was too young to take it in when her granny died. She was still just a baby. Well – a toddler.'

Dannie hadn't known Lottie then. She wondered how Rosa had coped with losing her mother and minding an infant all on her own. She knew that Rosa had had no support from the father, had never even approached him for help. She wondered now about the man who'd fathered Lottie. How many countless thousands of men were out there in the world, going about their business without having an inkling that somewhere on the planet was a son or a daughter belonging to them?

What about *her* baby? The one that was taking

shape inside her now? Would she ever tell her child the true story behind its conception – the story of how she, gullible Dannie Moore, had been hoodwinked and shafted by an unscrupulous slimeball with a mean line in chat-up and no heart? What sex was her baby? she wondered. If it was a boy, what would she call him? Not Jethro, after his father, that was for sure, even though she rather liked the name 'Jethro Moore'. It had a kind of gravitas to it. She knew her own name had posed no problem to her father. Daniella, after her mother. Daniella was really quite a lovely name. Sometimes she wished that her brothers had never come up with the diminutive 'Dannie'. But, of course, the nickname had well and truly stuck, and she'd be Dannie for ever.

'How did you choose Lottie's name, by the way, Rosa?' she asked now. 'Carlotta's such a beautiful, unusual name.'

'I know I should come up with some wildly romantic story, but I'm afraid it's pretty mundane. I bought a book of babies' names, and I went for "Carlotta" because of what it means.'

'What does it mean?' asked Michael.

'"One who is all that is feminine, but who rules and controls".' Rosa gave a little laugh. 'Sometimes I wonder if I did the right thing. She's certainly living up to her name. She has me wrapped around the proverbial.'

Dannie wondered what the name 'Jethro' meant. Bastard, probably. What if she had a little girl? Paloma, of course. Paloma Moore? Um, no. It didn't really work. Paloma Palmer acually sounded much better . . . Oh! Don't go there, Dannie! But she couldn't stop herself . . . Would she be dark, like her, or would she inherit Jethro's reddish-blond hair?

As she stirred the sauce and allowed herself to dream a little, she became aware of the direction the conversation in the sitting room was taking.

She heard Joe saying: 'Has that scandal blown over in the Hamilton, Rosa?'

'Scandal?'

'I heard a rumour from a journo pal that someone involved in that big budget movie mauled a member of staff.'

'I'm not at liberty to comment,' said Rosa. 'I'm not allowed to discuss the goings-on of the clients.'

'But I am,' said Dannie, with vehemence. 'And you're right. One of the chambermaids was sexually abused by the film's director.'

'The director? Surely not? My pal would have said. The director's Jethro Palmer, isn't it?'

'Jethro *Bastard* Palmer,' said Dannie crisply.

Joe shot her a curious look, but the expression on his sister's face warned him not to ask too many questions. 'Well, it definitely wasn't him,' he said with authority. 'It was a much more ordinary, Joe Bloggs kind of name. Tom some-body or other.'

'What?' Rosa had clamped her hand over her mouth and was staring at Joe with wide, wide eyes. '*What?*'

'*What?*' echoed Dannie. She dropped the spoon she was holding and grabbed the edge of the cooker for support. Her legs felt as if they had turned to water, and white noise was buzzing in her head.

Rosa and Dannie exchanged frightened looks, then Rosa turned back to Joe and said: 'Call your friend, Joe. Call him now.'

'What? Why? What's going on?'

'Just do it, Joe. It's important. Please do it now.'

Looking flummoxed, Joe took out his phone and pressed digits. 'Andy? Joe here. Can you clear something up? The geezer who was said to have abused the girl in the Hamilton – who was it? No, no. Strictest confidence. Mm hm. And you say he was the second unit director? Tom Smith. Right. Thanks, Andy.' He put his phone down and said: 'Well, that's cleared that up. It was the second unit director.'

Rosa turned her stricken gaze back to Dannie. 'Oh, Jesus, Dannie. I'm so, so sorry,' she said in a voice that had gone whispery with shock. 'Miriam pointed him out to me when he was in the pool one day.'

'Jethro doesn't swim in pools.' Dannie's voice

was as whispery as Rosa's. 'He has an allergy to chlorine.'

'What's all this about?' asked Michael.

Dannie couldn't think. The sudden blind panic she felt frightened her. It was as if an abyss had suddenly opened at her feet, and the monster who lived there was waiting for her to lose her grip on reality and plunge herself into its maw. She lurched away from the cooker and ran to her bedroom.

'Women's stuff,' she heard Rosa say behind her, and then Rosa was there with her in her room, sitting beside her on the bed.

'Oh, Jesus,' Rosa said. 'Oh, Jesus, I'm so sorry, Dannie. It's all my fault. I made a dreadful mistake. I'm so, so sorry,' she said again, putting a hand on her friend's arm. Her face was still white with shock.

'What'll I do? What can I do, Rosa?'

'Can you phone him?'

'Oh, God, no! What would I say to him? "Sorry, Jethro, I made a big mistake. I mistook you for the kind of neanderthal gombeen that sexually assaults women."'

'Or e-mail him. Whatever. Just get it sorted ASAP, don't you think?' Rosa was quivering with anxiety.

Dannie put her head in her hands. 'I don't know what to think,' she said. 'My brain's banjaxed. Oh, Christ. Oh – *how* did I get him so wrong? I just assumed he was another bastard like Guy – another fecker doing a typical bastard bloke thing.'

'Why don't you just go to him. Go to him now, Dannie. He's in a place called Gozo – Calypso was over there with him before her accident – I got a postcard from her.'

'I know. He told me he was going to take time out there until he got a call from LA. I even had the feeling he was going to ask me to come and join him.'

'Then book a flight out there tomorrow, before he goes back to the States.'

Dannie bit her lip. 'I suppose Gozo's more accessible than LA.'

'I don't think you should let the grass grow under your feet on this one.'

'I don't have his address.'

'I'll phone Calypso and ask her for it.'

'Jaysus, Rosa – we can't be bothering Calypso for an address when she's in hospital!'

'Then I'll phone Dominic.' Rosa dashed back into the kitchen, where Michael was now stirring the pot on the stove.

'Everything all right?' he queried, looking helpless.

'Not yet. But I'm going to make damn sure it will be. It's got to be perfect.' Rosa grabbed her bag and disappeared back into the bedroom, rummaging for her mobile phone as she went.

She pressed in Calypso's home number, hoping to God Dominic would be there. He picked up the phone almost immediately, and Rosa just resisted the temptation to blurt out 'Thank God'. Instead she said: 'Dominic, it's Rosa. How are things with Calypso?'

'She's doing all right. She's sleeping a lot, but getting stronger.'

'Is she receiving visitors yet?'

'No. Not till next week.'

'Can I be the first?'

'Of course.'

Then Rosa took a deep breath. 'Dominic, I really hate to hassle you right now, but an emergency's come up, and I need to get an address for Jethro Palmer in Gozo ASAP. Have you any idea what it might be? I don't want to bother Calypso in hospital.'

'There's no hassle. I have his card right here in front of me. I'm in Calypso's study, packing up her laptop. She wants to try and get some work in tomorrow.'

'Oh! The bold girl!'

'Tell me about it. I tried to dissuade her, but you know Calypso. Nothing holds her back when she's got a bee in her bonnet, and there's a casting coming up soon that she wants to get sorted. Have you a pen handy?'

'Yes. Shoot.' Rosa tore a sheet of paper from her Filofax.

'It's Mediterranean Heights, near Xlendi, Gozo.'

'Thank you, thank you, thank you, Dominic,' said Rosa, scribbling more furiously than Picasso. 'Kiss that bold girl from me and tell her I'm dying to see her.'

'I'll do that.'

Rosa depressed 'end call' and handed the scrap of paper to Dannie. 'There. Go for it.'

'Should I?'

'Please do. I feel so guilty. This is all my fault.'

'No, it's not. Anyone could make a mistake like that. Oh, God – what should I do, Rosa? I don't know what to do any more. I'm pregnant.'

'What?'

'Oh, shite. I didn't mean to tell you that. It just slipped out. But it's true.' She studied Rosa's aghast expression with mournful eyes. 'I'm having Jethro's baby.'

There was a loaded silence. Then: 'Are you – are you going to keep it?' Rosa asked finally.

'Yes.'

'Well. Congratulations!' said Rosa, switching on a bright smile and aiming a kiss at her friend's cheek.

'Oh, Rosa!' Dannie flung herself back on the bed and contemplated the stars on the ceiling as if she were an astrologer and they could tell her future. 'Oh, *Janey*! This is a fucking awful complicated situation. This is the proverbial can of worms.'

'Well,' said Rosa. 'You know what they say about fucking awful complicated situations?'

'No,' said Dannie, miserably.

'They say: "Keep it simple, stupid." '

And that's exactly what she did. She simply phoned her assistant Laura the next day and told her she was taking a week off work. And then she booked herself into the hotel Calypso had stayed in on the island of Gozo, and took the first available flight out of Dublin. She flew to Gatwick, and then she flew to Malta, and then she took a helicopter from Malta to Gozo. By the time she arrived at the hotel Ta'Cenc it was late, and she felt grimy and tired and scruffy from too much travelling. She decided to wait until tomorrow to go grovelling to Jethro – she didn't have the stamina to do it this evening. She showered, then poured herself an orange juice from the minibar – wishing she was allowed a stiff drink – and ordered something to eat from room service.

The waiter who arrived was efficient and polite without being obsequious. As he set the table on the private balcony of her room, Dannie found herself thinking absently that she'd love to come back here some time to enjoy a proper holiday – it seemed mad to be staying in such a classy joint with no friend or loved one to share the gorgeousness of the Gozitan evening. It was obvious the waiter felt the same way, because behind the smile he gave her when she tipped him Dannie sensed there was a little 'ouch' of pity for the loser who was dining all alone. If she were the kind of person who indulged in self-pity Dannie supposed *she'd* feel sorry for herself. Here she was – sitting on a balcony in a balmy hibiscus-scented dusk, eating delicious food without tasting it, contemplating a glorious sun-set without appreciating it, listening to the stirring strains of a distant violin without being moved by it. It could have been dead romantic. And later, as she slid between the sheets on the king-size bed in her beautifully appointed room, she found herself wishing she'd contacted Jethro after all.

To distract herself from the unwelcome thoughts, she reached for the book she'd bought earlier in Gatwick and hadn't opened yet. Flicking quickly through the pages that listed babies' names and their meanings, she soon came to the one she wanted. Under the letter 'J', she read the following: 'Jethro. Excellent; without equal. A man outstanding in all his virtues.'

The next morning, she took a taxi to Mediterranean Heights, and instructed the driver to wait. She didn't want to run the risk of

Jethro not being at home – or worse, of him telling her to fuck off.

A polite, Gozitan-accented voice came over the speaker when she pressed the bell on the security gate.

'Um – could you please tell Mr Palmer that a Dannie Moore is here to see him?'

'I'm afraid Mr Palmer isn't at home right now, madam.'

Oh, feck it! Trust her luck! 'When do you expect him back?'

'He should be back for lunch quite soon.'

'Oh. OK, then,' she said inadequately. 'Thank you.'

'I'll tell him you called, Ms Moore.'

'Thank you.' Dannie stood there on the dusty road, deliberating. Should she go back to the hotel? No. It was lunchtime now. He couldn't be much longer. She'd wait. She explained the situation to the taxi driver, and he shrugged. There was no problem for him – he was at her disposal.

Dannie sat down on a low wall across the road from Jethro's house and thought. She wished she had a present for him, but she had had no time to put the energy and effort into choosing something that would have to be just perfect. She sat there, blind to the beauty of the surrounding countryside and deaf to the birdsong, and rehearsed the speech she'd soon have to make. What could she say? How about: *I have been a fecking eejit*. Well, yes, Dannie Moore – that just about summed it up. Oh, God! What demon had come calling, whispering in her credulous ear that Jethro Palmer was just another bastard out to get her? Why had she not just trusted her instinct about him, the instinct that had allowed her to invite him into her life on only their third date? What else could she say? *Please, please take me back*. For sure. She'd have to crawl for the Olympics if she wanted her überdude back. And the third thing she was going to have to say was this: *I love you, Jethro Palmer.*

I love you. She knew the words were true, and they were going to be the bravest words she had ever spoken in her life. She might as well remove her heart from her chest cavity and hold it out to him on a plate. It was up to him then whether to accept it as a rare gift, or whether to reject it outright with contempt. She wouldn't blame him if he opted for the latter response. She'd treated him like a jerk.

A car was approaching. It slowed as it reached the bend in the road where Jethro's tall front gates were located, and Dannie got to her feet, aware that the palms of her hands were clammy with nervous sweat. But the driver was a monkey-faced lech who leered at her – nothing like her gorgeous Jethro – and the car continued on down the hill.

There was sweat under her arms now, too. She

could feel a droplet trickle along the side of her breast. She hoped it wouldn't leave a mark on the pale blue silk of the bra she had chosen to wear that morning – the bra he'd been brave enough to buy for her in scary Agent Provocateur. It hadn't joined its comrades on the bonfire she'd built in her fireplace only because she'd been wearing it that day, and later she was glad she'd resisted the impulse to trash it because it was the prettiest one of them all. It had embroidered forget-me-nots on it.

She went to sit down again, and as she did, a flicker of movement caught her attention. A tiny khaki-coloured lizard was basking on the plump green leaf of a nearby prickly pear, gorging itself with noonday solar energy. It sat still and un-obtrusive as a stone before tweaking its tail once, twice, then darted with such mercurial adroit-ness into the shade that if Dannie had blinked she wouldn't have believed it had ever been there. Now when she did blink, she realized that there was a sting of tears in her eyes. The stupid sun was blinding her. She rooted in her shoulder bag for sunglasses and tissues, wishing she had thought to bring a bottle of water with her. Her lips were dry as dead leaves, her tongue was parchment. She blew her nose, wiped her eyes, and as she went to slide on her shades, she became aware that there was a figure in the landscape, that the figure was moving towards her, and that it was Jethro.

The next thing she knew, she was moving fast towards him down the hill, oblivious to the whiplash sting of the scutch grass on her bare legs. The speech she'd prepared earlier never made it out of her mouth. She launched herself into his arms and he enveloped her, gathering her into him, inhaling her scent – and it was the most romantic thing that had ever happened to her. And because she knew with absolute, blinding certainty that the words she'd rehearsed earlier weren't necessary, she simply burst into a Niagara of tears.

They were lying in Jethro's enormous bed, the sheets of which were gratifyingly tousled and tossed and trailing all over the place.

He was fiddling with her ear. 'D'you know how I first caught sight of you this morning?' he said.

'How?' She was tracing the line of his jaw, relearning the geography of his gorgeous, beloved face.

'I was photographing the landscape, and suddenly I saw a forlorn figure sitting all alone on a wall. Shall I show you the photo I took?'

'Mm hm,' she said meekly. She was still feeling humbled by her absurd good fortune.

He left the bed and fetched his camera, which hung by its strap over the back of a chair. 'Look,' he said, positioning the viewfinder so that she could peer at the image he'd clicked on. 'Look how lonely you are. Lonelier than Greta Garbo.'

The photograph was a close-up of her face. Her eyes were enormous with worry. 'I really *do* look lonely, don't I? Oh, shite, Jethro – I might have looked that way for the rest of my life if I hadn't discovered my mistake! Oh, thank you, thank you, Jethro, thank you for having me back.' She didn't care that she was abject. She had her überdude back, and all was well with the world.

'The pleasure's all mine,' he said. 'I'm a lucky man to share a bed with a broad who wears stuff like this.' He stretched out a hand and picked up the baby-blue panties that he'd thrown onto the floor earlier. 'I bought these for you, didn't I? What knock-out taste I have.'

She didn't want to tell him that these particular underthings had narrowly missed going up in smoke with all the other frothy, frivolous stuff she had set light to in her fireplace on the evening she thought he was a worse bastard than Guy. She also thought with sorrow of that other gift he'd given her: the beautiful blue Karmann Ghia. 'Whatever happened to the gorgeous car?' she asked.

'I had it sent back to the dealers.'

'Oh! How sad.'

'Serves you right for being such a wuss. What possessed you to think I was the kind of sicko who'd perpetrate shameful acts on chambermaids?'

'That's exactly what I asked myself earlier. I don't know, I don't know! Oh, shut up, Jethro, and don't be reminding me of that!'

'I'll remind you of it any time I feel you need punishing. I hope you've learned some kind of a lesson.'

'Oh, I have!' she said, kissing him fervently. 'Indeed, and I have.'

'And what might that be?'

'All men are *not* bastards,' she said meekly, then steeled herself. It was her cue to say something like 'And I'd prefer it if our baby wasn't one either,' but she wimped out. She'd already put her heart on a plate once today; she couldn't start pestering him to marry her at this stage.

On the bedside table, the phone purred. Jethro checked the display. 'Hot damn,' he said. 'I'll have to take this. It's from my line producer. We've problems.' He picked up the receiver. 'Louis?' he said. 'Bring it on.'

As he listened to a lengthy soliloquy, interspersing it with the occasional 'Shit', or 'Too bad', or '*Damn*!', Dannie wandered naked to the window and looked out. The view was astonishing. As she surveyed it, she realized that despite the palm trees and the cacti and the bright oleander and the olive groves and the wind-borne scent of wild thyme and all the other sundry unfamiliar exotica, this landscape reminded her of Aran – the islands off the West Coast of Ireland that Joe had taken her to visit all those years ago: Inishmaan, her big sister Inishmore, and her baby sister Inisheer. This island of Gozo was greener than her big sister Malta, greener than her baby sister Comino. But unlike the Arans, which were habitually clawed and gouged by the hostile Atlantic Ocean, these islands were cradled in the lap of the benign blue Mediterranean Sea.

She thought of her home, by the sea in Connemara. The terrain there was ribbed with drystone walls: it was a geographical hotchpotch of stone and grass, of sepia and verdant green, of barrenness and fecundity. And when she crossed the room to look at the view from the opposite window, the window that faced towards the land, she saw that, looking down from Mediterranean Heights, she could have been looking down from the mountain near her father's farmhouse. Had she come home at last?

She thought of her father, and of what Joe had said about him, and in her head she started to compose the e-mail that she determined to send winging its way to Connemara this very evening. *Dear Dad. I hope you are all well in Kilrowan. Sorry it's been so long . . .*

Chapter Sixteen

Sunday morning dawned, and for the first time
in ages, Rosa had no hangover. She'd deliberately avoided drinking any alcohol at all
yesterday because she knew she needed to be on
the ball today. It hadn't been easy, but she'd
managed to block her ears to the sound of
Wine box singing his catchy siren song from the
cupboard in the kitchen by keeping herself very
busy indeed with very necessary housework.
She'd known that Sunday was going to be a big
enough headache without having a hangover to
contend with on top of everything else. Her displacement activity had worked. She was feeling
OK today – the only jitters being the jitters of her
nerves. Today was the day Lottie was coming
home. Today was the day of the Mysterious
One's funeral.

She had made a coffin from a shoebox. She'd
padded it with cotton wool, and tucked an old

silk scarf around the padding, making a smooth bed for the Mysterious One's final resting place. She'd unearthed some silk flowers from a drawer and placed them round the sad little corpse, and she'd found a postcard reproduction of a statue of Isis for Lottie to write her epitaph on.

Now she'd finished making the coffin, and there was no more housework to be done, and she had no distractions. A book? No. She'd never be able to concentrate. Maybe she should have a glass of wine to calm her nerves? No, no. She knew that one glass of wine wouldn't be enough. What, then? Oh God, this was awful. If Dannie had been there she would have gone up and begged for one of her homeopathic calming tablets, but Dannie wasn't there. She was in Gozo.

What to do? She was dreading the expression she knew she'd see on Lottie's face when she broke the news. How could she make it up to her? Could she maybe treat her to the movies and a McDonald's? She wasn't sure how much cash she had. As she scrabbled in her bag for her wallet, the notebook she used to jot down ideas for Lottie's bedtime story fell out, and suddenly she was hit by an inspirational idea. Could she pay tribute to the Mysterious One by including her in the story? By making the Map Girl and the Mysterious One cohorts, somehow? She could start the story all over again and put the Mysterious One in at the very beginning!

Rosa went into the kitchen and sat down at the table. Then she picked up a pen, and opened the book at a blank page. The blankness stared at her, mirroring her expression, and she felt self-conscious, even though there was no-one there to see her. This was stupid! Pointless! She forced her hand to move to the top right-hand corner of the page where she executed a little series of ooooooo's – as if by doodling something, *anything*, the blankness would stop being so scarily – well – *blank*.

And then she started to write. It felt weird at first. The words came much more slowly than they did when she was telling her story at bedtime, and it was funny to see the actual physical shape of them on the page in her roundy writing, but after a while a sort of rhythm established itself, and the words turned into sentences, and the sentences turned into paragraphs.

When the phone rang some time later, its jangle completely disoriented her. It took her some moments to drag herself out of the Map Girl's cabin back into her kitchen. How strange, she thought, as she stretched out an automatic hand for the phone. It was as if she'd been inhabiting another world . . .

'Rosa? It's Michael here.'

'Oh.' She felt a brief flutter, as if a humming-bird had taken flight inside her. She'd given him her phone number at Dannie's the other night, so that he could arrange when to pick her and Lottie up in order to take them out to the country for the funeral. The funeral! Oh God! Now she was well and truly back in the real world.

'Um . . . I was wondering was Lottie back yet, and what was the word on her funeral. Oh, God – sorry! A slip of the tongue! I meant the Mysterious One's funeral, of course.'

'I know, I know. Don't worry.' But Rosa lunged for the table and touched wood just in case. 'She still hasn't arrived back from Wicklow.' She looked at the clock on the kitchen wall. Lottie would be here very soon. 'Maybe you could call back in an hour or so?' she suggested hesitantly. Was she pushing things here?

'Or would you like me to call round now?'

'That's really kind of you, Michael, but I'd prefer to tell her the bad news on my own.' The doorbell rang. 'Oh, God. Here she is. Wish me luck.'

'Good luck, then, Rosa. I'll see you later.'

'Yes. Thanks for everything, Michael.' She put the phone down, ran to the door and pressed the buzzer.

Seconds later, Lottie was trailing down the corridor towards her, lugging her backpack and clutching a hideous green teddy bear.

'Darling!' Rosa stepped into the corridor, hunkered down and held her arms out. 'Oh, how I missed you! You were away a whole fortnight!' She covered the child's cheeks with kisses, then held her at arm's length so she could look at her. 'Where did you get the teddy bear?'

'I won him at a funfair.' Lottie dropped her backpack and leaned against her mother.

'You're a bit droopy,' remarked Rosa. 'I suppose you and Roxanne have been awake every night until all hours.'

'Mm. I'm glad I'm home. I missed you. Me and Roxanne had a row. She promised to lend me her X Box and then said she wouldn't, after all.'

'Uh-oh. I'm sure it won't last long. Your rows with Roxanne never do.'

'Mm.' Then came the question Rosa had been dreading. 'How's the Mysterious One? I missed her too.'

Rosa stood up and hefted Lottie's backpack. 'Come inside, baby. There's something I have to tell you.'

'What? Is it about the Mysterious One?' Alert, suddenly, Lottie followed her mother through the door of the flat. 'It is, isn't it? People always say "there's something I have to tell you" when something awful's happened. Is she sick? Oh!' Before Rosa could prevent her, she had run into her bedroom. She re-emerged looking distraught. 'Where is she? What's wrong? Oh – oh! Oh, no! She's dead, isn't she?'

Rosa sat down on the sofa and faced her daughter. 'Oh, Lottie. I'm sorry to have to tell you this, but yes, angel. I'm afraid she is.'

Nothing in the world could have prepared Rosa for the child's reaction. Lottie's eyes closed and her mouth opened slowly, and an awful, awful sound emerged. It was the most chilling sound Rosa had ever heard; it was more chilling to her ears than the wail of a banshee. 'Lottie!' Rosa moved towards her to wrap the child in her arms, but Lottie refused to be held. She fended off her mother with surprising strength, then backed into a corner, where she huddled, rocking to and fro, mewling with grief. 'Oh, Mysterious One! Oh, Mysterious One!' she kept repeating, over and over again, and each time she said it, Rosa felt a jab of pain.

'Darling! Darling! Think of all the fairies you're drowning!' She tried again to take her daughter in her arms, but Lottie stiffened and pushed her away. Rosa remembered how she had felt when her mother had died. She had been inconsolable, unapproachable, just wanting to be left alone with her grief.

There was nothing she could do. There was no way of comforting her child. The only way to handle the situation was to wait until the weeping subsided. It took a while, a racking, bloody awful while, but finally, finally the sobbing ceased, and she knew it was time to talk.

'Where is she?' was the first question Lottie asked.

Rosa took Lottie's hand and led her to the table, where the shoebox coffin was resting on a cushion. 'She's in there. Can you bear to look?'

Lottie nodded. She relinquished Rosa's hand and lifted the lid. A little cry escaped her when she saw the dead animal lying on its bed of silk. 'Oh! Beloved!' She took the gerbil between gentle hands, and raised it to her face. Rosa didn't stop her. She knew that the child needed to do this. Lottie kissed the creature and stroked its fur, all the time crooning to it in the secret language she had always used when talking to her pet. Rosa could hardly bear to watch. She was crying now too: great big splotchy tears were coursing down her cheeks, but they were nothing to the tears that Lottie was weeping.

'Oh! Look at you, beloved!' Lottie eventually said. 'Your poor fur is all soaked!' She dried the gerbil's fur with a sleeve, then set it back in its coffin, and tucked one of the silk flowers under its muzzle. 'Sweet dreams, little Mysterious One,' she whispered, and then she placed the lid back on the shoebox.

'There's a card for you to write a farewell note on,' said Rosa, indicating the picture of Isis. 'And your friend Michael the vet has offered to drive us out to the country to give her a proper funeral.'

Lottie didn't appear to be listening. She just stood there, staring at the Mysterious One's coffin. Then she turned to her mother. 'How did it happen?' she asked.

Rosa had been dreading this question as much as she'd been dreading breaking the grim news. She knew she had to be as economical with the truth as she could. 'She just got sick and passed away peacefully. These things happen, darling.'

'Oh, no. She was pining for me.' Fresh tears rose to Lottie's eyes. 'I shouldn't have gone away. It's all my fault! She must have thought that I was never coming back. Oh! Mysterious One!' And Lottie flung herself on the sofa and started weeping again.

Oh God. This was awful, awful! What to do? What to say? She couldn't allow Lottie to think that she'd been responsible for the animal's death! But how to tell her that she, Rosa, was the guilty party? She sat down beside her daughter on the couch and racked her brains for a way of consoling her.

'I think it's a lovely idea to bury her in the countryside. And maybe we could drive out and visit the grave from time to time and—'

'No! The Egyptians didn't bury their dead

in the earth! I couldn't bear to think of her underground.'

Hell. This was intolerable. 'Honestly, Lottie, we have to be sensible about this—'

'I can't bear to think of her pining away, Mum! I *murdered* her!'

'No. No, Lottie, you didn't. You mustn't think that. Michael told me that she died of a condition known as dehydration.' Rosa was praying that Lottie wouldn't understand the word. But as soon as her daughter raised her appalled face to hers, Rosa realized that she knew only too well what it meant.

'Dehydration? That means dying of thirst?'

'Yes. Wow. I'm impressed that you know such a big word. You are a clever girl.' Rosa was rambling now, stiff with unease. 'Where did you learn it?'

'All Will's marijuana plants died of it at the weekend.' Lottie's voice was automatic, toneless. 'How could the Mysterious One have got dehydrated, Mum?'

'Oh, God, Lottie. I'm sorry. I'm—'

'You did it, Mum, didn't you? You forgot to give her any water. You killed her.'

'Oh, God, I – I don't know what to say. I – I'm so sorry, Lottie, I—'

'No. I don't want to hear you.' Lottie got to her feet and went over to the table. Then she picked up the box containing the remains of her pet, walked towards her bedroom and shut the door.

Oh God. Oh God. Her heart pounding with painful panic, Rosa followed her and knocked on the door.

'Go away.'

She couldn't go away. Her heart was bleeding for her daughter. She opened the door. Lottie was standing white-faced in the middle of her toy-strewn floor. 'I said to go away.'

'Darling, I want to help. Please—'

'I don't want to see you.'

Rosa's desperation was mounting. She'd have to try another tack – any other tack. Maybe a good dose of plain old-fashioned, politically incorrect anger would do the trick. 'Oh, for God's sake, Lottie! Calm down, will you, and put things into perspective. It was only a bloody gerbil! It's not as if your best friend had died!'

It was the worst thing she could have said. Lottie looked as if she'd been struck across the face. 'She *wasn't* only a bloody gerbil! She was the Mysterious One! And she *was* my best friend, and you killed her! I hate you! I wish *you* were the one who'd died!'

'Lottie—'

'No!' Still clutching the shoebox, Lottie pushed past her mother, ran the short distance down the corridor to Rosa's room and slammed the door. Before Rosa could get there, she heard the key turn in the lock.

'Lottie!' she cried, thumping uselessly on the door. 'Lottie! Let me in! Unlock the door!'

Desperate now, she thumped and thumped and called ever more urgently to her daughter, but there was no answer. The only sound that came from behind the locked door was the insupportable keening of a child whose heart had been broken. Rosa could no longer bear to listen. She made her way to the sitting room, wishing there was vodka and making do with a glass of that nasty Côtes du Rhône instead. It wasn't six o'clock yet, but she didn't give a fuck. This had been one of the worst days of her life, and she needed something, anything, to numb the pain. If there had been nothing but a bottle of meths in the house she'd have drunk it.

She curled up on the sofa, nursing her wineglass and cursing herself for the crap person she was. What a fucking mess her life was. She couldn't even get being a mum right. Her own daughter had just told her she hated her and wished she was dead. And now there was nothing she could do but listen to Lottie's anguished sobbing and wait for her to cry herself out. And then she remembered her inspired idea of putting the Mysterious One into the Map Girl story, and she went into the kitchen and threw the notebook with its pages of scribbled writing into the bin. What had she been *thinking*! What a stupid, stupid bitch she was.

About half an hour later came the sound of a door unlocking. Rosa unburied her head from her hands and gave thanks.

'Mum?'

She looked round. Lottie was standing in the doorway of the sitting room, looking paler than Rosa had ever seen her.

'Oh, my darling girl! I'm so glad you've come out. Will you forgive me? I am so, so sorry about the Mysterious One, I really am. Will you allow me to hug you now?'

'Mum. I just threw up in your room.'

'Oh, God, Lottie! You've made yourself ill with all that weeping. Come here to me.'

Lottie shook her head. 'No. I think I—' She was beyond ashen now, and her breathing was coming fast and shallow. Her hands went to her mouth as she threw up all over the carpet. 'Oh, Mum. I'm sorry. I couldn't help it.' There were tears of shock in her eyes. 'I don't know what's wrong!'

Rosa sped across the room and took her daughter in her arms. 'There, there,' she said, smoothing Lottie's hair. 'Come. Lie down on the sofa.'

'But what if I get sick on that too? I've a feeling I might get sick again soon.'

'It doesn't matter. You're what's important.

You're a million trillion times more important than a silly old sofa.' Rosa swung her daughter up in her arms, carried her across the room and laid her down against the cushions. Then she ran to fetch a basin from the kitchen.

She was just in time. Lottie vomited again, then leaned her head back against the arm rest and turned stricken eyes on her mother. 'I'm sorry, Mum. I – Oh! I need the loo!'

Rosa supported her as she stumbled down the passageway to the bathroom. As Lottie sat on the loo Rosa studied her face with an apprehensive heart. She could read no pain there. The expression on her face was one of bemused incomprehension. The child simply couldn't understand what was happening to her. When the spasms ceased, Rosa undressed her and stood her in the bath so that she could wash her with the shower attachment. She then went to get a nightdress from the airing cupboard, but in the short time it took her to fetch it, Lottie had soiled herself again.

'I'm sorry, Mum, I really am. I—'

'Don't apologize, sweetheart. You mustn't fret. It's not your fault.' She wrapped her daughter in a dressing gown and carried her back into the sitting room. 'I'll cover the sofa with a towel, just in case you have another accident.' Rosa spread a bath sheet across the cushions, and Lottie curled up on the sofa. She was sweating profusely now, and it was clear she had a temperature. Rosa stuck the thermometer in the child's mouth and instructed her to keep it under her tongue for three minutes, hoping she wouldn't suffer another attack of nausea before she could get a look at the instrument. Lottie's temperature was one hundred and three. Oh, sweet Jesus.

'I'm calling the doctor, sweetheart,' said Rosa. 'But first, can you tell me if you might have eaten anything dodgy today, anything that might have disagreed with you?'

'Mm hm. Will and Sonia had oysters for lunch, and Roxanne dared me to eat one. She said I could borrow her X Box for a week if I did. It was the most disgusting thing I've ever tasted, Mum. I'd rather eat—'

'OK, sweetheart. That's obviously what the problem is. The oyster was a bad one, and it's given you a nasty dose of food poisoning. The doctor can fix that with an injection. I know that because it happened to me once.' Rosa's head was spinning with relief at this diagnosis. The 'meningitis' word had been banging relentlessly around the inside of her skull since Lottie had first thrown up.

She grabbed the phone and dialled the doctor's number, scribbling down the emergency mobile number with one hand while smoothing Lottie's hair back from her forehead with the other. Lottie was bent over the basin again, labouring to expel the poison from her body, in awful paroxysms of physical effort.

Rosa listened again to the number that was being carefully rearticulated on the doctor's answering machine, then punched it in. 'Hello?' she said into the phone. 'My name is Rosa Elliot. I have a very sick child here. Can you make a house call?' Rosa strove to keep the panic out of her voice. She didn't want to alarm Lottie, who, between her bouts of nausea, had really been disconcertingly calm. There had been no complaints, no querulousness, no moans of pain or discomfort.

The doctor reassured her that she'd be with her soon, and advised her to sponge Lottie, so as to keep her temperature down. Rosa fetched another basin, filled it with tepid water, and wrung out a flannel. 'There, baby. There, there, my baby. The doctor will be here soon,' she soothed, as she gently ran the flannel along Lottie's limbs. The child was trembling and goosebumpy now. She had wrapped her arms around herself, and was hugging herself for warmth. 'No, Mummy! Why are you doing this! It's cold!'

'But you're burning up, sweetheart, and I don't want your temperature to go any higher. I'll tell you what. We'll sing a song while we wait for the doctor, will we? What'll we sing?'

'No, Mum. Not singing.'

'What, then? What can we do to distract you?'

'Go on with my bedtime story, Mum. Please. That'll work better.'

'OK, toots.' Continuing the story of the Map Girl was the last thing Rosa felt like doing, but if it would help take Lottie's mind off her hellish predicament, then it was worth doing well. 'Where were we?'

'Um. Carlotta had made friends with that centaur, remember? Bob. She was riding through the forest on his back, and it had just started to rain.'

'Oh yes.' Rosa cast her mind back to their last storytelling session. 'Um. OK. Here goes. Had I got to Bob and the puddles?'

'No.'

'Well, Bob had one rather annoying habit, which was this. He loved to go splashing through puddles, and every time he did it, water would shower up all over Carlotta. She wished he'd stop, but she didn't like to say anything to him because he was, after all, doing her a big favour by giving her a lift. "Hey! Another big one! *Yeah!*" he'd shout when he spotted a puddle, and away he'd charge. He'd even dive down other path-ways if he saw a puddle that looked worth investigating, and by the time they reached their destination, Carlotta was soaked to the skin . . .'

Rosa went on and on, racking her brains for

ideas that she hoped Lottie would find entertaining. She dreamed up a walking, talking kettle, a bald cat, and a fairy called Narcissa, who was so vain she had a dress made all of mirrors. Narcissa had just burst into tears of rage because the talking kettle kept steaming up her mirrors, when the doorbell finally went.

Rosa let the doctor in, feeling shaky with relief. 'Thank you so much for coming. The invalid's through here,' she said, leading the doctor into the sitting room.

'Hey! You're the foxiest doctor I've ever seen!' said Lottie from her sickbed on the sofa.

It was true. Dr Jay was young, foxy, and very good at her job. She examined Lottie, took her temperature, and told her that she was going to have to give her a little injection that would help her to stop getting sick. And if she was brave about the injection, Dr Jay would give her a bunch of lollipops that she could eat when she got better. And Lottie *was* brave, and as well as the lollipops Dr Jay gave her a sticker to wear that read 'I was very brave at the doctor's today'.

As Rosa gibbered her thanks and wrote out a cheque, Dr Jay extracted some sachets of Dioralyte from her bag and told Rosa to phone her if the anti-emetic injection didn't seem to be working, and if she had any cause for concern.

Dr Jay may have been young, foxy and good at her job, but the anti-emetic she'd administered didn't kick in. Lottie had drunk down the Dioralyte and promptly thrown it all up again. Rosa kept running for more towels. She filled the bath and soaked the soiled ones in it, but no sooner had she spread fresh ones out on the sofa for Lottie than she would have to dump them in the bath along with the others.

She was becoming more and more agitated, and the more agitated she got, the more she tried not to show it. But she knew the anxiety must show on her face every time she looked at her daughter, who was paler than ever, and gaunt-looking. There were great dark rings under her eyes, and Rosa could almost see the skull beneath the skin. She remembered the dream she'd had, where Lottie and her mother had walked away from her hand in hand on the Silver Strand looking like ghosts, and the thought filled her with such horror that she lunged for the phone and pressed 'redial'.

'She's dehydrating,' said Dr Jay. 'You'll have to get her to hospital right away. She'll need to be isolated – can you get her to the Cherry Orchard in Ballyfermot?'

'Of course I can.' Rosa could get her daughter to the moon if necessary. 'I'll go at once.'

She helped Lottie into clean clothes, murmuring endearments and reassurances as she did so. Then she wrapped a bath sheet round her, and took a spare from the airing cupboard. It was the last one. She stuffed it in a plastic bag, then rinsed and wiped out the basin, dumped the bag with the towel into it, and instructed Lottie to hold it. Rosa located her car keys, her phone and her wallet, lifted Lottie, who was still stoically clutching her basin, and carried her clumsily out of the flat.

She was heading towards the car park with the child in her arms when a car horn arrested her. There, a little further down the road, was Michael Luque. He'd parked in the side street by the Londis shop and had rolled down the driver's window. 'Rosa!' he called to her. 'Hang on!' He slid out of the car, waited for traffic to pass, then sprinted across the street to her. 'What's the problem?' he asked.

'I've to get Lottie to Cherry Orchard,' she said, as calmly as she could. 'She's dehydrating.'

Michael simply took Lottie from Rosa, and indicated to her to follow him to his car. He set Lottie in the back seat, and Rosa got in beside her, putting an arm around the child's shaking shoulders and holding the basin under her chin. 'Connect me to the Cherry Orchard Hospital, please,' Michael said into his mobile. He checked his rear view mirror, indicated, and slid into the traffic. 'Hi,' he said after a couple of beats. 'Could you instruct a nurse to have a drip ready to go? I have a dehydrated child here. I should be with you in about twenty minutes. Thanks.'

'How can I thank you, Michael?' said Rosa weakly from the back seat. 'I don't know how I could have managed this trip alone.'

'It's lucky I caught you. I'd just nipped into Londis to get a present for Lottie.'

'Oh! What kind of a present?' Lottie managed to gasp.

'Sweeties, unfortunately, sweetie. But you won't be eating them for a while.'

In the back seat, Lottie leaned over the basin again. 'Mummy?' she managed to say after another dry heave. 'I'm dying to know how Narcissa gets rid of the steaming kettle. Carry on telling the story, Mum, will you? Please?'

And Rosa did.

It was agonizing watching the drip being attached. Lottie was so dehydrated that the doctor could not find a vein, and it took him three attempts before the apparatus was attached successfully. Rosa could scarcely bear to look, but she sat through the whole ordeal, holding her child's hand, and going on with the story. And all the while Michael listened too, and the doctor and the nurses, and sometimes they laughed, and sometimes they said: 'Oh, dear!' and sometimes they said: 'Wow!'

Lottie was finally wheeled into her room. The nurses told Rosa that she could stay overnight on a camp bed, and she was beyond grateful for this. The idea of the child in an isolation ward all on her own was unendurable. She tucked Lottie in, stroked her pale cheek and told her she'd be back soon to tell her her story, and then she went out to where Michael was waiting in the reception area. And when she saw him sitting there with his dark hair flopping over his anxious face, she burst into tears.

He stood up and took her in his arms, and he didn't say anything – he just held her for a long, long time until she stopped crying. Then he said: 'Let's go for a walk in the grounds. You could do with some fresh air, hen.'

'Hen?' she asked stupidly.

'It's Scottish for "darling".'

They walked out into the evening sun. Michael kept his arm around her, and Rosa loved it so much that she dared to lean her head on his shoulder, and when they'd strolled a little further, Michael stopped and turned to her. He took her face between his hands and looked at her questioningly before kissing her tentatively on the lips. And after some moments the kiss wasn't tentative any more – it was ardent. Rosa sensed that if they continued to kiss like this, the kiss would suddenly become as passionate as the way he moved when he danced, and she knew that that would be *dangerous*, and that it was time to stop. So she broke away and smiled up at him, and said: 'That was lovely. Thank you.'

'Thank *you*.' He returned the smile, and then said: 'I'd better let you get back to her.'

'Yes. You better had.'

But neither of them moved. They just stood there looking at each other with their rather goofy smiles still in place.

Finally Rosa said: 'I'll walk you to the car park.' And when he slung an arm around her again it felt even better than it had done the first time round.

'D'you fancy doing something tomorrow night?' he said. 'Like a movie, or dinner or something?'

'I'd love that,' said Rosa. 'But not tomorrow. I'm going to stay here until they let Lottie out.'

'How long did they say she'd have to stay in?'

'Four nights. Maybe five.'

'How about next weekend, then, if she's out and feeling better?'

'Yes, please.'

'Dinner?'

'Yes, please.'

'How will you manage till then? I mean, clothes-wise and stuff?'

'I'll take a taxi into town tomorrow and pick things up.'

'Why don't you let me pick you up instead of going to the expense of taking a taxi? And write me a list of any supermarket stuff you need and I'll get it for you.'

Rosa looked at him and smiled. 'You're very kind, Michael.' She rooted in her bag for her pen and notebook to write him a list, then remembered that the notebook was in the bin in her kitchen. 'Have you anything I could write a list on?' she asked.

They'd reached his car, and Michael zapped the locks. He reached into the glove compartment and took out a biro and a diary. MACKEY VETERINARY PHARMACEUTICALS was stamped on the *faux*-leather cover. 'Write it in this,' he said. 'What will you do with yourself this evening, by the way? You've no books or anything to keep you entertained. Tell you what – I'll lend you a copy of *Irish Veterinary Monthly* if you like. There's some riveting reading in that.'

Rosa laughed. 'Thanks. I'll probably just get an early night after I've told Lottie her story.'

'It's something else, that story. I want to know how it ends.'

'Even I don't know that,' she said.

Rosa started writing her list. She'd need lots of juice for Lottie, and some kind of tempting titbits to encourage her to eat. She didn't reckon that Lottie would find hospital food that appetizing, somehow. And what did she need for herself? She was feeling pre-menstrual, and wasn't sure that she had any tampons at home, but she couldn't ask Michael to buy tampons for her. He'd die of embarrassment. Perhaps she could get them in the hospital shop.

She felt wrung out now. It had been a fuck of a day, and she didn't even have the prospect of a glass of wine to look forward to. How would she get through the evening without it? But she'd got through the previous day without her chum Wine box, and had turned to him today only when she'd been at her wits' end when Lottie had locked herself in the bedroom. And then she remembered how she'd coped earlier in the day, when she'd been pacing the flat, fraught with nerves, anticipating how she was going to break the bad news to Lottie: she'd distracted herself from her worries by writing her story. Something clicked into place in her brain and she found herself giving it a name. 'Displacement activity,' she said out loud.

'Sorry?' said Michael.

'Nothing,' she said, furrowing her brow and looking hard at the book in her hand. Then: 'Michael?' she asked. 'Do you need this diary?'

'No,' he said. 'It's last year's.'

'Can I keep it?'

'Be my guest. Why do you want it?'

'I just had an idea. I wanted to write it down.'

She finished writing her list, tore out the page and handed it to him. 'By the way,' she said. 'Remember you offered to have the gerbil incinerated?'

'Yes.'

'I think that's our only option now. Do you mind?'

'Not at all,' he said.

They stood looking at each other for a moment or two and then Michael said: 'Do you mind if I kiss you again?'

And Rosa echoed his 'Not at all'. He kissed her quite, quite, beautifully, and when they broke the kiss, an elderly couple walking through the car park broke into a round of spontaneous applause.

Later, when Lottie was sleeping, Rosa opened the *faux*-leather diary and wrote the following words: *Carlotta opened her eyes and stretched herself. And this felt very strange, because she had never done it before. And even as she was thinking this thought, she was thinking how strange it was to be thinking. And she blinked, and thought that was strange too, and she blinked again and found herself looking at a thing that was hanging on the wall of the cabin. And even though she didn't know how she knew this, she knew that the thing on the wall was called a map.*

After three and a half hours of non-stop writing, Rosa crawled onto the canvas cot that had been set up beside her daughter's bed in the isolation ward of the Cherry Orchard Hospital feeling as tired and fuzzy as she'd done on other nights when she'd used alcohol to blur the edges for her. Except this time the fuzzy feeling was good.

Rosa had a light heart the next morning, and a clear head, even though she'd been woken three times during the night by a nurse coming in to change Lottie's drip. 'Good morning, Ba-Ba!' she said when Lottie opened her eyes around seven o'clock. 'You slept well!'

'I'm not a ba-ba,' said Lottie sleepily, rubbing her eyes.

'Yes, you are. You're like Ba-Ba Black Sheep. You had three bags full of saline solution dripped into you last night.'

'Did I? Cool.' A big yawn. 'I'm hungry.'

'Good. That's the best thing you could have said to me. Let's see about some breakfast.'

Lottie didn't take much breakfast, but it was reassurance enough for Rosa that she was eating anything at all and – more importantly – managing to keep it down. She was also relieved that Lottie made no reference at all to the Mysterious One – except for once, obliquely, when she'd caught Rosa looking at her with tragic eyes.

'Don't worry, Mum. I don't hate you. I know I said it yesterday, but I lied. And I'm sorry about the other thing I said. That was a lie too – you know – about wishing you were—'

'It's OK, Lottie. You don't have to apologize. We all say things we don't mean when we're upset. Lies are allowed sometimes when you love someone. Sometimes you need to hurt someone as badly as you're hurting yourself, to make yourself feel better.'

'I do love you, Mum.'

'I know. And I love you too, baby. Now, eat just a tiny bit more.'

A little later Michael picked Rosa up and they drove back to her flat as fast as the early-morning traffic allowed them to. She picked up the stuff she needed – Lottie's battered teddy bear being the number one priority – and afterwards she kissed Michael goodbye in the hospital car park, which she had now decided was the most romantic place on the face of the earth. And after she'd delivered Ted and books and fresh pyjamas to Lottie, she took her phone outside and sat down on a hospital bench to ring her agent. She filled Sally in on the Roydon Sneyde fiasco, and asked her to handle it for her. And of course Sally said 'No problem', and when Rosa pressed 'end call' she felt a bit baffled by the number of times she'd been too intimidated to pick up the phone to someone who was not only happy to do her bidding – but who was actually *paid* to do her bidding. Rosa had just learned that taking the initiative made her feel kind of empowered. It was a nice feeling.

Around midday, Michael arrived with a bag

full of all the things she'd asked him to buy for her, and they couldn't stop smiling at each other – even though Michael's smiles were still rather shy. 'I brought you a magazine, too,' he said, indicating a rolled-up glossy that he'd tucked down the side of the bag.

It was *Cosmopolitan*. Rosa tried not to laugh at the eager-to-please expression on his face, and tried not to laugh even harder when she got a load of the explicit contents splashed all over the front cover. He registered her expression. 'What is it?' he asked, and when she showed him the cover, he went puce. 'Aw, Christ,' he said, looking mortified. 'I was in a hurry – I just grabbed the first women's magazine I saw. Sorry, Rosa – I didn't mean it as a big hint or anything, I—'

'I know you didn't,' she said, laughing openly now, and standing on tiptoe to kiss his cheek.

They managed another snog in the beautiful, rose-tinted car park before he drove away again, and Rosa found herself looking forward to the weekend more than she'd looked forward to anything in her life for a long, long time. Michael had told her he'd booked a table for Saturday night in a restaurant in Temple Bar, and Rosa had rung one of the Motherhood and asked her if Lottie could stay over – if she was well enough, of course – and the mother had agreed. Rosa remembered what Dannie had told her about sexy underwear, and found herself wondering if she'd get a chance to nip into Marks & Sparks and stock up on new stuff between now and then.

Later that day, with Lottie engrossed in a book, she was sitting in a sunny spot on the grass outside the hospital scribbling away in Michael's old diary. When her mobile rang it took her some moments to shake herself out of the strange, trance-like state she'd drifted off into while writing. 'Sally! Hi!' she said into the phone. 'How'd it go with Roydon?'

'It didn't,' said her agent down the line. Rosa had never heard Sally sound so ferocious. 'He is categorically the rudest man I have ever had the misfortune to deal with, Rosa. He's flatly refusing to write you a cheque. And do you know what he said when I came down heavy on him? He said: "Oh, stop pissing me off with your nagging, you boring little *woman*." And then he put the phone down on me.'

'Oh! How *dare* he speak to you like that! How dare he diss you!'

'It's not just me he's dissing, Rosa. Because I'm your agent, by implication he's dissing you, too. If I get the OK from you, I'll take this man to the cleaners. I am going to sue the ass off him.'

'Oh.' Rosa didn't much like the sound of this. 'Do we have a case?'

'Oh, yes. He's just such an arrogant fuck that

he doesn't think that "little women" like us will have the balls to go for it. But he's going to have to pay you eventually, Rosa, and I'll make damn sure that he forks out more than just the amount that's due. He'll pay the solicitor's fees, and he will damn well compensate you for the stress and inconvenience he's caused you.'

Rosa balked. 'So this'll go to court? Will I have to take the stand?'

'Not a chance – it'll be settled out of court. His superiors won't be at all happy with this – can you imagine how they'd appear in the newspaper coverage? A multinational computer components manufacturer shafting a near-penniless actress? The tabloids would have a field day, and I'll be very happy to let them know all the details if I feel you haven't been adequately compensated.'

'So what's the procedure now?' Rosa asked. She was feeling fearful. Legal stuff terrified her – she'd been sole executrix of her mother's estate, and dealing with all of that so soon after her mother's death had been a nightmare. It had been like trying to learn a foreign language that you knew you were never going to master.

'I'll get in touch with my solicitor straight away, and I'll keep you posted.'

'Oh, God. Are you sure I'm doing the right thing?'

'Absolutely. With a bit of luck Roydon Sneyde

and his like might learn a lesson from this – the lesson being that you don't get anywhere in this life if you don't treat people with respect. Bye, Rosa.'

'Bye, Sally.' Rosa stuck her phone back in her bag, thinking how weird it was that things should have come to this. She was the least litigious person in the world! And then she found herself thinking that the only alternative would have been to sit back and let Roydon Sneyde and his ilk continue to trample all over her, and she knew that that alternative was no longer an option. She remembered something she'd read in one of the legion of self-help books she'd dithered over in Eason's one day. *If you're going to change your life, you're going to have to make changes in your life.* Sitting on the lawn with the afternoon sun on her face, Rosa thought long and hard about the direction in which her life had been going, and then she made a solemn vow. She was going to make some changes.

She had clocked the look of delight on Lottie's face when she had told her that Michael Luque was taking her, Rosa Elliot, out to dinner in a posh restaurant in Temple Bar on Saturday night. 'Only if you're feeling better,' she'd assured her, and something had told her that this was the best incentive Lottie could possibly have to get better.

Astonishingly, everything had worked out according to plan. Rosa put it down to the fact that she'd been touching wood all over the place all week. Lottie had gone off to her chum's house under strict instructions that she was *not* to stay up all night chittering, and Rosa told the chum's mother not to hesitate to phone if she had any worries. Lottie was still feeling a bit cotton-woolly after her food poisoning, but she was bored blue being an invalid. She'd been given the all-clear in the hospital on Thursday, had spent all day Friday in bed at home, and now she was dying for an opportunity to show her friend the photographs Rosa had taken of her hooked up to her drip.

On Saturday evening Rosa got ready with a girlish heart. She put Dido on the CD player and sang along as she had her shower. She used up lavish amounts of expensive Chanel 19 body lotion and didn't care. And now she was performing clumsy dance steps as she selected her outfit for this evening's date. What to wear, what to wear, what to wear? Something told her to go for the girly frock that she'd worn to Dannie's last weekend, even though Michael had seen it before. She laid it out carefully on the bed, and she checked her shoes for scuffs, and then she went to pour herself a glass of wine – just a tiny one – to sip while she did her make-up. And suddenly that voice was in her head, the horrid, nagging one she hadn't heard for some time, and it was saying: *No!*

Not even a tiny one? she asked in a rather taken aback, pretty-please tone.

Not even a teeny tiny one, replied the voice, sounding scarily categorical. *You want to change your life? You want to change it by blowing your chances with Michael Luque? You know there's no such thing as just a 'tiny one'. You know that an entire bottle won't be enough. It's your look-out, Rosa. You want to get pissed and make an eejit of yourself tonight? Go ahead, then. Go ahead and change your life for the worse.*

Rosa sat down heavily on a kitchen chair. She knew the voice was right. She knew it. She knew with blinding certainty that she had a problem with alcohol, and that it was up to her to do something about it. No-one else was going to do it for her. She thought of the awful fortnight when she'd stayed in her flat drinking, and what the consequences of *that* had been. She'd killed her daughter's single most beloved possession through neglect. And she remembered how, last Sunday afternoon, she had automatically poured herself a glass of wine when she had no longer been able to bear the sounds of Lottie's sobbing coming from behind the locked bedroom door, and she thought: What if Lottie hadn't got sick until much later in the day? What if I'd been too pissed to handle the situation?

What if I'd been comatose when Lottie started to dehydrate? The worst-case scenario she envisioned made her almost reel as she got to her feet.

She took the wine box out of the cupboard, and located the kitchen scissors in the cluttered cutlery drawer. She cut away the cardboard carton from around the silvery bladder that contained the cheap Côtes du Rhône, and then she stabbed a great hole in the bladder and watched as its life blood flowed out into the sink. She knew in her heart of hearts that this was her first real change for the good, and as the last of the red wine ran down the plughole, she prayed that changing her life wasn't always going to prove so dauntingly, desperately hard.

Michael had told her that he'd ring her doorbell at around half-past seven. He was only two minutes late. Rosa took the lift down and pulled open the door of the apartment block. He was standing there self-consciously holding a little coffee bouquet of parti-coloured daisies that had obviously come from Florabundance.

'Is it the right thing to do?' he asked. 'I wasn't sure whether flowers were a good idea. My granny always told me it was a mark of respect, but then she's from a different generation.'

Rosa smiled at him. 'Your granny had the

right idea. It's a very good thing to do.' She wouldn't – couldn't – tell him that she had never had flowers from a man before in her life.

As they strolled down to Temple Bar they started to talk. They talked about everything. They discovered things about each other that they had in common, and smiled every time one or other of them said: 'Oh! I love that too!' or 'Oh! Don't you *hate* that!' They discovered that they both enjoyed Moby, they both read Roddy Doyle and Marian Keyes, they both adored watching old *Father Ted* and *Trigger Happy TV* videos, and they both despised pretentiousness of any kind.

Rosa ordered Ballygowan to drink, and avocado salad followed by pasta, and he ordered a half-bottle of white, and nettle soup followed by lobster – which she found quite surprising, given the unhip contents of the shopping trolley she'd once seen him fill; and he didn't comment on the fact that she had ordered water, and she was glad, because it had been quite a brave thing for her to do. By the time they were polishing off their main courses, they were still finding out things about each other.

'There's one thing we definitely don't have in common,' she said, sucking a strand of tagliatelle into her mouth. 'I can't dance.'

'Course you can,' he said. 'Everyone can dance. Everyone has their own internal rhythm.

It's here –' he placed his hand on his breastbone '– in the heart.'

'Then my heart's out of sync. I used to have to go to Modern Movement classes in college and fling myself around to bongo drums on a sprung wooden floor all decked out in a leotard and footless tights. The memory makes me practically faint with embarrassment. All I can say is the poor bongo man must have been a bloody good poker player.'

Michael gave her a questioning look, and she laughed.

'He actually managed to keep a straight face as I cavorted to his bongoing like some deluded latter-day Isadora Duncan. If he'd had any cop-on he'd have taken pictures with a concealed camera and blackmailed me with them.'

Michael was studying the stem of his glass. 'You could dance if you had the right teacher,' he said. 'I can tell by the way you move.'

They looked at each other, then immediately looked away again. 'I suppose it's a specifically Spanish thing, isn't it?' said Rosa, after a beat or two. 'That all-consuming passion for music and dance.' She hadn't really a clue what she was talking about – in fact she was spoofing her head off – but she just needed to talk about *something*.

'Not at all. You have it here, in Ireland. That's why I decided to come here to live. The Irish are much more passionate about their song and

565

dance heritage than the Scots are. We're a bit dour in Scotland.'

She remembered how she'd thought him a dour individual when she'd first met him, and took a sip of water to hide her smile. 'I suppose you're right. I have friends who travel miles for a good trad session,' she said. 'But if it was heritage you were after, why didn't you go back to Spain?'

He laughed. 'I'm almost too embarrassed to tell you.'

'Oh, go on! Please! I love finding out embarrassing things about people! And I just told you an embarrassing story about my lack of physical co-ordination. You owe me one.'

'OK,' he conceded. 'It's this. I don't speak the language well enough. I'm second-generation Spanish. And living in Glasgow and desperate to get out of there, I had more pressing priorities than learning Spanish.'

'Why were you so desperate to get out of Glasgow?'

'I hated it. I hate cities in general.'

'So what made you come to this grim metropolis?'

'Because I was offered a share in a good practice, and because you can get to the seaside in thirty minutes. Living in Dublin city centre may be as bad as living in the Gorbals, but at least it's easy to escape.'

'The Gorbals? There's a brilliant theatre there, isn't there?'

'The Citizens', yeah. Unfortunately, some people in the Gorbals think all performers are poofs. I got a lot of stick on account of my dancing.'

'Oh? How did you cope with that?'

'I developed street cred. The boys who took the piss didn't do it twice. People forget that dancers are athletes.' He cracked a lobster claw, and sucked out the meat. Oh, God! She'd have to think of something to say to distract her from the lovely sensation of sexiness that had just engulfed her.

'Kids can be vile, can't they? There was a bad case of bullying at Lottie's school recently. Luckily, she wasn't involved.'

'I bet she's a popular pupil.'

'Yes. She is – with the teachers as well as the students. She's very easygoing.'

'You've done a great job with her, Rosa. As my granny would say, she's a credit to you.'

'Thank you.' Her pasta was nearly finished now, but Michael was still working on his lobster. She noticed that his fingers were suckably slippery with juices.

'It can't have been easy,' he remarked, sucking one of his fingers as if on cue. 'Do you get support from her father?'

'No. She's all my own work.' Stop looking at

his fingers, she told herself crossly. Look at some other part of him. He was leaning back in his chair now, and the way his T-shirt clung to him afforded her a terrific view of the musculature of his chest. Oh God. Look elsewhere. His mouth. No! You eejit! His eyes. Look at his eyes. 'Although I have to say I couldn't have done it without a little help from my friends. Dannie's been amazingly supportive.'

Michael was running a finger round the rim of his wineglass. 'Dannie's terrific, isn't she? Very kind of – eh – vibrant.'

Rosa smiled.

'What are you smiling at?'

'Nothing, really. It's just that – the first time we met – that time I got so desperately drunk in the Clarence, I thought that you fancied Dannie.'

'No,' he said. 'I don't fancy Dannie.' He was looking at *her* mouth, now. 'There's a wee bit of something – a trace of sauce – just there, above your top lip.'

She looked away from him as she wet a finger and rubbed the area just above her mouth.

'Why did you get so drunk that night?' he asked when she looked at him again. 'I wanted to chat you up, but by the time I got round to it you were out of it.'

'Why did I get drunk?' Rosa took a sip of her water, and then decided to go for it. 'I got drunk because I fancied you and I was nervous.'

'You fancied me? That's dead ironic.'

'Why?'

'Can I be straight-up, now? I fancied the arse off you. I've wanted this to happen for ages – I just wish I acted sooner. I'm very shy when it comes to chatting up women – I've always been crap at it.'

'You're not crap at it right now. You can carry on.'

He grinned at her. 'Really?'

'Really.'

Michael studied the rim of his wineglass again. 'I'm glad you allowed me to kiss you in the hospital that time. You might have given me a dig and told me to mind my manners, for all I knew.'

'How could I tell you to mind your manners? You have lovely manners. It's unusual for a man to have manners, and it's very – um – sexy.'

He looked at her, and this time they maintained eye contact, and Rosa felt swamped with sexiness. 'Will I get the bill?' he said, extracting a credit card from a sleek leather wallet. Rosa remembered the little-old-lady's tasselled purse she'd once seen him fumbling with in Tesco's, and wondered about it. Maybe the purse had been a gift from a niece or nephew or something. She was occasionally obliged to sacrifice her street cred to Lottie's gifts from her arts-and-crafts workshops – she had once even courageously sported a green and pink knitted scarf with pompoms on for two whole weeks before she 'lost' it.

'Yes, please,' she said.

And then they said nothing for ages. He paid the bill and they walked back to Rosa's place hand in hand. When they got to the door of her apartment block she said: 'Will you come up?'

And Michael Luque said: 'I'd love to.'

It was weird to wake up with a man in her bed. Rosa raised herself from the pillow inch by inch, determined not to disturb him, wanting to watch this precious person sleep. She thought of all the other couples waking up in bed together at this very moment all over Ireland, and she wondered if they ever stopped to consider how lucky they were. It might be routine for them, but for her it was wonderfully, magically novel.

Michael had been right when he described dancers as athletes. Last night's lovemaking had been sensational. Afterwards he'd held her and they'd talked some more before finally drifting into sleep. Rosa thought how wonderful it would be to fall asleep that way every night, and she allowed herself to dream a little that maybe they could fall asleep that way again some time soon. Now, looking at his face, she saw how sensual his mouth was in repose, and she marvelled at the self-discipline she exercised in resisting the impulse to kiss it. And then *fuck self-discipline!* she thought, and she half closed her eyes, leaned towards him, parted her lips and – froze.

She lay back against her pillow again, biting her lip. Maybe she was just a notch on his bedpost? She'd had enough evidence of that in the past, when men had shagged her and done a runner the next day. Not that many men, to be fair – in fact, she could count them on the fingers of one hand. Rosa had had few opportunities for sex in her life because she had made it a rule that she would never, ever invite a man into her bed when Lottie was around. She bit her lip harder. What was she thinking of? To indulge in silly, rose-tinted dreams of a future together was like asking for a puck on the jaw. No man in his right mind would want to saddle himself with a cash-strapped single mother.

And then Michael moved beside her and stretched and took her in his arms and said: 'Good morning, beautiful,' and all her fractured thoughts flew out of her head.

Later in the kitchen she made coffee while Michael poured himself a bowl of Lottie's Frosties and browsed through one of Rosa's cookbooks.

'I haven't had these for years. I'd forgotten how good they were,' he remarked, then gave a burp. 'Excuse me, please, madam,' he said, slanting her a smile. 'See how well I'm minding my manners? I'll be minding them even more now, since you told me they were sexy.'

She laughed and set a mug of coffee in front of him. 'Where did you learn those gorgeous manners of yours?'

'My granny was a stickler for them, and there was no arguing with her. She was a scary mix of Gorbals Glasgow and Andalusian Spanish. She told me that if I wanted to succeed in life I would have to smooth off the rough edges.'

'You did that all right,' she said, remembering the posy of flowers he'd presented her with last night. 'I'm glad you don't talk too proper, though. I love your Glaswegian burr.'

'And I love your soft posh.'

'It was very useful once. I made a lot more money as a voiceover artist than I do now as a masseuse. It's weird, Michael, isn't it? How we end up drifting through life with no real control over what happens to us? I never really dreamed I'd end up as a masseuse.'

He stretched as he considered what she'd just said. 'I was damn sure I was going to take control over *my* life,' he said. 'My da was a complete control freak.'

'Oh? In what way?'

'He was a big traditionalist – he was the one who insisted on me carrying on the family tradition and becoming a dancer.' Michael picked up his mug of coffee and blew on it. Then he shrugged. 'Still – he was a brilliant teacher, I'll say that for him.'

'So why didn't he teach you Spanish?'

'He was a man of few words. I suppose you could say he spoke with his body.'

A man of few words. Dour, arrogant and evasive. That's how she'd first perceived Michael. In the course of less than twenty-four hours she'd found out that, in fact, he was a man of loads of words, and she still hadn't found out everything she wanted to know about him. 'What made you decide to become a vet then, instead of a dancer?'

'Loads of reasons. I wasn't earning enough money teaching dance. I had to supplement it by doing cabaret, and I *hated* cabaret. Eh. What else?' He furrowed his brow momentarily, thinking. 'I preferred animals to most humans—'

'I can relate to that,' said Rosa, thinking of Roydon Sneyde.

'So once I'd earned enough cash to see me through college, I more or less gave it up. Professional dancers have a short shelf-life, Rosa.'

She *loved* the way he pronounced her name! 'So have actors. But what I'm doing now is hardly an ideal way of earning a living. What would be *your* idea of a perfect job, Michael?'

'I'm pretty happy doing what I'm doing. What would yours be?'

'Wow. Let me think.' She cast her mind back to that day – months ago, it had been – when someone had stuck a flyer through her door, inviting her to begin 'A Brand New Life of Freedom' by joining a network marketing group. Network marketing wasn't something she'd ever contemplate doing, but she remembered how alluring 'A Brand New Life of Freedom' had sounded . . . Being your own boss! Being liberated from having to work with bullies and misogynists, not having to say 'Absolutely' every time someone asked you if you were available . . . 'I've never really thought about it,' she said now. 'But I think I'd like to earn an income from doing something creative.'

'Wasn't acting creative?'

'Not really. It's interpretative rather than really creative. You have to work for some awful eejit directors, and it's insecure and badly paid. No, I think I'd like to earn a living doing something like painting, or composing music. Or writing.' She took a deep breath and then: 'I'm writing a book in my spare time,' she said in a rush.

'Are you?' He raised an eyebrow and shot her a smile. 'I'm impressed. What kind of book?'

'A children's book.'

'Well, if it's anything like the story I heard you

tell Lottie, you definitely have a talent for it.'

'I dunno. I've only just started. Loads of people start books, and then get discouraged. I'll probably never finish it.'

'I'll encourage you.'

'Will you?'

'I will if you allow me to see you again.'

'I will. Allow you to see me again, that is.' She moved to where Michael was sitting and slid onto his lap. Then she wound her arms around his neck and rubbed her face against his shoulder. 'I'd love to see you again,' she said in a tiny voice.

Michael parted her robe and kissed the hollow of her neck. 'And I'd love to sleep in your bed again tonight.'

'Oh – I'd love that too! But we can't.'

Michael raised his head and looked at her. 'Because of Lottie?'

'Mm hm.'

They were silent a while, and then Rosa took another deep breath. 'If I'm going to see you again, Michael, there's something I have to tell you.'

'Fire away.'

'I have a problem with alcohol.'

'Aye. I know.'

Oh! 'Because of that night in the Clarence?'

'Partly. But I kept an eye on you one week. You were looking a bit rough, and I was concerned. And then I overheard one of the girls in the supermarket talking about the amount of alcohol you were buying.'

'Oh, God!' Her face was so hot that she had to hide it against his shoulder. 'And you still wanted to get to know me? Even though you knew I was a lush?'

'Why wouldn't I? Having a problem with alcohol doesn't make a person a monster.' He took one of her hands and kissed it. 'I noticed you stuck to water last night.'

'Yeah.' She forced a laugh. 'I'm going to be a boring water-drinking type from now on.'

'As a matter of fact,' said Michael, 'you're much more interesting when you stick to water.'

'Am I?'

'Aye. In my experience, all drunks get dead boring as the evening draws on.'

She snuggled into him even more, and kissed his chest. 'In that case, since you've said you'll encourage me to write, maybe you could encourage me to stick to water, too? I think it's going to be a bit tough for me, to begin with.'

'Of course I'll encourage you. I know you can do it, Rosa. You're a responsible type, and responsible people are good at regaining control over their lives.'

'Responsible? *Me?* I'd never have called myself that. Dannie's more the kind of person I'd consider to be "responsible". She's decisive and brave and – and – independent.'

'And you're not? You don't think that rearing a child single-handed is brave and independent?'

'I suppose.' She licked his neck. 'D'you know something else that might make it easier for me to give up alcohol? I have this theory about displacement activity. You know – keeping busy doing other things so as not to keep thinking about wanting a drink.'

'That sounds like a very good idea. In fact, I'm thinking of an excellent kind of displacement activity right now.' He tumbled her off his lap.

'Oh? What?' asked Rosa disingenuously, suspecting it involved going back to bed, and hoping she was right.

'I'm going to teach you how to dance,' said Michael Luque.

Chapter Seventeen

Calypso wore her wound well. It was taking its time to heal, but the surgeon had assured her that after a few more sessions with him it would be virtually invisible. She didn't know that she cared, anyway. For the first time in her life she was sublimely content, secure in the knowledge that she was loved unconditionally.

Watching people's reaction to her ruined beauty even afforded her a wry amusement. Most people attempted to hide their sense of shock by focusing very intently on her eyes when they were talking to her, but inevitably their gaze would flicker to the scar emblazoned upon her right cheek. She preferred it when people were upfront with her. Rosa had flinched when she'd first seen it, then crooned sympathetically and enquired how much it hurt, and what kind of treatment Calypso would need, and she had clutched squeamishly at Calypso's hands when reminded of a documentary they'd once watched together about women and their facelifts. Calypso, who was far less faint-hearted than her friend (she'd had her fair share of facial peels and botox injections), had remarked: 'Remember the way they pulled the flap of skin up?' She'd smiled as Rosa had blenched at the memory and said: 'You're so *brave*, Calypso O'Kelly!' And Calypso had remembered the night she'd gibbered and sobbed at the thought of life without Dominic, and said: 'No. I'm not really.'

She seldom thought of Leo Devlin now, and when she did, she contemplated him and the degradation she'd suffered at his hands quite impassively, without shame or even very much remorse. The sense of liberation this afforded her had been – well, liberating. In a funny way, she suspected that he'd actually helped her. She'd once heard some psychologist on Radio 4 talking about how coming to terms with child-hood trauma can be facilitated by emotional catharsis. Perhaps Leo had been that for her? Perhaps, ironically, *she* had been using *him* to help her heal the psychological wounds that had been inflicted by her father and mother? Calypso didn't dwell on it too deeply – she couldn't understand why people felt the need to read books with titles such as 'How to Blame Your Parents for the Fact That You've Ended Up Being Such a Completely Crap Person'. She had tried hard all her life not to look back – she just got on with things. She was doing that now – getting on with things. She was even working on healing the rift with her mother, who had come to visit her in hospital and cried.

She had also discerned another irony the day the bandages were removed, and it was this: her emotional damage was now mirrored in the physical scar that she'd taken to wearing like a badge of honour. The beauty products ranked like artillery on her bathroom shelves were finally out of commission, and the war with herself was over.

Irony abounded: but the worst joke of all was that, if it hadn't been for Leo, she might never have found out how profoundly she was loved by Dominic, nor, indeed, how profoundly she loved him in return. In those moments when she felt giddy and weak with happiness, she was almost tempted to write Leo Devlin a thank-you note. But, because she had plans for her erstwhile protégé, she resisted the temptation.

Calypso had dusted herself off and gone back to work two weeks after the accident. Dominic had suggested a holiday, but there was something she wanted to do first. She wanted to cast her next movie.

Dannie had been staying in Jethro's house in Gozo for over a week. She'd phoned Laura, her second-in-command, in Dublin and asked her to take control of things until she got back. She wasn't sure how long she intended staying: every day some major work-related event threatened to drag Jethro back to the States, so she reckoned that she'd return to Dublin when he eventually decided that he had no choice but to fly back to La-la Land. So far he had managed to juggle everything from his Gozitan eyrie, but he was busting a gut work-wise. She had never seen him so stressed. He apologized, and made extravagant promises that as soon as things calmed down they would take a holiday together in some exotic utopia.

She had still said nothing to him about the baby. There just hadn't been an opportunity. She wanted to break the news to him over a candle-lit dinner, or while walking along a beach, or after a glorious lovemaking session, but there had been no time for leisurely meals or moonlit walks, and their lovemaking was so vigorous that poor, knackered Jethro generally fell asleep immediately afterwards. Pillow talk was the last thing on his overwrought mind.

Because she'd brought very little in the way of clothes with her, Dannie had made a trip early in her stay to the neighbouring island of Malta to shop and do some sightseeing while Jethro made back-to-back conference calls. She'd helped herself to a couple of sundresses and a bikini, loads of sun cream, sunglasses, sandals, and a floppy sunhat made from the local Maltese lace. She'd also visited a stationer's in Valletta to stock up on books and magazines before taking the ferry back to Jethro's island retreat. She had a feeling that she'd be spending a lot of time reading.

The balcony, with its spectacular view of the Mediterranean, was the place in the house where she felt most comfortable. Jethro's house was so modern and so masculine and so very, very *alien*! It stood like a glass sentinel on the cliff top, and from wherever you looked the stunning views were framed by stark concrete or shiny gunmetal-grey steel or unyielding Perspex. Even his furniture was hard-edged and clean-lined. She'd asked him about his house in LA, and had felt a deep stab of disappointment when he told her that it had been designed by the same architect.

One morning she woke after a dream of her baby. The babby had been asking her who its dada was, and Dannie had been going 'Um. Um,' not knowing what else to say. She knew this meant it was time to tell Jethro. She turned to him in the bed, but he wasn't there. Well, she knew where he'd be. He'd be in his fecking edit suite so he would, talking on the phone to some Hollywood hotshot. Feeling pissed off that she'd actually summoned up the courage to tell him about the baby only to be thwarted in her intent, she shrugged into his oversized towelling robe and went down to the kitchen, where his Gozitan major-domo, Roberto, was making coffee.

'Please go and relax, madam,' he said. 'I'll bring breakfast out to you.' Oh, how she hated being called 'madam'! It made her feel like a complete impostor. 'I bought some magazines in Valletta yesterday, as requested,' continued Roberto. 'I left them on the table on the balcony for madam.'

Dannie had asked Roberto to bring her a fresh supply of magazines because she found it difficult to concentrate on the books she'd bought while this baby business was preoccupying her thoughts. She spent most of her balcony time leafing through magazine after magazine – the more frivolous the better, as far as she was concerned. Oh *Janey!* she thought, as she remembered the hefty stack of glossies and gossipies she'd dumped in the bin yesterday – she'd *have* to broach the subject with Jethro soon or she'd be responsible for the destruction of an entire rainforest.

Helping herself to a bunch of grapes from the aluminium fruit bowl, she thanked Roberto, then trailed off to the balcony and flung herself down on the aluminium sunlounger to gaze over the aluminium railings at the by now very familiar Mediterranean view. She was starting to feel like a kind of a prisoner, she realized, remembering the daguerreotype Jethro had bought of Calypso's bereft, castaway namesake. A very privileged prisoner, of course, she reminded herself, as Roberto set a tray down on the table, but there was only so much pampering a gal could take. She'd love to *do* something! Maybe she should go to the hotel Ta'Cenc for a massage? Pah. No. She was feeling too restless for that.

The major-domo poured coffee and retreated, and Dannie steeled herself to sit down on the aluminium chair. She helped herself to freshly squeezed peach juice, and to a croissant fresh out of the oven, and to the topmost magazine of the selection that Roberto had fanned out for her along the tabletop. It was *Hello!*, and there on the cover was none other than Pelagia Brookes. Oh! *My Life After Guy* she read. What? Hel-*lo*? Quickly, Dannie turned to the story.

There were a couple of full-page photographs of beautiful glossy Pelagia holding her three-month-old baby girl, and at least half a dozen smaller pics. Skimming the copy, Dannie read the beans that Pelagia had spilled to the *Hello!* journalist. 'I feel such a failure having to admit that my marriage is over so soon,' confessed Pelagia. 'But Guy was just never there for me. Before little Luana was born he'd been offered a job as host of a new political talk show, and I tried to persuade him to take it so that he could spend more time at home with me and the baby. But the lure of live war reporting was just too strong for him to resist. Guy is a man married to his work. Little Luana and I will struggle on on my trust fund . . .' Pelagia continued in smilingly unironic mode for several further pages. On the last page there was a picture of a beaming 'Guy and Pelagia in Happier Times' that had obviously been taken around the same time as the spread Dannie had seen in *OK!*

Something made her reach into the Perspex storage box that contained her stash of reading material, and draw out the book of babies' names that she'd bought at Gatwick. Under 'L' she found the following. 'Luana (Teutonic): graceful army maiden', and Dannie found herself wondering if Guy had chosen the name, or if poor Pelagia had a better sense of humour than she'd originally given her credit for.

The sound of footsteps clanging up the staircase to the balcony warned her that Jethro was approaching. Dannie tossed the book back into the basket and tried not to look furtive.

It was doubtful that Jethro would have noticed whether she looked furtive or not. He was looking dog-tired. 'Hello, darling,' he said, dropping a kiss on her shoulder. He sat down opposite her, rubbing his eye with a finger. Instantly Roberto materialized with another cup and poured coffee for him. 'You got e-mail from your father at last,' he said, handing her a folded sheet of paper. 'I printed it out for you.'

'Oh, thanks!' said Dannie, unfolding the A4 sheet and spreading it out on the tabletop.

'Dear Dannie,' she read,

I'm sorry I haven't answered your e-mail sooner, but I don't check it more than once a week or so. It was good to hear from you. I hope you're having a nice break in Gozo. The weather has been grand here, and we've started to save the hay. Minnie had pups – a litter of five. The cottage beyond that your brother Michael was having fixed up as his holiday home is finished, but the bank has decided to post him off to promotion in Bangkok so all that work is wasted. All the boys are well, and Joe was telling me that he'd seen you in Dublin, and how well you were looking. Isn't it the grand girl you've become, with your city centre apartment and your foreign holidays! I suppose a holiday in Connemara wouldn't appeal to a high-falutin career girl like yourself, but you are very welcome. Try writing to me again, and I might get used to this computer yoke yet, and become an expert at the electronic mail! Very best from your old Dad.

Oh! Dannie felt tears well up in her eyes. She bit her lip, then folded the sheet of paper and slid it into the pocket of her robe.

'Bad news?' asked Jethro.

'No. I just had an awful wave of homesickness come over me, that's all.'

'Homesickness for Dublin?'

'No. For Connemara.'

He leaned back in his steel chair, and Dannie couldn't help wondering how he managed not to wince. 'Why don't you take some time out and go back there?' he asked.

'Yes,' said Dannie slowly, fingering the letter in her pocket. 'That's exactly what I'm thinking I should do. I think it's time to go home.'

'I'm glad you said that,' said Jethro, equally slowly. 'Because I just got word that I'm needed in LA. I'm booked on a flight out tomorrow.'

'Oh.'

They looked at each other, and it was obvious from their helpless expressions that neither of them had a clue what to say. Jethro broke the awkwardness by saying: 'I've told my people in LA that I'll be incommunicado for the rest of the day. I'm having the afternoon off. I want to take you for a walk along my favourite beach. But first – lunch in the most special restaurant on Gozo. It's tiny, but the food is delicious. It's all home-cooked by the proprietor and his wife. They run the joint single-handed – the proprietor even plays the violin to his customers.'

'It sounds dead romantic.'

'It is.'

It was. And she could easily have told him what he needed to know over lunch. The walk along the beach afterwards was dead romantic too, and she could equally easily have told him then. Or during the leisurely love they made later that evening. The entire day had been the most preposterously perfect one of Dannie's life. And when they'd finished making love around midnight, and Dannie was lying cradled in Jethro's arms in the emperor-sized steel-framed bed, she knew that the time had come at last to break the news to him. 'There's something I have to tell you, Jethro,' she said. 'Something really important.'

'Sounds scary. What is it?'

And Dannie hadn't been able to look him in the eye as she'd answered. 'This isn't going to work,' she said.

Calypso's casting session was not going well. She tired easily and felt a little woozy from the painkillers she was still taking, but she was determined to get it right this time. She was further disadvantaged by the fact that Viv was off sick, and she'd had to rope in Iseult as her assistant instead – as well as organizing a temp to man the office. Viv's timing could not have been worse.

Calypso always, always tried to find something positive to say to each actor she saw at a session, because she knew from experience what a grim ordeal auditions could be. She remembered the insecurity she'd felt during her own stint as an actress and the awful debilitating nerves that had afflicted her: nerves that could transform a reasonably intelligent, confident, attractive person into a clumsy, sweaty, stammering, stumbling thicko.

But today she was finding it difficult to say anything positive or encouraging to *any* of the actors at this cattle call. She was actually finding it more and more difficult as the afternoon wore on to resist the impulse to roll her eyes to heaven and shout: '*Next!*' Time after time the door to the studio had opened today to admit someone who was quite plainly wrong, wrong, *wrong*.

'More coffee, Iseult, please,' she said, wearily handing her assistant her empty mug and pressing her fingers against her eyelids. 'Hell. Since Leo's big success story, half the actors in Dublin clearly think it's a good idea to come in looking mean and moody and smoulder all over the place. Thanks.' She took the proffered mug and heaved yet another heavy, heartfelt sigh. 'Hell's *teeth*! I *still* haven't found what I'm looking for, for Dakota!'

Iseult gave her a sage look. 'In that case you're in illustrious company. Think of Bono. He penned that very lyric – without the Dakota bit, of course – and he's the most positive person in the world. I think of him when I do my affirmations every morning. He's my role model!'

'OK, Iseult, enough.' Calypso took a swig of very strong black coffee, then stretched and yawned and winced as the muscles in her cheek protested. 'OK. Send in the next one,' she said.

Iseult left the studio, and came back looking animated. 'I know Jason Byrne is next on the list, but—'

'Oh, no, no, *nooooo*!' fretted Calypso. 'Jason is at least ten years too old! What was his agent *thinking* of when he decided to send him along? He's just wasting my time.'

'But,' resumed Iseult patiently, 'there's a guy out there I've never seen before. He's not on the list, and I know it's not our policy to see anyone who turns up on spec, Calypso, but I think it might be worth your while having a look.'

'What's his name?'

'Ben Tarrant.'

'Mm. Good name.' Calypso gave her secretary a speculative look. After a beat or two she said: 'OK, Izzy. Send him in.'

Iseult danced out of the studio and re-appeared with an undeniably beautiful boy. This Ben Tarrant was a cross between a young Brad Pitt and Travis. He was lean and golden and wholesome-looking, with wonderful teeth and a gorgeous, crinkly smile.

'Hi,' he said, moving towards her and extending a hand. 'I'm Ben Tarrant. I hope you don't mind me gatecrashing your session. I know it's not a very kosher thing to do, but I thought I'd take a gamble.' His grip was firm and assured, his smile confident but not cocky. In fact, his entire manner was appropriately and pleasingly just on the right side of deferential. This boy was eager to please.

'Nice to meet you, Ben,' said Calypso, sliding into professional mode. 'Have you a CV and a ten-by-eight for me?'

'Sure.' He set a manila envelope on the table. Calypso drew his CV out and scanned it while Iseult issued instructions, directing Ben to sit on a stool in the centre of the studio floor, and to make sure that he answered all the questions she was going to put to him directly to the camera, not to her.

'Rolling?' Iseult asked the camera operator.

'Rolling.'

'And your name is?' questioned Iseult, re-embarking for the twenty-seventh time that day on her standard list of questions.

Calypso studied his image on the monitor in front of her. Mm. Not bad at all. He was what some women would describe as 'cute', she supposed, and yes, he had an undeniable sex appeal. And while he might not leap out at you from the screen the way Leo did, she knew that an excellent screen presence was something that could be acquired if an actor was hungry enough and sussed enough to want to learn fast. He followed Iseult's directions to the letter. Biddable, too. Good. Biddability was the very quality she was looking for this time round.

Calypso started to smile. She'd come here looking for a new star to eclipse Leo Devlin – someone as different from him as it was possible to be. Ben Tarrant fitted the bill to a T. He was day to Leo's night, angel to his demon, heaven to his hell. Her smile grew more thoughtful and her eyes narrowed with concentration as she considered the state of play. The war with herself might be over, but the game of chess with Leo Devlin most certainly wasn't. Now the High Queen of Casting had not only a king in the gallant form of her husband Dominic to help her win it; she also had a knight in shining armour to be her champion. It was her move, and it rather looked as if endgame was in sight.

It wasn't long before Michael moved in with Rosa and Lottie. Initially, Rosa had been very circumspect, making sure that Lottie was asleep before sneaking him into her bedroom, and only allowing him to stay the night if Lottie was away at a friend's. She felt the same way she'd felt when she'd brought boyfriends home to her parents' house for sneaky petting sessions after teenage discos. The idea that it was her own daughter she was now trying to hoodwink almost made her laugh – but of course there was no hoodwinking Lottie for long.

They were sitting watching a travel programme together one evening when Lottie said: 'Are there any nudist beaches in Ireland? Every other country seems to have them.'

'Not as far as I know,' said Rosa. 'Do you know of any, Michael?'

'Um. No.'

'I'm sure Mum'd love to go skinny-dipping with you, Michael. She's not a prude like some mums, and *anyway*,' she slanted an oblique look at her mother, then at Michael, 'I've a feeling that you've already seen her with no clothes on.'

'Lottie!' Rosa's mouth dropped open with indignant surprise.

Lottie raised her eyes to heaven. 'Mu-*um*. I'm not a baby. I've heard you two sneaking into your bedroom when you thought I was asleep. Anyway, from what I know about the sex thing, I can pretty well understand why you'd like to do it with Michael.'

Michael had gone very red, and all Rosa could do was blink and say: 'Um.'

'I'm not shocked at all, you know,' continued Lottie. 'I'm really glad you have a boyfriend at last, and I'm even more glad that he's Michael. My friend Jemima hates her mum's boyfriend, so you're dead lucky that you have me to like Michael.'

There was a rather awkward hiatus, then: 'Oh, Carlotta Elliot – what a minxy thing you are!' Rosa sat down beside her on the sofa and adopted a put-it-there kind of tone. 'Does this mean that we don't have to carry on sneaking around on tippy-toes at night?'

'Yep. But you will remember to keep the bedroom door shut, won't you? I'd hate it if I heard any actual – um –'

Rosa put out a hand and covered her daughter's mouth. 'It's cool. You don't have to be any more specific.'

Shortly after that, Michael moved in.

He offered to cook the first meal they were to share together as a family. When he told Rosa he intended doing roast lamb, she was surprised. 'I wouldn't have thought that you had much interest in cooking,' she said. 'I remember the first time I met you, you had a supermarket trolley full of crap.' Michael laughed. 'I remember that too,' he said. 'I was so embarrassed I wanted to explain. But I could hardly turn round to a virtual stranger and say: "By the way, this shopping isn't mine. It's for my elderly neighbour who's stuck in bed with the flu."' Rosa had laughed back, remembering his 'gay' purse and his Silk Cut and his scratch cards, and said: 'So the moral of the story is, "Never judge a person by the contents of their shopping trolley".' And then she'd gone down to the local Londis and come back with a bottle of red wine for him and a bottle of Aqua Libra for herself.

'Are you sure you don't mind?' he asked as he poured himself a glass of wine to drink while he cooked. 'Are you OK about keeping alcohol in the house?'

'I'm sure,' she said, clinking her tumbler of alcohol-free fizz against his wineglass. 'This is a special occasion. There's no reason for you not to enjoy a glass of wine just because you're living with a lush.'

'Well, thank you.' Michael raised his glass to her. 'Here's to sobriety.'

'Haven't you worked it out, you klutz? I'm trying to get you drunk so that I can seduce you after Lottie's gone to bed.'

'Mm. So there's some displacement activity to be looked forward to this evening?'

She gave him a foxy smile. 'Lots of it.'

Rosa's displacement activity seemed to be working rather well. The only time she really missed a drink was when she went to one of Calypso's do's, so she'd taken to saying no to those invitations. She still did girly stuff with her friend, and dropped into her office any time she was passing, but she didn't see as much of her these days because she was spending most of her free time indulging in her very favourite displacement activity of all (apart from sex with Michael), which was her story. Rosa had discarded her old notebook and the diary Michael had lent her, and was now using the word-processing facility on Calypso's cast-off computer. The words just seemed to flow straight out of the tap of her imagination onto the screen. Sometimes hours went by without her noticing. It became a form of escapism: the real world receded whenever she entered the world of the Map Girl.

One day she went down to Londis and came back with another bottle of red wine and another bottle of Aqua Libra. When Michael came back from work that evening and saw the table set with wine and flowers and candles, he said: 'OK. So what are we celebrating today?'

And Rosa pointed proudly towards the coffee table, where a big stack of printed pages stood next to a jiffy bag with the address of a literary agency on it, and said: 'Look.'

Michael looked from Rosa to the pile of paper and back again, and a smile spread slowly across his face. 'You've finished,' he said. 'You clever, clever girl.'

Back in Dublin, Dannie did some complicated legal stuff. She transferred the running of Florabundance over to Laura and sold her assistant some shares in the business. She put her flat on the market and got a good price for it. And then she did the most difficult thing of all. She said tearful farewells to Rosa and Lottie and Calypso and her ex-staff.

This new life-enhancing decision had been a surprisingly easy one to make. She loved her flower shop in Dublin, and she was proud of all she'd achieved on her own, but the baby meant that it was time to move on. It was time to go back to Connemara and move into the restored cottage that had been intended as a holiday home for her brother Michael and his family. She had felt a bit uneasy about telling her father she was pregnant, but she needn't have. When she'd dropped the bombshell, dived for cover and finally dared to peek out from between her fingers, Frank had just smiled at her and nodded benignly.

Dannie put her own creative stamp on the pretty place that was now her home, and worked back-breakingly hard in the garden until her pregnancy started to show and her father commanded her to stop.

She was happy in a listless way as she waited for her baby to be born. She spent days walking the beaches around Connemara – Lissnakeelagh and Lissamore – and she revisited the place in the rocks where she'd had her hideout as a child, thinking there was nothing on earth quite so satisfying as seeing nobody's footprints bar her own on an expanse of golden sand. She went back to her school in Kylemore and took tea with Sister Benedict, she looked up childhood friends, and she got better acquainted with the inhabitants of the village. People were obviously dying to know who the baby's father was, but Dannie told no-one. Not even her brother Joe knew.

And then one day she answered the door of her cottage and found Jethro Palmer standing there.

'Oh! It's you!' she said stupidly. 'What are you doing here?'

'You surprised me in Gozo once, Miz Moore,' he said. 'I'm returning the compliment.' He bent his head to hers in the cottage doorway that had pale pink roses clambering round it, and kissed her. And at first she resisted because he was no longer her man, but when he persisted with the kiss she realized that she couldn't resist him any more because she was still quite hopelessly in love with him.

'How did you know where to find me?' she asked some minutes later. She hadn't much wanted to break the kiss – it was the most gorgeous one she'd ever had – but she needed to know things.

'Rosa contacted me. She told me she'd wrestled with herself for months, and finally just couldn't bear the idea of me not knowing that you were going to have my baby. She says she'll understand if you never want to speak to her again.'

'Of course I'll speak to her again.'

'She did the right thing, then?'

'She did. Oh, God, yes she did!' said Dannie, feeling little bubbles of happiness rising within her, like the fizz in a flute of champagne. Endorphins! And she dissolved in a positive soup of endorphins as she stood on tiptoe and snaked her arms around his neck so that he could kiss her again. And again. And again.

Later, in bed under her embroidered velvet throw, he stroked her belly and asked her why she'd done what she'd done, and she told him. She told him that to her mind LA was no more a suitable place to rear a child than city-centre Dublin, and that she wanted her baby to grow up surrounded by the wild beauty of Connemara. When he suggested that she move into the house in Gozo, she laughed out loud at the notion of Jethro's cool, contemporary interior being compromised with protective corner-covers on the angular furniture and baby-gates on all those balconies and stairways. 'Jethro. No toddler would survive a week in that house,' she said. She reminded him that she couldn't live with a man who would never be there for her, the way Guy had never been there for Pelagia Brookes.

And then she'd asked him to make love to her again.

That evening they wandered down to O'Toole's seafood restaurant in the nearby village of Kilrowan for a bowl of chowder and a glass of Guinness, and they sat by the open fire at a candlelit table and listened to a fiddler play traditional Irish laments in the bar next door. It was so perfect that Dannie couldn't help blubbing a bit. And afterwards they wandered back home through the village, and Dannie told him stories about the places they passed, and what they had meant to her in her childhood.

'What was that?' asked Jethro, stopping outside a small boarded-up shopfront with peeling paint.

'That was O'Flaherty's – a grocer's shop. It's been closed for years. I remember when I was little getting dead excited when they got satsumas in at Christmas time. It seemed so exotic.'

'I like to think of you as a little girl.' He slung an arm around her shoulders. 'What do you reckon? Will we have a boy or a girl, Dannie?'

'I'd like a girl. I know it's silly, but I love the idea of dressing her up in tiny pretty things.'

He gave her a lovely, indulgent smile, then: 'Will I meet your father before I leave tomorrow?' he asked.

'Janey Mackers – no way, Palmer! He might take a shotgun to you.'

'Why?'

'For not making an honest woman of me.'

'I would, you know. If that's what you wanted.'

'I know, Jethro. Please don't make me cry again.'

Later, when Jethro was sleeping, Dannie did cry again. In fact, she bawled. So that Jethro wouldn't hear, she wrapped her velvet throw around herself and crept out into the garden where she could weep freely. Under the apple tree at the bottom of the garden she revisited each of the scenarios that were open to her, as she had done most nights since she had left Gozo. She pictured herself and her baby living in his bachelor pad on the island, with Jethro flying in occasionally to visit, and she knew it wouldn't work. She pictured herself and her baby living in LA, in a culture at the opposite end of the spectrum to Connemara, and she knew that that wouldn't work either. And then she pictured Jethro exchanging his überdude status and his jet-setting lifestyle and coming here to live with her in her pretty country cottage so that he could be a hands-on, stay-at-home father, and if she hadn't been crying, that might actually have made her laugh out loud.

And there, under the heavens' embroidered cloths, Dannie Moore shed copious tears for the perfect man she knew she had to let go.

It was 17 March, and Calypso was decked out in Salvatore Ferragamo, drifting towards the *porte cochère* of the Four Seasons hotel where the party to celebrate the première of *Don Juan's Double* was being held. Beside her, Dominic looked dashing in his tux.

Calypso had been dreading this evening. She wasn't sure how she would feel on seeing Leo again for the first time in nearly nine months, so when his image had hit the cinema screen earlier at the showing she'd been glad to find that she could regard him now with more or less impervious objectivity.

She accepted a glass of champagne from a waiter who was standing to attention in the doorway of the function room where the party had already got into swing, and then she turned to Dominic, who patted her flank and said: 'Off you go and network, darling.'

'Won't you come with me?'

'Calypso – you know very well that I despise these occasions.'

'But what will you do?'

'I shall make myself comfortable in a corner of the room and derive huge enjoyment from observing all these luvvies drink too much and make horses' asses of themselves.' He gave her a saturnine smile and backed away from her through the crowd.

Calypso stapled on her best party face and worked the room, manoeuvring as adroitly as a chess player. The usual adjectives were being bandied around – 'triumphant', 'sensational', 'astonishing' – but she couldn't manifest much enthusiasm – particularly when these adjectives were used about Leo. She just nodded and 'mm'd' and came out with the right responses, and was relieved when she finally spotted Jethro. He was talking to a debonair silver-haired man who was wearing an exquisitely tailored Nehru jacket in ivory-coloured silk. 'Please forgive me for interrupting,' she said. 'I just wanted to find out if you're a daddy yet, Jethro. Dannie must be due very soon, isn't she?'

'The baby is imminent, ma'am. I'm expecting a call from her any day now.' He indicated the person to whom he'd been talking. 'Allow me to introduce you. Calypso O'Kelly, this is Gordon DeLapp.' Calypso inclined her head politely at the man who was now shaking her hand, wondering why the name seemed familiar. 'I know you consider Leo to be your protégé, Calypso,' continued Jethro, 'but strictly speaking he's Gordon's. Gordon was the man responsible for encouraging his interest in acting.'

'Really?'

'Yes,' said Gordon DeLapp with what could

only be described as an infernal smile. 'I'm very, very proud of him. For a boy to have come from such a cruelly deprived background as Leo's, he's accomplished quite an extraordinary amount.' Gordon DeLapp's voice reminded Calypso of the snake's in Disney's *The Jungle Book*.

'D-deprived?' Calypso faltered. 'So Leo actually *does* come from a deprived background?'

'Oh, yes. He makes no secret of his appalling childhood.'

'I thought you knew about it, Calypso,' remarked Jethro.

'I – I know nothing about Leo, really,' she said. And now she knew it was absolutely true. She knew *nothing* about him. 'I just thought maybe the stories were – you know – a little, well, *exaggerated*, that's all.'

'Good God, no. And I should know,' said Gordon DeLapp. 'I've known Leo nearly all his life. He had a perfectly ghastly time growing up. He never knew his father, and his mother was a chronic alcoholic and desperately, desperately poor. But there was something about Leo – some *quality* that made him special, that set him apart. Other boys were lazy – or quite simply stupid – but Leo was *very* hungry to learn. Voracious. He'd come to me after school—'

'You were his teacher?'

'No. But I'd like to think I was his mentor. I

opened doors for him, showed him all the fascinating things that life and art had to offer. My library became his home from home, and of course I lent him books. He was reading Dostoevsky at the age of twelve. A precocious little thing he was in those days – but just look how it's paid off!'

Gordon DeLapp. Suddenly Calypso remembered where she'd seen the name before. It had been on the flyleaf of the edition of *Crime and Punishment* that she'd seen in Leo's apartment the last time she'd been there. *For my dear friend Leo, as a token of my appreciation. Gordon DeLapp*. And she remembered the graffiti that had covered the inside of the front cover. *Leo Devlin. Leo DeLapp. Leo DeLapp-Devlin*. What the hell was going on? What *was* Gordon DeLapp to Leo? Mentor, friend, lover, confidant, puppet-master? And then she knew with blinding clarity that he was all these things and more. Gordon DeLapp was an abuser.

She couldn't handle the overwhelming sense of confusion she felt. The rules in the game of chess she'd been playing had been changed, suddenly. And something about this DeLapp person – something about the way he was look-ing at her, as if he *knew* things about her – was making her feel deeply uncomfortable. She decided it was best to back off. 'Oh!' she said brightly. 'There's someone I need to talk to just coming through the door. Will you excuse me, please?' She didn't need to talk to anyone, but she *really* needed to get away from Gordon DeLapp. Abruptly she broke away and negotiated her way back through the crowd, deciding that she'd ask Dominic to take her home. She'd had enough.

'What a peachy fucking scar. It really suits you, Calypso.' A familiar, silky voice came from behind. She turned to find Leo looking down at her. There was a dangerous glint in his anthracite eyes, and his beautiful, sensual mouth was curved in a sardonic smile. 'You must have changed your mobile number, sweetheart. Fed up with getting juicy text messages, were you? Pity you didn't get the one I just tried to send you. You'd have found it a huge turn-on.' He bent his head to hers and muttered something quite unspeakably lewd in her ear.

Once upon a time she would have gone into a virtual swoon at what he'd just said to her. Now she turned to face him. 'Fuck off, Leo,' she said, returning his smile with one that was blatantly insincere.

He didn't smile back. 'Why didn't you cast me in the David Marchant film, Calypso?'

Calypso regarded him levelly and said: 'Because you weren't right for the part.'

'I damn well was, and you know it. That gleaming blond boy you went with doesn't have an ounce of what I have.'

'He's learning fast, believe me. And he has beautiful manners.'

Leo gave an unpleasant laugh. 'Since when did you start finding *manners* a desirable trait in a man, bitch? And why haven't I had a call from Sally about your next casting? I would have thought an invitation to lunch with the director should be on the cards.'

She shrugged. 'I'm afraid you're not right for that either, Leo. Now fuck off and leave me alone.'

'Cal-yp-so?' He succeeded in investing the three syllables with real menace, and she felt a flash of fear. 'How would you feel if your husband got wind of what went on between us? I really think it would be a very wise thing indeed to invite me to lunch, darling, or hubby might get very explicit details in the post.'

'Leo. My husband already knows what went on between us. I told him myself.'

He gave a laugh that sounded more like a bark. 'You expect me to believe that?'

'I swear it. And if you have any problems with my testimony, Leo, why don't you check it out for yourself. Ask Dominic.' She raised an arm and waved to her husband, who was lounging in a chair on the other side of the room, looking more saturnine than ever. Dominic got unhurriedly to his feet and started to move towards them through the mass of prattling party-goers.

'You wouldn't dare do that. You're calling my bluff.' Leo narrowed his eyes at her, but she knew she was winning.

'Try me,' she said, then added in a venomous, urgent hiss: 'You blew it, Leo. You messed with my mind and you treated me with disrespect. *Nobody* messes with Calypso O'Kelly. Now, are you going to fuck off or not?'

'Ooh. How you must hate me, Calypso.'

It was Calypso's turn to give a bark of a laugh. 'I don't hate you, Leo. Hate is too passionate a word for what I feel for you.'

'I don't believe you. I know if I propositioned you now, within minutes you'd be up against a wall somewhere with your legs wrapped round my hips.'

'Then you know nothing, Leo.' He curled his lip at her, and she noticed for the first time that his teeth were stained. She wouldn't bother advising him to get them bleached. 'But I *want* you to know something,' she continued, in the kind of tone she'd reserve for a particularly stupid actor during a casting session. 'I want you to know something very, very important. I want you to know that I pity you. That I feel really, truly sorry for you.'

'Get lost, Calypso.'

'No. Listen. I know where you learned your tricks, Leo, and if you were fucked up as expertly as I was, it doesn't surprise me that you're damaged goods. I'm glad to say I've come through. There may even be hope for you, yet.'

Now Leo looked as if she'd slapped him. Quickly he hid his expression by looking away towards Dominic, whose progress towards them had been stalled: he was talking with a fellow gallery owner. A muscle in Leo's jaw clenched and unclenched, and when he turned back to her he'd resumed that expression she knew so well of studied indifference. '*Hope?* Where the fuck does *that* come in your skewed scheme of things?' he sneered.

She looked back at him levelly and said: 'Oh, poor, poor you. How *wretched* it must be to live in your head.' This time her tone was the pitying one she'd use to an injured opponent, and from the look in his eye she might just as well have said 'Check'.

In that instant a woman bedecked in diamonds worthy of Liz Taylor approached and asked Leo for his autograph in the most flagrantly French accent Calypso had ever heard. Calypso never forgot the look that came into his eyes as he turned his attention away from her to bestow it upon Madame. It struck her in that split second that he resembled a seasoned hunter deftly readjusting his sights.

He took the proffered pen and sheet of paper and said in his most velvety voice: 'With pleasure. What is your name, madame?'

'My name is Marguerite, but the autograph is not for me.' She pronounced the word 'is', 'eez'.

'Marguerite? That's the French for "daisy", isn't it? Coincidentally, I once had an older sister called Daisy.'

'Oh?' The woman put her head on one side and regarded him quizzically. 'You – *had* a sister? She is no longer with you?'

'Sadly, no. She was killed in a boating accident when I was ten. My entire family was.'

'Oh! How *tragique*! You poor boy! I am so sorry.' The woman called Marguerite pouted with sympathy so that her mouth looked even more sensual.

Leo gave her a melancholic smile, then pulled himself together. 'And your daughter's name is –?'

'Is Claudine.'

'What age is she?'

'She is just sixteen.'

'No! You have a *sixteen*-year-old daughter! Impossible!'

Madame Marguerite slanted him a look, then cast down her eyes with a demure smile, putting out a hand for the safe return of her autograph. But Leo didn't give it back. Instead he set his head at an angle and looked down at her with interested eyes. 'Please allow me to get you a drink, Marguerite. There's a buffet over there, with oysters. *Champagne et huîtres. Vous aimez les huîtres?*'

'*Oui. Je les aime beaucoup.*'

'*Et vous savez ce qu'on dit sur le sujet des huîtres?*'

Calypso's schoolgirl French effected a rough translation: 'You know what they say about oysters . . .'

'*Je le sais bien.*'

He gave her a slow, vulpine smile. '*Allons, donc.*'

As he laid a hand on the small of her back to guide her across the room, Calypso saw the woman judder visibly at the contact, just as she had once done. He turned back briefly to Calypso and waggled his tongue at her. 'Daisy's ripe for plucking,' he hissed in an undertone, sending her a meaningful wink. And then Leo Devlin was moving away from her, moving out of her life, paw firmly on the back of his latest victim. It was checkmate. The chess game was finally over.

On 17 March, Dannie gave birth to her baby. It was a girl, and she was perfect. Quite, quite perfect. Dannie had done all the things she'd been told that new parents do – counting fingers and toes, checking for birthmarks, assiduously avoiding any contact with the soft place on the skull (the fontanelle: she knew all the technical terms now!) where the bone had yet to knit – and she could find no flaw in the infant at all. Dannie and Jethro's baby was perfection personified.

Three days after she was born, Dannie's father came to the Galway University Hospital with a gift-wrapped something for her, and a garage shop mixed bouquet.

'What will you call her?' he asked, sitting down next to the bed and peering at his new grand-daughter.

'Paloma.'

'Paloma? What class of a queer name is that?'

'It's Spanish. It means "dove".'

'Sure they've called a soap that.'

'It also means "a gentle, tender girl", Dada.'

'Ah. Now you're talking. Hello, little Paloma! Hello, my gentle girl, my tender girl, my little dovey!' Her father leaned towards her and prodded the baby gently, and Dannie smiled at the uncharacteristically soppy expression on his face. Then he straightened up and handed her the gift-wrapped package. 'Here,' he said. 'A few things for the babby.'

Dannie opened the clumsily sellotaped parcel to find sundry items of baby clothes in a tissue-paper nest. There was a preponderance of tiny pink and white smocked dresses, trimmed with lace and ribbons. Some had little rosebuds scattered on them, some had pictures of teddies, and some had bunnies. They were the silliest, frilliest, most girly baby clothes Dannie had ever set eyes on.

'Oh, Dada!' she said. 'Thank you!'

'I wanted to get proper girl-baby stuff. Did I get it right?'

'Oh, yes – indeed and you did!'

'It's just that I never had much truck with that class of stuff when you were growing up. That was women's stuff. You missed out on that class of a thing through not having a mammy. I wanted to make up for it with little Palomina.'

'Paloma, Dad,' she corrected him.

'Paloma.'

Just then the baby blinked, wriggled, opened her mouth and let out a roar.

Frank looked aghast. 'The lungs on her!' he said. 'Will you listen to that!'

'She's hungry, Da. She's due a feed.' Dannie quickly started to undo the buttons on her nightdress in order to produce a breast for her hungry daughter.

'Ah, now,' said Frank, getting to his feet, clearly discomfited by the idea of witnessing a display of breast-feeding. 'It's time I was off. Oh – I nearly forgot. This arrived for you this morning by special delivery. Good day to you, now, Daniella. I mean Dannie. Yes. And to you, um – Pamola.' He drew a big brown envelope out of his overcoat pocket before turning and lumbering out through the door.

Dannie delayed opening the envelope until Paloma had finished feeding, which was about an hour later. This baby clearly relished her grub! By then more stuff had arrived – flowers and chocolates and baskets of fruit – and it was some time before she turned her attention to the brown envelope her father had given her. Inside it there were two more envelopes. One was cream vellum, the other was the long manila kind favoured by lawyers. The vellum one had her name inscribed in Jethro's distinctive slanting black script. She slid out the card it contained, and smiled. It was a reproduction of the Klimt painting she'd once told him she loved – the breathtakingly romantic representation of mother and child. Inside he had written the following words.

Dearest Dannie. Enclosed is a gift to mark the birth of our daughter. I know you told me that you were going to devote yourself to full-time motherhood, but when Paloma has grown up a little and is going to school, you may change your mind, and if you do, I'd like to think that you might resurrect your not inconsiderable business acumen. I am racing off to Australia to start work on a new epic. When it's finished, I would dearly love to spend some time with you and our daughter in Connemara.

With warmest wishes to you and Paloma,
Jethro.

PS – Please send photographs of mother and child ASAP.

With curious fingers, Dannie tore open the second envelope and withdrew a legal document. Paper-clipped to it was a card bearing the legend *Florabundance Two?* Flummoxed, she ran her eyes down the legalese. It took her some moments to realize that what she held in her hands were the deeds to the old O'Flaherty shop in the little village of Kilrowan.

On 17 March, Rosa received two phone calls.

The first one had been from her agent to advise her that it would be a good idea to agree to Roydon Sneyde's latest offer of compensation. Letters had been toing and froing between their respective solicitors since Rosa had issued proceedings. Sally had scoffed at the derisory amount initially offered, but Rosa had been secretly thrilled, because among all the legal bumph in that very first letter she'd received admitting liability, the following words had leapt out at her: 'Mr Sneyde wishes to unreservedly apologize to Ms Elliot . . .'

She'd phoned Michael at work to tell him to bring back a bottle of wine and one of Aqua Libra so that they could celebrate the long-awaited victory over the tyrant Sneyde, but she hadn't mentioned the second phone call she'd had later in the day. She wanted to tell her lover and her daughter that particular piece of news face to face.

Now she was waiting with mounting impatience for Lottie and Michael to come back from the surgery, where Michael had been showing her some weird furless oriental cat.

She'd tried to distract herself with displacement activity, but she hadn't been able to concentrate on the new story that was taking shape on her computer screen, so she just sat in front of MTV worrying a fingernail with her teeth until she drew blood. She'd rung Michael twenty minutes ago to be told that Lottie was drooling over some puppies, and she'd told him quite categorically that Lottie had drooled enough, and she wanted them back home *now*.

'Mum! The cat was so *cute*!'

At last they were back! Lottie came racing through the front door.

'You should have seen it, Mum! Its eyes were so big it looked like it was wearing make-up! And it was so snuffly with the cold! And so kind of sweetly bald! It was just like the cat in your story! And there were puppies!'

Michael came in behind her, and gave Rosa the kind of look that said 'Sorry!' 'She'll want one now, I'm warning you,' he said.

'When we move to a house with a garden, maybe,' said Rosa.

That was enough to arrest Lottie. 'A house with a garden? Are we moving?'

Michael and Rosa exchanged looks. 'Well, we've been talking about it,' confessed Rosa. 'It seems to make sense. If we both sell our flats we could afford something bigger, with a garden. The house I grew up in had a garden and a garage – and an attic where I had a playroom, and I always thought that that was what a home should be for a little girl. Maybe we could find something a little nearer your school so you don't have so far to travel. And I do feel guilty about you not having a pet.' Rosa had, of course, never got over the guilt she'd suffered after the death of the Mysterious One. 'I might even consider some kind of cat like Calypso's nice Burmese – definitely *not* a bald cat, though,' she added hastily, seeing the expression on Lottie's face.

'A Burmese? But aren't they dead expensive?'

'Your mum got some good news today,' said Michael. 'When do you think that gobshite Sneyde will pay up, by the way?'

'I haven't a clue. I got even better news, though, about an hour ago.'

'Oh?'

'I got a phone call from that literary agency. They want to represent me.'

'Hey, Mum! Cool! So you *could* be the new J. K. Rowling!'

'Sorry to disappoint you, babe. I'll be lucky if I get as much as a couple of grand as an advance. But it's a start.'

'Christ, Rosa! That's fantastic news. All that displacement activity paid off!' Michael looked amazed, and then he grabbed her and kissed her until Lottie said: 'Oh, stop it, you two. It's disgusting,' and headed for her bedroom.

Rosa laughed, then detached herself from Michael's embrace and extracted her Aqua Libra and his Bordeaux from the Londis bag.

'Christ, Rosa!' said Michael again. 'I'm so proud of you.'

'And I'm so lucky to have you,' she said, handing him his celebratory bottle and a corkscrew. 'Because I couldn't have done it without you. Without you I could be a lush on skid row with a daughter in care. And look at me now.' She set the bottle of Aqua Libra down on the dining table and drew herself up into an arrogant pose, raising an arm above her head in the manner of a matador. She gave him a beautiful smile. 'I remember what you said once, the first time I saw the real you.'

'What did I say?'

'You said: "Flamenco isn't shy – it's *bold*!" You said: "You have to believe you are beautiful."' Rosa executed a short series of rapid steps, beating out a thrilling rhythm with confident heels against the hard wooden floor, and then she clapped her hands – once, twice – above her head and lifted her chin even higher. 'You taught me to have faith in myself, Michael Luque. You taught me how to dance.'

One summer evening later in the year, after settling Paloma for the night, Dannie poured herself a glass of wine and curled up in her favourite armchair with one of her botanical books to do some homework. She was spending a lot of time tending her garden these days, spreading La Paloma's rug out under the shade of the apple tree where the baby could lie on her back and play with her perfect toes, which she'd only recently discovered.

She was planning ahead, thinking about next year and what the garden might look like when her daughter's first birthday came round. White flowers felt right – snowdrops and lily of the valley and white crocuses. White for innocence and purity – and, she thought with a smile, for Paloma: for the white dove of peace. She'd need to get the bulbs into the earth come October.

She reached out a hand for the well-thumbed book she'd kept in her flower shop – the illustrated *Language of Flowers* – and started to leaf through it, searching for 'C' for crocus. 'Crocus (spring)', she found, meant 'youthful gladness'. And this reminded her of her friend Lottie, and she wondered how she and Rosa and Michael were getting on in their new home, and if Lottie had got the hairless cat she'd set her heart on. And she wondered too about her other friend, Calypso, from whom she had recently received a postcard. It had been sent from the Seychelles, where she and Dominic were renewing their wedding vows.

Leafing idly through the pages, Dannie's eyes were drawn to the words 'Balm of Gilead. Healing. I am cured.' Nothing could be further from the truth. And then she turned her attention back to the matter in hand, looking under 'S' for snowdrop. Snowdrop, she read, meant 'hope'.

'L' now for lily of the valley. Running a finger down the alphabetical listing on the page, she found that imperial lilies meant 'majesty', white lilies meant 'sweetness', and yellow lilies 'falsehood'. Lily of the valley was next. She read on, almost fearful of what she might find. She wanted no ill omens.

Her fears were groundless. Lily of the valley signified 'return of happiness'.

Hope. Return of happiness.

Dannie finally allowed herself to think of Jethro Palmer.

She reached for the phone.

THE END

Kate Thompson would like to invite you to visit her website at www.kate-thompson.com

STRIKING POSES
by Kate Thompson

When you're burdened with the name of a goddess and your mother's a flamboyant actress, the last thing you want is a career in the limelight. So Aphrodite Delaney opts for a job backstage, grafting as a stylist on cling film commercials, a forlorn Canderella with no invite to the ball until – ping! – the handsome prince of Irish fashion, Troy MacNally, appears centre stage. Suddenly this Cinderella is snowed under with fairy-tale threads and invites to the ball – and the spotlight's right in her face. But there are big bad wolves and spiteful pixies lurking in the dark beyond. Pitted against the bitchiest of witches, Aphrodite develops a rare flair for wickedness herself . . .

From the author of the number one bestselling *The Blue Hour* comes a modern-day fairy story – a tale of love, sex, revenge and intrigue set in the glittering *demi-monde* of the Irish fashion world.

'Sublimely addictive'
Marian Keyes

A Bantam Paperback

0 553 81431 1

THE BLUE HOUR
by Kate Thompson

'A rare novel. Beautiful, powerful, unashamedly romantic'
Marian Keyes

Maddie Godard: chief copywriter, The Complete Works advertising agency. Smart. Sussed. Scared. Because when your self-esteem's been trampled and your world is overturned, you have to act fast. Maddie escapes from busy Dublin to seemingly tranquil Saint-Géyroux, an idyll in rural France. There, she is led into temptation by beautiful, roguish Sam, cajoled into becoming a life model by renowned artist Daniel Lennox, and haunted by a portrait of a mysterious beauty with a secret to share. Can she help Maddie exorcise her demons?

In this sexy, bittersweet, joyously romantic tale by the bestselling author of *Going Down* and the *Mischief* books, Maddie Godard confronts her innermost fears, makes new friends, and learns that life really is worth living . . .

A Bantam Paperback

0 553 81298 X